He lay back against the headboard. Stared up at the ceiling, an unreadable expression in his distant gaze.

She sensed his turmoil. And his pain. And a whirling storm of confusion too tangled for her to unravel. His emotions pressed like a weight upon her chest.

Her heart fluttered queerly just imagining that knife blade entering a few inches lower. A few inches deeper.

"I'm getting damned tired of apologizing," he said, breaking into the awkward silence. "Damned tired. Especially when you won't believe me." He swung around to face her, his eyes as angry as the storm-tossed loch. He lifted a hand as if he might caress her cheek. Pull her close.

She swept to her feet, away from the tantalizing heat of a body she knew too well. Hands that knew her every secret place. Lips that could tease a scream from her.

Away from a man that could love her until she shattered into a million pieces or hurt her more deeply than any other person alive.

BOOK YOUR PLACE ON OUR WEBSITE AND MAKE THE READING CONNECTION!

We've created a customized website just for our very special readers, where you can get the inside scoop on everything that's going on with Zebra, Pinnacle and Kensington books.

When you come online, you'll have the exciting opportunity to:

- View covers of upcoming books
- Read sample chapters
- Learn about our future publishing schedule (listed by publication month *and author*)
- Find out when your favorite authors will be visiting a city near you
- Search for and order backlist books from our online catalog
- Check out author bios and background information
- Send e-mail to your favorite authors
- Meet the Kensington staff online
- Join us in weekly chats with authors, readers and other guests
- Get writing guidelines
- AND MUCH MORE!

**Visit our website at
http://www.kensingtonbooks.com**

Dangerous As Sin

Alix Rickloff

ZEBRA BOOKS
Kensington Publishing Corp.
http://www.kensingtonbooks.com

ZEBRA BOOKS are published by

Kensington Publishing Corp.
119 West 40th Street
New York, NY 10018

Copyright © 2009 by Alix Rickloff

All rights reserved. No part of this book may be reproduced in any form or by any means without the prior written consent of the Publisher, excepting brief quotes used in reviews.

If you purchased this book without a cover you should be aware that this book is stolen property. It was reported as "unsold and destroyed" to the Publisher and neither the Author nor the Publisher has received any payment for this "stripped book."

All Kensington titles, imprints, and distributed lines are available at special quantity discounts for bulk purchases for sales promotion, premiums, fund-raising, educational, or institutional use.

Special book excerpts or customized printings can also be created to fit specific needs. For details, write or phone the office of the Kensington Special Sales Manager: Attn. Special Sales Department. Kensington Publishing Corp., 119 West 40th Street, New York, NY 10018. Phone: 1-800-221-2647.

Zebra and the Z logo Reg. U.S. Pat. & TM Off.

ISBN-13: 978-1-4201-0453-0
ISBN-10: 1-4201-0453-5

First Printing: July 2009
10 9 8 7 6 5 4 3 2 1

Printed in the United States of America

For Mom & Dad

They always believed

Chapter 1

Somewhere in Wiltshire, March 1815

He came to with a jerk as the sack was ripped from his head. Still groggy, he peered through the dark, but he may as well have been blind. He couldn't see a damn thing. Not where he was. Not who had cracked him over the head in the alley and brought him here.

He shifted, coming up hard against his bonds. Rope, thick and rasping, bound his wrists. Another cord lashed him at chest and ankles upright against a wall or a building. The stones bit into his back. Dug into the flesh of his thighs.

"Ha, ha, chaps. Very funny," he called out. "Joke's over." This was just like Geordie and Rolf. He'd only been late for parade once, and they hadn't gotten into that much trouble. "Point's made. Now untie me."

No one answered, but he sensed them watching.

"I'm waiting," he shouted. He deserved it. Fine. But enough was enough. He was stiff. The goose egg at the back of his skull hurt like hell. And it was cold without his jacket. He struggled against the rope.

"If all goes as planned, Private, you'll be able to tear those ropes loose yourself."

A voice, but not Rolf or Hughie. Not anyone he knew. For the first time, fear prickled his spine.

A man stepped into his line of sight. Four or five companions ranged behind him. All of them dressed in regimentals, their faces hidden behind white greasepaint.

Only the leader remained unmasked.

He'd seen him before. He couldn't remember where, but he'd recognize him again. He was sure of it. And when he did . . .

The moon chose that moment to break through the clouds. Now he knew where he was. The Stones. Only three miles from camp. But the moon also revealed the glitter of unsheathed steel. The inhuman shine of the man's eyes.

"Look long and well at the *Morkoth* blade. Like a mother, *Neuvarvaan* will create you anew. You'll become a child of the sword. An Undying."

What the hell? He struggled harder. But it was worse than useless. He was trussed like a pig for slaughter. "Who are you?" He hated that his voice cracked on a sob.

"A soldier like you." The man held his sword at his side. It seemed to glow with a cloudy gray light. "Someone who knows intimately the terrible price that comes of war. But spear point and rifle will be nothing to a new generation of warriors. All of you christened in blood by *Neuvarvaan*, the goddess blade."

Sweat poured off him. Terror soured his stomach. Closed his throat. He tasted it in the bile gagging him. Heard it in the rush of his breathing.

"Prepare for strength unchallenged. Agility unmatched. Immortality rivaling the *Fey* themselves. You'll find all these things within the blade's cut."

The man brought the sword up in front of him.

He fought. Screamed. Pleaded. This was insanity. He wasn't about to be skewered on a hilltop not half a league from his billet. Not by soldiers of his own army. This was a dream. A drunken nightmare. A hallucination.

The other men remained like statues, their hollowed eyes unmoved. Emotionless. Were they really going to stand there and let this madman murder him?

Piss drenched his breeches. He swallowed over and over.

Only the leader moved. Raised the sword high. Drew it back. "You'll be the first among my army of heroes. Be proud."

And with a mighty thrust, the sword flashed forward.

Slammed home.

Edinburgh, Scotland

Cam stepped off the stair, everything about him gleaming. From his guinea-gold hair to the dazzling swath of braid across his uniformed chest to the champagne shine of his cavalry boots. Even the hilt of his dress sword twinkled in the lights from a thousand candles.

Admiration prompted Morgan to catch his eye. Impudence made her hold his gaze longer than proper.

Cam never batted an eye. A flicker of recognition, and then he moved on to be swallowed by the crowd.

Just as if they hadn't been in bed together only hours earlier.

He'd gleamed then too. But then it had been the bronzed sheen of his muscled body, damp from lovemaking. The flash of white teeth as he rolled off her, laughing, before he pulled her against him. The spark of desire in his eyes as he took her once more into his arms.

She snapped her fan up and open, flapping it in a sad attempt to cool the heat just the memory of him created.

All around her, comments buzzed and swirled like a spriggan's wind.

An elderly gentleman in conversation with two older matrons. ". . . heard he made quite a name for himself . . ."

Two giggling girls in virginal white muslin. ". . . dashing. Mother says he's just home from the wars . . . wounded at Toulouse . . . a hero . . ."

Three young bucks watching him with envious eyes. ". . . helps to have the Sinclair fortune behind you . . ."

And the words that doused her flaming cheeks like a bucket of ice water spoken by an insipid, spinsterly woman amid a crowd of similar pinch-nosed females. ". . . scandalous . . . say his wife's a prisoner while he beds a string of mistresses . . ."

Wife. The word screamed in her ears. Drowned out everything else.

Wife.

Oh Gods, what had she done?

For the briefest of moments, Cam's head surfaced, and he sought her out. Gave her a conspiratorial wink. Conspiratorial as in conspiring. Plotting. Conniving. Against a wife. A woman who until this moment, Morgan hadn't even known existed. She forced herself to smile back even though it felt like her cheeks would crack.

"Pardon me," she mumbled, diving back into the safety of the swarm of guests.

They obliged, curling back around her like an inrushing wave. Anonymous among so many in the ballroom. Although in this scandal of a dress, she doubted she'd remain anonymous for long. The fabric clung to every curve—hampering her usual ground-eating stride—and the smoky blue silk wasn't exactly lost amid the sea of bland pastels. She'd worn it for Cam. Wanting him to see her as he thought she was. Elegant. Daring. Beautiful. But it had been just as much an illusion as his desire. His freedom.

They'd both been pretending.

She tore the combs from her hair as she went. Let the heavy fall mask her humiliation and her fury.

He followed. Not far behind. But the blinding attractiveness that had dazzled her hindered him. He was caught. Held. There was conversation. Introductions. His adoring admirers would keep him busy while she made her escape.

The terraces were quiet. The party hadn't progressed this far yet. Flambeaus guttered and smoked. Lanterns bobbed in the trees on the lawn. But the benches were empty. The arches and summerhouse waiting.

A sweep of the gardens revealed the paths to the park beyond. And once there, she knew her way off the grounds. Had marked the routes as she entered. The professional at work, even then.

She rushed down the stairs. Pretended she didn't hear Cam call out. Beg her to stop.

There was nothing he could say that would make her feel less like a fool. It was her fault she'd fallen for the gloss and ignored the rot beneath. And it was her fault she'd dared to dream. Because, after all, he'd never promised anything. And too infatuated, she'd never asked.

He called out once more. But by now, she'd concealed herself among the trees. Swift and silent as the wolf, she sped. The gown tore. She reached down, barely drawing breath, and ripped it farther up the side. Immediately, her stride lengthened.

But he was still too close. And a part of her ached to turn around and let him explain.

So she did the forbidden. She murmured the words. Felt the power shiver through her. And dropping the *feth-fiada* around her like a cloak, she vanished.

Chapter 2

Strathconon, Scotland, six months later

"Wake up, Cam. Time to return to the land of the living."

A cold blast of air and a nudge at his shoulder jarred him awake. Or at least back into semiconsciousness. He rolled over. Threw up into a slops jar he'd kept handy—this wasn't the first night hammering himself into oblivion. Wiped his mouth with the back of one sleeve.

"Go away, Brodie," he snarled. "Don't you know it's sacrilege to disturb a corpse?"

"If it were up to me, I'd let ye sleep it off, but a messenger's come from General Pendergast."

The chipper matter-of-factness of Brodie's voice grated on Cam's nerves.

"You're to be scraped off the floor, poured into your uniform, and driven to London by the end of the week. Big meeting at the Horse Guards. Very hush-hush."

Cam thought of heaving a boot in his direction, but his brain and body weren't cooperating yet. Too much Sinclair whiskey. On top of too much Sinclair whiskey. On top of . . . well, he couldn't remember quite that far back. But, no doubt, it had been something equally potent. "You said Pendergast?"

The general had put in an appearance at Charlotte's funeral. Offered his gruff condolences and immediately moved on to the subject of Napoleon's return to France, Wellington's strategy, and the prospect for renewed war.

Cam could have kissed him for his lack of sympathy.

It was bad enough he'd felt nothing at his wife's death but relief. As if he'd been sprung from prison after a sentence of seven long years. But the weepy, emotional grief he'd been showered with only made him feel worse.

Cam sat up, instantly regretting the impulse. His head throbbed, and his mouth tasted like vomit and alcohol.

"Have ye been sober at all since ye got home?" Brodie pushed a glass into his face. It smelled disgusting. "I'd say it was Charlotte's death had ye depressed, but I ken she only set ye to drinking when she was alive."

Cam gulped the drink down without stopping. He'd learned the hard way if you came up for air, so did everything else.

He finished it. Threw his wobbly legs over the bed. Waited for the room to steady. "You know too much for your own good."

"What are friends for?" Brodie banged through the room. Throwing a clean shirt onto the bed. Fussing. It was like having a really efficient, really annoying valet. "So what has got ye searching for the bottom of every bottle ye pick up?"

"Friends. Hmmph." Cam yanked his soiled shirt over his head. Sniffed himself. A bath was definitely in order. "Let's say it was a poor choice on my part."

Brodie finally dropped into a seat, his frenzied mother-hen behavior apparently at an end. "Was it the blonde or the brunette poor choice? Ye make a habit of them."

"Am I that obvious?"

"Oh, aye." Brodie MacKay flashed that devilish smile that misled so many women into thinking he was a sweet young man. How wrong they were. "But it's all right. So many of your poor choices end up being consoled by your understanding best friend."

Cam stood up. Brodie's mystery elixir was doing its work. His stomach had the squashy fragility of a gelatin, but the whirling room had settled. He squinted. Now if only his eyes would focus. "She was a redhead. But you didn't have the chance to console her. You were in London."

"So it *is* a woman that's got ye crying in your whiskey. I thought you'd had your fill with Charlotte."

"I had. I have." Just mentioning her name tightened his stomach into new spasms. As if any moment she'd come through that door. The eternal martyr. The deserted wife. She had the act perfected. What a load of shit. "Stop pestering. You think you'll get me to spill my guts. But it won't happen. And it doesn't matter anyway. She's long gone."

Cam stripped out of his breeks. Kicked them into a corner next to the shirt. Even in high summer, the breeze off the loch was cool. Beyond the window, it glittered icy blue and clear as glass. And breath-stealingly frigid. But that was all the better. One plunge into the water would cure the last of the whiskey fog from his brain.

Brodie threw himself to his feet. Made for the door. "Well, the reprieve is over. So finish getting dressed and meet me downstairs. We need to be on the road by noon."

"Gone responsible on me?"

Brodie looked over his shoulder and laughed. "Bite your bluidy tongue."

London, England

As he shifted in his seat, Cam caught the woman watching him.

It was an unnerving stare from an unnerving figure. Ornately dressed in a silver-girdled robe of royal blue, she was tall—well over six feet—and with the sturdy, muscled build of a wrestler. It was almost possible to forget the leather breeks peeking from the slit skirt or the long hip boots or the dagger's hilt Cam swore he glimpsed as she sat.

But surely he'd mistaken that.

With the exception of a white streak, her hair was black as sin. Black as her eyes. Eyes that flicked from him to General Pendergast to the door to the general's adjutant, Major Eddis. Never resting for more than a moment on any of them as if they were beneath her notice. As if she were running this interview and not the general.

Cam had arrived in London before dawn this morning. Taken rooms at Stephen's Hotel long enough to rinse off the grime of the road, change clothes, and catch a catnap of minutes before heading here to the Horse Guards. It hadn't been nearly enough. As he waited patiently for the start of the general's meeting, he fought the cotton-headed feeling that came with lack of sleep. Only the disturbing presence of the strange woman kept him alert and on edge.

"We should fill the colonel in, General Pendergast," she said, breaking into the long awkward silence. "My . . . representative has already been briefed."

Her voice was as unsettling as her stare. Deep and throaty. It seemed to echo off the walls of the office. Reverberate through his skull as if it were made of paper. After his last bender, not an impossibility.

Pendergast cleared his throat. Shuffled his papers. "Yes, of course."

Mayhap she was in charge. The general certainly jumped at the crook of her finger.

Cam leaned forward. "I assume it has to do with the deaths I've been investigating."

"Is that what you call it, Colonel?" Major Eddis interrupted. "It's been five months and you've learned nothing more than we knew after the first soldier turned up dead."

The taunt was obvious, but Cam refused to rise to the bait. Eddis was entitled to be a pain in the ass. The disfigured face, the empty boot—the man had paid his dues.

The general pushed a paper across the desk toward Cam. "The latest list of victims. The last one just two weeks ago."

He read the names, but he already knew all nine by heart. All but for the last. Sergeant Tucker. Thirty-fourth Foot. There was nothing linking these men. No commonalities. No ties between them. Nothing but the manner of their deaths. A grim bond, for sure. But it had led him nowhere.

"Whispers are beginning among the ranks. Rumors of an evil infecting the army. Napoleon's curse on the soldiers who destroyed him," the general told him.

Cam looked up. "That's madness. The first deaths were months before Waterloo."

Pendergast steepled his fingers, his eyes solemn. "You're right. It has nothing to do with the little emperor or any outside enemy. This cancer eats us from within."

The woman's gaze was upon Cam. Even without looking over his shoulder, he knew she watched him. Sized him up. Who the hell did she think she was? And for that matter, why was she here? The army hadn't begun admitting women to the ranks, had it? God, that was a thought to make him shudder. "Sir, I just need more time."

"Time is a gift we do not have, Colonel Sinclair." The soft pad of her boots was almost silent as she moved into his line of sight. "The general and I have consulted. We've decided the moment has come to join forces before *Neuvarvaan* is used again."

He braced his hands upon the arms of his chair. Tired of being played for a fool. "And who are you? What forces could you possibly bring to this? Some kind of ladies' aid society? A bevy of matrons armed with teacups and chicken skin fans?"

"Sinclair!" Pendergast barked.

Eddis smirked, the scarred side of his face twisting his smile into a grotesque mask.

"General." The woman spoke over him. Still frustratingly calm. Unfazed. "It is all right. He is *Duinedon*—mortal. He does not understand." Then her gaze swung to him, and if he hadn't been sitting, his knees would have buckled at the weight and power in her limitless black eyes. *I know you hear me. And I know in your heart you see the truth of my words. The men of Caithness have long been friends of the Fey.*

Cam almost bolted out of his chair. It was her voice. But in his head. He looked wildly from the general to Eddis. Neither one seemed the least bit concerned. Couldn't they hear her? Or was she poking into his brain alone. *This can't be happening. I'm losing my mind.*

No, not your mind. But you do walk a razor-thin path that will lead you further into darkness do you not turn aside.

Had this woman been talking to his aunt and uncle? He'd had enough carping from them to last a lifetime. *Sober up, boy. Look at yourself. Remember your name. Your position.*

His gaze narrowed, anger making him face her without flinching. *Don't talk to me of things you know nothing about.*

She is dead, Sinclair. And the war is over. You can begin again. Or is that what you fear?

This was crazy. He tried ignoring the voice, but it was insistent. He'd swear it was a drunken hallucination except he was stone-cold sober. Unfortunately.

He shook his head, trying to clear the snaky feeling of having her there. Seeing things he'd hidden from everyone. But fighting it only made his temples throb. A sharp pain lanced the space behind his eyes.

"Scathach, why don't you tell the lack-wit what's going

on?" The general's voice when it came—overloud after the soft vibration of the mind-speech Cam had been focused on—startled him back to the present. "He mayn't believe, but he'll sit for it"—he shot Cam a warning glance—"if I have to bind him to his chair."

Shaken and still refusing to acknowledge the woman's power, Cam decided to humor the general. The man had suffered enough in the last few months. Not one but two sons killed in Belgium. Another lost in the early days of the war. It was no wonder he'd cracked.

Mayhap Cam had cracked as well. He'd been riding close to the edge for months now, he'd not be surprised if he'd started to hear voices.

The woman—Scathach the general called her—closed her eyes as if summoning patience before she spoke. "Have you heard of the *Other*, a race of mortals bearing *Fey* and human traits?"

"My grandfather told me stories."

Your seanair knew the old ways. It is not his fault he could not make you accept them as true. Times have changed. And the mortal world has moved beyond us. And we have let them.

There she was again. This time, he gave in. Let the words wash over him. It didn't hurt so much that way.

"They are more than stories," she said aloud. "The Order of *Amhas-draoi* is home to many of these. Men and women trained in weapons and magic. Bound to protect both realms; *Fey* and *Duinedon*."

"Does anyone else realize how insane this sounds?" He looked around for support.

"You would not be the first to deny our existence. But belief will make your task easier."

"And what is my task? Dragon slaying? Virgin rescuing? Mayhap pulling a sword from a stone?" Cam looked from Pendergast to Eddis waiting for them to laugh and begin the

DANGEROUS AS SIN

real meeting. But both men were grim-faced. Not a chuckle between them.

She ignored his mocking tone. "You know of *Neuvarvaan*, the great sword belonging to the warrior-goddess Andraste."

Cam shrugged. "I know the legend. The sword's touch gives immortality."

"The tale has been twisted like so much of our history. It requires more than a touch to gain the gift of undying. *Neuvarvaan* must deliver the ending stroke. The wound that kills. And it must be done in accordance with the laws of the *Fey*. But 'tis not just undying the sword bestows, but great strength. Agility. Speed. All skills a soldier would covet. Any army would long for."

"You're telling me the soldiers were killed with this sword?"

"Aye. Someone wields it. Someone who knows the truth of its power but does not fully understand how to harness it. These deaths were his attempts at mastering the weapon. Experiments, to put it crudely."

"It's *Fey* legend," Cam argued. "A faery story." He stood up. Enough was enough. "If this is your way of showing your displeasure at my work, General, I've got it."

"General Pendergast," the woman snapped. Her first hint of annoyance. Her first hint of any emotion, for that matter, "you told me this man would do what we asked. No questions."

"He questions everything. But he knows his duty. And he'll do what the army asks of him. For king and country."

Sinclair felt the sting of the general's reprimand even through his anger.

For king and country.

Words he'd lived by for over fifteen years. Words he'd clung to for the last seven when everything else had gone to hell.

Eddis stepped up, his expression as infuriatingly pompous as his voice. "Sir, may I—"

The door opened. "I apologize for being late. They didn't want to show me up here at first."

Cam knew that voice. He spun in his chair, the wind kicked out of him.

Great. God. Damn. It *was* her.

Miss Morgan Fucking Bligh.

Morgan had prepared herself.

When Scathach had ordered her to London, the head of the *Amhas-draoi* warned Morgan who awaited her. But the sight of Cam still caught her off guard. Punched through the defenses she'd thought she'd built up over the last few months.

Her first thought was he looked like hell. Still too damned gorgeous, but definitely lacking the Adonis quality she remembered.

He was pale as if he hadn't seen the sun in weeks. Tight lines strained the corners of his mouth. Hollows shadowed his red-rimmed eyes. And he'd lost weight. Probably not noticeable to someone who didn't know him well, but she could tell. The hard soldier's body had softened. Lost its edge.

She was glad. Served him right. She hoped it was fatal.

That last thought checked her. Drew her up short. Gods, was she becoming one of those women? Sour? Spiteful? Angry at the world? Bitterness only sapped energy better used for more important tasks. Cam Sinclair was not important.

Not anymore.

"Forgive me for being late. The sentries stopped me downstairs. It took a bit of persuading for them to let me pass."

"No problem, Miss Bligh," the general said. "We were just telling Sinclair what we know to date."

Scathach caught and held Morgan's eye. A telling look, letting her know the *Fey* hadn't revealed everything. Doran

Buchanan's treachery remained a secret known only to the *Amhas-draoi*. Morgan meant to keep it that way.

She shot a quick glance at Cam. He was trying hard to keep the surprise from his face. But she knew. His shock vibrated in the air like a plucked wire. "By the looks of him, you hadn't gotten as far as explaining me."

"Miss Bligh will be joining you on this assignment." General Pendergast put up a hand, cutting off Cam's sputtered outrage. "I know it's unusual. But the *Amhas-draoi* don't work under the same restrictions as the British Army. And I've seen firsthand what they can do. As an *Other* and as an *Amhas-draoi*, Miss Bligh is well up to the task."

Morgan straightened. She'd better be. She'd been training for this moment since she was eighteen and realized she'd rather be wielding a sword than a needle. And she was a damn sight better with the sword.

"*Amhas-draoi*? Sir, please. No disrespect intended, but, sir, she's a female. And she and I . . . we . . ." Cam's confusion would have been funny if it hadn't been at her expense. She almost felt sorry for him. "We've met before."

"Good," Pendergast said. "That will make introductions unnecessary."

"How can she possibly help? And how will we travel? She's unmarried. She'd be ruined within a day of being with me unchaperoned."

What a bloody hypocrite. He certainly hadn't been concerned over her reputation last winter. "You worry about your own skin, Colonel," she snapped. "I can take care of myself."

Pendergast rubbed the side of his nose. Adjusted his spectacles. "But that does bring up a problem. Despite the freedoms women enjoy among the *Amhas-draoi*, normal society does not look kindly on single young females gallivanting alone across the country. Major Eddis has solved this problem in a simple, if unorthodox, fashion."

The major stepped forward. Morgan had barely noticed him up to now. She'd been so busy not noticing Cam.

"It's easy enough," Eddis explained. "The two of you will travel as a couple—a married couple." His pale, clever eyes raked her over. Made her want to give him a taste of the steel hidden by the *fith-fath* she'd woven around it. If the men downstairs had thought a woman entering the Horse Guards was strange, one with a scabbard strapped to her side would have really set the cat among the pigeons.

Cam shook his head. "Won't work. Everyone knows my wife just died. I'm still officially in mourning."

Eddis sniffed his disapproval. "Those same people also know you're no grieving widower. They'll simply believe you've hitched yourself to another in an indecent span of time."

Scathach had also explained this part of the plan to her. She hadn't liked it any better than Cam. But she knew better than to fight it. She'd been entrusted with this mission. She'd do whatever it took. No matter how much she hated the thought of being within two counties of Cameron Sinclair.

"So it's settled, then." The general straightened his papers. "You'll leave for Devonshire tomorrow."

"Devonshire?" Cam asked.

"We got word this morning of another victim. That makes ten."

"The list showed nine dead, sir."

"I didn't say this victim had died. He's alive and hopefully will remain so until you get there. Perhaps he can give you something to go on. Anything. We need to find that sword, Colonel. We need to locate it. And return it to the *Fey*. And we need to do it soon. If its mysteries are solved before we find it, we could have a far larger problem on our hands."

"Sir?"

"They aren't called Undying for nothing."

Chapter 3

They'd barely hit the corridor outside the general's office before Cam grabbed Morgan's arm. Spun her around to face him. He'd forgotten how tall she was. How her eyes could flay you with one scathing glance. "Is this some kind of joke?"

She yanked her arm away. "Do I look like I'm having fun?" She straightened the short crisp jacket she wore—a far cry from the sheer silks and bodice-hugging muslins he remembered. "I don't like this pairing any better than you, but there's nothing to be gained by snarling at me like a rabid animal."

"And I'm supposed to credit you're some kind of Amazon? Damn it, Morgan. What's going on?"

"Scathach and Pendergast explained."

"No. They gave me some cock-and-bull story about swords and magic and *Fey* and mysterious military societies who accept women as if they were the equal of men."

"As if they were equal?" She sniffed her contempt. Motioned toward the stairs. "Come. There's a pub across the way. We can get something to eat." When he raised a skeptical brow, she offered him a cool smile. "Don't get too excited. I haven't eaten yet today. And just so you know, I'm letting you pay."

The pub was quiet. Few customers this early in the afternoon.

In the light of such normal surroundings, it was hard to believe what had just occurred. If it hadn't been for that voice in his head he'd have discounted the whole episode. But no matter how he tried, Scathach's words remained. Echoing into corners of his mind he'd slammed shut long ago—and for good reason.

Cam waited as Morgan ordered before he followed it up with a call for beer. The pint when it came slid into his stomach, easing the anxious tension banding his shoulders. Tightening his back. He ordered a second.

She watched him over the top of her own glass. "When did you start drinking so much?"

"Well, you've got the wifely nagging down already," he grumbled.

She glared back at him. "You'd know all about that, wouldn't you?"

He put the beer down. Pushed it away, no longer thirsty. "I tried to apologize. I came to see you after Charlotte's death to explain. You wouldn't listen."

She sighed. "I didn't want your excuses, Cam. I don't want them now. Let's just pretend last winter never happened. Move forward."

"Can you do that?"

"Do what?" She offered him a confused look.

"Forget last winter?"

Her brow wrinkled. "What happened last winter?"

"We . . ." He smiled. "Ah, very nice."

"You see? Easy as falling off a log."

She dug into her meal with relish when it arrived. The aroma of fried potatoes, steak, and steaming wheat bread slathered in butter made him realize how long it had been since his own breakfast, but too much had happened. Food could wait.

He rested his elbows on the table. Settled in. "All right, if that's out of the way, you can tell me what's going on."

"What do you want to know?" The worst of her hunger obviously sated, she sat back. Crossed her arms matter-of-factly on her chest. All business. This Morgan was so different it was almost easy to forget what they'd shared in Scotland. Almost.

He plowed an impatient hand through his hair. "In the general's office . . . while we were talking . . . that woman—"

"Scathach."

"Right. She spoke to me."

"I know. I was there."

"No. I mean here"—he tapped his temples—"like she was in my brain. Can you do that?" God, that was a thought. Morgan plucking thoughts right out of his head. He polished off the end of his beer on that frightening image.

"No, I can't mind-speak. Only the true *Fey* have that ability."

"Then what can you do?"

She leaned forward, her whiskey-gold stare fired with hostility. "I can separate your head from your shoulders before you have time to blink. And I can track. That's why Scathach chose me for this mission. I can track magic. What's known as a mage chaser. It's a gift. If they use *Neuvarvaan* and I'm close enough, I'll feel it."

He snorted. "Magic. Right."

She offered him a thin smirk. "A nonbeliever?" She looked around. "See the two men over there in the corner? Keep your eye on the man in the blue coat. He's going to spill his drink."

Morgan focused her gaze on her chosen victim. Her lips moved in a silent whisper.

The man across the way raised his pint to his lips, but before he'd taken a swallow, his arm jerked. The tankard sloshed. Fell to the floor.

Cam flashed back to Morgan. "Keep watching," she urged. "Now the man in gray is going to order fish. Wait for it."

Again came her whispered words. Again he watched.

The man's laughing companion waved for the barmaid. She hurried over with a towel. As she wiped up the mess, he said, "Cod if you have it. And another beer for my friend."

Cam's stomach rolled. It wasn't possible. But he'd seen it with his own eyes. The evidence was piling up. Pointing toward a conclusion that made no sense.

Morgan laughed. "I added that last bit spur of the moment. I felt sorry for the blighter who'd lost his beer to prove my point."

"That was your doing?" His throat was dry, his heart thudding at a strange galloping pace.

She gave him a sympathetic look. "There's a whole world out there you know nothing about. And you don't have to believe, Cam. I don't blame you. As *Other,* I've lived with magic my whole life. It's second nature. Like breathing. I forget not all mortals understand."

"Scathach used that term—*Other*. My grandfather told me tales of half mortal/half *Fey*, but is it true? They exist?"

"You're staring at one—rather rudely, if you must know."

He blinked. Dropped his gaze.

"We're not monsters, Cam. Or freaks. The *Fey* blood can manifest itself in any of a thousand ways. Sometimes so subtly, the talent isn't even realized." She grimaced. "Or in my case, it's just who you are."

"I thought I knew who you were."

"You didn't know anything about me." She shook her head, shadows hovering at the corners of her gaze. "We were both pretending, Cam. It just caught up with us in the end."

He clutched his empty tankard.

How right she was.

They stopped when the rain grew so heavy it was impossible to see. The toll road was a swamp of mud and debris, the rutted lane branching off toward the inn, even worse. Morgan had vague ideas of shaming Cam into pushing on through the worst of it. But even that seemed too much effort after hours of huddling in the saddle, her hands slippery on the reins, her eyes scratchy and heavy from trying to peer through the gloom.

She pulled the oilskin boat cloak tighter around her—*thank you, Ruan*. Her older brother had given it to her for her last birthday. An odd present, but Ruan knew her better than anyone. And cared less for convention than she did. It was just what she'd wanted.

The yard was packed. A heavy coach sat unharnessed in a corner. Gentlemen's phaetons and curricles had been pulled willy-nilly wherever there was room, crushed against smaller gigs and even a few wagons. Ostlers hung at the stable doors, just out of the rain. Others moved up and down the aisles checking on the horses, fretful in the storm. She grimaced. Perfect. A crowded yard meant a crowded inn. She'd hoped for the luxury of her own room. Not completely out of the question, even for a married couple. But hope was fading fast.

A beefy, bearded man stood up from his crate. Wiped his hands down his trousers. Spat into the mud.

"Why the crowd?" Cam asked, his tone clipped and short. Even soaked and filthy, he carried an aura of command. An authority that made people snap to attention. Morgan would give him that, if nothing else.

The stable hand seemed to straighten, eye them in a new respectful light. He pulled his cap off his head. "A boxing match, sir. This afternoon. The place is packed with visitors from as far away as Bournemouth."

"Any rooms?"

"If ye're not too picky, there may be a place in the attics. But it'll be dark"—he cast a doubtful look in her direction—"and musty. Not fit for the lady."

Morgan dismounted. Tossed her reins to the man. "This lady's slept in worse."

Cam cringed, but followed suit, tipping the man as he led both horses away.

Anger burned through her exhaustion at Cam's involuntary shudder. As if he were ashamed of her. Well, to hell with him. She was who she was. She'd tried pretending at being Miss Femininity and been kicked in the teeth for her trouble.

The inn was as packed as the stable hand had warned. Cam pushed his way through toward the bar, the crowds parting as much for the scarlet jacket as the tall, elegant gentleman wearing it. Waterloo had made heroes out of anyone in military braid.

Morgan shed her cloak, smoothed her hands down her damp, clinging skirts. Wished for the millionth time since leaving London for the comfort and ease of her leather breeches. She'd settled on a simple riding habit for travel. Disguising her breeches beneath the *fith-fath*'s mirage would have taken considerable concentration. Easier to conform, if less convenient.

The publican stood in the bar, busy filling glasses for the rushing barmaids.

"My wife and I are looking for a room," Cam said.

The man gave a sheepish look. "This prize fight has filled me from rafters to cellar. I've just one left. More a box room than a proper chamber. It's under the eaves. Awful small. And only one narrow bed."

He wiped his hands as he showed them the way, each flight of steps narrower, each corridor dimmer as they climbed. Finally they came to the room, a tiny space beneath the roof, as spartan as the innkeeper had described.

Morgan threw her satchel on the bed. Tried not to dwell on how small it was. How there was no possible way she'd be able to lie there without being uncomfortably close to Cam.

She glanced up. Caught the look on his face telling her he was thinking the exact same thing.

She sighed. It was going to be a very long night.

Morgan went to bed early, hoping to be asleep before Cam joined her. Laughter floated up from the hubbub downstairs. Men's voices raised in loud talk and celebration. Bets won and lost. And occasionally a snatch of song.

She flung herself from one side to the other, trying to focus on the pound of rain overhead. The rattle of gutters. The rumble of distant thunder. But her mind kept skipping back to nights not so long ago when she'd gone to her room in inns similar to this one, Cam's hand pressed to the small of her back, his voice low and seductive in her ear.

The risk of discovery and subsequent disgrace had worked on her like an aphrodisiac, making everything about their relationship brighter, sweeter, more intense. The knowledge that under Cam's oh so proper uniform was a body molded by training and hardened by war had created a shivering heat that started low in her belly until she ached to peel off the layers of his respectability, each discarded piece of clothing firing her with anticipation. The jacket. The shirt. Running her hands over the gilded expanse of his chest, across the washboard muscles of his abdomen, and down to trace the line of golden hair from his belly button into his breeches only made the heat spread faster.

Time stretched as together they undressed. In her case, swift and urgent. In his, slow enough to draw out the exquisite torture until she thought she might explode with wanting him.

Naked, they fell laughing to the bed, a tangle of arms and legs. He came over her, curved his hands around her breasts as he bent to suckle them. She arched her back, begging him to take more of her into his mouth. His tongue laving her nipples until they were hard as pebbles.

She combed her fingers through his hair, caressed the stubble of his cheek. Smelled the crisp sweat and soap smell that was uniquely Cam. His hands explored her as his mouth devoured. She drowned in his kisses while his touch set her on fire.

Even now, she tingled, rubbing her hands over herself in memory of a yearning that never fully left her. Her breasts throbbed with a pleasure she'd become used to and now missed. She closed her eyes, trying to recapture that wild, frenzied lust that tore into her like a dagger's plunge. Passed through her, leaving only a shadow of joy behind.

If she concentrated, she felt again the close of her muscles around him when he'd slid into her. The slow, steady need building in her center as she rocked up to meet his every thrust. He watched her. With eyes as cool and blue as an eagle's. And in that focused stare burned desire and passion and beauty—her beauty. Because that's how he'd seen her. And how she saw herself when she lost herself in his gaze.

All sensation rushed to the core of her being. She was light and fire and yearning. The edge loomed close. One rock of his hips would send her spinning over. She tried holding back. Wanted the exhilarating freedom to remain always, but he thrust harder, and she tumbled through. The world tilted, and she cried out.

He drove into her again and again, drawing out the ecstasy until he found his own release and the two lay sated and spent in each other's arms.

Alone tonight, she pressed her hands to her breasts, rolling her nipples until they hardened. She choked on the lump in her throat. Tears stung the corners of her eyes as she dropped her hands lower. Skimmed her stomach, her hips. Lower still, her folds throbbing and wet with the memory of him.

Cam's face swam before her. The soft, rolling Scottish burr of his words vibrated through her head. "*M'eudail*. My darling."

And she'd believed him.

She swiped at the disgraceful tears. What a wretched weakling she was. All it took was seeing him again to recall that crazy, blood-pumping joy. She'd blithely insisted she could handle this assignment. Cam meant nothing to her. Well, damn her for being wrong. And damn him for being here.

Sleep was definitely lost.

Cam knew he couldn't put it off any longer. He had to go to bed. It was after two, and he needed at least a few hours of sleep if he was going to be alert enough to confront the only surviving victim of *Neuv*—no, he wouldn't even dignify the theory by naming it. It was too preposterous. He didn't care what parlor tricks Morgan had managed back in London to try and convince him. The *Fey* world was stories told by his gran-da. Relics of a time long past when people believed in the power of faery rings and saw shapes in the mists shrouding the Highland lochs and valleys. These attacks were being carried out by men. Real blood-and-bone humans with a thirst for murder. And when he found them, he'd prove it.

The chamber was dark, not even a sliver of moon to see by. He stumbled against the foot of the bed. Pain shot from his shin straight to his brain, where hours of hanging with the boys had caught up with him. Stifling a curse, he closed his eyes until the worst passed.

"I can light a candle if you need it," Morgan suggested, cool amusement coloring her words. Her voice was untouched by sleep as if she'd been waiting for him or—like him—had been too troubled by this awkward arrangement to sleep.

"No, thank you," he grumbled, spreading his bedroll on the floor, using his pack as pillow. He'd fared worse on campaign.

He undressed down to his breeks. Lay back, one arm flung over his closed eyes. His other hand unconsciously found the gold chain around his neck. Played with the jet cross hanging there.

He'd never felt completely right after he'd lost the necklace to Charlotte. It had been a part of him too long. One of the few links to his parents. To his childhood in Scotland. To a time when he'd lived life, not just marked time.

With her death, he'd gotten the cross back. And this time he'd make sure it stayed with him. He'd not foolishly hand it over to another grasping female.

The bed creaked, and a match flared.

"You've been drinking."

He dropped his arm. Looked up. The dim light harlequined Morgan's face, her eyes narrowed on him with that same critical stare she'd worn since London.

"A few. Not enough to matter."

"And if an enemy chose this moment to attack? You're hardly fit for a fight."

"We're safe enough here." He shot her a look. "Unless you're afraid of ghosts. Or is that your latest theory as to who's killing these soldiers?"

"Go boil your head," she muttered. "What I ever saw . . ." Her words grew too low to hear, but he could imagine.

This new Morgan was as far from the passionate, sexy hoyden he'd known in Scotland as one could get. How could she have hidden so much of her true self from him? Had he been blinded by her looks? She was, after all, the most stunning woman he'd ever seen. A jaw-dropper, for sure.

No dimpled elbows. No luscious female curves. No coy flirtatious glances.

Instead, she carried herself with the confidence of a lioness, her lean, supple body made to be caressed, her red-gold hair running like silk through his fingers. And a fire smoldering in her honey gaze. Had the physical jolt of her been enough to delude him into only seeing what he wanted to see?

The silence seemed as charged as if a slow fuse had been lit between them. The air grew oppressive as each tried to outwait the other. See who broke first.

His hands grew clammy. The floor began rocking as if he were shipboard. He rolled himself onto his side, almost knocking himself out on the leg of the bed—this really was a bloody small room. But even after he stopped moving, his stomach didn't. He closed his eyes and gritted his teeth until the urge to heave passed. It must be the gin. It had been foul, but the others had been drinking it and had urged him to join them. Not the smartest of moves, but he'd already been hazy with brandy fumes and hadn't been thinking completely straight.

Try not thinking at all.

Of all the people to be paired with, couldn't Pendergast have found him someone he hadn't exchanged body fluids with? The next few weeks were going to be sheer hell.

". . . drunken sot . . . get us killed . . ." she grumbled.

He pounded the lumps in his pack into submission. Lay back down. "Have you always been this self-righteous?"

"Have you always been a drunk?" she snapped back.

"No. And I'm not one now. Damn it, woman. You're as bad as my wife. . . ."

If the air had been thick before, now it froze ice-solid. His words hung suspended within the chill, spinning out over and over until his head swam, and he wanted to be sick all over again. "I'm sorry, Morgan. Even on your worst day times ten, you were never—could never be as bad as her."

He didn't know if she would answer. And if she did—in her current frame of mind—it wouldn't be good. He cringed, waiting for the eruption. But nothing happened. Not a sound came from the bed.

His shoulders relaxed a fraction. "Morgan?" he whispered. "I'm sorry."

"Did you think I wouldn't find out?"

The quiet reproach was worse than any fireworks would have been. He could have handled those. This slid between the cracks in the armor he'd built around himself over years. Pricked at the tattered remains of his conscience.

"Or didn't you care? What was one more notch in your bedpost? One more jest with your friends?"

"It wasn't like that."

And it hadn't been. Oh, there had been plenty of women before her. That much was true. His sham of a marriage had been over long ago. Charlotte had wrought her havoc early on. Pulled his life apart strand by strand until nothing had been left of the impetuous young man who'd pledged himself in a fit of youthful ardor. Until his only way out of her personal blend of guilt, accusations, blame, and petty cruelties had been into the cannon's mouth. An escape, he'd come to find, with its own devastating costs.

But Morgan had been different. Mayhap it was her beauty. He'd never seen a woman who could have a roomful of men watching her every move and be completely oblivious of the attention. Or a woman who could make him hard with one slow, level stare. But then there'd been the laughter and the ease he felt when he was with her, as if maybe—just maybe he could tell her about his war. And she might understand. Not shrink away in horrified shock. Or watch him with fear and loathing in her eyes.

His hand went to the long, puckered scar that started at his shoulder. Ended just before his spine. Aye, Morgan had definitely been different. But being different hadn't been enough in the end.

"What hurt the most was knowing afterward that even if everything you'd told me was truth . . ." She paused for what seemed like an eternity. "Even then, it wouldn't have made a difference. You were still married. And I was still just your latest whore."

He drew a breath. Felt his hands tighten again around the cross at his neck. "I'm not married now."

"And I'm not your whore, Cam. Not anymore." Her voice hardened. "Not ever again."

Chapter 4

They arrived in Tavistock as the parish clock tower struck two in the afternoon.

The lodging house where the latest victim Ensign Traverse was quartered smelled of boiled onions and dirty laundry and echoed with the shouts and cries of children from the floors above. A faded woman hitching a baby on her hip opened the door to them, her gaze sharp as she raked them over. Not even Cam's most captivating smile was enough to thaw the chill in her eyes.

"I've no rooms to let," she announced, beginning to close the door even before she'd finished speaking.

Cam slid his foot into the crack. "We're not here to rent a room. We're here to speak with Ensign Traverse. Has he rooms here? Is he at home?"

She frowned, pushing away the baby's hand as it reached up to grab at her cap strings. "And where else would he be? Not exactly fit for battle, is he?" She laughed at her own joke as she swung the door wide to admit them. "I just took him his dinner." Without checking to see if they followed, she started up the stairs. "He's a bit better today. Not raving, at any rate."

The seductive sway of her hips told Cam she wasn't as

hostile as she made out, though the baby's loud squawking took away from the overall enticement. A swift glance at Morgan showed him she was as aware of the silent flirtation as he was—and highly amused by it. She rolled her eyes. Shook her head. "Are his wounds bothering him?" she asked.

The woman stiffened as if just reminded that Cam wasn't alone. She stopped at a closed door, equal parts annoyance and suspicion clouding her face. "Wounds? Has he been filling your head with his stories too? The ensign's not hurt. Not as I can see."

"We were led to believe—"

Ignoring the baby's cries, the woman leaned in close. Whispered, her eyes flashing from Morgan to Cam. "An opium eater, he is. That's my guess. And sickly with the drug from what I can see. It won't be long now." She rapped on the door. "Mr. Traverse? Visitors for you." Motioned them in with a nod of her head. "It'll be dark. Take no notice. It's as I said. Not long now."

The room they entered was dim and hot as an oven. Curtains drawn even though the afternoon was fine and cloudless. A fire burning low and smoky in the grate.

Immediately, sweat dampened Cam's back. His heavy wool jacket clung to him, and the heat made breathing difficult.

Morgan crossed to the windows to push open the heavy drapes.

"Keep them closed," a voice snarled from the corner. "No light. I've told them. No light."

Even in the gloom, Cam could make out the humpbacked shape of an old man seated by the meager fire, a shawl across his knees. His knobbed hands opened and closed in agitation on the arms of the chair.

Dread settled in the pit of Cam's stomach. "They told us Ensign Traverse lived here."

The man in the chair turned his head from the fire. Young, terrified eyes in an ancient, ruined face. "I'm Traverse."

Horror crushed the final shreds of Cam's disbelief.

Magic. Swords. Curses. The undead. Every tale his granda had related at the nursery bedside come to life.

And if that was real . . .

He pulled his gaze from Traverse. Settled it on Morgan.

. . . that meant the *Other*. The *Amhas-draoi*. All of it was real. She'd been telling him the truth. She really was a bloody great Amazon.

Hysterical laughter bubbled up. Threatened to spill over. He was chasing a damned *Fey* legend. With a half-blood warrior. That he'd slept with.

Could his life be turned any more upside down?

While he stood like a clod, Morgan poured out a cup of tea from the pot on the table. Brought it to the man. Returned with a tray of food. Helped him juggle his tea and his shawl and his plate. No false sympathy. No bumbling platitudes. She just did it. Comfortable. Efficient. And the awkwardness passed. She pulled up another chair. "Do you mind if I sit, Traverse? We've been traveling since Tuesday with few breaks." Her casual tone implied there was nothing odd about a twenty-four-year old in the body of an octogenarian.

Maybe not in her world.

"Help yourself."

Traverse's gaze followed Morgan. And Cam couldn't blame him. The landlady's try at temptation was amateurish compared to Morgan's silky movements. The starched, military cut of her jacket and brisk demeanor in contrast with the graceful tilt of her head, the sweep of cheekbones, and those pouty, kiss-me lips did things to a man's insides that ought to be illegal. And the killer was, she did it all with an unconscious elegance. It wasn't a pose. It wasn't an act. She had no idea what she did to him—he shuddered. He meant Traverse. Definitely Traverse.

Cam could tell the man was already smitten. Morgan had

that effect. Like a blow between the eyes. It was the follow-up punch to the gut you had to watch for.

"I don't get visitors," Traverse apologized. "Except for Mrs. Brumby, my landlady. And she only comes to bring me my dinner. She's scared. They're all scared. And I don't blame them."

Cam took up a position by the window. Adjusted the curtains to keep an eye on the street. Traffic was steady. Carts and wagons. An occasional carriage. Pedestrians threading their way between them all.

"You were attacked a week ago?" Morgan asked.

Traverse nodded. "Ten days. And since then . . . well, you can see for yourself."

"Do you remember anything?"

He ignored the food. As he raised his tea to his lips, his hands trembled. He dropped the cup back into its saucer as if self-conscious. "I've already spoken to my commanding officer. And the physicians. They thought I was making up stories."

"Will it bother you to repeat it?"

He took a slow, wheezy breath. "No. I'll tell you everything I remember if you think it will help."

She offered him an encouraging smile. "It might."

Oh, she was good. Traverse was eating out of her hand. Cam glanced back to the window. He could swear he'd seen that peddler pass by once already. His gaze narrowed, his attention split between the street and Morgan's questioning.

"It was late. I was coming back here after meeting friends when I was jumped." Like his eyes, the ensign's voice remained disconcertingly boyish. Reminded Cam of his younger brother Alisdair. They'd be about the same age, though Al would die rather than get within twenty leagues of the army. Especially after rumors revealed Cam's dirty little part in it. "They must have knocked me cold. When I woke, I was tied. It couldn't have been long. It was still dark. The moon was high."

"They?"

"Aye. There must have been three or four men. Mayhap more. It was too dark to see."

"Could you tell where they'd taken you?"

"Out on the moor. There's a group of stones. The locals call it the Giant's Fist. A place near where we run exercises. I recognized it. But then the men . . ." His words faded as his memories took hold.

The peddler passed by again, and this time glanced up at the house.

Cam broke in. "Did they have the sword?"

"What?" Traverse jumped, his eyes unfocused. Confused.

Morgan glared at the tactless interruption. "Colonel Sinclair wants to know if any of the men carried a weapon."

Cam gave Morgan a look that meant something was up. She frowned. Nodded her understanding.

"It burns," Traverse hissed. His face went deathly white, his hands gripping the chair arms, his plate sliding unnoticed to the floor with a crash. "It burns still. Here." He pounded above his heart. "I told the doctors what they did. The captain. My friends. I even told Mrs. Brumby. None believed me. They think I'm mad." He looked from Morgan to Cam, his voice growing louder. Stronger. Almost frantic. "But you believe me, don't you? You know what they did to me."

As if possessed, he ripped his shirt open. "Look for yourself," he shouted.

A pale silver scar slashed its way across the left side of his chest. But he said he'd been attacked two weeks ago. This scar looked as if it had healed over years hence.

"The sword glowed. I swear it glowed. And just seeing it, you knew you were in the presence of death. It was like the first shovelful of dirt just hit the top of your coffin."

Cam was grim. "They did this to you that night?"

"He told me it would be all right. That to be struck by the blade wouldn't kill me."

"Who was he?"

"I don't know. The leader, I expect. The other soldiers seemed to obey his orders."

"Can you describe him?"

Traverse screwed up his face in concentration. "That's the funny thing. He wasn't masked like the others, but his face—it just never seemed to be clear enough to see. Blurry . . . or runny . . . or . . . it doesn't make sense, I know. But you have to believe me." His voice had grown loud again as if he could convince them through sheer volume.

"We believe you," Morgan said, trying to calm him back down.

A movement across the street caught Cam's eye. The peddler had been joined by another. A man in a scarlet jacket. An officer. Cam's hand slid to the hilt of his saber while he let Morgan pick up the questioning.

"You didn't see his face. What about his uniform?"

Traverse plucked at the fringe of his shawl. "It was old. Piecemeal. As if he'd worn it for years or picked up bits and pieces along the way. A faded jacket. An old-fashioned hussar's shako. Cavalry boots."

By the exaggerated gestures and the curious glances of passersby, the peddler and the soldier were arguing. Cam would have given a small fortune to know what they were saying.

"Did he sound cultured? Rough? An accent?" Morgan continued.

Traverse took time to think. "No accent, but the others were frightened by him. I could tell."

"Anything else?" Morgan pressed. "Anything that might help us identify him?"

He squeezed his fingers to his eyes as if trying to focus. "Nothing. I saw the sword. And then he lifted it." His voice shook. He sobbed, drawing Cam's attention away from the window. "I didn't believe it would happen until he slammed it into me. I don't remember much after. The pain. The blood . . ." By the time Cam looked back, both the peddler and the soldier had vanished. ". . . and then it was like acid running through every vein. I broke the ropes . . . there was a man. I caught him. He shouted, but I had his neck. . . . The others scattered . . . I . . ."

He'd held together this long, but the memories unmanned him. He broke down, dropping his head into his hands, his weeping loud and angry like a child's. "I don't want to be this way. I want my life back. My friends." He looked up, his wrinkled face splotched red. "My body. Help me. Can't you help me?"

Cam felt an unexpected rage churn his stomach. How would he feel if this were Alisdair sitting here sobbing his guts out and cursed by some magical sword? He looked to Morgan. She was the damned sorceress. Couldn't she *alacazam* Traverse back into his old body? He waited for her to say something helpful. More of the quiet kindness she'd shown earlier. Instead she sat, biting her lip, looking everywhere but at the broken-down, old-young man. As if she didn't care. Couldn't be bothered.

The room was silent but for the ensign's gulping sobs until Cam couldn't stand it. "It'll be all right," he said gruffly.

That got Morgan's attention. She rose. Motioned him toward the hall. "Excuse us. Colonel Sinclair and I need to speak privately." Taking him by the arm, she dragged him to the door. "What do you mean telling him it'll be all right?" she demanded in a hoarse whisper.

"You saw him," he said so only she could hear. "I couldn't just leave him in that state. You're the witch. Fix him."

"Keep your voice down." She pursed her lips. Looked over to the ensign and back. "It's not that easy. If my gram were here or even my brother . . . They understand this sort of thing. Not me. I don't know."

Unease settled across his shoulders. "But you *can* fix him. Right?"

"I. Don't. Know," she repeated slowly. "I don't want him to think we're here to heal him. We're here to find out what we can about the men who attacked him. That's all."

"So once you've found out what you need, you just walk away?"

"I came to do a job. Find that sword. Get it back to the *Fey*. If I succeed, no one else will suffer like he's suffering. Isn't that enough?"

Cam turned to go back to Traverse afraid that if he stayed he'd answer Morgan's cold-blooded logic with some choice words of his own. Still, he couldn't leave without saying something. His emotions were too charged. His body strung tight.

He spun back to face her, fury licking his words. "Take a good look at him, Morgan, and you tell me. Do you think it's enough?"

Chapter 5

Doran polished the long obsidian blade of the Aztec dagger. Until recently, the most prized possession among his rich and varied collection. Three other blades and an ornate Byzantine fighting axe taken from the storming of Seringapatam lay on the table in front of him already sharpened and oiled.

"So they've come, have they?" He carefully placed the Aztec dagger back among the rest. "I knew it would take the *Fey* this long to admit they'd lost control over . . ." He paused. ". . . over Andraste's sword. I wish I could have seen Scathach explaining that little failure."

He never referred to *Neuvarvaan* by name if he didn't have to. He'd found out months ago that speaking it aloud seemed to strengthen its already considerable influence. His head would buzz for hours with the black speech of the *Morkoth*, the forgers of the blade and the ones who'd imbued it with the power of undying.

In their hands, it had been a weapon of destruction. In his, it would be a keeper of the peace. His peace. For who would dare challenge a ruler with an army of immortals?

"I'm surprised the *Duinedon* army colonel's in league with

Scathach, though," he continued. "Can't say I saw that one coming." He gave a snort of astonishment.

Captain Burfoot shifted uncomfortably, threading his hat brim through his hands. As if he were on trial. As in a way, he was. There was always a need for—volunteers. *Neuvarvaan* demanded it. And who was Doran Buchanan to deny the sword anything it demanded if it gave him what he wanted in return?

"Do you want us to deal with the colonel and his woman like we did Hurley?" the captain asked.

Burfoot had described a fiery-haired beauty with the focused eyes of a hunter. Had to be Morgan Bligh. There weren't two such among the ranks of *Amhas-draoi*. But did Scathach really think an untested mage chaser had a chance against him? It was almost insulting.

Doran raised an amused brow. "This woman's no common soldier's trull. Haven't you learned anything I've taught you? Bligh's *Other* like us. And more than that, she's *Amhas-draoi*. You may be able to take Sinclair. But she'd fry you before you got within fifty yards of her." At Burfoot's look of skepticism, Doran laughed. "Don't let her sex fool you. She may look like a good ride, but she'd strip the meat from your bones in less time than it took you to mount her."

Even as his mind turned over the implications of this odd pairing of mortal and *Fey*, he felt the tug of *Neuvarvaan*. It called to him. A thread of ancient words beckoning him to unsheathe it. Admire it.

He needed to hold the inlaid hilt. Marvel at the mastery of silverwork. Feel the rush of power burst through him when he gripped it. Andraste's sword whispered to him. Tempted him with unimaginable rewards. And he knew he was close. So close. The gift of immortality was in his grasp. The dark magics that ruled the goddess blade almost clear to him now.

And once all had been revealed, he'd begin the recruiting. He'd be swamped with enlistees, for certain. And why not?

No more death by cannon or bayonet. No more maiming from shrapnel. His army would be the best of the best. Respected. Feared. And completely unstoppable.

All *Neuvarvaan* asked in return was blood.

A bargain at any price.

Burfoot fidgeted as if he too felt the sword's influence. Heard its whispered words. He cleared his throat. "So what are my orders?"

"I don't want to leave town," Doran answered. "I need the deeper *Fey* magics that surface at the Giant's Fist." He stared hard at the shadows of death gleaming in the black heart of the Aztec dagger as if the answer were writ within. "Watch them. Don't let them out of your sight. But don't get too close, and for damn sake don't use magic. Bligh will sense the mage energy and be on to you in a flash."

"And if they start to get too close?"

Doran couldn't help himself. He glanced at the locked cupboard. His body hummed with an almost sexual need to curl his fingers around the hilt. Caress the sharpened steel.

The sword responded to his attention. A crackle of black speech leapt into his mind. Buried its hate. Made it his own.

He offered the captain a thin, cruel smile. "The sword hungers again. Mayhap we should invite Colonel Sinclair to dinner?"

Cam slid into the seat across from Morgan, his face gray with fatigue, a slightly wild look in the blue chill of his eyes. He immediately searched out the barmaid, waving her over.

Morgan's temperature rose, her hands tightening around her glass. She was already in a foul temper after being left behind. Cam had convinced her Traverse's commanding officer would never speak freely in the presence of a woman. And though she wanted to argue, she knew he was right.

Instead, she'd spent her day exploring the town. Starting at the heart of Bedford Square, she'd ranged outward, investigated every alley, dead end, and blind corner. She'd scouted the water's edge, up- and downriver before falling back to note where the soldiers gathered. Taverns, inns, and a rickety, dingy set of barracks still inhabited, though most of the militias had been disbanded.

Where could Doran be hiding? He'd cloaked his magic, a task requiring discipline and great strength. Both qualities the man held in abundance. But it made her hunt that much harder. She'd not felt a trace of mage energy. Not caught even a hint of a trail to follow. Worse, if he were disguising himself beneath a *glamorie*, he could be anywhere. Anyone.

"You're late," she complained. "You said six. It's almost eight."

A corner of his lip twitched. "Miss me?" He downed the whiskey—the barmaid ogling him like a piece of raw meat—and ordered another. When the woman pranced off to fill his empty glass, Cam gave Morgan an apologetic smile. "You can't snarl at me forever, can you?" When she glowered even harder, he grimaced. "Apparently, you can."

This time, she fought a smile. Pursed her lips together, fully immune now to the Sinclair charm. "I was worried." His brows rose in amused surprise. "Yes, worried," she repeated. "Obviously we've been followed."

Cam grew serious. "Obviously. The man Traverse said he caught—I checked with the major. His name was Hurley. A private from the Eleventh Foot."

"Was?"

"Hurley's been murdered."

Her stomach plummeted, the hope of an easy break vanishing. Hurley had been a connection to *Neuvarvaan* and Doran. A connection severed before he could tell them anything.

She was saved from responding by the return of the

simpering barmaid. Gods, had the woman never seen a good-looking man? She was doing everything but exposing herself. And with Morgan—Cam's supposed wife—sitting right there. She could only imagine what the slut would attempt if he were alone. She gritted her teeth. Flashed the woman a dangerous look that sent her scuttling back to the bar. "So what the hell happened to Hurley?"

Cam winced at her language, which only served to raise her temperature another notch. "He was unconscious and under guard. They'd found him after Traverse arrived back in town raving about the attack on the moor. But of course since Traverse had no obvious wounds and Hurley was nothing but broken bones, Traverse was arrested. Later a guard was placed on Hurley as well. When Ensign Traverse . . ." He paused. ". . . aged, the military were more baffled. Downright scared, if you ask me." Cam slammed back the second whiskey, only now beginning to lose the strung, haunted look he'd carried with him into the taproom. "The major in charge was happy to wash his hands of the mess and hand it off to us. This is the second incident at the Giant's Fist in two months. The first soldier died."

"And Hurley's actual killing?"

"The guards don't remember anything. According to them, they never left their posts. Never slept."

"Magic. I'd bet my life."

Cam didn't argue. Just stared into the bottom of his empty whiskey glass.

Prepared for a fight, Morgan felt deflated. As if he'd cheated her out of something. Frustration pounded through her with every breath. Resentment at being left behind. Cam's embarrassed reactions to her lack of refinement. And now exasperation that the only link to Andraste's sword was dead. Anger clawed at her, demanding an outlet. An escape.

Cam was the perfect target. She knew if she picked at him,

he'd give her the fight she wanted. And her scorn and annoyance would remain alive. Hard emotions. Safe emotions. "Ready to believe now, are you?" She sneered. "Not so quick with the snotty comments after seeing *Neuvarvaan*'s power."

He lifted his head, and for a second, he looked like he wanted to throttle her or kiss her—or both. His eyes glittered, silver blue like the heart of a flame. She could drown in those eyes. Had once.

Her skin prickled as her stomach gave a strange, lurching plunge. She blinked and looked away. Ashamed of her petty needling. More ashamed of her unbidden reaction.

"Have you sent word to your family about Traverse?" He'd chosen to ignore her waspish comment, but his expression was stern, almost disappointed, which only infuriated her more. As if she were acting the child.

Her jaw clenched, her stare as icy and forbidding as she could make it. "I told you I would. But don't expect an answer right away. And even if my grandmother comes, that's no guarantee."

He shrugged, a grim smile curving the corners of his mouth. "No guarantee, but it's a hope Traverse didn't have before. Thank you."

She knew what he was thinking. That she was cruel. Heartless.

It wasn't true.

She liked to think of it as single-minded. Driven. Focused on what needed to be accomplished. And those were positive traits, weren't they?

"So, have you checked on Traverse?" she asked. "If those men silenced Hurley because of what he might tell us, the ensign could be in danger."

"That's why I'm late. I've had Traverse moved and posted a guard. The major didn't like me commandeering his men, but mention of General Pendergast's authority didn't leave him a lot of choice."

"How is he?"

"The ensign? Holding his own. He's tough. He's needed to be."

Was he trying to make her feel worse? "I told you I wrote, you can't ask more—"

"Morgan," he interrupted. His steel-blade gaze softened. "I said thank you." There was no attitude behind the words. He meant it. And that confused her more than anything that had gone on before.

Her stomach did that uncomfortable tumbling again. She felt as if she'd passed a test. Gained his approval. But when had Cam's good opinion become so important? And what would he think of her when he found she'd been lying to him? Keeping secrets?

Cam's hand rested on the table. Close enough that she could brush it if she wanted and it would look like an accident. The long, clever fingers, absent of any adornment—not even a signet ring. The faint scar across three knuckles he'd told her he got from a fishhook when he was nine.

There was strength in those hands. There had to have been to fight and survive as he had on the bloody heights around Toulouse. Salamanca. Badajoz. And dozens of other battlefields through six long years. And yet those same hands could bring her to climax with the gentlest of touches. Play her body until she cried for release.

She shifted in her seat. Wished she had something as strong in her glass as Cam's whiskey. She needed to get a hold of herself. Cam was just using her. Like he'd done last winter. Like he'd do again in a heartbeat. But she was ready this time. On her guard.

And there was no way in this world—or any other—that Cam was going to sneak his way back into her bed—or her life. They'd find *Neuvarvaan*. Restore it to the *Fey* and go their separate ways. Period.

She snatched another look at him, but this time he caught her. And she couldn't look away. His face held a wistful, far-away expression, but his eyes had grown dark as slate. A purpose in them lost to even her powers.

She threw herself to her feet. Left the table, Cam's intense gaze boring into her back.

Distance, her final refuge.

Cam pushed his way to a table past a crowd of soldiers. And whores. And those who enjoyed the company of both.

The public tap of The Forlorn Hope reeked of smoke and sweat and male bravado. The tavern's private parlors offered space for gambling. Other chambers, even more private, offered sex. Women wove their way between the tables, serving drinks. Advertising what could be had for a price. And vice here came at a premium. This was no run-down gin shop. Nor was it a posh officers-only gentlemen's club. The owner had carried off his establishment with style, keeping his high-class guests as happy as the lowest privates. If there was information to be gathered, it would be found here.

And though Cam tried not to dwell on it, it had the added benefit of being away from Morgan. The long days of constant confrontation and endless nights spent in enforced proximity wore on his already frayed nerves. He'd even begun dreaming again. Fragments of memories he'd locked away when he'd stepped off the boat in Portsmouth. Things he'd done. Things he hadn't. Both haunted him on occasion.

He drowned his regrets with shot after shot until he went numb. Until the hollow ache of guilt didn't bother him anymore. He felt as if he'd tumbled into one of his nightmares. That same sense of unreality. Of impending doom. As if somewhere normal had taken a horribly wrong turn and ended up in a place where he was pretending marriage with a woman he'd slept with and lied to—and, oh, by the way, she came armed and dangerous.

He needed another drink. Or barring that—something to take his mind from the churning confusion. Get him back on solid ground. He focused on the tangible. The rational. A mysterious soldier. A missing weapon. Find one, the other, or both, and he could go home to Strathconon. Put this whole bloody awful mess behind him.

He stood, his whiskey binge making itself felt in the swaying of the room. The sudden unevenness of the floorboards. The new attractiveness of the women.

One peeled herself away from a nearby table of officers. Sauntered his way, her body brushing suggestively against him. "You look as if you've seen a ghost," she said, her voice a gravelly whisper.

As things were shaping up, not an impossibility.

"Not interested, but I appreciate the concern," he said, squaring his shoulders.

He squinted. Tried concentrating on one spot to keep the rest of the world from spinning. It helped. He knew if he could just make it outside, he'd feel better. Fresh air. A long walk. Both would dilute the worst of the alcohol. Always had before.

The woman followed, coiling herself against him, her body soft, her face decent, her morals nonexistent.

Without quite understanding how it had occurred, by the time they'd hit the door, he'd wrapped an arm around her waist and she'd giggled her assent, her breath hot against his neck. "Name's Lucy. And I can make you forget she ever existed."

He frowned. "How do you know I want to forget?"

Her lip curled in a pouty smile. "Because if you didn't, you'd never have come with me."

The street was dark, the sharp breeze like a slap in the face.

Lucy pulled him toward an alley running between the pub and a tall, narrow stone house. A set of stairs climbed the outside of the building to a landing and a door on the second floor. She glanced up, but instead of heading to the stairs, tugged him behind the building with anxious, greedy hands. "I've a room next door, but I share it with another girl. She's using it. We'll have to make do. But don't worry. I'll cut you a deal on the price."

Pushing him back against the wall, she fumbled at his breeks.

Cam closed his eyes. Tried to forget everything that had led him to this place tonight.

His tortured memories dredged up Morgan. Not as she was now, sulky and ill-tempered, but as she'd been in Scotland. Laughing up at him, her hair spilling across her naked shoulders. Her eyes—the exact shade of his family's malt whiskey—bright with lust and joy.

The world tilted out from under him, and he groped to find purchase on the wall. As he stumbled, the back of his head connected with the bricks. Lights burst in front of his eyes.

Lucy sidled against him, her breasts pushed up into his face, as she untucked his shirt. Her smell of stale smoke and greasy food turned his stomach. Exploded through his pathetic imaginings like black powder.

What the hell was he doing? Had he gone mad? Sunk to the point where a quick bang in an alley was necessary to keep body and soul together? "No," he said, grabbing her arms.

She ignored him. Knelt.

"I said no." This time louder. Stronger. "Get off me." He yanked her to her feet, repulsed at the fear in her eyes.

She backed away, her alarm swiftly becoming anger when she realized he wasn't going to come after her. "Where's my money? You owe me." Her earlier sultry murmur had risen to a fishwife screech.

Cam dug in his pocket. Tossed her the first coin that came to hand. She caught it. Dropped the half crown into her apron with a mingled look of surprise and disgust. She shook her head. "You stupid prat! You asked me out here. Remember?"

He didn't, but that didn't matter. He plowed a hand through his hair. Took a steadying breath. "You told me I wanted to forget. You were wrong. There are some things I want very much to remember."

Chapter 6

Morgan had been sitting in the taproom for an hour. By now she was certain. The man at the corner table watched them.

He sat far from the fire to hide his features. And alone, although men had invited him to share in a drink or a game of draughts. He'd turned all offers down—using his untasted pint as little more than a prop. He'd already waved the barmaid aside twice.

She wasn't certain what had alerted her first. The inn's taproom had been full and there had been nothing to distinguish him as odd. But she'd been on edge since this morning. Looking for trouble. And so she'd remained alert. Watchful. Picking up on signs and signals until she'd narrowed it down to him. It must have been the precision of his movements. The careful way he handled himself. It spoke of training. And ability. Cam had that same quality. Though in his case, it was honed to diamond perfection. Buffed to a high shine.

At least it had been.

She snuck a glance at him. Frowned. He'd been drinking again. A lot. She'd known it was bad as soon as she'd seen him come into the room. But she'd bitten her tongue this time. If he wanted to pickle his liver, so be it. So long as he didn't get in her way while she retrieved the *Fey* sword. But damn it, did he have to look so god-awful miserable and vulnerable and good enough to eat all at the same time?

It plucked at a long-buried maternal part of her that wanted to smooth the lines from his face, take him in her arms, and let him know everything would be all right. Even if it wasn't. Not a part of her she wanted to explore too closely. Or get too comfortable with. She returned to watching the man in the corner. Kept her eyes and her mind firmly off Cam Sinclair.

But in the seconds she'd been mooning, the man had disappeared. The table stood empty. She scanned the room, but there was no sign of him.

"Cam. He's gone."

"Probably gone out back to take a piss."

That was a possibility, but she doubted it. He hadn't taken more than half a dozen sips from his beer. "No. He's gone. I'm going to follow him."

"Morgan. Wait. I need to say something. . . . I . . ." Cam grabbed her wrist. Met her gaze. And for a moment, it was the man she remembered. The silver blue chill in his eyes like tempered steel. The determination in the chiseled angles of his face. She swallowed around the lump that sprang into her throat.

She paused. Waited.

And then he opened his mouth. "Don't be daft. You can't go wandering out by yourself. It's not safe for a woman alone." And the moment passed.

She shook him off. Pushed back her chair. "Coming?"

His hesitation told her everything. She couldn't say she was surprised. But she was disappointed.

She didn't wait. Grabbing her cloak, she left him behind. Stepped into the dark. And didn't look back to see if he followed.

The streets were almost deserted. Low clouds covered the moon, and a brisk wind plucked at her cloak. Morgan slid from shadow to shadow, keeping no more than twenty paces between her and the man. He crossed through the market square, making no attempt to evade any followers. He obviously didn't realize she'd noticed him. That was good. It was tempting to conceal herself within the invisible security of the *feth-fiada*, but she didn't want to use magic if she didn't have to. If she was dealing with Doran or one of his men, they might sense the mage energy released. Know she was on to them.

Rain began, a sprinkle at first that grew to a downpour, shielding her footsteps, but also making it hard to track her quarry. His pace quickened as he moved farther from the inn. Was he on to her? Or was he just impatient to reach his destination?

She followed him into a rabbit warren of alleys, each one more filthy, cramped, and crooked than the last. The dark buildings leaned drunkenly over the streets. A cat lurked by a stack of broken crates.

She paused. Listening. Hoping for a betraying footstep telling her which way he'd gone. A flash caught the corner of her eye. Lamplight. A torch.

Hurrying after him, she vaulted a low stone wall, ducked down a narrow lane close to the river. Dank fetid air rose from the mudflats, and she caught the scrape of a boat against a piling. Wiping the rain from her eyes, she broke into a jog, slamming to a halt at the end of an alley. A dead end. But just beyond was the river where her man was obviously making his escape. How had he arrived there?

She whipped around. Of course. She knew where she was. She'd been here before during her earlier scouting. She was behind Church Lane, the river no more than a few hundred yards beyond. High walls ran the length of the cramped passageway. Above could just be seen the roofs of sheds, outbuildings. The spire of a church. Gates studded the wall, giving access to the yards and enclosures. She dashed back up, trying every one. Rattling the latches. All locked.

"Damn."

Reaching the gate that led into the churchyard, she pushed on it. A sharp tingle zinged up her arm as if she'd hit her funny bone. Her fingers went numb. "Magic," she ground out through clenched teeth.

Someone knew they were on the hunt for Doran. Someone with knowledge about the traitorous *Amhas-draoi* and *Neuvarvaan*.

And he was getting away.

She put her shoulder to the gate, slammed it open in her haste to catch her target before the river carried him beyond her sight. If he put in farther downshore, she wanted to see where.

As she raced across the church grounds toward the river gate, long grass dragged at her wet skirts. A low branch whiplashed her cheek. She dodged a headstone, her breathing overloud in her ears. Surely she'd be heard.

She reached the river gate. Tried it. Locked.

"Shit."

How had he escaped? She backtracked, but by now it was pointless. He was long gone.

"Hello, pet. Lost yer way, have ya?"

Figures melted out of the shadows. Street thugs by the coarse, half wild look about them. Unpredictable. Overconfident. "It's not wise fer a pretty young thing to wander alone."

She counted five or six of them, cutting off her escape. No weapons in sight, but doubtless they were hoping sheer terror would be enough to quell any fight in her. An easy mark.

She smiled. Their mistake.

"I'm safe enough," she answered, drawing herself up. Weighing her options.

The heaviest of the group gave her a gap-toothed leer. "You've a sharp tongue."

"You should feel my blade." She flung her cloak away, revealing her dagger.

It was a game of who bluffs best. She had a weapon, but didn't want to use it unless forced to. Dead bodies meant questions she didn't have time to answer. A fireworks display of mage energy was equally chancy. Meant a whole different set of questions she couldn't answer. But perhaps a more subtle show of power would be enough. Now that her target had escaped, she didn't have to worry about giving herself away.

"I don't want to tangle with you." She pitched her voice to the correct key. Allowed the persuasive magic of the *leveryas* to infuse her words. Suggestion would become compulsion, would become an irresistible command. "Let me pass and go on about my business."

The men hesitated. Some fought the spell, their eyes darting, their limbs twitching. Others—more pliable—simply gave up. Stepped out of her way.

She slid past, keeping up a steady stream of quiet talk, nothing to rouse them out of their stupor. Just enough to hold them within the *leveryas*' grip. "I'm no threat to you. I'll disappear. You won't remember I was even among you."

She'd not gone more than ten paces when one of them—stronger than the others—broke free. He straightened in lethal challenge. "What tricks are you playin', bitch?" he growled, reaching for his weapon.

A shout drowned out her response. Someone ran toward them. "Get the hell away from her!" The dark figure materialized into Cam. He flung himself among the crowd, his sword drawn. Ready for any of them to make an impetuous move. "Go, Morgan. While you can."

Her concentration broken, the spell dissolved. "What the blazes are you doing?" she hissed.

"Thank you is the usual response," he snapped.

The villains stirred and regrouped. Wary but instantly on

guard. Weapons appeared. Restraint vanished. One of them advanced, fisting a crude knife.

Cam, surprisingly agile despite the alcohol, parried with a twist of his blade that disarmed the attacker.

The others had hung back as if waiting to see how the feint would be met. But no longer. She had to admit, numbers were on their side. Six on two made odds pretty good. But then, they were assuming she was a typical female and Cam—indistinguishable out of uniform—more bravado than skill.

As the gang closed around them, training took over, and thought became instinct. It would be so easy. Just a slight draw on her gifts and she and Cam could be free and clear. No looking back. But no. Battle magic was out. Nothing to bring attention to themselves. Nothing to delay their ultimate goal. She hated it, but so it must be.

She ducked a dagger strike. Swung with a fist, connecting with her attacker's jaw. He howled, spitting blood and a broken tooth. Spinning on her heel, she slid her dagger through another's shoulder. Screaming and clutching his wound, he splashed back up the alley. Lost himself in the downpour.

Cam shouted for her, but she couldn't speak. Breath clogged her throat. Her lungs burned. He was in trouble, cornered against a wall. He fought well, but there were too many.

Rage screamed through her veins. She dove amid them, her dagger a silver arc of steel that wounded when a bit more strength would kill. They wouldn't appreciate the mercy, but it might keep her from the questions a pack of corpses would require.

Cam was down, a hand to his chest.

Oh gods. He was down.

Blood and rain soaked his shirt. His eyes stared through her, shock and pain whitening his face. He looked at the growing scarlet bib spreading across his front as if confused.

It's not serious. It's not serious. She kept the refrain going in her head. Forced herself to look away. Pushed the panic deep where it wouldn't distract.

Two men remained between her and safety. Fighting to keep her voice steady, she drew once more on the *leveryas*. Faltered when she glanced at Cam's slumped body. Then gathering herself together, she let the magic take hold. Used her words to calm the situation to manageable.

They retreated, their slack jaws and mesmerized gazes evidence that this time, she'd succeeded in gaining full control.

She dropped to her haunches beside Cam. "Can you walk?" she asked, hating the frightened waver in her voice.

He nodded, his jaw clenched tight. His eyes closed.

Looping her arm under him, she let his rest across her shoulder. Struggled to her feet, bent under his weight. "Don't you die on me, Cameron Sinclair."

For a split second, mischief sparkled in his pale face. "I'd have thought you'd be glad to see me go to the devil."

Afraid to admit the fear that weighted her stomach like lead, Morgan sniffed. "Oh no. If anyone sends you to hell, it gets to be me."

A strangled laugh was his only answer.

Cam hissed as Morgan peeled off his blood-soaked shirt, exposing the jagged, torn flesh left by the villain's knife.

He felt a complete fool. What the hell had he been thinking charging into that brawl like some green recruit? Acting the reckless swashbuckler when the situation called for the stealth of the assassin?

He glanced up at Morgan, rummaging through her bag, her back to him. There stood his reason. He'd seen her surrounded, and every instinct had flown. This wasn't a clinical kill. Not a planned execution. This was Morgan. And all his effort had been to get between her and them. Not the smartest of ideas, as it turned out.

"An inch or two lower and you'd have bled to death in that alley," was her grateful comment.

"Sorry to have disappointed," he replied, taking the cloth she handed him. Gritting his teeth as he pressed it against the gash to stanch the blood.

His whole shoulder throbbed where the knife had bounced off his collarbone. Nausea rolled his belly, and the room wavered like water on glass. He bit his lip, refusing to pass out. Morgan would never let him hear the end of it. She was bad enough now. After the momentary truce when she thought he'd been dying—and wasn't that interesting?—she'd returned to being surly as a badger.

"The next time I rescue you," he said, "I'll try to get it right."

She threw up her head at that remark, a dangerous flash in her eyes. "You rescue me? If you hadn't come blundering in like a drunken bull in a china shop, I'd have been away without a memory to mark my passing. I had the situation under control. It was only your meddling that nearly got us killed."

His startled reaction sent a spasm of pain from his shoulder down his right side. Threw pinwheels of light across his field of vision. "And how did you expect to get away from a gang of cutthroats? Turn them into toads?"

She'd discarded her skirt. She stood now, hands on hips, in leather breeks. Tall boots. Her hair bundled into a loose braid. He'd be appalled—or excited—at her appearance if he didn't hurt so damned much.

"I've told you before, Cam. I'm not some simpering miss who can't break a nail without fainting. And you should be glad of my strength. You'd be dead otherwise."

"So you're saying you rescued me?"

The flash in her eyes had become a red-hot boil. She looked ready to explode. "You deserved to get hurt. Mayhap it'll knock some sense into you. Look at yourself. You're worthless to this investigation like this."

The accusations slammed into him like bullets. And hurt all the worse because she was right. He drank too much. Slept too little. Had done so for months. Drinking had been the easiest way to forget how much he'd lost.

At least it had been.

Until tonight.

Tonight had marked his ultimate low. A dingy alley. A whore on her knees. With him too full of self-pity to care.

He tried meeting Morgan's scowl, but couldn't hold it. It was as if she knew his thoughts. And despised him for them. It was just as well he'd kept his mouth shut in the taproom earlier. He could just imagine the scorn she'd have heaped on him for that moment of sentimentality.

Her point made, she spun away to rummage in her bags.

Resentment mingled with his pain. Why did he care what Morgan Bligh thought of him? She was everything he hated in a woman. Brash. Willful. Pushy. Arrogant.

And worst of all—right.

He watched her with growing anger as she worked. Grabbing up a leather drawstring bag from her traveling case. Pouring out a small amount of red powder into a cup. Adding water from the basin on the washstand. Every action abrupt. Meant to show her displeasure and her scorn.

Well, fuck that. It was her fault. She shouldn't have wandered off alone. If she'd stayed put like he'd told her, he wouldn't have had to chase after her. Wouldn't have had to take on an entire damned gang of thieves to save her skin. It was her fault. Not his. And he'd be damned if he'd play the chastened schoolboy for her.

Rescued? By Morgan? Not bloody likely.

"Here. Drink this." She shoved the cup of thick, viscous liquid at him.

He wrinkled his nose. "What is it?"

"Trust me. You don't want to know." She tipped it up, making him swallow. "But it will speed the healing charm."

He gagged, his fragile stomach revolting at the smoky-chalky-pepper taste of whatever she'd just forced down his throat. It was worse than Brodie's hair-of-the-dog elixir, and that was saying something.

"Lie back. This may hurt before it's over. Now, let me see the wound." She pushed his hand away. Moved aside his necklace chain. As her fingers brushed the cross, she jumped, her eyes widening in surprise.

"What's wrong?"

She pursed her lips, her eyes staring beyond him for a moment, and then she was back. "Hmm? What? It was nothing. Just a . . ." She fumbled, obviously troubled. "I thought I saw . . . It was nothing." She frowned. Once more all business.

He shivered. When had the room grown so cold? And when had the lights gone so dim?

She examined the stab wound. Smelled it. Ran her fingers around the flesh where the knife had penetrated before striking bone.

Clenching the blood-soaked rag in his hand, he fought the sudden urge to vomit. "A surgeon too?"

She shot him a long-suffering look. "I have a little healing ability. Enough to do what needs to be done."

He waited for the scathing words to follow, but she'd passed through fury and come out cold and contained. He wasn't sure he liked this version better.

He let himself relax under her slow, steady scrutiny. In fact, it was hard not to. Lethargy weighted his limbs. His chill was gone. Replaced by a warmth spreading outward from his shoulder. Penetrating through his system. He closed his eyes, letting the pain recede into the background. Whatever she'd given him to drink was potent stuff.

"*Airmid gwithyas a'n fenten. Ev sawya. Dian Cecht medhyk a'n spryon. Ev sawya.*"

"What did you say?" His words came out slurred and thready.

"*Shhhh.*" Her voice was low and soft and captured the memory of past times. Lost moments. His body reacted with ridiculous ease, his groin tightening in instant arousal. If he weren't floating in a drug-induced haze, he'd have been embarrassed as hell.

A sultry-sexy laugh met his ears. "You must not be hurt as badly as I thought."

He tried grabbing her wrist. Pulling her down next to him. She smelled so good. And he'd missed her so much. If only she'd waited for him to explain. If only he'd been able to. But she'd run. And he'd let her go. And the chance for the two of them had slipped away—if it had ever been.

She yanked her arm away. "Lie still. I told you this might hurt before it's over. And you may feel sick and dizzy after. It takes some people that way."

The warmth increased. Grew hot. Intensified into a cauterizing burn that started deep in the injured tissue and muscle. He grimaced. Bit his lip. Groaned. Chills and fever swamped him simultaneously. The burning became unbearable as if she held an open flame to his skin. He refused to cry out, but his back arched off the bed. His nails dug into his palms.

She held him down. Kneeled across his thighs to keep him steady. And still the words kept going. "*Leuvyow. Hwythow.*" A drone that went on and on, shooting slashes of agony into him at every syllable. "*Goes. Keher.*" Far worse than the pain of the actual stabbing. "*Ev sawya.*"

And then it ended.

His limbs trembled as if palsied. His breathing came rapid and shallow.

She rose, shoving her hair off her face with the back of

her arm. Walked to the basin to pour him a second cup of water. This time with no added hallucinogens. "Drink it all. And then sleep. You'll feel better in the morning."

A few drops made it past his lips before exhaustion overcame him. His last dismal thought—she was right. He'd failed.

Chapter 7

Cam slept. His wounded shoulder still swathed in the bandages of last night; the arm held protectively across his chest. His other arm he'd flung over his face against the morning sun.

He'd thrown off the covers, exposing his lean, muscled torso. His long, powerful legs. But like his face, months of drink and self-destruction had left their mark. Had he cared for his wife so much that her death had wrought such a change? Or did something more account for his devastating free fall?

She should turn away. Just walk out. Instead, she knelt beside him, feeling his forehead. Checking the bandage. Naught but a pink, angry scar to mark the passing of the villain's blade. And even that would fade in time. Like the others.

She'd seen the scars the first time they'd lain together. A long puckered weal of raised tissue marking his upper back. Another ugly slash scoring his upper thigh. Mementos of the war, he'd told her. No spinning of a heroic battle story. No recounting of miraculous derring-do meant to impress. He'd shrugged them off. Dismissed them. And so had she.

Until today.

Around his neck hung a cross upon a chain. Simple. Well

worn. But a recent acquisition. He'd not had it when they'd lain together last winter. She'd have remembered. Would have felt its power. And power, it had. She'd barely touched it last night and the images had burst in her head like fireworks. It would take little on her part to see what memories lay stored within the shards of jet. What else Cam had hidden from her their few short weeks together.

She cupped the cross in the palm of her hand, the thin gold chain draped across her fingers. Closing her eyes, she let the rippling power of the scrying deepen. Take hold of her. Show her what she might see.

Mage energy sparked up her arm. Stung her neck. Set her scalp tingling.

As if drawn up through deep waters, objects swam into view. Dim and murky at first, the scene emerged, gilded with a hazy afterglow. Emotional echoes. Distorted reflections of the past.

A sea or a lake, so clear it mirrored the sky and the snow-capped mountains ringing it to the north and east. She was Cam. Seeing the moment through his eyes. The sleek perfection of a racing yacht's tiller beneath his hand as it cut through the water.

A boy of ten or eleven scurried with lines and sails while a young girl sat tucked in an enormous waterproof, her hand outstretched to catch the spray off the creaming waves, licking the water from her fingers. Hugh. Euna. Their names fell into Morgan's mind as if they'd always been there.

The wind kicked round, sending the boat heeling on its side, the shoreline whipping past in a blur of green and brown and gray. Hugh laughed, pointing skyward as they raced a V of geese.

Cam threw his head back. Shouted into the wind. He was alive and in his element. The freedom from books and tutors and school and authority made his heart leap in his chest. Any minute he might soar skyward to join the birds.

Father and Mother were coming home today. They'd have one whole week together before Cam had to leave. Before he was forced to return to the civilizing influence of the south.

Hugh frowned. Gestured at the growing swells. The darkening skies. A storm approached, drawn like a curtain across the body of the loch.

Needles of rain stung Cam's face. Slicked his hands, making his grip on the tiller unsure. The sailboat wasn't made for this weather. It tossed and pitched as he fought for control, urging it back to shore. He squinted, looking for lights from the house. Tried to judge his distance. Gauge the crosswinds. He gripped his cross—whispered a quick prayer to the god of his faith. Another softer one to the Good Folk like Gran-da always did.

Tears and water slid down Euna's face, her terror palpable. Yet she did as ordered. Scrambled across the deck to catch a runaway line. Caught and tied down a lashing sail.

Uncle Josh would kill him for taking his new yacht out. Probably a week of pottage and eels for punishment. Made his stomach turn just thinking about it.

The wind screamed through the rigging, pushing them farther away from shore, as whitecaps crested over the gunwales. Broke in rivers across the deck. Hugh slipped and fell, coming up hard against the railing, saved from washing overboard by a hairsbreadth.

Fear knotted Cam's insides, but he refused to let it take him over. It had been his idea to launch the boat without permission. He would see them safe.

"When did you get back?" The tired voice tore through Morgan.

As if she'd been pulled into the water beneath the boat, she felt herself falling. Sucked back into the present. The vision no more than a raging headache.

"What are you doing?" Cam's hand closed over hers. Eased the cross from her grip, the chain sliding free. "Morgan?"

She hid her purpose behind a bland smile. "How's the arm?"

"It's—"

"Here." She took him by the elbow . . .

"Wait!"

. . . shook his arm up and down.

Pulling free, Cam grimaced as he massaged his shoulder. "Could you give me some warning before you torture me?"

She tossed him a wicked smile. "You're fine. Naught but a scar."

At his look of disbelief, she laughed. "See for yourself." She unwound the bandage. Dropped it on the floor.

Cam's eyes rounded at the ugly, pink weal. "Incredible."

"Not really. You'll still be sore for a few weeks. I'm not an expert at healing. My gifts don't run that way, and it's hard to perfect a talent that doesn't come naturally."

He shoved himself higher on his pillows. Ran a hand through sleep-tousled hair, the barest hint of a smile in his eyes. "I thought you just wiggled your nose or crossed your arms and nodded your head. I'd no idea magic was so complicated."

She'd grown up with brothers so she recognized a barbed comment when she heard one. Cam teased, but this time not in a mean way. More to see what he could get away with. Even so, it caught her off guard. Cam was supposed to remain taciturn and unpleasant. Not charming. Or amusing.

Not in a way that might make her start to like him.

Unsure of how to respond, she let his remark slide. "We, *Other*, keep to ourselves. Most of us hide our abilities and our *Fey* heritage. Or use it in a way that the mortal world would never suspect the truth. Like a dark family secret. The mad aunt in the attic no one talks about."

"And your family?"

A shallow grief passed over her heart. "In our case the mad aunt actually lived in a comfortable set of apartments. But that's another story."

"I meant how do they handle their . . . *Fey*-ness?"

She'd forgotten he'd met her family once. In the spring. He'd been investigating the fifth death at a tomb near Lands End. And she'd been horrified by his invasion into what she'd always thought of as a sanctuary. The one place she could truly let her hair down. With his unexpected appearance, the world of *Other* and mortal collided head-on in one bloody awful mess.

It had collided again in General Pendergast's office, but at least she'd had some warning. Time to prepare against the pain of seeing him again.

Or so she'd thought.

She shrugged. "My family's a bit of both. My brother Ruan's always hated his *Fey* blood."

She paused, unable to tell whether Cam was really interested or whether he was just being polite. He'd never asked about her past before. As if their lives before meeting hadn't mattered once they'd found each other. Or—the more cynical side chided—as if he'd never meant for it to last long enough to bother.

Still, he asked now. That counted for something.

"And your other brother?" he pressed.

She shot him a look, but saw nothing but open curiosity in his question. "He's more like my grandmother. Jamys studied to become a physician, but left university before finishing. Now he tends to the health of the tenants and the villagers and those who've heard of his luck with even the most stubborn illnesses."

Cam shifted his shoulder. "No doubt."

She twisted the wolf-head ring—her family's emblem—on her finger, the citrine eyes of the beast winking up at her. Ridiculous, but she missed them. She'd fought her whole life to get away from her family's overwhelming, in-your-business closeness, and now when she'd finally won her independence, she wished she could curl up with Gram for a long heart-to-heart. Trade good-natured insults with Ruan and Jamys. Or fling her arms around her father and bury her face into the warm, pipe smell of his jacket.

And it wasn't just her family she ached for. She missed rambling Daggerfell's woods. Watching the ships pass east through the Channel. Rounding the last turn of the drive to have the rambling old house appear out of the trees as if conjured there, its lamplit windows beckoning her home.

"What about you?" she ventured, heading off a surprising wave of homesickness.

He went still, his eyes trained on some distant past. "My aunt and uncle had the raising of us after our parents died. They'd no children of their own, you see. As the oldest, I was supposed to follow into the family business. Marry the woman they'd picked for me. Raise a passel of little Sinclairs. Grow fat and respectable."

"I take it you didn't exactly fall in with the family plan." She could sympathize. She'd bucked tradition as well. First, by spending more time tagging after her brothers and cousins than attending to the proper pursuits of a young woman of quality. Later, when she'd made it known she wished to journey to Skye rather than London for the Season they'd planned for her.

Cam grimaced. "Wrong woman. Wrong profession—"

Morgan's gaze fell on the powerful muscles of his arms. The broad chest. "And nowhere near fat or respectable."

That drew a laugh. "Uncle Josh tried to understand, but . . . well, let's just say I've spent my life disappointing him."

"I'm sorry." A ridiculous response, but the only words that sprang to mind.

He shrugged. "It is what it is."

The regret in those few words was more convincing than any long-winded rant. And more powerful because she'd seen his family. Hugh. Euna. Memories of Cam's childhood in the Highlands of Scotland. It was plain they'd been close. As it was equally plain he'd been the wild one. Reckless. Bold. Foolish.

Nothing had changed.

Her thoughts trained inward, she started when he spoke.

"You did say you'd fixed it." Cam tested his shoulder, wincing as he lifted it over his head. Made a fist.

She shook off her musings, aware of their treacherous course. "Horrid man. You should be grateful I didn't let you bleed to death. It was your fault. All of it."

Prepared for a fight, she didn't expect the sullen "You're right" that followed.

"I'm sorry, Morgan." He lay back against the headboard. Stared up at the ceiling, an unreadable expression in his distant gaze.

She sensed his turmoil. And his pain. And a whirling storm of confusion too tangled for her to unravel. His emotions pressed like a weight upon her chest.

Her heart fluttered queerly just imagining that knife blade entering a few inches lower. A few inches deeper.

"I'm getting damned tired of apologizing," he said, breaking into the awkward silence. "Damned tired. Especially when you won't believe me." He swung around to face her, his eyes as angry as the storm-tossed loch. He lifted a hand as if he might caress her cheek. Pull her close.

She swept to her feet, away from the tantalizing heat of a body she knew too well. Hands that knew her every secret place. Lips that could tease a scream from her.

Away from a man that could love her until she shattered

into a million pieces or hurt her more deeply than any other person alive.

Morgan flung her bag onto the bed. Wiped her forehead with the back of a sleeve. She was a mess. Skirts sopping and muddy to the knees. Jacket torn and streaked with dust. And still she managed to look sexy.

Cam caught himself staring. Quickly refocused on working his stiff arm.

"Where have you been?" he asked, trying to keep the concern from his voice. If he hadn't known it before, this morning had shown him the ease with which he could slip into making himself believe he and Morgan were good again. That the past six months never happened.

"I've been down at the riverfront." She pulled the combs from her hair. Shook it out. Plucked a stray leaf or two from her head. She wasn't making this not-staring business easy. "I wanted to retrace my steps from last night."

"And did you find anything?"

He pulled his shirt on, careful not to jar his shoulder. Morgan swore he was fine, but it sure as hell didn't feel like it. His collarbone throbbed, and any quick movement sent slashes of pain on a straight path from his arm to his brain.

"I found traces of mage energy," she said. He must have looked confused, because she heaved a long-suffering sigh before continuing. "The energy used by *Fey* and *Other*—magic for want of a better term. When we draw on mage energy, residue is left behind. It can be used to track. Like a footprint. A blood trail. That's my expertise." She frowned. "The man I tailed last night was *Other*. No doubt of it. Someone knows we're here. And why. They're not taking any chances."

"How about the gang in the alley?"

"I'd like to say they were a coincidence. They couldn't

have known we'd be there." She seemed indecisive as if an unexpected problem had arisen. Her glance swept over him, a thoughtful look upon her face. Finally, she shrugged. Took off her soiled jacket.

"Unless that's why he showed himself," Cam suggested. "To entice us into following. A teaser to draw us out."

She cocked one more reluctant look at him and then—holy shit—began unbuttoning her gown. Neatly. Quickly. As if he weren't sitting two feet away. With his tongue hanging out.

"What the hell are you doing?" He threw himself to his feet, the pain from that ill-thought move almost enough to overwhelm the screaming blast of instant lust he was experiencing.

"My clothes are filthy. I have to change," she replied matter-of-factly, although challenge lit her burnished bronze gaze. "You're my husband. Get used to it." Letting the gown fall to the floor, she stepped out of it, clad in nothing but a shift. Skin he'd last seen months ago much too close for comfort. "It's not like you haven't seen me naked before."

"But that was . . . and now . . . shit, Morgan. You know as well as I do it's different now." He tried looking everywhere but at her. Failed miserably.

"Don't think about it. Pretend I'm a man."

Like that could happen.

"To answer your question, the men in the alley were no more than they seemed. A rabble of thieves. The *leveryas* worked too easily for them to be *Other*."

He concentrated. Pretended she was Brodie.

He could do this. He just had to ignore the hard-on that had him shifting uncomfortably, and pray she didn't realize what she was doing to him, although by that smug look in her eye, she knew exactly. In fact, she counted on it. "How do you know the men were waiting for you?" he asked.

She fumbled with the fresh gown she'd pulled out. Shot him a curious look. "For you?"

"Don't look so shocked." He forced himself to watch as she dressed, his gaze as calm as if this sort of thing happened every day.

In his dreams.

Long-since-discarded dreams.

"And they succeeded in that, didn't they? They stabbed me. Would have killed me."

"Only because . . ."

"Only because I jumped without looking. You can say it. I . . ." He shook his head. "Stupid me. I thought you needed my help."

She took a seat at a dressing table. Began violently brushing her hair until it crackled. Her face in the mirror was grim. As if he'd annoyed her. "Well, next time think before you act the hero," she snipped. "As you saw, I'm not helpless."

Here he was, trying to apologize and she was still carping at him. What did she want? A full groveling confession? Well, damned if he was going to give it to her. He didn't care how hard she made him. He clenched his jaw. Began working his arm again.

"No. I can see you do very well on your own."

Morgan avoided it as long as possible. But it had to be done.

She'd hoped to be alone. Hoped Cam would use the excuse of his injury to stay lounging in comfort at the inn. But he'd surprised her. Gritted his teeth. Shrugged into his clothes. And ridden the three miles with almost no complaining.

She would scry the stones. Pull the memories stored within the Giant's Fist and pray they showed her Doran. She needed to see his face. Or rather the *glamorie* he'd woven to conceal himself. He wouldn't keep to his true form. Not when he knew he was being hunted.

She'd last seen the rogue *Amhas-draoi* in Skye two years ago. A tall, barrel-chested man, he'd been polite, but distant. Holding himself apart from the daily life of the school. Spending long weeks away, or alone in his chambers. Yet when asked, he did what was demanded of him. And did it well. He was a skilled mage. An amazing fighter.

He'd been a man to respect. Now he was a man to fear.

Why? What change had occurred within the *Amhas-draoi* to send him down this path? Or had he always planned for this? Had his time with Scathach simply been a way to gain access to the knowledge he needed? She couldn't believe that. The head of her order would have read the signs and understood the danger. Doran couldn't have hidden so much of what he planned for so long. Could he?

The questions worried at her, but in the end they mattered little against the task she'd been assigned. Doran's motivations aside, he needed to be stopped and the sword regained. Why he did what he did could be left to others.

Her scrying might or might not work. Stone was the most impressionable, but only the most forceful emotions, the most powerful images would imprint themselves and remain. Whether Traverse's terror had burrowed itself into the rock he stood bound to was a big if.

Wind plucked at her as she climbed the rocky, scrub-covered hill to the group of five stones. Weathered and gray with moss, they seemed to have erupted from the landscape as if the earth had spat them out.

Once free of the sheltering valleys, the wind picked up. As it swirled through the stones, it became sour and cold, smelling of decay and death. The soldier's had not been the only blood spilled in this place. Only the most recent.

Morgan glanced over her shoulder. Still stiff, Cam followed more slowly, his blond head bent against the hillside.

He stopped halfway up. Called to her. "Was it worth the trip?"

She hoped to hell it was. Doran was good. She had no idea what form he had taken, and he cloaked his magic. The traces and glimpses of mage energy she'd tracked in town had been slight compared to what he would give off. And *Neuvarvaan*'s power would shout itself to her if it were unsheathed. But that hadn't happened. Which was a small victory. No sword. No Undying. She and Doran were at a standoff.

Cam joined her at the top of the hill. Looked around at the sweep of rocky wilderness. "Reminds me of Strathconon," he remarked. "So why are we here again?"

She had a sudden urge to reveal the truth. Doran's defection. The seizing of *Neuvarvaan* by force with three *Fey* killed in the ambush. All unimaginable offenses. Unthinkable to one of her kind. Yet Doran had done it, and taken pleasure in the heinous crimes by the accounts of those he'd left alive. Those sins would be enough in her eyes to take him down. But he'd gone one step further. Involved the mortal world in his madness. And that could not stand.

Would Cam comprehend the significance of Doran's betrayal? Or would he dismiss it as more of her nonsense? Or worse, run to General Pendergast with what he'd learned?

There was too much at stake. She couldn't risk it. Not with a heart so bruised that any glimpse of the old Cam was enough to make her forget all her well-founded intentions.

Stay away from him. Keep quiet. Once she'd found the sword would be soon enough for Cam to learn the truth. By then, it wouldn't matter.

Ignoring his question, she knelt at the base of the tallest stone. The ground was trampled. Torn. She closed her eyes. Traced the gouged dirt. Plucked a blade of wilted yellow grass, twirling it between her fingers. Circling outward, she followed the faded evidence of struggle. Time had passed. The marks left by men were scarce and told her little. But enough.

"Four men. Mayhap five. They came on horseback." She pointed toward the north. "Up through the ravine to avoid anyone on the cart track."

"You can tell all that from a few dusty smudges and a piece of gorse?" His disbelief was evident in the tone of his voice.

She'd been right to follow her instincts. It was obvious Cam couldn't be trusted with the truth. But disappointed anger flared within her. At herself for doubting. At Cam for making it all so hard. She stood up, whipping around. Shot him a withering glare, wishing it had the power to scorch the look of doubt from his face.

It must have conveyed every ounce of her fury because he stepped back, motioning her to continue.

Taking a deep breath—as much to calm herself as to prepare for the scrying—she closed her eyes, placing both hands palm-flat against the stone. *"Gweles. Klywes. Bos."*

She used the words to strengthen the focus, but there was no need. She staggered under the overwhelming images and emotions. Teasing the separate threads apart to reveal a clear picture took more concentration. Her heart pounded against her ribs. Throbbed up into her throat. Her skin prickled as the lightning flare of mage energy sparked and flashed through her body. Fear took her over. Claimed her for its own.

She was there. She was Traverse.

Chapter 8

Stars gleamed high and white in a black sky. Ropes lashed him at ankle and waist. Chest and neck. They chafed and burned as he struggled. Blood snaked from a cut on his scalp, and his head hurt from the blow that had struck him down.

He squinted, trying to clear his vision. But that only made his head hurt worse.

Men emerged from the stones. Stepped from the darkness to take form, wraithlike around him. Uniformed. Masked.

His panic increased. His heart strained. A wild pounding shook his limbs.

An enormous man stepped from the group, a sword carried erect in front of him as if on display. Death shone from his pale eyes. A ruthless self-assurance weighted his step....

Doran Buchanan.

Morgan knew him by many names. *Amhas-draoi*. *Other*. Now—enemy.

Morgan knew who she'd see, but still the shock of him standing mere feet away frayed her ties to Traverse. Her knowledge became his just as his terror fed her own panic.

Dark mage energy rippled off the goddess blade. The force of it enough to send a chill slicing through her.

She fought the urge to sever her connection to the stone. She needed more. She would hold out a little longer. She knew she could. Swallowing a breath, she forced herself to sink back into the memory. . . .

Doran approached, his weapon drawn.

Traverse screamed. Fought harder, but the bonds held him fast. Cut off his air until he sank against the ropes, coughing.

Doran spoke, his face wavering in and out of focus.

A trick of the light? A result of the crack on his head? His features shifted and warped, never resting. Young. Old. Blond. Brunette. Bearded. Clean-shaven.

Morgan concentrated on ripping through the *glamorie*. The confusion of faces slowed. Settled. Held still. She had only seconds left.

Doran held the sword aloft. The black speech of the *Morkoth* dropped from lips curled back in vicious anticipation.

The pounding of her heart vibrated through her. Traverse's terror had become her terror. But she wouldn't look away. She remained locked on Doran's face and not on the weapon aimed at her heart.

Heavy-lidded eyes. Dark hair. A scar down his left cheek. And most revealing of all—sergeant's stripes.

All this she glimpsed as *Neuvarvaan* was drawn back. The final incantation whispered to the sword's *Morkoth* creators.

Morgan fought to break the link holding her in the moment. But she hadn't counted on the tangle of mage energy. Too many forces hallowed the stone. Too many conflicting pulls on the deep magic bound to this sacred place.

She scrambled to protect herself from what she knew was coming. Braced her body and her mind against the explosion of past and present colliding. The sword bit dead-on into her chest. Tore through her heart. Pinned her to the stone.

She screamed as the whirlpool opened beneath her feet. Dragged her away.

* * *

Cam caught Morgan as her legs buckled, the sudden weight on his sore shoulder pulling them both down. They sprawled together against the base of the standing-stone, her eyes wide and staring, her lips parted on the end of the *caoineag* shriek she'd let out just before she'd collapsed.

He scrambled to his knees, his gaze sweeping the area. No glint of sun off steel. No telltale whiff of powder. No slide of shale. If a shooter had followed them here, he'd come and gone. Cam leaned over her. Began to examine her for a bullet wound.

Morgan jerked once, gasping as if all the air had been driven from her lungs, before hunching forward, drawing her knees up under her.

Steadying his shaking hand while trying not to dwell on how scared he'd been, Cam held a flask under her nose. "Drink this."

"I'm all right," she croaked, pushing it away.

"What the hell happened?" he snapped, still reeling with fear that had his palms sweaty, his knees wobbling.

Wind bounced and curled through the stone fingers of the Giant's Fist, carrying whispered voices in a language he couldn't understand. The hairs on the back of his neck rose. So intense was his feeling of being watched, he half expected a *Fey* to step from out of the stones' shadow.

Whatever watched also listened. The wind died away. The air grew heavy with expectation. Cam shivered in the sudden shade cast by the scudding clouds.

"Morgan? What did you do?" He pressed her for an answer.

"I scryed the standing-stone." She held up a hand as if she knew what his next words would be. "Objects hold memories. Emotions. I can draw them out. See the past. I saw Ensign Traverse's killing. Saw *Neuvarvaan* and Dor . . ." She stopped. ". . . the man who wields it. We can track him down. Find Andraste's sword and return it to the *Fey*."

She tried standing, but Cam was faster. He gripped her shoulder. Held her down. "It can't hurt to rest here for another minute. Until you get your bearings."

"I'm fine," she bit back.

"You're not fine. You screamed. It was . . ." How could he describe the complete helplessness he'd felt hearing her ear-splitting, anguished cry? Knowing there wasn't a damned thing he could do.

He couldn't. Not without sounding like he cared. Which would scare her away quicker than anything else. "You were loud."

"Brilliant. That's professional." She flushed before pressing the heels of her hands to her eyes. Whatever had happened had shaken her more than she'd admit. "I need that drink after all." Wrenching the flask out of his hand, she tossed back the contents. Wiped her mouth with her sleeve. "Shit, Cam. Stop staring at me. I told you I'm all right."

Their gazes locked, and Cam knew instantly Morgan tested him. Waited for him to react. With disapproval. Repugnance. And so much came clear. The foul language. Yesterday's striptease. The constant over-the-top bravado.

A reaction was just what she wanted. She wanted to see him flinch. Make him squirm. But it was all an act. A way to show the world—no, a way to show him—how tough she was.

Morgan might not be the pleasure-seeking Siren she'd portrayed in Edinburgh last winter. But she wasn't all hard-bitten, ruthless warrior-woman either. She was both.

One aspect of her personality hadn't changed. She was as unpredictable as always.

He stifled a laugh, sure that wouldn't go over well.

"What are you smirking at?" she asked.

"You scared ten years off my life."

Her gaze darkened, grew troubled. She fumbled with the flask.

He'd surprised her. Hadn't given her the response she'd expected. And Cam knew he'd won that round.

But what had he given up?

He leaned forward, wishing he had the right to offer comfort. A touch. A kiss. But he knew what that would get him. A scathing comment at best. A blow to his midsection at worst. He swallowed the impulse, though not the desire. Decided to confront her head-on. "Have you ever seen death? Violent death? Been close enough to smell the blood or watch the light fade from someone's eyes? Have you ever dealt it with your own hand? Looked a man in the face while his life drains in front of you?"

Morgan plucked a grass blade from the ground. Twirled it between her fingers. "I've seen . . . not . . . No."

Memories surfaced. Recollections that resisted all his drunken attempts to obliterate them. "I have. It sours your stomach. Makes your blood run fevered, then frozen through your veins. But you do what you have to do. You don't think. You don't care. You simply act or react. That's what makes a perfect soldier."

That's what makes a perfect killer. But he didn't say it.

Tossing the grass away, Morgan faced him, her eyes honey gold in the westering light. "What are you trying to tell me?" Her voice and her expression had lost their edge. She cocked her head as if trying to understand.

"I . . ." Just talking about it made him go cold. Made his gut churn. "I'm trying to tell you it's all right to be shaky in the knees and want to cast up your accounts. It's all right if you're not the dirtiest, meanest son of a bitch out there." He dropped his gaze to the ground. To a crush of pebbles. A broken stalk of grass. Anywhere so he didn't have to meet Morgan's eyes. That keen gaze of hers would pick out every crime he'd ever committed in the name of duty. See every man who hadn't been as quick or as cunning or as good as he was. And unfortunately for their sakes, he'd been damn good once.

"Cam?" Her hand on his arm snapped his head up. Her hair fell forward, a loose strand caught in her lips.

That simple gesture was all it took. He leaned toward her. Caught her face in his hands. And before she could resist, claimed her mouth in a hungry, desperate kiss. Her lips moving over his overpowered the raging flashbacks. There was no room for thought. Only sensation. The faint whiskey taste of her lips, the exquisite softness of her skin, the deep, spreading burn of his body as seconds passed and she didn't pull away. Could it be this easy?

She started in his arms. Shoved him away. "No."

Out of reach, she scrambled to her feet, dragging her sleeve across her mouth. Erasing all trace of him. Her expression was enough to tell him how badly he'd cocked things up.

Her voice trembled. "Thank you for your concern, but I don't need your advice. I can see where it's led you."

Cam plowed a frustrated hand through his hair. "Aye, stuck with the most stubborn, pigheaded pain in the . . . neck." He stood, faking a calm that took all his energy. Afraid of what he'd just done. The emotions he'd unleashed with one thoughtless kiss. But she'd felt perfect in his arms. Just as he remembered.

He wondered if she remembered too.

Cam sat—drink in hand, though he'd yet to take a sip. He'd ordered it more for reassurance. To have if he needed it. And the way this investigation was shaping up, he'd need it soon.

The message had been waiting for him at the inn when they'd returned.

Come to The Forlorn Hope at seven.
Take a table by the stairs.

Fingering his glass, he worked on blending in. Disappearing. Difficult because of the placement of his table, but not impossible. He'd not abandoned his battle skills when he'd stepped off the boat in Portsmouth. Just drowned them.

While he waited, he kept an eye on those coming and going. Counted the men heading upstairs. Made mental note of all exits.

A loud party of militia officers held court by the hearth. Near the back, a group of infantry sat, their attention all for their ongoing card game. Lucy and her kind served drinks as they sought customers for the tavern's upstairs rooms.

Cam couldn't help but compare their rice-powdered breasts and pasted smiles to Morgan's prowling grace, the huntress light in her golden stare. Even now, with all her efforts bent on proving herself one of the boys, she was the most feminine female he'd ever known.

Sex with a sword.

There was a dangerous thought. He glanced at his watch. It was long past seven. He'd give it another ten minutes.

The stairs behind him creaked as another satisfied john returned to the taproom from the brothel above. But halfway down, the footsteps slowed. A hoarse, gravelly voice sounded low in Cam's ear. "Remember me, Sin?"

He stiffened. Few people knew him by that name. And with good reason. It was a name he hated. A name that symbolized a time in his life he thought ended last year with a dagger thrust through his upper back. Another tearing into his thigh.

"Unfortunately, yes," Cam answered without turning around, his fingers tightening on his glass.

A soldier in the scarlet jacket and gosling green facings of the Fifth Foot dropped into a seat across from him, though it could just as easily have been the scarlet and white of the Third Dragoon Guards. Or even a French grenadier's bearskin cap and epaulettes. Cam had seen him in all of them.

Uniforms meant little to Rastus. A scrounger extraordinaire, he used what came to hand or what was most expedient under the circumstances. It's how he survived when others smarter, faster, or stronger didn't. "Welcome home, Colonel. Been a while."

"Not long enough, Corporal. I heard they shot you for a deserter."

Weedy and pouch-faced with a terminal shake in his hands, Rastus lit a cheroot. Closed his eyes as he inhaled. Blew the smoke out through his nose with a yellow smile. "Nah, just a mite of confusion. I decided to head back to Spain with my woman. You remember Dolores? There was a bit of trouble, but it come right in the end."

"Did you finally make an honest woman of her?"

"Ha," Rastus snorted. "Marriage? I ain't one for shackling myself. Dolores found herself a butcher in San Millan. Fought as a guerilla in the war. Lots of practice cutting meat, eh?" Rastus cracked his knuckles. Snapped his neck.

Cam cringed, remembering where he'd been and what he'd been preparing to do the last time he'd heard that incessant, aggravating one-by-one crunch of bone. He picked up his glass, knowing it wouldn't take much to push those thoughts away.

"I hear you're a free man again too, Sin," Rastus droned on. "That hag of a wife finally nasty herself into the grave? Or maybe you brought a bit of work home with you when they shipped you out?" He slid Cam a knowing look. Flexed his fingers. "Never took much, did it?"

Cam placed the glass back on the table with deliberate care, his fist crushed around it, the urge to pick the sleazy grub up by the collar and shake him until his teeth rattled burning its way up his throat. "You brought me here for a reason, Rastus."

Rastus stubbed his cheroot out on the table. Immediately lit another. "You're looking for a sergeant."

"I am. What do you know?"

"A man's got to live, and the army don't pay." Rastus's sob story was as familiar as his tobacco-stained teeth, the broken veins across his flattened nose.

Cam shrugged. "You forget who you're talking to. I know where the bodies are buried—so to speak. You're not starving."

Rastus grinned. "Ah, no, but that bit of sparkle's my retirement fund. I've got to have a little brass to live on day to day. What are you willing to pay me?"

"Depends on what you're selling."

"My life won't be worth a whore's promise if Buchanan finds I've spoken to you."

Cam flashed a dangerous smile. "Then you better hope he doesn't find out."

The corporal didn't flinch exactly, but his easy manner stiffened into something approaching fear.

Cam had him hooked. He just needed to ease him into the boat. "You've the lives of a cat. What have you got to fear from this Buchanan? Spill it, and we'll toast to old times. You and me." God, there was a thought to sour his stomach.

Rastus nodded slowly, his demeanor still cautious. His eyes scanned the room, much as Cam's had done earlier. He lowered his voice, forcing Cam to lean closer. "Buchanan ain't no ordinary sergeant, that's for certain. Can't put my finger on why, but it's a feeling I get. He's got a way of looking right through you like he was reading your mind."

That caught Cam's attention, though he never moved a muscle, not even a break in eye contact. Rastus would see it and up the price.

"You've seen him more than once?"

"Scads of times. He's tight with a group that lives in a set of houses by the canal. A queer bunch. Some are officers. Some no more than rankless lobster backs. I do a bit of work over that way from time to time. Just to keep my hand in."

Cam fixed the man with a deadly stare. "If you're setting me up . . ."

Rastus had the grace to look offended. "Would I do that to a fellow Serpent?"

In a knee-jerk reaction, Cam reached across the table, pulling the other man close enough to smell the sour odor of sweat on his skin, hear the terrified hitch in his breathing. Whiskey sloshed over the plate onto Cam's breeks. "Never speak that name again," he growled. Before any could note the strange behavior, he released him. Sat back. "The war's over. That's no longer who I am."

His jaw working, Rastus cleared his throat. "Is it, Colonel? You can pretend it's not a part of you, but the serpent's always there. Waiting."

Bands of pressure tightened around Cam's skull; his hands trembled despite his best effort at controlling the fury that narrowed his vision to a pinprick.

Rastus rose from his seat at the table. Straightened his stock, the seam of his jacket. "If I were you, I'd let it out, Sin. If you're set on tangling with Buchanan you're gonna need every trick you ever learned. The skills of the killer are all that's gonna keep you alive."

Chapter 9

Doran watched the slow crawl of the murky canal water past his window, digesting the news his last runner had brought.

Questions were being asked. Someone searched for a mysterious sergeant. Someone who paid well for answers.

The mistakes that had brought him to this point were his alone.

He'd left a trail when he left the last soldier alive. Trusting to the rapid decay of the man's body his first lapse in judgment. Death came slower than anticipated. He lived long enough to talk of what he saw before the goddess blade pierced his heart. But that was an oversight Doran could remedy.

His second mistake was underestimating the strength of *Other* and mortal combined.

Morgan Bligh was competent among the *Amhas-draoi*, though nowhere near the caliber of her cousin, Conor. Trading on her family's power among the *Other*, rather than her own skills, to advance.

Sinclair had been a thorn in his side for months now, but his investigation turned up nothing that Doran didn't want him to find. He'd become a joke. Referred to as the undertaker, his task reduced to finding and burying the abandoned bodies. The riverside attack had been a halfhearted ploy, the rabble Doran contracted to carry it out not worth the coin he'd paid.

Now the hunt grew serious. Pursuit became real. And he could afford no more mistakes.

He'd end the questions and the threat. Tonight.

Morgan never took her eyes from the tavern across the street. She'd traced Cam to The Forlorn Hope after waiting at their room for over an hour. She understood his reasons for leaving her behind. But still, it grated on her desire to keep busy. Stay involved.

Cam saw her as a helpless female. One who needed protection. Well, to hell with that. She'd been fighting that fight her whole life. First against brothers and cousins who tormented her until she landed her first bloody nose. Then against the men she trained with on Skye who paraded their physiques in front of her as if one look at their hard bodies would send her over the moon. The bloody noses there had been harder to achieve, but she managed to gain their grudging approval as well.

But both her family and the *Amhas-draoi* held an advantage over Cam. They'd grown up with capable women. As mothers, teachers, leaders. Cam was a novice. It was up to her to prove she could hold her own.

She shifted, trying to regain feeling in her right arm. Pressed back into a doorway, unmoving for what seemed a lifetime, she'd gone tingly and then numb. By now, it felt as if a dead fish hung from her shoulder.

September's chill stole in off the moors, dusting the ground with hoarfrost. Fog silvered her hair, dampened her face. She tried heaving the boat cloak farther over her, but the lack of mobility in her arm and the confined space made it impossible. Half numb, half freezing. Could it get any better?

Where was Cam? Had he slipped out the back, losing

himself in the smoky, gray cloud hovering ghostlike in the air? Or had something happened to him?

The image of him blood-soaked and horrified sent a lightning jolt of fear through her, bringing painful sensation back to her arm. Another part of her—the angry part—imagined him hunched comatose over a whiskey, or worse still, wrapped between the legs of some riverside whore.

No. She shook her head, ridding her mind of that unwelcome idea.

She'd not come out here to spy. She'd come to force Cam to see her as an equal in this fight, a partner. If they stopped Doran and retrieved Andraste's sword, Cam could skewer any whore who'd have him.

She straightened, new resolve firing her cold, stiff body.

She didn't have long after that to wait. Ten minutes after a loud group of drunks weaved off into the night, she spotted Cam. She recognized him as soon as he stepped into the street. If he'd been drinking it hadn't been enough to dull the controlled power of his movements, the aura of invincibility surrounding him. Despite his knife injury, there was just something about him that spoke of hidden strength—intense single-mindedness.

She held far enough behind that even if by chance he glanced her way, she'd have time to blend in with the darker shadows. Step into the gloom of an alley or a doorway. But he never looked back, his path steady on an unerring course to take him across town to the inn. Head down, hands shoved in his coat, he acted as if he were out for a Sunday stroll and not returning from a mysterious meeting with who knew what kind of scum.

This should be harder. Mayhap she needed to amend her first reaction. Mayhap Cam's aura was as superficial as the perfect uniform, the gold braid, the strong jaw.

Just more of the brilliance that had blinded her the first time.

She drew closer, now no more than a hundred yards separating them. She'd leave her gotcha moment for just before the inn. The pinprick of her dagger at his back. A whispered told-you-so in his ear.

Cam crossed the street, rounding the corner, still with no idea she followed only steps behind.

Morgan jogged to catch up. Too many side alleys and narrow lanes broke off from the main streets through town. She wanted to keep him in visual as long as she could. But rounding the corner, not seconds after, she slammed to a stop.

The street stood empty.

She blinked, narrowing her gaze as she scanned from corner to corner, but nothing moved. No telltale scrape of a footfall. No harsh breath giving away his position. Not even a print in the frost.

He'd vanished.

She swallowed an uncomfortable lump. This wasn't going exactly as she'd planned, her gotcha moment slipping away before her eyes. Picking up the pace, she hurried down the street, passing into a lane that brought her out close to the inn. She'd cut time and distance going this way, and be waiting when Cam arrived.

That's when it happened.

One minute she slid from shadow to shadow, the hunter on the trail of her prey; the next, a hurtling punch slammed her between the shoulders. Another smashed her in the small of the back. She landed with a head-cracking thud in the dirt, the wind knocked out of her.

A hand grabbed her, flipping her over. Her attacker straddled her hips, his knife inches from her face.

Eyes, gleaming with deadly purpose, stared down at her, before widening with a mixture of surprise, confusion, and horror.

She opened and closed her mouth, trying to work her crushed lungs. Pump some air back into her body.

"Shit." The knife clattered forgotten to the ground. "Morgan, are you all right?" Cam wiped a hand down his face. "Shit," he groaned again.

She tried croaking out an answer, but aside from her squashy lungs, Cam's weight still pinned her to the ground. "Fine," she managed to squeeze out, "I think."

The solid weight of him on top of her was doing crazy things to her earlier resolve to stay as far away from Cam's dazzle as possible. "Off," she gasped. "Off me."

"What?" He leaned toward her and those amazing lips drew closer, the stubble on his jaw within kissing distance. Delicious heat spread outward from her center, twisting through her, tying her in knots.

"Off," she squawked, thrusting up with her hips to dislodge him.

Oh, that was definitely the wrong thing to do.

Her body went on instant alert, as did his. But he got the message. He scrambled off her as if she'd caught fire.

She pushed up on her elbows, breath finally expanding to fill her airways. Doing her best to ignore the explosive mixture of pleasure at the closeness of his body and tension at what that pleasure might mean. When she spoke she tried sounding as if she'd meant for this to happen all along. "You're better than good. I never heard you."

He retrieved his knife. Shoved it back into his belt. "You weren't meant to."

"But how? You didn't learn that stalking deer."

"Forget it. It doesn't matter."

"But, Cam. That was amazing. It takes a hell of a—"

"I said forget it." He clenched his jaw, his tone curbing further questions.

She sat up, wincing as she felt the lump on the back of her head.

"Are you bleeding?" His hand stole around her neck, probed her skull as he checked to make sure she hadn't received anything worse than a goose egg.

She closed her eyes. Giving in would be easy. He held her in his arms. His hands were in her hair. What would he do if she kissed him? And expanding that thought, how would she react to his reaction?

Not exactly normal thoughts to have after an almost-death experience by an ex-lover, but she'd passed far beyond that about a week ago when she'd walked into General Pendergast's office.

"I could have killed you," he muttered. Low, apologetic, and thoroughly, completely annoyed.

She opened her eyes, her erotic fantasies shriveling under Cam's steel-edged gaze. Those were fighting words. "Do you think so?"

He sat back, checking her challenge with a raised hand. "No. You don't understand, Morgan. I . . . could have . . . killed you. It's what I do. What I did."

He dropped his head, his chest heaving as if he'd been the one to have the air punched out of him.

"Well, I'm still breathing. I guess you're stuck with me, killer."

Cam didn't seem to appreciate her attempt at humor. Ignoring it, he stood, helping her up after. "What the hell were you doing skulking around anyway?" he asked. "Playing cat and mouse? Your little joke on me?"

"No," she defended herself, though without much conviction. That had been exactly what she'd been doing. A stupid effort to prove something.

She'd proved something all right.

She still had it bad for Cameron Sinclair.

Now she just had to decide what to do about it.

"I understand, Morgan," he fumed. "You're Miss Warriorwoman. You don't have to ram the point down my throat."

Knowing he was right, she held silent, gritting her teeth, slapping at the mud on her breeches. Her scraped hands stung, and her legs felt wobbly, although whether her unsteadiness was a result of being plowed over or—more disturbing to her peace of mind—not being plowed at all, she couldn't say.

She swallowed hard, taking a few shaky steps.

"The inn's the other way," he said, the temper drained from his voice. Now all he sounded was tired.

She bit back her rude comment, especially when she noticed the shake in his hands as he guided her shoulders in the opposite direction.

"Don't ever . . . Morgan, just . . ." He stumbled over his words. Blew out a frustrated breath as he combed a hand through his hair. "I don't want to hurt you."

So much in those six little words.

She turned back, fixing him with a level stare. "Too late."

Cam pushed the door to their room wide, motioning Morgan through first. Not out of any gentlemanly attempt at gallantry, but because it kept her from seeing what a mess he was. The slender thread of her neck between his hands slithered through his mind. The ease at which he could have slashed the knife across it crawled over his palms, making him break out in a cold sweat.

Cameron Sinclair had become Sin. Again.

The present had faded. He'd forgotten where he was, who he was. He'd reacted on pure instinct. Pure survival. The need to eliminate the threat. The training of the Serpent Brigade living in his actions.

He'd recovered in time. It took only a moment before

he'd recognized the cloaked figure and realized she wasn't a danger to his safety.

To his sanity? Very much so.

Morgan unclasped her cloak, threw it across the bed, revealing her plain linen shirt worn over a pair of hip-hugging, leave-nothing-to-the-imagination leather breeks. Her hair, she'd plaited in intricate braids caught up with silver and bone combs. At her waist, a bone-handled dagger. Nothing soft about her. He should have been horrified or offended at her brazen appearance. Instead, reckless arousal flared through him.

Dainty. Sweet. Delicate. Words he'd once have used to describe how he liked his women seemed ridiculous now.

She lit the lamp by the bed, its glow illuminating the red-gold fire of her hair, bringing a dusky flush to her skin. "About following you tonight"—she plucked at the blanket's fringe, uneasy, awkward—"it wasn't the most intelligent of ideas."

Morgan? Apologizing? She must be as rattled as he was. Or else he'd cracked her head harder than he'd thought.

"Forget it," he said. "It was as much my fault as yours. More, because I know what I'm capable of. You don't—didn't." He busied himself undressing. Boots kicked off. Jacket flung over a chair. Shirt buttons one by one. Mundane tasks he could accomplish without thinking. Because thinking meant acknowledging what had just happened. He'd almost killed Morgan. And then he'd almost kissed her—again.

The second time in as many days.

Morgan's tempting presence. Devil's sidekick Rastus resurfacing. And a crazy, sword-wielding murderer with a taste for soldiers. This assignment was hellish in so many ways.

"So what are you capable of?" As if she knew how close he'd come—and maybe she did—Morgan rose from the bed, the only woman he knew who could dress, talk, and fight like a man and still carry herself like a queen.

Albeit a queen with attitude.

Mayhap the Celtic Boudicca who spent her days slaughtering Romans. He could definitely picture Morgan riding roughshod over a few dozen legionnaires.

Just before reaching him, she stopped, one hand poised to caress his bare chest, her eyes black with desire.

Meeting her gaze, he knew he hadn't imagined it. She'd been ready for him to kiss her back there in that alley. Had wanted it as much as he did.

And, damn, he wanted it. Bad.

Was this meant as punishment? To tease him with what could have been if only he hadn't been a rat bastard and told her up front about Charlotte? Did she wait for him to call her bluff so she could react like a wronged virgin? What did she want from him?

Did he care?

He needed an outlet for the crazy pressure building inside him, the tension banding his shoulders, tightening his gut. If Morgan was willing . . .

"Just so we're open about what we're doing here," he started, fumbling for words.

An embarrassed smile hovered at the corners of her lips. "No tricks. No strings. But I'm tired of pretending I don't want you in my bed. This way, I call the shots. I'm in control." Her hand splayed over his chest, cool against his burning skin. She ran her fingers over the thin chain, her touch featherlight as it brushed the cross.

He fisted his hand protectively around the necklace. "Is this a good idea? You're upset, maybe a little confused by the knock on your head."

What was he doing? Was he actually trying to talk her out of sleeping with him? Was he completely insane? Just the touch of her hand had his body reacting, the pressure reaching dangerous levels. One more provocative move on her part and all hesitation would be over.

Her gaze grew serious, almost sad. "Please, Cam. I know it's mad. I know it's probably the worst thing I can do, but"—her lashes swept down, hiding the ache in her gaze—"this way at least, I'm making the mistake eyes wide open."

He tilted her chin up so that she had to face him. "So you admit it's a mistake?"

She moved into him, pressing her body the length of his, letting him feel the soft crush of her breasts, her lean muscled legs, the luscious V of her crotch. "The most perfect mistake I could make."

All it took was one rub of her body and Cam's restraint erupted into white-hot need.

Gods be praised. If he'd left her standing there after she'd done everything but strip and stake herself out for him, she'd have felt a complete fool.

Morgan knew she'd snapped. Cam blamed it on the blow to her head. But it was more complicated. She couldn't say why she threw caution and her better judgment to the wind to follow the more elemental pull of her body. She just knew now she couldn't move forward unless the drive to find out if he'd been as exquisite as she remembered was put to the test.

And so far exquisite didn't even come close.

He devoured her with his mouth, his hands playing her body, awakening parts of her she thought dead forever. He smelled of sweat and strength, and she clung to him, her hands curving under his shirt, finding the broad, corded muscles of his back while she drowned in the wild power of his lovemaking.

Cam shoved her back against the wall, the swollen ridge of his erection jammed oh so deliciously between her legs. His hand dropped to the waist of her breeches. With an expert flick of his fingers, he'd opened the fall, dipped lower, tracing the folds of her woman's place, teasing the nub that lay hidden there.

She gasped, rocking forward against him. Her body nearing the edge of no return as he answered her thrust with his own, his fingers pushing deep inside her. She clutched his back at the savage need that tore through her with each stroke, the building ecstasy narrowing her focus to this room, this man, this moment.

The laughter when it came never registered. It was only the sneering contempt of the voice that followed that tore her out of her bliss. "Now, isn't this romantic?"

Then all hell broke loose.

Chapter 10

Cam reacted before she did.

In one sweep of motion, his hand slid to her waist, unsheathing her dagger, and, pivoting, he let it fly toward the man standing ten feet away at the open window, all while shoving Morgan farther behind him. As if that would help.

Any other time and with any other target, the dagger would have ended buried hilt-deep and dead-center. Instead, the blade sank quivering only an inch into Doran's metal breastplate.

"Am I interrupting?" He plucked her blade from his armor. Dropped it to the floor, kicking it into a corner. "You had me fooled, Bligh. I always imagined you the frigid man-hater type."

Humiliation and fury shriveled Morgan's insides, her earlier runaway need frozen needle-sharp in her veins.

Beneath her hands, Cam went completely still, his whole body coiling tight as a wire just before he sprang.

Caught by surprise, Doran allowed Cam to close the distance between them. The *Amhas-draoi* outstripped him in sheer bulk, but Cam's speed and ability made up for it. He swept under Doran's guard, landing a chop across his neck that carried enough force to crush his windpipe.

Doran fell to his knees, his hands grabbing at his throat as Cam dove for the corner and the discarded knife.

Weapon in hand, Cam adjusted his grip. Prepared to drill the blade into Doran's hunched, exposed back.

Then dropped to the floor as if his legs had been pulled out from under him.

At the same moment, dark mage energy ripped through Morgan, cramping muscles, numbing senses.

Cam groaned, rolling into a ball, his face blanched white, his jaw clenched in a grimace of agony.

Morgan shouted, casting her personal wards as wide as she could, praying her shields would be enough to protect them both from Doran's curse. Pain knifed through her, but she held steady, Doran's spell dulling to a roar in her ears, a twist of her insides.

Doran unfolded from the floor. Stood to tower over her. "Nice try, Bligh, but did you really think you had a chance in hell? Join me and I might let you live."

"Never happen, you son of a bitch," she spat. "I'm no traitor."

Her eyes darted around the room, searching for anything she could use as a weapon. Cam's knife was across the room. Her knife still lay clutched in his twitching fist. Both impossible to reach. Cam carried pistols. Useless to her unloaded and packed in his saddlebags. So now what?

"Implying that I am?" Doran's voice oozed menace. "You're the traitor. Betraying your race to uphold *Fey* supremacy. Doing their bidding like some groveling errand boy."

Did he hear himself? Did he hear how insane he sounded? "You're mad."

"Am I?" His expression seemed glazed with insane purpose. Alight with the rightness of his zealous obsession. "The true *Fey* have spent millennia gathering all the power for themselves. We *Other* left with the dregs and expected to be satisfied. No more. With the goddess blade, I'll create my own race. A power to rival the *Fey*."

His words echoed in her head like a pounding surf. Over and over. Pushing their way past her defenses. Was he right? Was she really only a lackey for the *Fey*? A cat's paw doing work too menial for the true *Fey* to bother about?

He nodded toward Cam. "Should I begin with lover boy here? My first Undying?"

Panic snapped her gaze to Cam. "No!"

The one word crashed through the fog of Doran's spell.

She shook her head violently. Pounded her forehead with her fist to jar the overpowering persuasion of the *leveryas* from her skull.

He sought to try his tricks on her. And naive her, she'd almost fallen for it. "Andraste will never allow it. She'll send her forces over. Drop the walls between worlds to stop you."

"Let her try."

"You'd doom us all to death?"

"Join me and there will be no death. No defeat. Only domination."

"I don't deal with traitors or murderers."

Doran's lips twisted in a smug, cruel smile. "A shame. But have it your way."

His words barely ended before his spell flung her backward like a puppet on a string, smashing her against the wall, lights bursting in her head for the second time tonight.

If Doran had been formidable before, now freed of the constraints placed upon him by the *Amhas-draoi*, he'd become unstoppable. The black magic he drew on could only have come to him through the *Morkoth*, the blade a conduit for their evil sorcery.

Blood dripped from her nose, her mouth. She wanted to scream, her body slowly breaking down under the force of Doran's power. But she refused to drop into the deep well rushing to meet her. Instead she met and matched Doran's attack with her own, stunning him with a counter spell, disrupting his hold on her.

It lasted only a moment, but long enough for her to throw herself across the room. Sweep the lamp off into the drapes. Feed the flames with a quick bit of household magic until they roared to life. Climbing the curtains. Spreading over the bed. The crackle growing to a roar.

She crouched by Cam's side as the flames rose around them, lapping at the rug like an orange-red tide, waiting for her moment. It had to come soon. Or by flame or by Doran, she and Cam were dead.

Her chance came as the fire leapt from the window to the ceiling beams, devouring the old wood in seconds. Smoke and ash floated into Doran's eyes, caught and smoldered in the wool of his coat. The flames forced him back, and the pain in her body eased, the poison of his magic withdrawn.

It was now or never.

Using both the invisibility of the *feth-fiada* and the sleight of hand of the *sprys-maclioar*, she hugged Cam to her while projecting the illusion of them both prone on the floor as if Doran had struck them down.

Screams and running footsteps sounded in the corridor and the rooms to either side, muffled by the snap and snarl of the growing blaze. Black smoke clung to her hair, her face. Singed her lungs with every breath she took. Blisters rose on her arms, her cheeks. Self-preservation hammered at her will as she dragged Cam through the heart of the inferno toward the window.

She'd never attempted anything like this before. Her brain felt split in half, thinned to a veil's thickness. One miscalculation and the weaving of spells would unravel. Their attempt to escape revealed.

Men pounded on, then forced open the door to the room. Shouting. Cursing. Buckets long past being useful.

Doran spun around, meeting them head-on. "Quick. There are people trapped in here. I've tried getting to them, but the fire's too hot."

Alarm and terror, grit and desperation. The emotions swirling through the inn stole between the cracks of her consciousness as the firestorm rose higher. Yet Doran stood, silent after his initial outburst, content to watch the figure he thought was her burn, his pale eyes empty of all but death.

The ceiling buckled as the window behind her shattered, sending shards of glass into her face, slicing her hands and arms. But no one saw that. Or heard her shout of pain. They saw only the bodies she wanted them to see, blackened and withered. They heard only the groan of the floor beneath their feet as trusses weakened and snapped.

At last, Doran lost himself among the crowd just as Morgan shoved Cam over the windowsill. Out the window. His body slid free into the darkness, and she slithered after.

The roof sloped low into a stockyard. Air boiled with soot and embers. Flames shot skyward through the roof of the inn above their room. Below in the yard, panicked neighbors rushed like ants to and from the building as contents rained from windows or were carried out to safety in bags and boxes.

Free of the rending of brain and body the dual magics imposed, she fell exhausted to her knees. Blood and smoke blinded her. She coughed until she heaved, her ribs straining. But she couldn't rest yet. They still weren't safe. Doran might be gone, but the fire still raged.

Taking Cam beneath the arms, she scrambled over the slates to the roof's edge. Judged the distance to the ground, then praying it wasn't too far, pushed him off. He fell spread-eagle amid a heap of dung and garbage. She groped for purchase with her legs, reaching out for a handhold. The slates gave way, broke like scree, tumbling toward her. Dragged her with them into the dark and the bricks of the yard below.

She lay beside Cam, feeling for a pulse, praying for a breath. But he was too still. His body cold. Or was that her?

Blood from cuts she couldn't feel dripped into her eyes. She wiped it away.

A silver glow hovered over them. Burned through the pain. She reached out, touching Cam. And let the light claim her.

Cam came awake, every nerve ending scraped raw, every part of his body seemingly twisted out of shape as if some force had wrung him like a sponge. He groaned, shaking the stench of death from his mind, though it lingered at the corners.

Where was he? He hefted himself onto his side, his hands encountering something oozy soft that stank to heaven. An acrid wind blew ash into his face, stung his nose. He was outside, looking up at the inn. Above him, the second floor glowed red, fire lapping out the windows, curling down the walls. Screams and shouts and smashing glass sounded behind him. What the hell had happened? He remembered a man. And a fight. And then . . . where was Morgan?

Oh, please don't let her be up there.

He sat up, his vision going dark as dizziness swamped him.

There she was. Curled on her side nearby, one hand outstretched, her wolf-head ring glittering in the light from the blaze.

"Morgan." He shook her, prayed she'd wake. Look up at him and smile. Hell, he'd settle for one of her scathing glares. "Morgan, we have to get out of here. Now."

He didn't know what had happened up there, but it hadn't been good. Successes didn't leave you tossed on a rubbish heap feeling like the bottom of someone's boot. If Buchanan found them like this, it was over.

He staggered to his feet, breathing through the pain until he steadied himself. Then kneeling, he gathered Morgan into his arms. She smelled of smoke, her hair, her clothing. Ash streaked her face, mingling with what he prayed wasn't blood.

"Cam?" she murmured, burrowing her head against his chest. "You're alive."

"And trying to stay that way," he ground through clenched teeth. "Hold on."

But she'd already drifted off.

Focusing only on putting one foot in front of the other, he carried her out of the yard and into the street. Plunged through the chaos of the firefighting. Just one more victim trying to escape. Unremarkable. Unremarked.

He needed a safe haven. A place where no one would ask too many questions. Would accept what had happened to them without thinking they were insane. He knew of only one place. One person.

Ensign Traverse.

Chapter 11

The target had been sighted. An open shot. An easy kill. Another body claimed by the Serpent Brigade.

Out of habit, he reached for his cross for one last good-luck rub before remembering. Charlotte had it. Locked away in a jeweler's box.

He was on his own.

His finger tightened around the trigger, his focus narrowed to the kill zone of the enemy's chest.

The report of the gun echoed across the rocky hills, followed by the anguished screams of a woman, her cream and gold gown, her glossy black hair, her dusky Spanish features—all spattered now with blood and bone and offal.

"Hábleme, Papa!" she wailed, bent over the dead man's corpse. *"Papa! Mi Papa."*

Others emerged from the church: the woman's new husband, the rest of the wedding party, the priests. The weeping and screaming and shouts for vengeance curled up from the valley like smoke, but he'd already slung his rifle over his shoulder, already erased the evidence of his hiding place.

Target eliminated. Mission accomplished.

The images followed Cam up and out of sleep, the gnawing

pain in his gut sending him rolling for the side of the bed to heave, the spasms clutching his stomach long after he'd thrown everything up.

Lying back, he shuddered, wiping a shaking hand down his face, his body clammy with sweat. A niggling thought teased the edge of his mind. Something he should remember. Something important that had only come to him in his sleep.

A woman's voice broke the silence, clear and sharp like a stone upon a sword, and the ghost of a thought vanished.

Do we blame the eagle for killing the hare? The wolf for bringing down the deer? We say it is their nature and accept. So it is with the soldier and his war. He does what is in his nature to do.

Scathach.

The warrior-woman stood at the window, arms clasped behind her, her black hair free and rippling down her back. She turned, and he realized by the expression on her face that her words came from within. She'd spoken to him mind to mind.

He flung himself forward, the room tilting, the pain in his head like a fork to the brain. "Where's Morgan? Is she safe?"

He'd risen halfway before she took him by the shoulders, eased him back onto the mattress, her grip like steel. Or he was a hell of a sight weaker than he thought.

Once he was back in bed, her inhuman gaze held him there. "She is with the young ensign. And she is well. We worried over you."

He tried remembering in reverse order.

The never-ending walk through town, Morgan's weight in his arms easy compared to the feeling that his body disintegrated with every footstep.

Back to the shocking intrusion of the giant in their room.

Back to—

He closed his eyes, groaned in disgust. Had he really been

caught with his hands down Morgan's breeks? Talk about the disaster of the century.

This whole working as a team thing was going so well to begin with. Why not add some meaningless sex to the mix? Make it really enjoyable.

"How long have I been here?"

"A day only. When you did not wake, Morgan grew worried and summoned me."

"So you know about . . ."

"She has told me everything." And he swore she smiled as she said it.

He took a deep breath, letting the slow expand and contract of his lungs calm his racing thoughts.

"You have hurt Morgan once, Colonel Sinclair," she said. "Who can say you will not do so again?"

This was definitely not the conversation he wanted to be having. And not now. There wasn't a point on his body that didn't ache. His head, especially, felt fragile as an egg. "I never meant to. And I'd make it up to her if I thought she'd listen."

She raised a surprised brow. "You've told her this?"

"She's been too busy telling me what a bastard I am to listen to anything I have to say."

A serene smile tipped the corners of her lips. Lit the inscrutable black of her eyes.

He met her gaze, refusing to be intimidated, though she was the most intimidating woman he'd ever met. His hand went to the cross at his neck as if it could ward her off.

"Your God has no fear of my power," she said indulgently, her voice soft with laughter, "yet neither do I fear him." Her face grew stern, the cold perfection of every feature almost painful. "Morgan will move on if she's given no choice. No encouragement."

"You think *I* encouraged *her*?" He started up, the throbbing stab in his head bringing tears to his eyes.

"Your presence is encouragement enough to one as volatile as Morgan." She moved toward the door like some great black cat, pausing to turn back before she left. "Just bear in mind, Colonel. She leads with her heart. It is a great strength, but it leaves her vulnerable to great pain. Betrayal—whether it be by friend or by lover—cuts her deeply. That is why this mission preys upon her so. For now, she is confronted by both."

Alone again, Cam was bothered by his earlier jangled senses. What had he missed? What had he discovered? It lurked at the corners of his brain, fading each time he reached for it. If he relaxed, thought of something else, mayhap the memory would clear. He lay back. Thought of Scathach. The idea that he'd encouraged Morgan. Hell, she'd done everything but beg for it. A few more uninterrupted minutes and—his mind jumped to the attack. To the muscle-bound giant with the power to strip Cam to bones. Skipped forward, clicking piece by piece into place like a puzzle. What had Scathach said? Betrayal by a friend. A warrior who commanded magic. One who'd called Morgan by name.

She knew who they were after. All this time. And she'd kept it secret.

Miss Morgan Fucking Bligh had set him up.

Cam looked like he'd been in a fight. And lost.

A fading yellow and green eye seemed the worst, but he held himself stiffly, favoring one leg over another. Old injuries aggravated by Doran's attack. The fall from the roof.

Morgan sympathized. She'd been hobbling around for the last two days like the walking wounded, snarling at anyone who dared glance in her direction. Ensign Traverse had finally given up trying to be nice and snarled back, which only made her feel guilty on top of miserable. After all, he'd taken them in. Let them hide in his rooms. And asked nothing in return, though she knew he held his despair in check by only the merest threads. She hoped Gram had received her letter by now.

Cam closed the door behind him, the snick of the latch making her jump. His face beneath the bruising hardened into strained lines, his lips pressed tightly together. Just as if they hadn't almost . . . as if she . . . and then he . . . Could this be more awkward?

She leaned back against a table, gripping the top with both hands, wishing the floor would open up and swallow her.

No embarrassment clouded his flint-hard gaze. He pinned her in place with the force of his stare, a muscle jumping in his rigid jaw. It reminded her of what he'd revealed in that alleyway. The skills. The violence. If she'd been hiding her true self, apparently so had he. "What the hell is going on, Morgan? And no lies this time."

He advanced toward her, murder in his tone, his hands clenched into fists he looked all too willing to use.

"What do you mean—this time?"

"You've been holding back since the beginning. You've known all along who stole the damn sword. Is he *Amhasdraoi*? A friend of yours? A lover?"

The words brought her up short like a slap to the face. The disgust in his eyes made her want to throw something heavy at him. He actually believed she'd slept with Doran. She'd think he was jealous, except jealousy implied feeling. And the only feeling evident in Cam's gaze was raw fury.

Hurt and angry, she met him glare for glare. "You filthy bastard. I hate you."

His brows rose in smug condescension. "Really? That's not the way it seemed a few days ago. But perhaps you go for the men you despise. Adds a little spice to the conquest."

He made it sound so sordid. And mayhap it had been. But for a single moment when he'd whispered in her ear, she'd come alive. She'd felt the chill of winter at the window, the heat of a roaring fire, and the security of Cam's love.

The present shattered her girlish imaginings. "Or was your little seduction just a game, Morgan? A way to distract me from what was really going on?"

He kept picking at her, knowing what words would punish the most. Knowing just how to destroy her. He had a gift for that.

"That's it exactly, Cam," she bit back, this new betrayal almost harder to bear than the first because she'd done it to herself. "You figured it out. Get you excited, and you wouldn't know whether you were coming or going. It was my plan from the beginning."

His shoulders slumped, the heat of his rage turning cold and hard. They stood inches apart yet the distance between them seemed unbridgeable. Too much held them back. Nothing held them together.

"I'm tired of being played for a fool. I'm running blind. And looking the perfect jackass. Must have been quite a joke to you."

"We had our reasons," was all she could say. Inadequate as it sounded.

"I'll bet you did."

He left her, the vacuum his sudden absence created almost painful. She wanted to cradle her arms to her body, squeeze her eyes shut. Instead, she remained stiffly upright against the table, her chin up. The picture of indifference.

He crossed toward the door. Definitely favoring the right leg now. "Well, you can keep your reasons. Joke's over. And so is this insane arrangement. You're on your own."

"Where are you going?"

He reached the door. Glanced back over his shoulder. "You're the tracker. You figure it out."

* * *

Scathach found Morgan in what passed for a back garden. She'd not left the lodging house since Doran's attack. If he thought she and Cam had died, so much better. He'd be off his guard. More confident. And thus easier to track. That was the conclusion she and Scathach had come to, but it didn't help her jumbled thoughts and boiling frustration. She needed to be doing something. Anything.

"The young soldier says you've been out here since breakfast."

"It's better than running into Cam."

Scathach folded her arms across her chest. "I heard about that as well."

"I've made a mess of everything. Cam hates me. Doran and the sword are long gone. I burned down half a building, for heaven's sake."

"You also saved Sinclair's life and your own. And did it in such a way Doran has no idea you are still alive. While tallying the pluses and minuses, let us not forget those."

"Cam doesn't see it that way. He's probably packing right now for London. Off to warn General Pendergast about the treachery of *Other*. They'll be on our doorstep with pitchforks and burning brands in a week."

"So stop him."

Morgan fiddled with her wolf-head ring. Dropped her hands to her lap when she caught Scathach's eyes on her. "You didn't see him. He was beyond furious. With all of us." Cam's hate-filled words echoed in her head. The blunt viciousness of his accusations still curdled her insides. "But especially with me."

Scathach swept up her skirts. Took a seat next to Morgan. Simple movements with the same contained precision she brought to the training field. "There is much you have to learn, but you do well under trying circumstances. I had faith you would rise to the challenge of seeing him again."

Morgan cocked her a quizzing glance. "So this was a test?"

"No test, but I desired to find out if your time with Colonel Sinclair had lessened your resolve to make a life with the *Amhas-draoi* your own. Zeal quickly fades. It is important to discover whether an apprentice truly understands what is asked of him."

"And what if I had given in? If the feelings I had were still there?"

"I knew you better than that. No *Duinedon*—no matter his attributes—would be enough for one such as you. Your grandmother may have turned her back on a life of the *Fey*, but the blood of the High *Danu* still runs within your veins. Even among the *Other* you are marked as special."

"So you think I was wrong to do what I did?"

"To take him as a lover?" She shook her head, an understanding smile curling the corners of her lips. "I am not of your world, Morgan. I believe in taking pleasure where you find it. If the colonel brings you that pleasure, so be it. I am only saying you must not let an entanglement of this kind affect your true purpose. It is within the brotherhood you will find your strength. And you have a duty to fulfill to that brotherhood."

Morgan picked at a corner of the broken bench, crumbled the stones in her hand. "Why must duty and love be separate? Why can't we have both?"

"Perhaps for some it is possible. But would your colonel allow you to continue on such a path once you became his wife? He would expect you to keep his house, rear his children. You have barely begun your life. I have lived a thousand and a thousand such. And in all that endless time, I have seen the way the *Duinedon* regard their females. Treasured pets at best. Prisoners and drudges at worst. Is this the life you would take upon yourself? The walls of your marriage would become the bars of your jail."

Morgan straightened, knowing the truth of Scathach's words.

Cam was amazing. There was no doubt. Just those few

minutes in his arms, the searing heat of his touch had been enough to throw all his past actions out of her mind. But the cold light of day had shown her Cam's true feelings.

She'd never be a proper lady. Saying the right thing. Doing it the right way. And she'd never yearned to be. Only Cam's arrival in her life had allowed her a glimpse of what might have been. But might-have-beens faded when touched by truth. And the truth was, she was *Amhas-draoi*. That was enough for her. It always had been.

"I can't let him go to General Pendergast with what he knows. Not yet. If he thinks things are bad now, the panic Doran's betrayal would cause could destroy the *Other*."

"If you can stall Sinclair, it will mean a reprieve. I fight the forces of Andraste. They wish to bring down the walls in order to find *Neuvarvaan*, and their voices grow louder among the court. We cannot let them cross over, Morgan. For the continued existence of both *Fey* and *Duinedon*. Tell your colonel that. He must be made to understand. An army of Undying under Doran's control would be disastrous. But a full invasion by the *Fey* would be Armageddon."

Morgan squared her shoulders, tossing away the handful of pebbles. Wiping her hands down her skirt, she stood. "Leave it to me. I'm very persuasive when I want to be."

Chapter 12

Morgan stood outside Cam's room, running through her mental checklist. Shaking off a sudden attack of nerves. She could stall Cam. She had to. She couldn't let him leave for London. Not like things stood now. Scathach was right. What she and Cam shared had been amazing. But she needed to put aside personal feelings now. Focus on the task at hand. Retrieving *Neuvarvaan* for the *Fey*. Bringing down Doran for the *Amhas-draoi*.

She'd mapped out her strategy. Plan A consisted of a sincere apology followed by rational arguments and an avoidance at all costs of a repeat of their shouting match.

If that didn't work, she'd move to plan B. Groveling on hands and knees. Not as highbrow but no less effective if carried off correctly. She'd even scare up a few tears. Men couldn't resist weepy females.

Halfway through her instructions to herself, Cam flung the door open, his expression making it clear she'd have to go straight to plan B or she didn't stand a chance.

Looking unsure whether to slam the door in her face, he hesitated for a moment too long. She took the choice away from him by pushing her way past, facing him with arms crossed. Just try and get her to leave now.

He shrugged. "Let me guess. You're here to talk me into staying."

"I'm here to say I'm sorry. I should have been honest about Doran's identity from the beginning, but I didn't see any other way."

"Did you hope I'd be too busy staying alive to notice he knew you? I deserved to know the truth."

"And what would you have done with that truth, Cam? Run to General Pendergast? I couldn't risk that."

"The general doesn't know Doran is *Amhas-draoi*?" He stiffened, his gaze drilling right through her.

"If he knew, do you think he'd trust Scathach? Or any *Other*? We half-breeds walk a dangerous line between acceptance and intolerance. Why do you think we hide what we are? Because to let people like you know the truth about us is asking for trouble."

"People like me?" His voice dropped, his tone ominous.

"The mortal world—the world of the *Duinedon*. To you we're freaks. Monsters. The devil's spawn."

"Don't lump me in with the narrow-minded and superstitious. I've been damned open to all you've thrown at me."

She rolled her eyes. "Fine. Not you. But the rest of them. It's only been a few years since they stopped burning witches at the stake. If Doran Buchanan's found to be one of us, the hunt will begin again, and anyone with *Fey* blood suspect."

Cam seemed to be considering her argument. A good step. He hadn't shoved her out the door, refusing to listen. Perhaps he wasn't as hardheaded as she thought.

"We're not a threat to the mortal world," she continued. "But do you think once we're exposed, your kind will believe that?"

"You could have told me at the beginning." He ran a tired hand down his face. Limped to a chair, leaning both hands on the top rail. Slower to recover than she'd expected. Or he'd been hurt worse than she'd known.

She met his stare, refusing to look away as if she were ashamed. "My friends. My family. My very way of life were at stake. They still are. I didn't trust you."

His jaw hardened. "You did once."

She dropped her gaze. "That wasn't trust. That was sex. And look where it landed us." She took a shaky breath, faced him again. "No, Cam. I did what I thought best. But Doran's stronger than I anticipated. *Neuvarvaan*'s power is enhancing his own. He's close to mastering Andraste's sword. Give me time. Two weeks. If we haven't tracked down Doran by then, you can go to the general. I'll even go with you."

He said nothing. The silence spinning out indefinitely until Morgan wanted to scream. Finally he shifted, a grimace washing over his face. Cleared his throat, his words coming slowly as if he'd thought about them a long time. "If I agree, you'll do things my way. No more lies. No more secrets. I'm in charge. When I say jump, you ask *how high?* Deal?" He held out a hand.

What would she be giving up by allowing him to call the shots? Or did he expect her to turn down his offer? Not a chance. She met Cam's stare, ice blue and completely unreadable.

Before she could change her mind, she accepted his hand. Gave it a firm shake. "Deal."

The corporal—dressed today in the scarlet and white of the Thirty Second—threaded his way through the market crowds, to stand beside Cam's bench. Never once did he look in Cam's direction or acknowledge his presence aside from a tipping of his hat. Instead, he chose to watch the traffic beyond the low iron fence. Crowded stalls, shouting vendors with packs slung over their backs, wagons, carts, and drays pushing through the choked streets.

Who would notice two men among so many?

Cam pulled a newspaper from his coat pocket. Flipped it open as if he prepared to read. "I need you, Rastus." His words came low, but he knew the other man heard him. "I'll pay. Well."

Rastus braced himself, hands behind his back, eyes front. The picture of a proper English officer. "I heard you were dead, Colonel. You and the woman."

"You heard wrong. But that's why I need you. You're going to follow Buchanan for me. Find out where he's gone."

"I know where he's gone. London. Alone."

"Why?" Cam shook out his paper. Turned the page. "What's in London?"

"Bloody hell if I know," Rastus groused. "He and I aren't exactly mates."

"Follow him. Find him. I want Doran Buchanan, Rastus. I'm going to enjoy putting a bullet in his brain. What do you say?"

Cam had come to Rastus as a last option. The only one he knew with the unmagical ability to ferret out Doran's hiding place. And already close enough to the *Amhas-draoi* not to arouse suspicion if he were spotted. If Morgan proved incapable of tracking the bastard, he wanted to have a backup plan in place. It was always well to have two strings to your bow.

He clenched his hands on the edges of his paper until it tore, hating every second he spent in the ex-Serpent's presence. "You give me Buchanan, you can name your price."

Rastus rolled forward on the balls of his feet. Cleared his throat. "I don't come cheap."

Cam's lips thinned. "I don't want cheap. I want good."

"In that case, why not find him yourself? You was always the best, Sin."

A dubious compliment, considering what he'd been the best at. Eliminating problems. Terminating embarrassing entanglements.

During war, alliances formed and dissolved. And those

favored one day could become liabilities the next. The Serpent Brigade made it their mission to clean up the army's messes in deadly fashion. A responsibility Cam never questioned. A duty he excelled at until the injury that almost killed him. Only then had his sense of mission begun to unravel. The ghosts rising up in the haunted hours before dawn.

"A year and an attempted murder ago, I may have been the best. But not now. Things change."

He'd changed. He wouldn't let that part of him take hold again. He'd not give in to the natural-born killer living inside him. Sin was dead and buried. And Cam meant to keep it that way. He'd lost too much to that side of himself to allow it full rein again.

He shifted, biting back an oath at the painful twinge from neck to knees. "So, do we have a deal?"

Rastus gave a curt nod. "I'll be in touch."

Cam folded his paper. Shoved it back in his pocket. Stretching his sore leg, he rose carefully from the bench. "We'll use my club as our drop point for messages. Arthur's in St. James Street. Do you know it?"

Rastus gave a low whistle of admiration. "Aye, I've heard of it."

"Leave any messages for me with the porter there. He'll see to it I get them. Send word as soon as you've run Buchanan to ground."

"Nice address, Colonel. Always figured you for a gentleman. Never realized you was a regular out-and-outer. Should I be calling you Lord Sin?"

"No, Corporal," Cam snarled. "You should be calling me sir."

Cam glanced around the room one last time. Not that he could have missed anything. He had exactly the clothes on his back, a borrowed shirt from Traverse—tight but workable—

and a few items he'd picked up to last him until he could purchase better. Knife, sword, pistols. All gone. He'd have to completely rekit in London. An added complication.

He hefted his bag to his shoulder, bracing himself for the long jarring ride ahead.

Morgan sat at the table with Traverse, a game of chess between them.

The ensign's time-ravaged looks no longer shocked, and his mood had grown less strained since their unannounced arrival. Almost as if offering them safe harbor had jarred him out of his self-pitying desperation. He gripped a walking stick in one gnarled hand, his fingers drumming against the wood, his piercing green eyes fixed on the board. Moving his piece into position, he sat back. Gave a ghost of a smile.

"Any ideas why Doran would flee to London?" Cam asked.

"He's from there," Morgan answered, moving her pawn to the middle of the board to counter Traverse's bishop. "Wapping. East of the Tower."

"So he knows the area."

"He also knows it will be impossible to track him. In a city that size, with that many *Other*, I'd never be able to pick up his trail. Even if he uses his powers, so much mage energy in one place will drown him out. It would be like looking for a needle in a haystack."

After another prolonged drumming of fingers against the stick, Traverse's queen joined the battle.

"He can't just disappear."

Morgan took her turn. Then watched as Traverse's queen slid down to checkmate her king.

Picking up the piece, she rolled it between her fingers, before laying it flat on the board, her gaze somber. "You forget. He's *Amhas-draoi*. If anyone can just disappear, he can."

Chapter 13

Fog thickened the air to soup, making breathing difficult and seeing impossible. She'd no idea where they were in this maze of buildings. One London street looked like every other street. Houses rose up and disappeared behind them into the swirling, gray-green miasma. An occasional corner held a lamp flickering like foxfire from out of the gloom.

Cam had no trouble. Ahead of her, he sat stiff and silent, his muscled back swaying with his horse's steps, his head erect and untiring. She'd long ago given up trying to navigate on her own. Instead, she'd thrown her reins away. Let her horse follow Cam's on a straight path to somewhere. She only hoped she got there soon.

Grit and sleep stung Morgan's eyes. Her body ached from the long, unending hours in the saddle. No breaks. Little rest. Cam drove them with a firm whip hand, his own endurance making complaints impossible. He had to be as sore as she was—if not worse, his leg slower to heal than expected. But he'd never once whined. And the hours had passed. Through scant meals eaten on horseback. Through changes in mounts with five minutes to stretch her legs and empty her bladder.

His expression through the whole hellish journey made it

plain he expected her to rebel. Call off their deal. Which, of course, only made her more determined. She squared her jaw and refused to give in. She'd agreed to this devil's bargain. If Cam thought a few uncomfortable days were going to break her, he was dead wrong.

She closed her eyes, secure in the knowledge her horse was as exhausted as she. Just a few moments wouldn't hurt. And in the dark, Cam would never know this one small weakness.

"We're here," Cam announced. His first words in at least ten miles.

Her horse jostled to a halt, sliding on the cobbles, breaking Morgan's doze. She looked around at the gray, shadowed shapes of tall, elegant town houses. Candle shine spilled from a few windows, but for the most, they were shuttered and dark. Knockers removed.

"Where's here? I thought we were taking rooms."

"It's my house," he answered, dismounting. "At least it is now. We'll stay here while we're in town."

"But servants," she argued. "And neighbors. Talk will spread. Doran will find out." She slithered to the ground, thankful her legs didn't give out under her. Surprised at Cam's steady hand at her elbow, though it was withdrawn almost immediately.

"It's just Amos and Susan." As if she should know who they were. "I haven't lived here since . . ." Since his wife's death, but he didn't say it. "And few neighbors. It's going on October. Most have already left for the country. Doran won't find out because Doran isn't trying to. He thinks we're dead."

"And if he does realize the truth?"

"Even better. He'll seek us out. And once he's flushed into the open, we deal with him." Few words holding an infinite amount of vicious finality.

In a strange way, reassuring.

They entered through a back door into the kitchen, her boots ringing hollow on the stone floor. In the center of the room stood a scrubbed worktable. Cupboards and racks lined the walls, stacked neatly in preparation for no one. A hearth yawned, cold and black.

Cam fumbled through a drawer, coming up with tapers and a flint. Even in the friendly glow of candlelight, the space seemed forbidding. The other rooms hardly better.

Furniture in Holland covers. Chandeliers draped in dust sheets. The place held the damp must of abandonment as if someone had simply given up. Walked out and locked the doors behind them.

A flutter of white caught the corner of Morgan's eye. The creak of a floorboard. "Cam," she whispered.

He looked up as the apparition materialized into a middle-aged woman in a nightgown and wrapper, her graying hair tucked neatly under a nightcap.

"It's Susan. She keeps house. Or did when there was a house to keep. We must have woken her up."

Holding her candle high, the woman surveyed them with a critical eye. "Colonel? That you? You never sent word you were coming. The house isn't ready. I've barely food enough in the larder for Amos and me. And the rooms aren't aired. You'll catch your death between damp sheets."

Her squint took in Morgan's less-than-respectable attire, making her wish she'd donned a gown or run a comb through her hair or at least washed her hands and face before arriving.

Cam put a possessive arm upon her shoulder, drawing her in close. No softness to his touch. His body remained as unyielding as his manner. "Susan, I want you to meet the new Mrs. Sinclair. We married a few weeks ago."

Whatever the woman expected to hear, this wasn't it. Her shock was clear. "And the last Mrs. Sinclair not in her grave more than a few months? The gabble-mongers will be jawing about this one, Colonel. No mistake. If you ask me—"

"Which I didn't," Cam replied, cutting off any more discussion.

Susan closed her mouth with a snap. "No, sir." She offered him an overly done curtsey before adding under her breath, "Nor did you the first time and look where that landed you."

If Cam heard her, he gave no sign. He released Morgan, almost shoving her away from him before standing rigid, a white-knuckled hand upon the staircase newel post, the weight off his injured leg.

Susan started back up the stairs. "I'll have your rooms readied quick enough. And the mistress's chamber—"

"No." Cam's vehemence echoed like a shout in the quiet room. "No. That room stays shut. Put her in the back bedchamber for now."

"It's awful small," Susan argued, "and there's no view. It's not comfortable like the front rooms."

"We won't be here long enough to notice."

Not exactly the manner of a besotted bridegroom. And so the old retainer must have thought as well. She eyed Morgan again, lifting her candle and motioning her to follow. "As you wish, Colonel. This way, mistress."

Morgan cast a swift glance at Cam's tight-jawed face, his grave expression. A desperate, lonesome need clouded his gaze before vanishing, replaced once more by the familiar brutal arrogance.

She'd wished him to the devil since Devonshire, but now that she'd the chance to leave him, reluctance seized her.

The housekeeper seemed to understand. Her manner softened.

"Don't worry over him, mum," Susan tsked, climbing the stairs. Leading Morgan down a long narrow hallway. "It's this house. Always puts him in a temper. Nothing a good dram of Sinclair whiskey won't cure."

Morgan grimaced. "That's what I'm afraid of."

Susan pushed wide the bedchamber door, peering around with pursed lips. "It's small. A bit dark. Nothing like the front rooms."

At this point Morgan could have happily curled up in a corner on the floor, but she kept her mouth shut. Tested the mattress. Lumpy, smelling of camphor, and absolute heaven to her tired bones.

Susan rubbed her arms briskly, the chilly room's hearth as black and empty as the kitchen's. "I'm sorry about the state of things. But I expect now that you're here, the colonel will reopen the place." She sounded disappointed. "A shame. He should sell it and be done, if you was to ask me."

Morgan straightened. "Why would he sell it?"

"Isn't it obvious? He bought it for her, didn't he?"

And with those cryptic words, she left.

Morgan surveyed her surroundings, the papered walls, the fancy scrollwork on the mahogany bed frame. The heavy damask drapes.

Fashionable. Refined. Stylish.

And completely unwelcoming.

What happened within these cheerless rooms to make Cam flee the first chance he got? Had Charlotte been the victim everyone rumored? Or had there been more to it than that?

Life was rarely black and white. Right and wrong. Could Cam's marriage to Charlotte fall into that same state of gray? And what did that mean for her own rocky relationship with him?

The ghost-feel of his hands lurked in the corners of her mind, the fierce need for him left unsatisfied. Her body still yearned to finish what they'd started. Know once more the mind-bending thrill of climaxing beneath him.

She shook off the craving and the questions at the same time, chalked them both up to bone-weary exhaustion.

Tomorrow, she'd wake and Cam would still be the jackass she barely tolerated.

He had to be.

Cam pressed the heels of his hands to his eyes, exhaustion rushing in to replace the dogged silence he'd managed for the last days. He'd known Morgan was tired. Hungry. Sore. But he pushed on, refusing to lessen his pace or give in to his urge to call a rest before she dropped in her traces. He wanted to say he did it out of necessity. That they needed to be in London as soon as possible, but he couldn't convince himself that was the only reason. It was to punish as much as anything else. Unfortunately, all he did was make his own injuries worse. His thigh burned as if a knife twisted its way through him.

Again.

Stretching his leg out in front of him, he massaged the ache in an effort to work the kinks out.

Susan would be here any minute. As soon as she'd settled Morgan, he expected the old busybody to clatter in, demanding explanations. A privilege of lifelong familiarity. And one she enjoyed a little too much.

"Well?"

Right on cue. "Well what?" Cam shifted in his chair. Curled his fingers around the whiskey he'd poured and then ignored.

Susan folded her arms across her chest. Settled on the corner of a chair. "The girl. Who is she? And none of this song and story of an anvil wedding. I've known you for too long to be listening to that kind of blather."

He toyed with the idea of revealing everything to her. Discarded it immediately. There'd be questions. Pointed looks. He wasn't up to her inquisition. Best to stick with the ridiculous story of an impetuous marriage.

"It's as I told you, Susan. Morgan and I wed a few weeks ago."

Her squint grew more pronounced, her foot tapping impatiently. "She's not some tart you've brought home, I hope. I won't have it, Master Cameron. Not under my roof. What would your aunt and uncle say?"

A muscle in Cam's jaw jumped. "They won't say anything because they won't know. The last thing I need is Uncle Josh and Aunt Sylvie bearing down on me. Keep it quiet for now, Susan."

Her mouth folded into a deep frown, her shrewd gaze suspicious. "A new bride and you don't want to be showing her off to the family?"

He thought of Morgan as she looked tonight. A slit skirt for riding, breeks beneath. A narrow-waisted jacket that highlighted her slender hips, the unusual breadth to her shoulders. Tried not to remember how she'd looked the night of the attack. Her burnished gold gaze awash with desire, the supple arching column of her back. The hot, wet center of her sliding against him. Wanting more. Wanting him.

He swallowed hard on the sudden craving to have her that way again.

Morgan. Double-sided as the claymore. And either facet of her personality enough to cause her ruin among the society sausage grinder where any newcomer was fresh meat. He should know. He'd been chewed up and spit out already.

"Does she look like the kind you show off?" He tossed back his whiskey, let the familiar heat ease its way through his system.

She shrugged. "I'm not the one running helter-skelter back into marriage. But if you loved her enough to marry her, seems to me you should love her enough to not be ashamed of her."

Was that a dig at his family? They'd professed to love him.

Until it grew too uncomfortable. Then they'd scattered like rabbits. Left him to find his own way through the growing rumors, the recurring nightmares. His war following him even into the drawing rooms of London. A titillation. A morbid curiosity. The burden of his crimes almost killing him. Literally.

"The situation's . . . complicated. Let's leave it for now. Just do as I say. Keep it to yourself. Morgan and I aren't here. You haven't seen us."

She rose. "As you say, Master Cameron. I'll not say another word, though I know a havey-cavey business when I see it."

Cam gripped the arms of his chair. Hard. "She's my bride, Susan. Believe me."

"As you say, Colonel," she repeated, muttering low in her throat as she left him. "And that's why you're down here and she's up there and both miserable as two people can be."

Morgan punched the lumps from her pillow. Lay back to stare up into the bed curtains, willing herself to fall asleep.

Only stubborn pride kept Cam unbending. Foolish arrogance that would see them both killed if they weren't careful. In battle, Cam might be a match for Doran. In some ways even, she'd admit, he was superior. But Doran wielded *Neuvarvaan*. And with it, the black spell of the *Morkoth*. It would take more than skill with blade and pistol. It would take magic. Something she held in spades whether Cam liked it or not.

She returned to her bed. Lay listening to the city sounds. Muffled through the heavy shutters across her window and lessened by the hour, but still present. A low grumbling roar like the breath of a living creature. She imagined the giant red dragon of England curled tail-tight beneath the ground, the soul of the *Duinedon*. Would it come alive at the booted tramp of Undying? Would it feel the panic such an army would create among the mortal world? And would it arise, taking shape as vengeance meted out on the *Other* by the *Duinedon*? Magic against mortal? Until all that was *Fey* was wiped clean from the earth?

She threw herself to the far side of the bed, wishing her mind hadn't reached that grim conclusion.

The house settled itself. Susan's footsteps going past her door on her way to the attics followed soon after by the slow uneven tread of Cam, making his way to his own rooms.

She rose, padding across the floor, lifting the latch to peer out into the gloom. A crack of light slid down the hall as he opened his chamber door, gilding his blond hair, throwing hard-edged shadows across the planes of his face.

Morgan held still, her newfound dedication hanging by the merest fingertip. A part of her wanted to confront him. Force him to accept her apology. And another part—the soft, sentimental part—wanted to chase the shadows from his eyes. Brush the strands of gold from his forehead. Let him escape with her back into a past where they were both happy.

She did neither.

He paused in the doorway, his hand on the knob, his head bowed. "Sleep well, Morgan. *Oidhche mhath, m'eudail.*"

Those words delivered so softly caused the blood to pound in her ears.

Slamming the door, she pressed her back against it, her hands shaking, the thread of his endearment ribboning her heart. Had it been a slip of the tongue? A cruel sarcasm meant to wound?

Or had he too felt that strange reluctance to part? As if their very lives depended upon this enforced solidarity.

She crossed her arms protectively over her chest, hating the low, crushing ache beneath her breastbone. She'd done with grieving. Had buried those few short weeks with Cam, hoping never to feel this misery again. And yet a few honeyed words battered straight through every good intention.

She dropped her arms to her sides. Straightened. No. She refused to be sucked back in. It would take more than a few vulnerable moments to make her go against her better instincts. Scathach was right. Cam was complete poison.

Chapter 14

Morgan came awake to the clank of a coal scuttle. A man bent at the hearth, coaxing a fire to life, his dark hair silvered with gray, his limbs large and gnarled as he worked the bellows.

He stood, wiping his hands on a rag, brushing soot from his sleeve. "You'll excuse me being here, mum. Not proper, but Susan was busy in the kitchen, and the master told me it would be all right." His broad face cracked into a smile, welcome after the housekeeper's suspicious glowers last night. "I tried not to wake ye, but . . ." He shrugged his apology. "I've left ye a basin and ewer of hot water on the table there. And there's tea on the tray. If ye need anything else, just holler. The name's Amos."

Morgan stretched and sat up, daylight making everything look brighter. Scathach had been right. She could indulge her desire for Cam, but never at the expense of what was truly important. A life among the *Amhas-draoi*. A life she'd wanted for as long as she could remember. Cam might not be poison, but he wasn't her white knight either. And she did her own rescuing, thank you very much.

"Susan and I are a bit shorthanded," Amos continued. "We never expected company. Couldn't have been more flummoxed to see ye and that's a fact. Never expected to have the colonel bring home another wife."

Wife. The word sent a shiver of panic up her spine. Or was that excitement? Both feelings so tightly wrapped she couldn't tease them apart. "He loved her that much?"

Amos choked. "Love? If ye can love a wasp, knowing one wrong move will get ye stung."

Morgan hugged her knees to her. "Then the stories were true? He did discard her for a string of mistresses?"

Amos's eyebrows shot so high they disappeared into his hairline. "Where'd ye hear such palaver? The colonel's no saint—I served him for all his years in the army. Could tell ye stories that'd curl your hair. But if anyone did the discardin', it were her. Not him."

"But—"

He grabbed up his broom and pail. "No more I'll say on that. It's not seemly to be talking of her with ye. She's gone. You're here. And the colonel's due a bit of peace if ye ask me. He's earned it times ten." He tipped his head. Banged toward the door.

"What happened to him during those years away, Amos?"

Her words drew him up. His hand clamped around the pail's handle, an uncomfortable flush creeping up his neck.

"He barely speaks of it, but it's enough," she went on. "You were there."

He turned back, old sorrows dulling his gaze. "The colonel, he knew how to shoot. How to stalk. Things he'd learned back at home in the mountains around Strathconon. First at his father's side and then his uncle's. Those men in charge. They saw that, and they twisted it. They took a man already on the edge and pushed him over."

"I've seen glimpses of what he must have been like. But was it so bad?"

Amos nodded. "Aye, it was. By the time we'd reached

France, murder and savagery were all the colonel knew. He ate, drank, and dreamed them." His words grew harsh, his face hard with pity. "Did they think once he'd come home, he'd forget? He'd just go back to the man he'd been? They were fooling themselves. They've created a killer. Now they've got to live with it." He swallowed. "But, then, so does he."

Cam flipped open the morning paper Amos had brought. What he'd hoped to find he couldn't say. Stories of unexplained magic. Legions of young-old men springing up like mushrooms across London. But nothing of the sort caught his eye. Just the usual scandal and speculation from the upper strata. Lord Tabberner caught in a revealing position with Mrs. Nowell. A banking scandal ruining two members of parliament and an undersecretary in the Foreign Office. The elopement of a young heiress to Gretna Green with her footman.

The notices of murder and mayhem from the lower classes were no more helpful. Bodies discovered washed ashore near Southwark Bridge. A doctor with his head crushed as he returned from a call near Holborn. A break-in and robbery at a gentleman's home in Cheyne Walk, his housekeeper murdered in the attack.

Pushing the paper aside, he spread the map of the city out on the dining room table. Placed his cup and saucer on one curling corner. The butter dish on the other.

He'd been awake since before dawn, but lay abed listening to the city, a garbled, dissonant roar of warring sounds.

He hated it. Just like every other morning when he'd lain in his room, waiting for the house to wake around him.

The ancient rhythms of the mountains. The purr of the fathomless gray loch, and the lyric sigh of the ever-present wind. The scream of the wildcat as it hunted and the mountain hare as it died. That was the music of his world. Not the incessant, ugly chorus of millions living cheek by jowl.

This was his uncle's world. This had been Charlotte's world. And now it hid a madman.

What drew Doran here? No standing stones. No barrow mounds. But he came with intent. Cam was sure of it.

He scanned the map with no clue to what he searched for. Then reaching the bottom right corner, began again. A name. A street. Anything that jumped out at him as a possibility, he wrote down to be checked later. He'd hired Rastus. But that didn't mean he'd leave the search to the wily, old corporal.

"You're up early." Morgan stood in the doorway, a hand on the knob, uncertainty in her eyes.

He should never have spoken those words last night. Never let her see how much he wanted her. But the look she'd given him had offered hope that mayhap she wanted him too. It had taken all his self-discipline not to go to her. Bury himself inside her and end the unceasing torment of those few unfulfilled moments.

Taking a deep, steadying breath, he motioned her in. Prayed she didn't notice the hunger in his gaze. "I don't sleep well. Thought I may as well be doing something."

She took up position at the opposite end of the table. Stood, looking down at the map, her body rigid.

She wore a gown today. A simple sweep of celadon green that clung to every curve. Emphasized her high round breasts, her mile long legs.

Which was worse? The leave-nothing-to-the-imagination breeks or the hidden curves and tempting flesh of the morning dress? His whole body throbbed. He straightened, plowing his hands through his hair. He had no answer. Both left him hard as a rock.

"How's your leg?" she asked.

His gaze narrowed. "Better. Why?" he snapped, his nerves frayed by the memories this bloody house brought back.

Sparks fired her own eyes. "Just trying to make conversation. I apologize for asking."

He clenched his jaw. Took firm hold of his seesawing emotions. Morgan didn't understand. She couldn't. "No, I'm sorry. Can we begin again? Pretend I didn't just bite your head off?"

A faint smile curved her lips. "We can try."

Thank God she wasn't sulky. Probably helped to be raised with a household of brothers.

She paused. Heaved a deep breath. "What have you found so far?"

And just like that, they were back on solid footing.

"Absolutely nothing." Cam jerked a chin toward the sideboard. "There's coffee. I had Susan make it for you. And I think the eggs are still warm."

She shot him a look of gratitude as she poured herself a cup. Fixed a heaping plate, bringing it back to her seat at the table.

"Here's us." He pointed to a spot near the park. "The only place we can say with certainty Doran isn't. Everywhere else is suspect. If he's smart, he'll go to ground until he thinks it's safe."

Morgan shook her head as she nibbled on a piece of bacon. "No. The goddess blade hungers for blood. Doran will need to appease it with a sacrifice."

Cam dropped heavily into a chair. "The damn sword's alive?"

She swallowed her forkful of eggs. "Not alive. But *Morkoth* magic lies behind its power. Their spells required the spilling of blood. Pain. And blind obedience. *Neuvarvaan* will require that as well."

It just got better and better. The moment he thought he'd wrapped his head around the whole magic aspect, Morgan dropped another bomb in his lap. He felt he played a continual game of catch-up where everyone knew the rules but him.

"If this weapon is such a menace, why doesn't Andraste look for the bloody thing herself? Why send us?" His words came fast and angry.

Morgan's lips thinned with annoyance. "She would. It's only Scathach's influence that keeps the *Fey* from crossing the divide. Bringing down the walls between the worlds to search for the sword. This is why the *Amhas-draoi* have been brought in. It's our job to see to it those walls remain secure."

"Not because Doran's one of you?"

Rage flickered at the corners of her gaze. "He's not one of us. Not anymore." She paused, taking a swallow of coffee. When she spoke again, she'd regained her composure. "I'm doing my best. You gave me two weeks, Cam."

He wished he could settle as easily. He felt jumpy as a cat, edgy and tense. This house. This mission. Morgan. It felt as if the walls closed in on him. "I could give you two months and it would still be impossible to find him in this labyrinth. It's up to Rastus now, God help us."

"Do you trust him?"

He shot her a wry smile. "Rastus? Not an inch. He'd sell us out if he thought he could get away with it."

"So what's keeping him from doing just that?"

"Self-preservation and greed. Rastus will find Doran for the money. He'll stay loyal out of fear."

"Fear of Doran?"

"No, Morgan." Cam met her gaze. "Fear of me."

He waited for the flash of alarm, the sudden distancing. Instead, Morgan rested her head on her elbows, watching him. "Do you do that on purpose?"

"What?"

"That look-at-scary-me act."

He shoved his chair back. Prowled the room, the need to be away from this house overwhelming. His throat closed, his heart banging wildly against his ribs. "It's not an act. You said yourself we lied to each other in Edinburgh. You're right. I lied about Charlotte. And about me. About who I am."

Morgan followed his restless pacing with her eyes. "You're Cameron Sinclair. A colonel in the dragoons. A society blueblood."

He stopped behind her chair, making her twist in her seat to face him. "That's not everything. That's not even the most important thing."

She lifted her chin, her eyes gleaming yellow gold as suns. Her scent filled his nostrils, a subtle mix of woodbine and meadowsweet that immediately made him think of Scotland and Strathconon. "This is me you're talking to, Cam. It might frighten some sweet, young thing—"

"It frightens me, Morgan."

He fixed his stare on the wall opposite, remembering long-ago meals. The arguments and screaming matches. The angry weeping and the cold brittle silences. If events had not sprung him from the death spiral of his marriage, would he have simply snapped? Ended it his way?

He told himself it would never have gone that far. But in the darkest watches of the night, the doubts surfaced. And he couldn't be sure.

In the end, Charlotte hadn't been sure either. Which is probably why she did what she did.

"Don't you see?" he urged. "It's in me now. The brutality's a part of me. I can't rid myself of what I know. What I've done."

"Then embrace it," she answered softly, bringing a hand up as if she wanted to catch him to her. Stopped before her fingers brushed his cheek.

"What the hell's that supposed to mean?"

"It means that for good or ill, this is who you are now. There's no going back. But you decide what you do with this knowledge. Not them."

"And that's supposed to make everything better?"

"Not better," Morgan conceded. "But you did what you had to, to survive."

"Perhaps. But as it turns out, there are far worse things than death."

The map of London had long since dissolved into a wavy jumble of lines and squiggles. Names and numbers. But Morgan kept at it. Waiting for that instantaneous spark that would let her know what Doran was up to. Why he'd escaped to the city.

Cam had left her at it hours earlier. Mumbled something about going out, a swift bark of an order to stay put just before he slammed the front door. No doubt, he thought she'd disobey. But no. Two weeks was their agreement. And for two weeks, she could bite her tongue.

It was just as well. A dull ache pressed at the base of her skull, the drone of mage energy saturating the air, penetrating the earth. It pushed upon her from all sides, making it nearly impossible to concentrate. She closed her eyes, pinching the bridge of her nose. Wished she were back on Skye. Climbing the peaks around Dunsgathaic. Watching the roll of breakers, smashing against the cliffs with the force of thousands of miles of ocean behind them. Not so many people. Not so many warring magics shouting in her head.

"'Tis all right, Susan, I promise. I'll just pop in and say good afternoon."

A voice in the hall—but not Cam's. A stranger. Though one comfortable with the household if he knew the housekeeper by name.

Morgan swung around as the study door opened. A man stood on the threshold, dwarfing the doorway with his stature, the perfection of his features enhanced by the somber cut of his clothes, his dark hair pulled back in a soldier's queue.

Even among the dazzling good looks of her brothers and cousins, this man would stand out. And tower over.

Ducking to enter the room, he laughed at the expression she must have shown. "I owe it all to a simple diet of bannocks and mutton stew. And a wee dram of whiskey before bed."

She shook off her surprise. Stepped forward, seeking to turn off the charm before he started. She wasn't in the mood for gallantry. "I'm Morgan Bligh—forgive me, Sinclair. The colonel and I just wed."

"Did ye, now?" He surveyed her, frank admiration in his gaze, and a slow knowing smile lit his gray eyes. "Cam's mystery redhead," he muttered.

"I'm sorry?"

He offered her his hand. "Captain Brodie MacKay. The roguish best friend. And if ye were able to drag Cam back to the altar, you've got a will of steel." His eyes narrowed, more to his glittering gaze than boyish charm. His grip upon her hand tightened. "But I'm thinking mayhap it's all a hum. And you and Cam aren't quite as shackled as ye say."

She pulled away, aware of the heat that spread up her neck. Burned her cheeks. How the hell had he guessed? And now what was she going to do?

Faced with this formidable Highland giant in front of her, she wasn't sure, though the same storm-cloud intensity of his stare that unnerved her, also dared her to call his bluff. Mayhap she'd reveal the truth. See what happened. "You're right. I'm Morgan Bligh. Sinclair and I are . . . traveling together." Let him make of that what he wanted.

"Captain MacKay. You've gone and frightened the young lady," Susan scolded from the doorway.

Morgan jumped. Prayed Susan hadn't overheard.

But she bustled in with a tea-laden tray and scones fresh from the oven, seemingly unaware of Morgan's confession.

Brodie scooped up a scone as she passed. "Do ye think so?

Somehow, I dinna think this young lady frightens very easily." He caught Morgan's eye. "Or am I wrong?"

She squared her shoulders, a sly smile curving her lips. "You've been correct on every count. Are you a gambling man?"

He offered her a teasing smile. "Me? I only wager what I can afford to lose, which makes me a very dull boy since I've barely a feather to fly with." He crossed to the table, grabbing a second scone.

Susan stood back, hands on hips. "Now, don't go running yourself down, Captain. Riches aren't everything in this world. You're as respectable as the next." She slapped his hand away before he could take a third. "You eat them up so fast, you won't even taste them."

She glowered, but was obviously smitten with the captain. Still vowing displeasure, she grumbled all the way out the door, leaving them alone.

He laughed. "Forgive Susan's blunt speaking. She's more a mother to me than my own mother ever was."

"To you?"

"And Cam. She served as wet nurse to both of us. You could say we're milk brothers. And later, I was fostered to Strathconon and Sir Joshua's household."

Raised together? Lord help the women of Scotland.

If Cam traced his icy blond brilliance back to his Viking forebears, Captain Brodie MacKay was all Celt with his dark brooding looks and chiseled features. She could only imagine what trouble two such young men got up to in that isolated corner of Scotland. Probably wenched their way through every lass within two hundred miles.

With that disturbing image uppermost in her head, she focused on the aroma of hot scones. Food would take her mind off Cam's oversexed past. Place it back where it needed to be. On the map in front of her.

Taking a seat by the tray, she smeared jam on one. Wished she had some of Gram's thick, creamy *dyenn molys* to spread as well. "How did you know we were here? Cam assured me no one would notice our arrival."

"Dodging the in-laws? Dinna blame ye. Lady Sinclair's a dear, but Sir Joshua's another kettle of fish." Brodie dropped into a chair, his stature dwarfing the delicate white and gold piece. She waited for its inevitable collapse. "He's proper as a Puritan."

"You haven't answered my question."

He poured himself a cup of tea. Looked as if he wished it were something stronger. "Nor you, mine. Should we exchange confessions?"

"I've already confessed as much as I plan to."

"Verra well. You're too well spoken to be some Covent Garden bawd. But ye dinna look the type to lie about, deciding what expensive bauble ye want next and waiting for your protector to snap his fingers either."

"So I'm not a low-class whore or a high-class mistress."

He grazed a hand across his jaw in thought. "No. I can't say with certainty what ye are. But I intend to find out."

"Then if you're finished cross-examining me, it's my turn. How did you know we were here?"

"Amos," he said simply.

"What about him?"

"I ran into him this morning. To anyone who doesn't know him, nothing strange in his manner. But I've known him since I was born. He looked cagier than usual. Full of something. A little prodding and he told me Cam was back in town. When I came round and saw the house still shut up, I got curious. Susan let me in through the kitchen. And here we are."

A pounding on the front door threw Morgan to her feet.

Susan rushed to answer, her mumbled yes, sirs and no,

sirs carrying through the house as she fought to fob the visitors off.

Finally a voice rang clear, and Morgan's heart dropped into her boots. "I know he's at home. Don't stand there sputtering. Get me my nephew."

So much for stealth.

Chapter 15

Cam left the gunsmith's, the second of his errands complete. A Baker rifle ordered and a new pair of pistols in his possession. If Doran came within five hundred yards, Cam would take him down. He didn't care how much magic the *Amhas-draoi* wielded, a well-aimed bullet to the head would stop him as easily as the next man.

He only wished his initial destination had been as beneficial. General Pendergast could tell him nothing of use. And Cam's deal with Morgan meant he couldn't share the information he did have. It made for stilted conversation and long uncomfortable pauses with Major Eddis's sneering, know-it-all glances making Cam's fists itch.

"I'm counting on you to find me that sword, Sinclair." The general eased back in his chair, hooking his thumbs in his waistcoat. "You were highly recommended for this assignment. Your wartime service made you of particular interest."

"Did it?"

He didn't like where this was going, though he'd suspected it from the minute the army had brought him in last spring. Something in the careful way they handled him. The way they danced around his past experience or didn't speak of it at all.

As if the dirty part of war was something gentlemen didn't discuss. Or even acknowledge.

"Your years abroad prepared you well for this type of mission, though it's been hard to take advantage of the brigade's expertise in peacetime. Few members of your outfit remain. And those who survived the campaigns aren't exactly . . ." His voice trailed off.

Cam knew what words the general didn't say.

Stable. Balanced.

Sane.

Supposedly he was all those things. Though what that said about him when the work of the brigade had ruined so many others, he wouldn't look into too closely.

He tried to ignore the tension banding his shoulders, the dead weight settling across his chest.

"Doran's from the Wapping area," he said. "We're assuming that's where he's gone. He'll know every bolt-hole. Miss Bligh is currently mapping the area. We'll flush him street by street if we have to." He kept his agreement with Rastus quiet.

"That's right." Pendergast nodded, adjusting his spectacles. "You and the young woman. How is that arrangement working out?"

Eddis's expression went from merely contemptuous to outright insulting. "Yes, Sinclair. How is she?"

Three little words and the weeks of pressure tore through him. Like a gun going off, Cam snapped. He lunged for Eddis, conscious thought lost amid the animal need to hurt. "You fucking prick," he snarled.

Eddis stumbled back, catching his wooden leg on the edge of a chair. He brought up his cane in defense, but Cam slid beneath his guard. He'd show them how bloody well the brigade had prepared him.

"Enough!" Pendergast bellowed, slamming his open hand

on his desk. The sound breaking through just moments before Cam's fist connected with Eddis's jaw.

Cam fell back, his whole body knotted with unfulfilled rage. "You speak that way about her again, I'll rip your head off—Major."

Eddis hobbled out of range, his own fury showing in the squint of his eyes, the tic in his jaw. "They were right about you. You're insane."

Cam's chest heaved as he tried slowing his breathing, tried slowing his racing heart. "Damned right. And don't ever forget it."

"Sinclair, that's more than enough. I'll handle my own staff, thank you."

"If you don't, General, I will." He knew he skated on thin ice. The general could reprimand him for insubordination. Hell, he could arrest him for treason if he chose.

He did neither. "It's that kind of spirit I'm expecting out of you, Colonel. That's what will find us this sword. And end this threat once and for all."

They wanted him this way? On a hair trigger and ready to explode? The demons so close to the surface he saw their faces and heard the whispers every time he closed his eyes?

Just knowing that held him together long enough to get out of the office and hail a cab, sending the driver toward Whitechapel and the gunsmith's. The army had nearly destroyed him once for their own purposes, yet he'd crawled back. Now they wanted to destroy him again.

He wouldn't give them—or the demons—the satisfaction.

"And when did you say you married my nephew?" Sir Joshua Sinclair asked, his tone strained in an obvious attempt to remain civil.

Morgan never batted an eye, though she felt Captain

MacKay's gaze boring into her back, waiting for her answer. "I didn't, sir."

Cam's uncle turned out to be all voice. As diminutive in stature as the captain was enormous. But despite his size, his manner brooked no nonsense. A man used to being in charge. Much like his nephew.

He'd ensconced himself in the fanciest chair in the drawing room, the rest of them ranged around him as supplicants. Lady Sinclair perched nervously on the edge of a settee. Their niece took up her subservient position on a bench near the window, strips of shuttered light falling over her delicate features, the pale blue of her dress. Even Brodie seemed cowed, his great frame ranging near the doorway as if he might bolt if given half a chance.

Only Morgan held her ground under the onslaught. She hadn't lived for twenty-four years under the stern discipline of the triumvirate—as she'd dubbed her father, her uncle, and her grandmother—without learning a little bit about self-composure.

"Well, I'm asking you now. When were you and Cam wed? And why weren't we told of it? We're family. You'd think he'd feel at least a slight obligation to let us know when he takes a wife."

"Cam and I have only been together a few weeks." Not a lie. Not a truth. She thought she threaded it nicely. "There wasn't time to send word."

"No time for the only family he has? Why, Euna's his own sister"—he motioned to the young woman at the window—"and she hears of his marriage for the first time from a stranger. I have to say this is all highly irregular. Not at all what I expect from a Sinclair."

Morgan's gaze fixed on the retiring blonde with the downcast eyes. This was Euna, the spunky child of Cam's memories?

Any backbone had been sucked out of her in the intervening years. She looked like she had all the pluck of a baby mouse.

"Did you send letters to your family while on your marriage tour, sir?" Morgan responded, every ounce of Bligh pride coming through in her cool tone.

"No, but I had no need to. Those dearest stood witness to our joining." He rubbed at his chin as if digesting an unexpected problem. "A second marriage . . . what can that boy . . . just like his father . . ." He gave a long-suffering shake of his head.

The captain came forward to stand beside Lady Sinclair. "She can't be any worse than Cam's first."

Thank you, Captain. And this was supposed to help her cause?

Lady Sinclair shifted in her seat. Placed her hand over the captain's. "Brodie, please. Charlotte's only been dead for a few months. It's unseemly to speak of her in such a way."

A mumble that sounded to Morgan's keen ears exactly like good riddance came from the direction of Euna Sinclair. Mayhap not so mousy after all.

Sir Joshua pounded his fist on a table as if calling the unruly room to order. "We can all admit Cam's marriage to Charlotte was an unmitigated disaster. But she's not the reason I'm here this morning."

Morgan crossed her arms over her chest, her spine straight as a saber. "Exactly why are you here? And how did you even know Cam and I had arrived? The house remains shut. We've told no one."

"I heard it from a gentleman at my club," blustered Sir Joshua. "A major on General Pendergast's staff. Edwards . . . Edgars . . ."

"Eddis," Morgan supplied.

"That's him. Fellow said he saw Cam this morning. Congratulated him on his wife and Cam attacked him like some common ruffian."

Morgan could guess what the smarmy Major Eddis had really said. But to set Cam off? It must have been particularly awful.

"So why would my nephew attack a fellow for wishing him well on his marriage? That's what I want to know."

Morgan's patience and her good manners were lessening by the second. The steady pound of her head had flared to a bass-drum crescendo. The map lay untouched. Doran remained uncaught. And the longer she stood here defending herself to Cam's inquisitive relations, the longer she'd have to remain his faux bride. "Your questions keep mounting. But I can't help you. One—I don't know why Cam didn't inform you of our marriage. Perhaps he didn't want you to know. Perhaps he didn't care whether you knew or not. Perhaps he wanted to tell you in person. And two—I wasn't with Cam this morning when he encountered the major in question. I can tell you the man's a right bastard, and I'd love to see Cam plant him a facer."

Brodie's laugh turned to a cough. Lady Sinclair's shocked gasp almost drowned out Euna's murmured giggle. Only Cam's uncle remained silent, a tight, white line ringing his mouth, his peat-brown eyes shooting arrows.

He rose from his seat like a king coming down off his throne. An old, tired king. "We've warned Cam about his volatile nature. He rushes headlong when patient thought would avail him more." Even his voice seemed weighted with exhaustion. "Does he take advice? Take his family's concerns into account? Of course not. Never has. Like his father in that regard. More's the pity." He ran a hand through hair thinning at the crown and silvered with age. "Can you tell me that a marriage to you will restore his reputation? Erase a disreputable past that threatens not only himself with social exile, but his sister and brothers as well? Or is it simply another case of Cam acting less than he is?"

Morgan's hands clenched to fists at her side. How dare they run Cam down as if he were some sort of blight on their grandiose family tree? "Less than he is? What the hell is that supposed to mean? Mayhap a little less scolding and Cam would let you know what was going on in his life. Do you even know your nephew?"

"Only too well. And what we know becomes harder and harder to forgive."

Morgan drew herself up, every ounce of *Amhas-draoi* power in her stony gaze. "Then you—sir—know all the wrong things."

Halfway down Fenchurch Street, a prickling sensation slithered up Cam's spine. Buried itself in his chest like a blade. Someone trailed him.

And this time, not Morgan.

He turned onto Lime Street, passed St. Dionis Backchurch just as the bells chimed three. Turned again at the next corner, kept walking. Noting who followed. Noting who didn't. He held to this routine block after block, narrowing the field of possibilities while at the same time leading his stalker away from the house and Morgan. Aldgate. Back to Whitechapel and through. Onto Shadwell. The streets grew narrower. Dirtier. The fishy, muck smell of the Thames overpowering the scents of garbage and excrement littering the rowdy, bustling riverside.

By the time he'd reached the congested wharfs and warehouses of Limehouse and the entrance to the still-under construction Regent's canal, he'd focused in on one man. And it became time for the hunted to become the hunter.

With ruthless precision, he turned the tables. Dropped back out of sight, his steps going silent, his movements invisible until he chose to be seen.

How many times had he done this? A hundred? A thousand? And every time, it grew easier. Less thought. More instinct. He almost wished he had to fight for the ability. It would ease the part of him that shrank from this talent.

Sliding behind his pursuer, Cam remained hidden, knowing he'd confused him. The man faltered, his gaze traveling the length of the lane. Up and down before moving on. More slowly now. More cautious.

Cam held to this course, feeling the man's growing uncertainty, his mounting fear. Finally as the lane converged to barely more than a neck of brick between two buildings, Cam sprang his trap. His shadow stretched between them, and his would-be tail knew he'd been snared.

The man whipped around, shock and panic whiting his eyes for a split second before narrowing, his scarred mouth twisting into a grim mask of hate. He bore the wild look of a street fighter. The stance of an ex-soldier. Both making him dangerous and unpredictable.

He lunged, hoping to lock his arms around Cam in a bear hug. Bring him down in a crushing wrestler's drop.

Cam stepped aside, tripping his attacker on his way by. Following it up with a quick twisting move that should end the fight before it started.

Scar-Face, more agile than he looked, dodged the blow. Dragged a knife from his coat.

Dangerous had become deadly.

Circling at a safe distance, the man searched for an opening in Cam's defense.

Cam held back. Allowed the man time to get comfortable. Then in the space between one heartbeat and the next, he closed. No time for finesse, he seized the wrist with the knife, dragged his attacker back against him, his arm around his neck in an unbreakable stranglehold.

"Who sent you?"

"Don't. Know." The man's words came out strained and broken as he gasped for air.

Cam squeezed. "Not the right answer."

Scar-Face's body flailed in a worthless attempt to throw Cam off. But he was ready for it. His grip firm. "A few seconds and you'll black out. Suffocation comes next." He jerked the man hard against him. Let the horrible panic of no breath sink in.

Just as the man started to go limp, Cam eased up. "I'll ask you once more—who sent you?"

Scar-Face coughed and heaved, sucking in precious air. "Don't know. He didn't give me a name. Just pointed you out. Told me to keep an eye on you. Tell him where you went. Who you talked to."

Doran? Rastus? The possibilities raced through Cam's mind. After all, Wapping lay only a little way to the west. Had they been discovered so quickly? Had Rastus given them up? Had he been too confident in his own abilities to keep them safe? "Describe him."

"Here, now! What's this?"

A voice from the far end of the lane broke Cam's concentration. Distracted him for the moment it took for Scar-Face to wrench himself from the choke hold. Tear his knife hand free. Slash Cam across the chest. Not a killing stroke, but enough to make Cam stagger back.

Like a shot, the man pounded back up the alley, shoving the intruder aside in a bid to escape.

Clutching his hand to the wound, Cam gritted his teeth. Forced himself to ignore the throbbing sting. He'd no time to waste. Any second and Scar-Face would have lost himself in the surrounding slums. Any chance of discovering where he'd gone and who had hired him, lost.

"Y'all right, guv?"

Cam's distraction still stood rooted to a spot at the top of the lane.

"Perfect," he snarled through pinched lips as he shouldered his way past the man. Followed in Scar-Face's wake.

Chapter 16

The front door slammed. Slow, heavy footsteps sounded on the stairs. Down the hall. Cam's bedchamber door opened and banged shut.

Morgan rose from her seat, relief and rage washing through her in equal measure. Cam had been gone since midmorning. Half the day ago. Dusk had fallen. Susan had lit fires. Candles. Made noises about preparing dinner. And still no Cam.

Now he'd come. But had he sought her out? Informed her about where he'd been and what had kept him all day? No. Just walled himself away. Still holding a grudge.

Well, to hell with him. She was tired of wearing a hair shirt for her supposed crimes. Crimes that in her eyes were completely justified.

She stormed down the hall, anger lending Dutch courage to her steps. No lock barred her entrance. She flung the door back. Stood, hands on hips, her demand for explanations dying on her lips.

Cam sat hunched on the bed, bloody shirt tossed on the floor, a rag pressed to his chest.

"What happened?" she asked.

"It's not as bad as it looks."

She crossed to the bed. Knelt beside him on the floor. "Let me be the judge of that." He leaned back, let her take over. Dried blood caked a shallow gash. Ugly. Almost certainly painful. But not serious. She started to move aside his necklace to get a closer look, but he grabbed it from her. Fisted his hand over the cross.

"I'm not going to steal it," she complained.

He offered a sheepish look of apology. "Sorry. It's been a part of me for a long time. I get jumpy without it. A goodluck charm, I guess."

"And last winter? I don't remember you wearing it then."

His gaze went hot and angry. "No . . . and look how that turned out."

She didn't want to think about how that had turned out. Or how things were turning now.

She focused back on the present. Changed the subject. "How did you get hurt?"

His muscles jumped under her touch, his flesh pebbling. "I was followed. He got in a lucky hit."

"But this cut is hours old. Where've you been since?"

"I followed him. Wanted to see where he went. Who sent him."

"And did you?"

"No. I tailed him as far as the London Docks—Ow!" He flinched as she dabbed at the wound with a damp towel. "Damn it, Morgan. That hurts."

She grabbed his arm. "Hold still, you big baby. You know, this is getting to be a bad habit with you."

He clenched his teeth. "Goes with the territory."

"So you made it as far as the docks . . ."

"A set of shipping offices connected to a warehouse. He went in. Never came out. But when I risked a look, the place was empty. There must be another exit. I'm going back there tomorrow."

Her eyes flicked up to meet his, the reason she'd barged in here snapping back into her mind. "You're not leaving me alone again. I'm going with you."

A smile tipped the corners of his mouth, softened the taut edges of his face. "Did the hours drag by without me?"

She rolled her eyes. "If you were hoping for secrecy, you failed miserably. I've been swarmed on by half of London."

He stiffened, his eyes going hard. "Who was here?"

"Who wasn't? First I had the dubious charms of a Captain MacKay."

"Brodie was here?"

"That was him. Then I was set on by the entire Sinclair clan. Or at least it felt like it."

Cam's expression went from merely annoyed to thunderous. "How the hell did they find out we were in town?"

"Your friend and mine—Major Eddis."

Cam let loose with a string of curses even Morgan found impressive.

"What's his game, Cam? Why would he sabotage the mission like that?"

Calmer after his explosion, he shrugged. "Eddis wouldn't be the first to hold me in contempt. Or want to twist the knife when opportunity arose. To most who heed the rumors, I'm no better than a government-sponsored assassin." He offered her a grim smile. "And my reputation wasn't sterling to begin with. So . . ." He spread his hands in surrender. "Eddis probably thought spilling our presence to my uncle would make me squirm."

Morgan's lips thinned in anger. "I wish you *had* landed a punch or two. He deserves them."

"You heard about that too, did you?" He sucked in his breath, flinching. "Careful. Don't take your temper out on me."

Sheepishly, she bit her lip. Gentled her touch.

"So what were my aunt and uncle doing here?" he asked.

"Looking for you. And demanding explanations I wasn't prepared to give. I'm afraid they went away with a very low opinion of both of us."

"No doubt they wondered what new folly I'd committed that would blacken the Sinclair name. Make them the subject of another round of gossip among those who've nothing better to do than shred their friends and destroy their enemies."

"The folly was marrying me. I don't think they've decided whether I wed you for your money or your winning personality."

That made him laugh. Amazing what a smile could do. Accentuating the golden perfection of every feature. Turning extremely handsome into wickedly gorgeous. Her whole body lit up, every nerve tingling. When had the space between them vanished to inches?

"And why did you marry me?" The evocative tone, like the whispered words of the other night, washed through her body in an almost painful wave.

She daubed at his gash long after the last blood had been wiped away. It gave her time to rein in her runaway emotions. Slow her galloping heart. "I'll get my bag. I can take care of the wound. Like last time."

He pulled the towel from her trembling fingers. "I've embarrassed you."

She lifted her face to him. Read the naked desire in his eyes. Clear as the heart of a flame. He didn't even bother to shield it. "Why do you have to be this way?" She hated the shake in her voice. "Why can't you stay horrible? Make keeping my distance easy?"

"Answer my question first."

She swallowed, grabbed firm hold of herself. If she took Cam to her bed, it wouldn't be when her rioting senses teased her with the what-ifs of old dreams. She threw up walls, using any defense—any weapon to hold him at bay. "I didn't. I screwed you. Charlotte married you."

It worked just as she thought it would. A chasm opened between them, immediate and unbridgeable. And Morgan regretted it as soon as the tired accusation left her lips.

Morgan opened her eyes, unsure of what woke her, but unable to drift back to sleep.

She lay quiet, listening to the deep growl of the city. Not the dull roar of the surf. That sound soothed her. Helped her sleep. This reminded her more of a snarling animal. A threat waiting for her just beyond the edges of her awareness. Beneath the city's noise, the buzz and hum of *Other* held to its dissonant chord. Muted, but constant as if carried on a current of air.

"No!"

The shout came from Cam's room. Sharp. Loud. Somewhere between a cry and a curse.

Morgan was up and moving before the sound died away. A robe across her shoulders. Every sense alive. She reached out, searching for echoes of Doran's magic. Nothing. Any intruder was of the mortal variety. The danger lessened, but not absent.

Shadows wrapped the corridor in darkness, a filmy light coming from a high round window at the end of the hall.

The shout came again. But with the angry call came understanding. The attack on Cam came from within where no amount of magic or swordplay could help.

She entered his room, the shuttered windows making the gloom here thick as the heavy carpet on the floor. Cam wrestled with his sheets, the carved muscles of his chest hard with tension as he fought his private ghosts, a grimace of anguish marring his face.

The pale slash of his latest injury was already fading into

the grim web of older scars. Ancient hurts. She'd done more healing since joining Cam than she'd done her whole life. As prone to getting into scrapes as he seemed to be, it was a wonder he'd survived without her for so long.

He groaned, thrashing against the restraints of the knotted sheets.

Unable to watch the battle continue, she ran to him, her only thought to pull him out of his nightmare. "Cam. Wake up."

Barely had her fingers touched him when he caught her wrist. Dragged her down onto the bed. Flipping her over. Straddling her hips. His forearm across her throat, his expression cruel and unfeeling.

"Drop it," he snarled, hate and agony equal in his broken voice. The promise of deadly violence ready to erupt. "Drop it, Charlotte, or I'll kill you."

He meant it. She felt the first squirm of panic as her lungs burned from lack of air. Throwing herself forward, she broke Cam's grip. Shocking him awake with a blow to the midsection.

Awareness flashed into his eyes, and then horror. He flung himself off her, his breath coming in sucking gasps as if he'd been running. "Damn it, Morgan. Damn it. I'm sorry."

"No permanent harm done." Morgan sat up, rubbing her neck. "I don't think."

Dragging the sheet across his lap, he sat on the edge of the bed, his head hanging, one hand clutching the cross at his throat as if for comfort. "You shouldn't be here. Not unless . . ." He paused. Took a long, unsteady breath. "Don't do this to me, Morgan. I can't take it. Not tonight."

She ignored his plea, too close to finding the truth about Cam's marriage. This house. "What did you want Charlotte to drop? What happened between you two? Really?"

She didn't think he'd answer. He sat, stiff and silent, for what seemed like hours while she watched him. Studied him, really. The curve of his ribs. The sculpted line of each perfect muscle. The arrogant line of his jaw. What he lacked in bulk and breadth, he made up for in lean, corded strength. Gods. He was beautiful. A quicksilver slash of form and grace.

"Cam," she said slowly, "dreams lose their power if they're spoken aloud. As do memories."

He ran a shaky hand down his face. Remained head-down, not meeting her gaze. "She hated me." His voice flat. Emotionless. "Not at first. But soon enough. She didn't understand. And I couldn't make her enjoy it. After a while, she shut me out, and I simply stopped trying."

Morgan closed her eyes. Wished she could close her ears. Now that she'd begun it, she couldn't tell him to stop. Secrets of the marriage bed were best left there. She didn't even want to imagine Cam with Charlotte. An emotion far too much like jealousy knotted her insides.

Cam kept on. "Countless marriages have weathered worse. But I was hurt. Angry. I fled to war." His words drawn out. Long pauses between. "I don't think she expected me to return. Perhaps in small part, hoped I wouldn't. But when I did, and she saw how I'd changed, she grew truly terrified. Got a notion I planned on putting her aside. Or worse. I don't know, mayhap she'd grown a little mad. Mayhap she'd heard rumors of the brigade and felt threatened by me, though God knows by that time, I wanted nothing to do with her." He inhaled a deep, shuddering breath. "I'll never truly know. But in the end, she decided to attack was her best defense."

The pieces fell into place. Hideous, twisted pieces. "The scar on your back . . . your leg . . . you said you got them in the war. . . . Your own wife did that to you?"

He turned to face her, his eyes diamond-hard yet containing a vulnerability that set her pulse racing. "She was never a wife to me. It was a sham of a marriage from start to finish." He dropped his head. "Do we have to talk about it? About her?"

"No, I didn't . . ."

"I'll ask you once more, Morgan. Leave, or I won't be able to let you go."

An unwelcome excitement surged through her. "You don't mean it. Not really. It's only because I'm here and you've been dreaming and . . ."

Her voice faltered and fell away. If she wanted, she could have him. Now. Tonight. Her body thrummed with anticipation. She knew what would happen if she stayed. And all of a sudden, she didn't care. She ached with unfulfilled need.

Torn between what she should do and what she wanted to do, she waited a moment too long. His hand came up, pushed the loose braid of hair off her shoulders. Caressed the long column of her throat. She shivered under his touch, her breath caught in her lungs. Her body flushed at the swift flash of desire in his gaze.

"I understand if you don't trust me." His thumb brushed away a tear she never felt fall. "I don't trust myself right now."

The strength of his touch. The savage vitality chained beneath an elegant facade. Held in check by only the thinnest of restraints. She struggled against the heady combination. Told herself to turn and flee. Escape before it was too late. But the blood roaring in her ears, the prickly tingle of her skin where he touched her drowned everything else out.

"We shouldn't," was all she could manage, and that came as a breathy whisper.

"You're right," he murmured. His hands were in her hair. His lips upon her throat.

Each second set her more firmly on the wrong path. Straight toward a cliff edge. Gods help her, but this was what she'd wanted for weeks. Now that she had it, she couldn't bear to let it go.

He pulled at the ribbons of her dressing gown, but she covered his hand with her own. "Wait . . . Susan . . ."

Laughter gleamed in his eyes. "We're married. Remember?"

Words failed her as did every good intention. Here it was, she and Cam. The solid feel of his chest. His heart beating strong and steady beneath her hand. She skimmed the sculpted strength of his body. Traced the hard-packed ridges of his abdomen. The brush of golden hair at his groin. Loving the way he jumped at her touch. The power that came with every slide of her fingers across his skin.

He covered her breasts with his hands. Caressed her through the thin fabric of her shift. Hot. Delicious. A leaping of senses. She arched into him. Greedy for more. "This doesn't mean anything." Her words came rushed. "It's not a declaration. Not a promise. It's a night. Just a night."

"Anything," he repeated, brushing his lips lightly across her mouth, down her cheek, into the hollow of her neck. "Doesn't mean anything." He pushed her back onto the bed. Came over her, the leaping pulse in his throat matching her own heart beat for beat.

She tilted her face to his. Fell into the gleaming flicker of his firelit eyes. She'd take what she could while she could. Tomorrow she'd gather up the mantles of duty and responsibility. But not tonight. Tonight she would revel in her wickedness. Drown in the intoxicating, sinful pleasure.

He found the hem of her shift, gathered it to her thighs, slid it over her hips and then up over her head. She lay naked beneath him, excitement shivering through her. Settling deep in her center until she was ready for anything he offered.

His mouth found her breasts. Tongued and sucked the ripe flesh until she moaned. Flames devoured her. A spark touched off by his mouth and the rough stubble of his jaw until it grew to a desperate blaze.

He dropped lower, his teeth skimming her stomach, her thighs. Grazing her sensitive flesh. Setting her stomach tumbling. He pushed her legs wide, dipping to tease the soft folds there, lapping the hot, wet center of her. She moaned, arching into him. Wanting him to end the sweet torture.

He chuckled, lifting his head. Filling her with his fingers. Pushing deep into her before withdrawing. Filling her again and again until she bucked against the spasms that spiraled through her. But he refused to give in, toying with her, holding her captive beneath him as he brought her ever closer to the edge. Sliding out of her, he allowed her space to gather her thoughts. Rolled her up and on top. Let her straddle him, the erect bulge of his cock nestled between her legs.

It was her turn to taste his masculine, sweat and sex-scented skin. To fall into his fathomless, azure blue eyes. She melted into him. Lowering herself onto his shaft. Watching his eyes blacken with need, the shudder ripple through his body as she closed around him. Already she felt the first tremors of climax twisting their way through her. Originating at the junction of their bodies. Racing through her at lightning speed.

She moved, let the slow steady friction build. Let her desire and his hunger grow and tighten like silken cords around both of them. The tempo of each thrust increased. The rhythm of their bodies growing like a rising tide until, crying out, the pleasure-pain ecstasy of joining crashed over her. Pulled her under with the same whirlpool force of a scrying.

Sex with Cam—potent as any magic.

As each successive wave dashed her under, he flipped her onto her back. Thrust into her again and again. Brutal. Angry. Staking a claim. The riptide of climax hit her fresh, and she bucked and cried out. He met her shout for shout, his whole body alive and quivering like a plucked chord.

Collapsing on top of her, his body and her body a tangle of limbs and heat and racing, pounding blood, she looked for regret. For guilt. For shame. And found only joy and a sweet satisfaction she'd not experienced since Edinburgh. All the better because this time she was Morgan. He was Cam.

No lies in bed between them.
They were alone together.
And complete.

Cam woke to darkness, but instead of a cold, empty room and a lonely bed, Morgan lay sprawled beside him, one hand thrown across his chest, her breath tickling his neck.

He pulled her close, resting his chin on top of her head. Savored the solid weight of her against him. No softness here. She had the lean muscles of a warrior. The curves of a courtesan.

Tracing her breasts, he felt himself go hard. He couldn't get enough of her. Like with an addict, giving in only made the yearning that much greater.

She chuckled, her hand capturing him beneath the covers. Making every sense come to painful life. "Already?"

"*Mmmm,*" he grunted. "I'm like a starving man. Not sure when or if I'll feast again."

Her hand slid the length of him. The cool deftness of her fingers a little too sure. A little too tempting. She rested her head on one elbow. Looked down into his face.

In the purple, predawn shadows, her eyes glowed smoky bronze. Almost feral in the way they pinned him in place. Picked out every hidden thought.

With movements as fluid as a cat's, she rolled herself on top of him, took him deep inside her.

He gasped, letting her control what came next.

She straddled him. Relaxed. Smiling. Infuriatingly unmoving. Closing her eyes, she withdrew until he wanted to scream in frustration, then slid home again, letting him fill every inch of her. Her neck muscles taut, her face delicious in its rapture.

He lay still while she rode him, caressing the long beauty of her torso, adjusting to this new and passionate Morgan.

Then just like that, her inner muscles spasmed around him as she clutched his shoulders, dug her nails into his skin.

He came, exploding inside her, the mind-blowing crash of sensations like being struck by lightning.

He reached up, pushing the heavy braid back over her shoulder. How had he found someone so utterly perfect? And how had he managed to bungle it so incredibly? He wouldn't look too hard. With the sun, his dream lover would vanish. He knew it. And he'd live with it. He had to.

Chapter 17

Using the honed skills of the hunter, Morgan slid into the house through the kitchen, snagging a biscuit from a tray on the worktable, Susan none the wiser as she banged her way through breakfast preparations. It was easier than facing the pointed looks and unspoken questions that marked every interaction with the housekeeper.

After last night, she probably didn't need to ask. Every answer was clear on Morgan's guilty face.

Crossing into the front rooms, she shook out her hair, drops curling cold and shivery down her neck. Wished for the hundredth time she'd not lost her treasured boat cloak in the fire.

Even though Morgan had awoken before dawn, Cam had been up before her, his side of the bed empty. Hoping to escape unnoticed, she'd crept from his room, down the stairs, and out into the cool, enveloping fog and rain.

Despite the gray, drizzly weather, she'd walked with no attention to direction or distance. Using the time to sort her scattered thoughts. To digest Cam's revelations. To wrestle her time with him into the proper box.

A life with the *Amhas-draoi*? A life with Cam?

No competition.

She'd come too far. Worked too hard. She wouldn't abandon her dream of a lifetime for one night's passion. All right, a lot of nights of passion, but it still wasn't enough to sway her.

Only when her stomach had begun growling and her sore muscles had grown wobbly did she turn her steps back toward the fashionable neighborhood of Cam's town house.

The warmth of a fire drew her into the study, though she knew who'd be waiting. Avoiding Susan was one thing. Avoiding Cam was impossible. She might not like it, but she had to face him sooner or later. Get past the awkward morning-after conversation. The second such in as many weeks. How pathetic was that? All it took was Cam crooking a finger and she fell into sex with him—again.

He raised his eyes from a piece of paper. The frown marring his features relaxing into a slow, lazy smile that spelled instant trouble.

She called on every ounce of willpower to keep the mental box where Cam and sex lived locked.

"I've had Susan make you a pot of coffee. It's on the sideboard," he said, motioning toward a table by the window.

"The surest way to my heart," she answered glibly. But she moved to pour herself a cup. Let the jolt of heat and flavor break the spell of rain-washed streets, cozy rooms, and gorgeous man.

He placed the paper on the desk. "Did your walk help?"

And she knew he understood. Everything.

"About last night, Cam . . . it was . . . I'm not sorry it happened, but . . . we can't . . . I can't . . ." She was making a complete mess of this. Awkward fast approaching humiliating.

He saved her. "If you think I'm looking for marriage or some kind of life commitment, then you weren't listening."

Heat flushed her cheeks, a twinge of pain at his words mixed with relief that he'd made it so easy. "I'm sorry, I know I've confused things, but—" she began, needing to explain herself. Needing to ease the hurt crowding the corners of his brilliant blue gaze.

He interrupted. Held up a hand. "Morgan, we're good in bed. No more, no less. That's enough for me if it's enough for you."

She looked around her at the culture and taste. The atmosphere of class that defined the house, the neighborhood. Hell, even Cam's family, despite the bluster, had oozed blue-blood refinement. She didn't have a refined bone in her body. Just ask anyone she'd grown up with. Any of the elegant mothers and their fashionable daughters who'd spurned her clumsy attempts at being one of them. Any of the young men who'd been scared away by her bold manner and frank speech. No, with the *Amhas-draoi* she'd found acceptance. With Cam she'd found pleasure.

She didn't need love.

She met his gaze. Let him see the truth of her words. "It's enough for me."

Cam dropped his uncle's letter on the fire. Watched the guilt-inducing words blacken and wither and turn to ash. Nothing he hadn't heard before. He only wondered why Sir Joshua kept up the barrage of thinly veiled disappointment and disapproval. At this point, bitter disdain would be welcome. It would give him the freedom to feel something more than the slow, soul-gnawing remorse that drained him of energy.

Why didn't Uncle Josh just write him off and move on?

Hadn't it been spelled out for him over and over—Cam was not the respectable up-and-coming officer his uncle had dreamed of? Charlotte's vindictive rumors coupled with the revelations of his less-than-savory war work had soured any hopes of a return to society's bosom. Fine with him. He'd never wanted to be there in the first place. It had been Charlotte's desire to remain in the circle of friends and family that had tied him to London and this house. He'd yearned for the pine forests and rocky crags of Scotland. The empty open sky, the silence, the freedom.

Near-death experiences had a way of focusing one's priorities. Waking on a Tavistock dung heap feeling as if his body had been crushed organ by organ, he'd felt a plan taking shape.

He'd find this damned sword. Kill the whoreson Doran.

Then disappear.

Back to Scotland. To Caithness. To Strathconon and the holding he'd inherited from his grandfather. A dot on the map. A place where he could breathe. Finally be Cam Sinclair. Not a dutiful colonel. Not a respectful nephew. Definitely not a cold-blooded assassin. Just a man.

He'd once dreamed of taking Morgan to the cottage. Showing her the place where he'd been happiest and most comfortable.

That part of the dream wouldn't happen now. But the rest of it?

He couldn't wait.

"Ah, the new bridegroom. I hear congratulations are in order."

Cam didn't exactly jump—Morgan had warned him that MacKay promised to return—but his heart did leap in his chest. He'd been too bound up with his own thoughts. Hadn't heard Brodie's approach until the deep voice rumbled behind him.

"Go to hell. You know damn well I'm not married." Cam's words came sharper than intended, Morgan's easy dismissal of him still rankling.

Brodie held up a hand. "Easy, old man. A little touchy, aren't ye?" He dropped into a chair, stretching his long legs out to the fire. "What's the story? Miss Bligh wasn't very forthcoming after the initial bombshell. She's your redhead, isn't she?"

Cam wished once more for the serenity of that distant farm. How had he ever thought he'd be able to hide here? Why not just put an advertisement in the paper?

Doran, we're here. Come and get us.

"You want the truth?"

"Talk about a teaser. Of course. Tell me everything."

Cam gave a grim smile. He'd hit Brodie with the truth. See what he did with it. How quick he ran. "Very well. Morgan's a sorceress. What's known as an *Other*. A real blood-and-bone witch. We're searching for a sword stolen from the *Fey* that can impart immortality to any poor bastard skewered with it. We've tracked the thief to London. To the area around the London Docks. I'm getting ready to head down there now. Scout around and see what I can discover."

Brodie glanced over at the desk and the pistol there. The open cartridge box. The powder bag. Then back to the knife at Cam's waist. His face dropped into stern lines. The responsibility-challenged scoundrel becoming the hard-bitten soldier. "When do we leave?"

He should have known. With Brodie it had always been that easy. The tension tightening his skull, twisting down his neck to clamp viselike on his shoulders relaxed. "You haven't told me I'm crazy."

"Ye haven't told me anything I can't get my head around yet."

"You believe me?"

"Ye weren't the only one raised on your gran-da's stories. And I never said anything, but once . . ." He waved it away. "Well, never mind, it's not important, but aye, I believe ye. It certainly makes more sense than ye marrying again. That was the tale that had me thinking you'd lost your mind."

Cam gave a gallows laugh. "No worries of a marriage with Morgan. She only wants me for my body."

Brodie's brows shot up. "Some men have all the luck."

Luck? Was that what it was? Knowing that no matter how he touched Morgan's body, he'd never reach her soul?

It felt more like one enormous cosmic fist to the jaw.

The man struggled against his bonds. They all did in the end. Definitely an example of being careful what you asked for.

Lester had agreed to join Doran months ago, lured by the prospect of invincibility. Power. A chance to live forever. Now he fought, screaming and crying, snot running down his nose, blubbering tearful pleas for mercy.

This was a mercy.

Doran had seen the wrenching violence of war. Had known the blood-searing agony and pain of battle. Both as soldier and as one left behind to bury his dead. He wasn't sure which was worse. But either way, Sergeant Lester would be spared that grief. He'd become a child of the sword. A creature of unnatural speed, unnatural strength. And unkillable.

A perfect soldier. A perfect weapon.

The man sank back upon himself, his face gone gray, mouthing inane prayers to some long-ignored childhood god.

Doran snorted his contempt. "You'll secure no help from that quarter, friend. Any deity listening is more likely to kill us both and leave the sorting to the devils."

Ignoring the animal moans from Lester, he turned his mind inward, forming a picture in his mind of the haze of magic that hung like fog over the city. Though instead of the putrid green funk that burned the lungs and stung the eyes, this fog remained pearly silver, sparkled like diamonds shot through with gold and green, crimson and deepest amethyst. So many *Other* living within London's limits. So much concentrated power. None would notice should he draw on such a deep well.

Gathering the power to him as if he inhaled a deep breath before plunging beneath cold waters, the mage energy settled over him. Sank beneath his skin, his muscles, his tissues. It drifted into his bloodstream, burning its way through his body. He felt it as a white-hot wire pulled inch by inch through each individual vein. He cried out, his eyes widening at the pain, the excruciating slow stab of heat.

Unsheathing the goddess blade, he gripped the worn pommel. Focused on the ridges where others had pressed their own fingers before him. Used it to keep his grip on sanity. This had to be the way. Surely this time *Neuvarvaan* would reveal its darkest secret. The sword recognized its name. Came alive in his hand, a living article of *Morkoth* hatred and corruption.

Voices called to him. Instructed him in the ways of Undying, even as others contradicted. Jeered. Taunted. Then offered their own secrets. Which voice to heed? Which words were real and which were meant to confuse? With no way to know, Doran chose the loudest voice. And plunged the blade hilt deep through Lester's heart.

The man let out a high, girlish scream that went on and on. Drowned away the voices. Echoed through Doran's head, the room. Hell, the whole city heard the keening as Lester sank against his bonds, his body caving in on itself, dark hair going instantly gray. Fingers shriveling into arthritic knobs, muscle wasting from his body.

Doran swung the sword again, this time severing the ropes. Lester fell to the floor, death already bluing his lips, glazing his eyes.

Morkoth laughter filled Doran's head, the black chorus of a million demons.

He'd listened to the wrong voice. And failed again.

* * *

Morgan slammed into the study, shock vivid in her pale face, her eyes flashing between Cam and Brodie.

Cam's gut kicked into his throat. "What?"

She slid to a stop. Hesitated in the presence of the captain. Cam sensed her reluctance. "It's all right. Brodie knows."

She threw the captain a wide-eyed look of surprise, but nodded. "I felt *Neuvarvaan*. I know it was the goddess blade. Doran's used it again."

Ignoring Brodie and the questions he sensed his best friend longed to ask, he took Morgan by the arms. Her eyes shone pale yellow in a face flushed with worry.

"Calm down. What did you feel? How do you know it was Doran? You said you couldn't pick out any one source of magic among so many."

She took a shaky breath. But when she spoke again, her words came clear and sharp. "I didn't think I could. But the pressure of the city's *Other* increased. Like the smash of a wave against the inside of my skull. Or the scream of a million people all at once. Every *Other* drawing on his powers at the same instant. Even I felt a tug, right here." She put a hand just under her ribs. "Doran's using us. He's harnessing our powers to focus his own. That's why he came to London. Not just to hide, but because the population of *Other* is better than any standing stone. We're a living source of mage energy."

It made sense. In a senseless sort of way. And that surprised him most of all. "Could you pick out Doran? Could you track him if you tried?"

"Not with certainty. But I can try to trace the mage energy back to its source. Like tracking the ripples in a pond back to the dropped stone."

With defiance burning in her clear gold gaze, the sexy-sultry, hot-blooded lover of his morning morphed into the cold, determined warrior-queen. No attempts to shock him. No in-the-face challenges to gauge his reaction. Her transformation was seamless and complete and just about the most erotic thing he'd ever witnessed. His groin tightened in instant arousal.

Shit. Was he losing his mind? The world stood at the brink, and all he wanted was to drag up her skirts, push her back against the wall, and drive himself into her, find for a brief moment the bliss he'd experienced last night in her arms.

With forced deliberation, he let her go before he made a fool out of himself. "Then that's what we'll do," he said.

Even as lust died away, another emotion sprang to life. The vicious creature—the part of him who'd hunted and killed and answered only to Sin—uncurled from its place in the darkest corners of his heart. Licked at Cam's soul. He pushed it down. Locked it away with ruthless finality. He'd not lose himself to the inhuman blood-thrill. Not again. Not even to stop Doran.

Morgan broke into his thoughts. Drowned out the slithery voice of savage temptation. "If we don't find Doran soon, he'll unlock the *Morkoth* magic. Create his army of Undying. And if we can't stop him, Andraste and the *Fey* will. The mortal world will become a battleground."

His voice was firm. Final. "Trust me. It won't get that far. I won't let it. All right?"

Their eyes met. The heat in her gaze locking on to the ice-cold freeze of his own. "I trust you."

Her words stunned him and terrified him and dropped his heart into his boots.

She trusted him? Was she insane? He didn't even trust himself. He was as strung out and off-balance as he'd been since the days of Toulouse. It wouldn't take much to send him tumbling.

He just prayed he wasn't setting them both up for the fall of the century.

Chapter 18

Morgan slowed, the scream of mage energy ripping through her, every nerve taut, every sense sizzling and alive.

"The source of the power is near."

She scanned the area. Rows of long, brick warehouses and offices, streets lined with dingy shop fronts, tenements, and low, dirty, seamen's cottages. Beyond the dock's high walls, the wharf stood congested with ships in various stages of loading or unloading. Lighters, barges, and colliers threading their way between the schooners and East Indiamen. Voices raised in Flemish, French, Italian, Spanish as ships' crews shouted and jostled against street costers and merchants, clerks and customs officers, the very air carrying the exotic tang of foreign ports of call.

A wild, rowdy marketplace of buying and selling.

The perfect place to disappear. And the perfect place to find the kind of men who'd sell their souls to join an army of Undying.

Doran was here. Or had been recently.

"This is where I tracked the bastard who jumped me," Cam said. "Looks like Doran's aware we're not dead." He came up behind her, his body reassuringly close. A step back would place her in the circle of his arms. She remained rigidly still until the temptation passed.

Unfortunately, even as the thought receded, a swamp of instant nausea took its place, the street and the buildings and the sky all swaying and swimming like water on glass. The pound of magic grew to a heavy beat threatening to shake her to her knees. She put out a hand to steady herself.

Cam was right there. "What's wrong?"

"I'm dizzy." She swallowed over and over. "It's the power. Raw. Overwhelming. It's too much."

"Brodie," Cam ordered, "stay here. Take care of Morgan. I'll be right back."

"No, I'm going with you," Morgan challenged, forcing herself to straighten. "You're not leaving me behind again."

Cam's gaze was glacial. And terrifying. Even Brodie took a step back. "You swore to do exactly what I said. To follow my orders."

How dare he throw that back at her now? Her fingers curled into her palms, her nails digging into the flesh as she fought her urge to tell him what he could do with his bloody idiotic bargain.

"Do you want to go back on your word?"

"No." She pushed the words out through tight lips.

"Then stay here. I'm going to take a look around. I can do that better without worrying whether you're going to collapse."

Before she could answer or offer any more resistance, he left her side. Passed into the street. And immediately vanished. As fully as if he'd called upon the invisibility of the *feth-fiada* to cloak his movements. It was impossible. And impressive.

Brodie gave a low whistle. "Damn. He's better than I thought."

Morgan kept quiet. She began to understand the toll Cam's abilities took on his soul. She thought with sadness of the reckless boy laughing into the wind. Racing the flight of wild geese. What chain of events had pulled him into the tangled tortured world of violence, death, and murder in the king's name? And had that boy been lost forever?

As she watched, a man appeared from the side of the nearest building. Ground out a cheroot as he scanned the street up and down. The crackle of familiar mage energy buried itself in her brain. She'd felt this thread of power before. Had glimpsed it for a hurried moment in the alleys of Tavistock just before the street thugs attacked.

Apparently satisfied he'd not been noticed, he entered the storefront. Banged the door shut behind him.

"Which building did Cam go into?" Morgan asked.

Brodie nodded. "That one, I think."

"That's what I feared. Doran's in there. Or one of his cronies. Either way, Cam's up to his ass in trouble."

The man's flicker of shock and confusion was quickly mastered, but Cam had seen it. "Surprised to see me, Rastus?"

The corporal raised his glass, taking a long, slow drink. Time to think and react. Wiping his mouth with his sleeve, he kicked the chair across from him out from under the table. Nodded Cam into it. "That I am, sir. You said yourself you was tryin' to stay under wraps. What brings you here?"

"You know what brings me. Buchanan's been here. And recently. Where is he now, Rastus?" Cam forced himself to remain civil, though it took every ounce of self-discipline not to lift the villain by his collar and shake the truth out of him.

"Gone. Left a few hours ago."

"Where to?"

"Don't know. He came in early, snappish and impatient. Looked as if he hadn't slept in days. A little wild, a lot dangerous, if you know what I mean." His sidelong glance assuring

Cam that he fell into that same category. "He and one of the girls went in the back. But not five minutes later, he was back. Black as a storm cloud and pulled tighter than whipcord. I followed him, for a bit. He went up toward Shadwell. And . . ." Rastus swallowed, his fingers rubbing nervously at a spot on the table. "And then I lost him."

"Why didn't you send me word?"

"I did. Sent a runner off an hour ago after Doran cut out. Probably passed you on your way."

Could they have missed the message? Could Rastus be telling the truth? Or was this a set-up? He was almost sure Rastus had hired Scar-Face to follow him yesterday. But to what purpose? He didn't like the smell this whole deal was giving off. "What's your game?"

"The sergeant's been keeping low. Moving about, ya know? He knows you're on to him. Got him rattled, it does." Rastus poured a second glass of claret for himself. One for Cam. "Drink up, Sin. To old times."

The man was tense. Not in an obvious way. But it was clear he waited for something or someone. He kept glancing toward the door, cracking his knuckles with annoying regularity until Cam actually thought of giving in to the desire to slit his throat.

A crude comment followed by overloud laughter drew Cam's eye to a table near the door. A group of men egged on one of their number who held a black-haired woman by the wrist with one hand, his other somewhere beneath her skirts. His face seemed familiar, dark eyes beneath thin brows, straw-colored hair. As Cam watched, the man leaned in close, his words quieter, but just as dirty by the look of shock on the girl's face. Where had Cam seen him before? Or had he? The man's hair, his face, his build. All were so ordinary, he'd fade into the background like wallpaper.

"Forget this devil's chase, Sin," Rastus urged, pulling

Cam's attention back to his own table. "Walk away. This is bigger than you. Bigger than the bloody army."

"You know me better than that. I don't walk away."

"This time, you better. Buchanan's on to something. He's got plans. And he's got the strength to follow them through."

"Decided to join his little gang, Corporal?"

Rastus offered him a look of shock, real or feigned impossible to distinguish. "I'm trying to save your skin. Get out. Convince your woman to get out too. It's going to happen whether you want it or not. You can't stop it."

Cam leaned forward, his gaze narrowed. "Watch me."

Morgan left the safety of her doorway, ignoring her unsteady steps, the way her vision blurred and darkened. Whatever Doran had accomplished here this morning, it had pulled so many differing strands of power together, just walking through the afterglow of mage energy took all her concentration.

As she staggered, she released a seeker spell into the air. Prayed to every god she could name that Doran wasn't near. Because if he was, how the hell was she going to stop him? And retrieve the goddess blade? Every use of *Neuvarvaan* drew more and more of the *Morkoth* magics under Doran's control. It was going to take all her power just to survive.

The spell returned, bringing with it the answer she'd hoped, though she knew it was a pitiful coward's wish.

Doran was gone.

Which meant the sword was as well. He'd not let it out of his sight, for certain. They had *Other* to contend with. But those she could handle. It was the black *Amhas-draoi* she feared. Even as she hated her own cowardice.

Threading her way through the crowded street, Morgan formulated and discarded plan after plan. Go in, magic blazing? Too flashy. If Doran wasn't here, a use of her powers would certainly alert him to their intrusion. She needed to ease Cam out of the building with no one the wiser. Now that they knew where Doran was hiding, they could come up with a way to wrest the sword away. But not now. Not like this.

She and Brodie reached the storefront. No sign hung from the broken bracket above the entrance. No way of knowing what lay beyond the grimy windows or the paint-chipped door. Brodie touched her shoulder. Jerked his head toward the side alley. "Back way in?"

She offered him a faint smile. Followed.

A narrow recessed door stood halfway down the alley. Locked.

Brodie pushed in front of her. "Allow me."

Drawing a thin-bladed dagger from his coat, he slid the blade into the lock. A few quick twists, a muffled curse, and the door cracked open. "Voila."

Her smile widened. "Hidden talents."

He dipped his shoulder in mock humility, his eyes alight with mischief. "You've barely scratched the surface."

The corridor they entered smelled of dank river water overlaid with the even more overpowering scents of roses and lilies combined with earthy exotic musk and patchouli. Enough to make her already swimming head light. Doors lined the opposite wall, behind which sounded muffled laughter, murmured conversation, and unmistakable rhythmic grunts.

She'd stumbled into a bloody brothel.

Brodie raised an amused brow. Shrugged. "Do ye think Cam is . . . ?" He gestured toward one of the doors.

"No," she snapped. "I do not." *He'd better not be*, she amended.

They followed the corridor to its end, where a curtain separated it from a larger room. A peek beyond revealed a sumptuous salon draped in velvets and silks. A fantasy boudoir. A sultan's seraglio. Every effort made to put a man in the mood for sex.

Women, dressed in the sheerest of fabrics, strolled from table to table or lounged upon couches. Their kohl-blackened eyes and hennaed skin paired with the high-waisted, low-collared gowns gave them the look of someone's idea of Eastern concubine meets French courtesan.

Not intended for the common sailor, the clientele here seemed made up of merchants and bankers, ship's captains and high-paid clerks with the occasional military braid thrown in.

"Cam's here," she whispered to Brodie. "Talking to someone." She glanced around the room. Spotted the man from outside alone in a far corner. "And there's the *Other*."

Brodie risked a look. "We need to let Cam know."

Morgan bit her lip, mind made up. "You get back outside. Keep the alley clear for our escape. I'll get Cam's attention."

"You're not exactly dressed like the rest of them."

She withdrew farther down the corridor. Stopped at a door. Listened.

Empty.

"I will be."

Cam looked up from the table to see a walking fantasy coming toward him. Red-gold hair loose in a heavy wave to the small of her back. A gown that must have been painted on, doing absolutely nothing to hide long, slender legs that seemed to go on forever. A sweet round ass. High, firm breasts. Both perfect handfuls and then some. He should know. He'd held them both only last night.

She approached, her gaze centered on him with eyes a man could drown in. Leaned in close to brush a kiss against his cheek, give him a bird's-eye view of all that could be his. For a price.

"Here, now, no one's asked for a poke." Rastus shooed her away. "We're doing business. Tell Molly we want to be left alone."

"It's all right. While I'm here, I may as well . . ." Cam let his gaze devour her. She was living, breathing desire.

And pale as a ghost.

But mayhap only he noticed the way her hands trembled, the unsteadiness of her gait ". . . I may as well enjoy my visit. Right?"

Rastus stiffened. Obviously unsure whether to let Cam leave with the whore or not. Finally, he shrugged. "Ride her all ya want. You can afford it."

"Expensive, is she?"

"Mrs. Molly Cabot's not in it for the good of mankind, I can tell ya that. She's made herself a tidy fortune runnin' this place."

"I'll be back." Cam stood, pulling the prostitute in close. Letting her feel the hard ache of his erection, the anger in his grip.

Her eyes widened as she motioned toward a curtained doorway.

"I'm not through with you," Cam tossed back at the corporal as he eased away from the table. Across the floor under the scrutinizing, suspicious eyes of the other women. The resentful eyes of their customers.

How dare she show so much of herself to this crowd of lechers? Let them ogle her as if she were no better than the women who worked here?

Possessiveness and—yes, damn it—simple jealousy lanced through him. Only he got to look at her like that. She belonged to him. His grip tightened.

She led him through the curtain. Dropped it in place behind them, leaning hard against the wall. Breathing heavily. "So far, so good."

Cam rounded on her, fury blazing. "What the hell are you

doing here, Morgan? And dressed like . . . like a bad version of the sultan's favorite."

She sniffed. "I thought my disguise worked out rather well."

"I just bet you did. You're about as inconspicuous as a swan among a roost of biddy hens. And every person in there knew it."

She looked surprised. "Really? That good?"

He shook his head, trying to gain some perspective. Some distance. Hard to do when she stood inches away from him in a gown that left enough to the imagination to make a man want to uncover the rest. Unwrap her like a gift. "You didn't dress like that for your health. What's going on?"

"One of Doran's goons. I recognized him outside. He's here."

"A redhead?" A voice sounded loud from the far side of the curtain. "I don't have any redheads here. The customers don't like them."

Morgan grabbed his hand. "This way." She pulled him down the corridor.

A man stepped from the shadows at the far end. Saw them coming.

"It's him." She stumbled back. Looked wildly around, her hand in his clutching him in a death grip. Unable to go forward or back, she stiffened. Stepped up to the closest door. Inhaled sharply before turning the knob and dragging him inside.

Thank the gods, it was empty. What she'd have done if the room had been occupied, she'd no idea. In fact, she was pretty much out of ideas. Caught between the brothel's abbess and the advancing *Other*, they'd run out of options.

She couldn't think. Her head felt stuffed with wool, her limbs dragging. *Neuvarvaan*'s effect wore off, but not near quick enough.

She was so far in over her head, it was laughable. Talk about the foul-up of all foul-ups. What had Scathach been thinking, entrusting Morgan with this task? It was obvious she couldn't do it. She'd bungled every step of this whole sad excuse of a mission.

"Was seducing me part of your plan?" Cam asked, dipping his head toward the silk-hung bed dominating the tiny cubby of a room, the enormous mirror on the far wall. How could he joke at a time like this?

"I'm making this up as I go," she shot back.

"Really? I'd never have figured that out." Now he definitely looked amused, damn him.

"So what's your big idea?" she snapped. Hating his smug superiority. Hating her helplessness. Hating the way he eyed her like a starving man eyes a meal. Hating the way she enjoyed it.

"First things first," he growled.

Without warning, he flung her down on the bed. Fell on top of her, fisting his hands in her hair, forcing her head back as he covered her mouth in a violent kiss of domination, his hand molding itself to her breast, his knee forcing her thighs apart as if he planned on dragging her skirts up around her waist and pushing himself inside her right here and now.

And if he did, she wasn't sure she'd be able to stop him. Her body seemed to have divorced itself from her brain. It welcomed his touch. Ached for it. A traitorous whimper of pleasure escaped her. They'd be caught. Revealed. But instead of embarrassment, that threat of discovery heightened her already dizzy senses. Somehow her hands ended up in his hair, her tongue in his mouth, her hand sliding downward to cup the hard bulge in his breeches. Oh yes. He might not actually mount her, but he certainly wanted to. A heady rush of power infused her panic.

The door slammed back on its hinges at the same instant she risked all with the most basic of *fith-faths* hidden under the thinnest of cloaking spells. It took every ounce of concentration to draw even that little bit of power. She just prayed it held.

Cam raised his head, his eyes black with need. "What the great goddamn?" he snarled, the venom in his voice completely convincing.

A buxom woman, dressed not in the exotic outfits of her girls, but in a prim gray linen gown and mobcap, curtsied, her cheeks flaming. "Excuse me, sir. My mistake. Looking for a redheaded imposter. Someone said she came in here."

"Does she look like a redhead to you?" Cam demanded, grabbing up a fistful of Morgan's hair, now black as ebony.

"No, sir. My mistake. Excuse me, sir. So sorry." She curtseyed her way out, knocking into the man standing behind her, his pale eyes raking them both with a hostile gaze. "Go on," the woman snipped, "you can see it's not her."

The man bowed and withdrew, but Morgan knew without a doubt, he'd be waiting. He may not have caught them redhanded—or redhaired—but he wasn't ready to dismiss them completely.

They were trapped.

Cam stared at the closed door as if deep in thought. Then as if a conclusion had been reached, he shrugged. Got to his feet, leaving her bereft. Stupid with abandonment. What was wrong with her? She should be working out a way to get them out of here. Planning their next move. Instead, all she wanted to do was pull him back into the huge bed. Watch him in that huge mirror as he pleasured her.

"Where's Brodie?" Cam's barked question jolted her out of her sexual stupor. Made her feel foolish. Until she caught the pained look in his eyes, the way he avoided touching her as if afraid he couldn't hold himself back a second time.

Morgan dissolved her spells. Hoped her magic had passed unnoticed. "In the alley behind the building. He's supposed to be guarding our escape."

"Well, we can't get that far without dealing with the man out there and any help he may have."

Morgan stood, adjusting her gown, trying to control her racing heart. She pulled her clothes out from under the bed where she'd stashed them earlier. "Let me change and I can—"

"No," Cam answered, his tone final. "You can barely stand. I'll get us out of here."

"How?"

His features seemed carved in stone, his eyes flat and staring. As if his spirit had fled. As if some dark demon inhabited his body. "Leave that to me. Get changed. I'll knock twice. Be ready to go."

She nodded, unable to argue with this new, implacable Cam.

And just like that, he was gone.

Piece by piece, she removed the whisper-thin silks. Dragged on the workaday gown, the comfortable jacket. Bundled her hair back into a quick knot at her neck. She regarded herself in the mirror. Looked down at the discarded clothing. And the truth hit her. She'd failed at being the elegant lady. And now she was failing at being an *Amhas-draoi*.

Neither fish nor fowl.

Tossing a curse to the empty room, she dropped onto the bed. Warrior or woman. *Duinedon* or *Other*. Where did she fit in? Who was she? Really?

A knock—once, twice—broke her from her thoughts. Cam.

She ran to the door, her childish worries forgotten. If they didn't get out of here, it didn't much matter, did it?

Cam stood on the threshold. Or a horrifying imitation of Cam did. He was frightening, his gaze flint-hard. His hands curled to fists at his side. His body poised to erupt if she so much as touched him. "It's done. Let's go."

She risked it, putting a hand out.

He flinched as if she'd struck him, his hand coming up, cuffs stained with blood.

"You're hurt."

"It's not my blood, Morgan." His words came slow. Heavy. As if just standing exhausted him.

Grabbing her hand, he dragged her from the room. Down the corridor. And out into the milky sunlight of the alley where Brodie waited.

"Take her home, Brodie."

Morgan grabbed his coat. "Don't give in to it, Cam."

He flung himself away from her. "Go, Morgan. That's a direct order." He stepped back. Looked to Brodie. "Take her home. And keep her there."

The captain offered a solemn nod. "You'll meet us there later?"

Cam gave a deep shuddering breath. Turned and walked away, shoulders hunched. "Much later."

Chapter 19

Morgan stood at the western corner of the house. Touched the foundation, closing her eyes. She'd always found it easier to focus this way, though it fell short of Scathach's high standards. The mage energy should flow without the need for tricks or crutches, her teacher chided her often enough. Still, if her only failing was shutting her eyes . . .

"Dor. Ebrenn. Dowr." The power swam to the surface, drawn by her need and the spell's chant. *"Tanyow. Menhir. Junya."*

A flicker of light burst, then dissolved as the last barrier went up. This incantation would complete the circle, and though her wards' crude protections would avail them little against a determined onslaught by Doran, it would slow him down. Give them time.

Time for what, she hadn't figured out yet.

She straightened, dusting her hands as if she'd built the wall with hammer and chisel instead of *Fey* magic.

"Bluidy brilliant." Taking Cam's instructions literally, Brodie had refused to let her out alone. He stood behind her, hands across his chest, a look of mingled disbelief and amazement upon his face.

Morgan gave him a sidelong glance. "You seem to be

taking it in stride. Most people would be crossing themselves at this point or readying their ducking stools."

Brodie led her back inside. "I'm not most people." Without being asked, he poured her a drink. Handed it to her with a tired smile. "He'll get over it and be home. He always has before."

Morgan let the smoky heat of the whiskey fill the worried, empty, frightened place. Dropping into a chair, she pulled her legs beneath her. "Do you think he gets over it? Or does he just bury it along with the rest of the pain he's carrying? His family's disapproval. The war." She paused. "Charlotte."

Brodie stabbed at the fire, the poker sending a shower of sparks snapping up the chimney. "Ye ken all that, do ye?"

"It's a little hard to miss. If the emotional scars aren't obvious, the physical ones club you over the head. She tried to kill him." Her teeth chattered despite the soothing fire in her belly. She saw again the horrible twisting scar down Cam's back, the rough healing on his thigh.

"By the time Cam came home, Charlotte had grown to believe her own wild stories." Brodie's gaze went far-seeing as he spoke. "He was a villain. A libertine and a rake. And when rumors of the Serpent Brigade began to circulate, she believed them too."

"With good cause. Those stories turned out to be true."

Brodie dropped the poker with a clang. Spun on her. "Charlotte attacked him in his bed while he slept. Did he tell ye that? Stabbed him in the back. And when he tried to defend himself, she stabbed him again. Amos found him, drenched in his own blood, more dead than alive. Did Cam lock her away? Reveal her as an attempted murderess? No. He let people believe what they would. If ye think Cam's a natural-born killer, you're a bluidy great fool, Morgan Bligh."

Her stomach turned, a shudder of nausea rolling through her. "I know what's before my eyes. He may not enjoy killing. It may tear him apart inside when he's called upon to do it, but it's there. It's as much a part of him as the boy on the loch or the amazing lover." She flushed at Brodie's startled look of surprise, but continued. "Cam's all those things."

Brodie's shoulders slouched. He poured himself another whiskey. Tossed it back. "Ye speak like ye love him."

She pulled herself into a tighter bundle, almost as if she protected herself from the tease of those words. "I'm not what Cam needs. He's not what I need. It wouldn't work. And love isn't everything."

Brodie's clear gray gaze sought hers. As sharp as a spear point. "Call me a hopeless romantic, but sometimes 'tis the only thing."

Cam fell in beside Rastus, the corporal's steps barely faltering at finding himself accompanied.

"I don't think we finished our conversation, Corporal."

Rastus's eyes slid over him, his face revealing nothing. "Thought you'd found Nirvana with Molly Cabot's newest slag."

"What's going on, Rastus? And no more song and story. You know more than you're saying."

Rastus dug his hands deep into his coat pockets. Shrugged. "I've told ya he's been hard to keep track of. I've done my best, but he's better. There's something more than man about him. Devilry. Witchcraft. He reeks of 'em both, Sin."

Cam felt the press of fear Rastus worked under. The old reprobate was scared. "You've discovered something. What is it?"

Rastus stopped dead in the middle of the street, his eyes raking Cam up and down as if seeing him for the first time, his jaw working, his gaze hesitant. Finally, giving his neck a decisive, bone-grinding crack, he motioned with a jerk of his head. "Come on, then. You won't believe me otherwise."

They walked in silence, dusk and fog casting the streets in

deepening gloom. But even that wasn't enough to dampen the surge of pedestrians pushing past. Or the constant stream of chaises, hackney cabs, drays, and coaches all making slow progress through the streets.

At a narrow tenement, its soot-covered facade and broken roof giving it a derelict air, Rastus stopped, grating a key into the lock at the door. Up and up, they climbed, their steps echoing off the bare plastered walls. Another door and another key and they entered a low garret. The only furnishings, a rough pallet on the floor, humped with blankets. A chair. A ewer and basin on a low table. And the musky sweet scent of recent death souring the air.

Cam's hand fumbled for his knife, but in no other way did he reveal his caution.

Rastus ushered him in. "I'd have called the Watch, but what could I say? They'd not believe me and with good reason. I'm not sure I believe it myself." He pointed toward the bundle of rough blankets. "He's here."

Not blankets, but the curled figure of an old man. Wisps of gray hair barely covered a freckled scalp, a face lined with at least eighty years of worries. Or so it would seem to someone who hadn't seen a similar old man before. Though one who'd escaped this poor bastard's fate.

"Who is he?"

"Name's Samuel Lester. Sergeant Samuel Lester. Or it was." Rastus's fear was palpable. His voice shook with it. "You'll not believe me, but that man's thirty-two. Or was till Doran got him."

"A sword through the heart?"

Rastus's whole body went still. "How'd you know that?"

"Why do you think I'm looking for Buchanan? I know what he's doing. Lester's not the first of his victims. And unless I find him fast, he won't be the last."

Rastus crossed himself. "This ain't for the likes of normal

people, Sin. This is devil's work. I've heard tales of these creatures. Even seen one once when I was naught but a lad. They dragged her by the cart tail. Stoned her and burned her cottage for practicin' such witchcraft."

To you we're freaks. Monsters. The devil's spawn. If Doran's found to be one of us, the hunt will begin again.

Rastus's fears brought Morgan's words to mind. Would things really come to such a pass? Neighbor turning upon neighbor? Brother on brother? He had only to glance at the misshapen hulk of the ravaged sergeant to know the answer. Who would feel safe knowing humans existed with that kind of power at their command? Even if they chose not to use it, they still posed a threat. Or that would be the argument.

"Tell me everything you know, Rastus. Leave nothing out."

Cam pulled off his knife belt. Let it fall to the floor. Wished he could drop the memories that went with it as easily. He'd walked for hours and for miles. Chewing over Rastus's revelations. And more importantly, what he hadn't revealed. Plotting and abandoning half-formed plans. All until the churning, blast of rage eased and wore away. Until once again, he was Cam. Exhausted. Hollowed. Alone within his own body.

No longer sharing it with the assassin that enjoyed the hunt, thrilled to the kill.

No longer Sin.

He shrugged off his shirt, the chill of the room barely touching him. His body numb, his blood cold and sluggish, his mind slow.

Tomorrow he'd begin again. Relate everything to Morgan. Begin to piece some kind of idea together. Tomorrow he'd be better. Tomorrow he could face her without worrying that she'd look into his eyes and see every life-ending action he'd taken today.

DANGEROUS AS SIN 187

"Are you coming to bed or not? You'll catch your death of cold standing there like that."

So much for tomorrow.

He closed his eyes, wishing for the power to turn and leave. He couldn't see her tonight. He didn't trust himself. He still hung too close to the edge. But he made no move to walk away. Like a coward, he stayed, knowing what would happen. And knowing he wanted it more than anything in the world right now.

He tried to make himself sound as close to normal as he could. "I didn't know you were there."

"You weren't supposed to." Amusement colored her words. "I have skill enough to be silent, if nothing else." For a moment, amusement faded to bitterness. He wondered at it, but didn't have the energy to ask.

He took one unsteady step toward the bed. Then another. And before he could talk himself out of it, he dropped to his knees beside her. Scooped her into his arms, crushing his mouth onto hers. Shock at the touch of her naked flesh burned away in an instant, leaving only the overriding need to feel the steady beat of her heart against his own. The heat of her body easing the chill that had buried itself so deeply into his bones, he never thought to be warm again.

His hands shook as he caressed the smooth slope of her shoulders. Cupped her breasts, rubbing his thumbs over the pearls of her nipples. Small moans broke from her as his lips teased her jawline, grazed her neck. To hell with the shimmering silks and flamboyant seduction of this afternoon, he preferred her naked, the scent of sex and desire rising off her more provocative than any perfume.

Surprise momentarily infused his lust as he noted the flame of her hair running over his hands, brushing his chest. She never left it loose. Braids. Combs. Pins. But today he'd caught a glimpse. And tonight, she'd left it free to flow like fire.

He dragged himself up long enough to ask, "Why?"

She caressed the long ridge of his scar, tracing the line of Charlotte's maiming as if she traced the route on a map. "Because tonight, you need me." He felt her shrug. "And because tonight, I need you just as badly."

He laid her back on the bed. Stripped out of his breeks before rejoining her.

Her eyes widened, her gaze running over his naked body with a sensual intensity that set off a low quiver deep in his being. Her fingers came up to caress the taut muscles of his stomach. Skim the length of his erection. But he caught her hand, rubbing his thumb across her sword-calloused palm before linking his fingers with hers. Easing himself over her, their bodies matched height for height, crushed skin on skin.

"You're frozen through," she said, squirming beneath him.

"Better now," he murmured.

She tasted like wine, her lips soft and velvety. He sampled, then devoured, his tongue sliding between her teeth, her whimper caught, then released into his mouth. He kissed her cheeks, the tip of her nose, nuzzled the curve of her throat.

"You can't do this alone, Cam." Her words gently spoken, but still carrying that hint of Morgan steel.

He met her gaze, flecks of gold burning through the dark whirlpool of desire. The corner of his mouth twitched. "It's possible, but not near as much fun."

That made her smile. She fondled a strand of his hair, pushing it back off his face, her hands warm against his frozen skin. "We're in this together. You need to ask for help."

Where the hell had that come from? And why was Morgan bringing this up now of all the god-awful times? He wanted to forget. Not analyze. And, for God's sake, not now. "I'm fine."

Letting his exasperation fall away, he skimmed his hand down her side as his lips trailed a path down her neck. Across her shoulders. Over her breasts. Prayed she'd give up. Give in. Let the matter drop.

"You're not fine. You're not sleeping. Barely eating." She shuddered at his touch, and her words came breathy and fast, but they came just the same. Accusing. A steady barrage of blame. "You're surviving on coffee and nerves. You can't last."

He rolled off her, lust sucked out of him. Her words as effective as a cold bath. Was this her idea of sweet torture? Get him close to exploding and then knock him over the head with questions and finger-pointing? Well, if she wanted to play that game . . . "You really want to talk about this now?"

She stiffened under the checked anger in his voice, her gaze cautious "I . . ."

"Fine. We can talk about this. How about you?"

That got her. She sparked, answering his annoyance with her own. "What about me?"

"You hide behind that hard-nosed, approach-if-you-dare attitude. That's not you, and you know it. It's a disguise you've learned to use to keep everyone at arm's length. To keep yourself from getting hurt when the man you fall in love with lies to you and breaks your heart."

She shot up, the swirl of her hair cascading around her shoulders, falling across her breasts. "You never broke my heart."

"Right." He snorted his disbelief, knowing he'd effectively killed the mood, but now that he'd begun, he was bloody well going to finish. "I know how you felt because I felt it too. We were this close, Morgan." His index finger and thumb were an inch apart. "But we let our pain and our pride get in the way."

"If you'll remember, it was your wife who got in the way." She threw her legs over the bed. Stood, glaring down at him. No effort to shield her nudity. Instead she seemed to gather strength from that pose as if showing him what he was about to lose.

He sighed, suddenly wishing he'd kept his mouth shut. Paid lip service to Morgan's worry and moved on. If he had, he'd be inside her right now. Not hard as a rock with nothing to look forward to but a cold bed and painful frustration. "Charlotte wouldn't have been an impediment if we hadn't let her."

"This is about you." But her words came less sure.

"It's about us," he replied. "Tell me you don't want me when I do this." He reached up to stroke his hand over her belly.

She stood rigid as a statue, her eyes shooting fire. "Stop." But she made no attempt to move away.

"Or this." He dared more. Covered her woman's place with his hand, his fingers gently probing, knowing immediately she wasn't as indifferent as she wanted him to believe.

A tremor ran through her body at his touch, but she held firm. "It's not true," she said, though her words held little conviction. "I never loved you." She squeezed her eyes closed. But when she opened them again, anger fired their glittering depths. "Why don't you just enjoy what we have? Why do you have to confuse it with emotions that no longer apply?"

Why did he need an admission from her that they'd been more than casual lovers once? What did it matter now—so many months after? She'd made it clear that she'd not make the same mistake again. Her heart remained closed as an oyster, only her body willing to renew their relationship. And God knew he didn't look for another wife.

The space between them quivered as if the very room held its breath.

"Let it be enough, Cam. Please." A hitch in her voice as heartbreaking as a child's plea.

A part of him wanted to punish—to send her away from his bed and out of his room. Show her how little she meant to him. But desire raged too, his body no longer restrained by subtle diplomacy or blatant mind games.

He pulled her into his embrace and back into his bed so that he lay between her legs, the sweet friction almost enough to end things before they even began. Her hair lay fanned against the pillow, her breasts upthrust, the dusky nipples puckered tight and completely suckable. The heat in her eyes matching the inferno boiling through him.

He could fool himself and call it love. Or he could take it for what it was—pure lust.

Right now, lust suited him fine.

Morgan opened her eyes to a spill of moonlight washing across the floor. Up the walls. For a split second, she was home. Surrounded by childhood mementos, the discarded pieces of an awkward adolescence.

A breeze curled over her bare skin, bringing with it the city smells of coal smoke, wet brick, and humanity. Church bells rang the hour of one. Awareness seeped through her dreams, and she knew where she was. Whose bed she slept in. Her hand reached for him, but came up empty. Again.

She sat up, pushing her hair off her shoulders, wonderfully sore, the languor of lovemaking still causing every muscle to tingle with satisfaction.

Cam sat by the window, the shutters thrown wide, the casement open. A blanket lay draped over his shoulders, but in every other way, he remained nude as a Greek god. The stern perfection of his profile edged in silver from a moon, round as a coin.

She'd known men with that kind of self-contained confidence her whole life, but in Cam, somehow the polished elegance overlaid with the coiled animal intensity touched a chord deep within her. Taunted her with every girlish fantasy she'd ever harbored and had dashed.

Could Scathach be wrong? Could Cam accept her—proverbial warts and all? The idea hung before her like a prize on a string. All she had to do was reach for it.

If she dared.

"Did it rain?" she asked, pushing the temptation away with the merest of commonplaces.

His gaze never left the window, his eyes trained on the darkness beyond. "Aye. But the wind should blow it off by dawn." He dragged the blanket farther up around his neck. "We'll go back to Wapping in the morning. Try and pick up Doran's trail from there. I want to end this. I need to end this. Soon."

Before she thought about it, she opened her mouth. "Which this are you referring to?"

He turned, his face tangled in shadow and light, the gleam of his blinding blue gaze burying itself deep within the hard nugget of her heart. "Doran. You. Take your pick, Morgan." His hands curled to fists. "I don't know how much longer I can hang on. I don't how much longer I want to."

Chapter 20

Doran watched the man with the cool appraising eyes of a serpent. Ironic since the weasly little corporal confessed to being a member of that infamous brigade.

Rumors of their exploits had reached even the weathered climes of northern Scotland. Touched the ears of the *Amhasdraoi* and been dismissed as the stuff of *Duinedon* spleen. But if this man, Rastus, were to be believed, they not only existed, but the annoying thorn in his side, Sinclair, had been a member as well. An assassin with a ruthless efficiency rivaling Doran's own.

Rastus sat across from him, anxious under Doran's stare. He shifted on his seat, cracking his knuckles, his hands shaking. Waiting on Doran's reaction to the explosive shell dropped in his lap.

Doran took the last sip of ale. Placed the cup on the table. Signaled for another before turning back to his guest. "You say he lives?"

"Aye, him and the woman both."

Bligh had tricked him. Somehow she'd faked her death and tracked him as far as London. Impressive, if annoying. "How do you come to know this?"

"He hired me to follow you before you left Devonshire. And he found me again at Mrs. Cabot's. Wanted to know where you were. What you'd been up to."

"And I imagine you told him, of course."

"Enough to keep him satisfied."

Doran's eyes narrowed as he leaned forward. "So why tell me this now? If, as you say, you're in Sinclair's pay, revealing yourself to me would seem an imprudent move."

Rastus's eyes flickered as if he was gauging the best way to answer this. Finally, he offered a cool smile. "Not if my work for the colonel might benefit yourself. You want to put the hurt on Sinclair but don't know where to find him. I do. I've been following him. I can tell you where he is and what he's up to."

"And you do this all out of concern for my well-being?"

Rastus cleared his throat. "Well, if you were to reward for service, I wouldn't be amiss at accepting a kind . . . word, if you know what I mean."

"Oh yes, Mr. Rastus. I know exactly what you mean. And for the time being I'm interested enough to keep you alive and . . . rewarded." Doran sat back, drumming his fingers upon the tabletop.

"Good. Then, well, if we've come to an agreement, if I may be so bold, what are you goin' to do about them?"

"It's obvious, isn't it?"

"Kill them, you mean?"

"Oh yes, death awaits anyone who stands between me and my goal. But a quick death is too good for them. They've plagued me for too long—Sinclair especially. No, I want them to suffer before the end."

The need to hurt iced his heart over, a sadistic evil that enjoyed watching others' pain froze out any differing voice. Every day spent in the company of *Neuvarvaan* strengthening the bonds and blurring the lines between the violence of the

Morkoth and his own motivations. He'd even forgotten his stricture about use of the sword's true name. What did it matter? He and the sword were one now.

Rastus slurped down his cider. Wiped his mouth on his sleeve. "Sin will be hard to kill. He's as canny a customer as any that served."

"And Morgan Bligh's abilities, though hardly a match for my own, still hold the potential for trouble."

"So then what?"

"We show them what happens to those who oppose me. Sinclair suffered a recent bereavement, I'm told. His dear wife taken from him last spring. It would truly be a tragedy if he suffered a second such loss. And one just as close to him. A sister or brother, perhaps? Thieves abound in London's mean streets and if they don't kill you . . ." He sent a mere thread of his power, winging across the table. Let Rastus feel the sudden weakness, the nausea, the chills, the shutting down of his body. The man went deathly pale, gripping his chest, his stomach. ". . . if they don't kill you, a mysterious disease can threaten at any moment."

Rastus's eyes bulged as he fought for air. His hands scrabbled against the table, his nails scratching furiously at the wood, knocking silverware and plates to the floor with a crash. He reached for Doran, his lips blue, his face gray.

With a flick of his wrist, Doran released the vile turncoat. He might appreciate his information, but he detested the ease in which Rastus gave it up.

Rastus coughed and heaved, his face etched in lines of horror and renewed fear, his hands shaking so badly he couldn't lift his glass to his mouth without slopping it on his vest. "What did you do?"

"A taste only, but you'll do exactly as I say, or suffer another such attack, and this time I shall not be so quick to ease your agony."

Rastus wiped a shaky hand down his gray face. "What do you want to know?"

"I know about Bligh. Tell me about Sinclair."

"Getting to him won't be easy. Sin's as good as they come."

Doran smiled, let the full melding of *Morkoth* and *Amhasdraoi* show in his expression. Enjoyed the man's shrinking reaction. "Meet someone better."

The rain-slicked streets teemed with as much activity as yesterday. More if that were possible. An East Indiaman—the apparent reason for this new frantic rush of energy—lay at anchor, its web of masts and lines and sails dwarfing the huddle of rooftops surrounding it.

Morgan felt like nothing so much as a hound on the scent. She stood, hands on hips, gazing up and down the street as if Doran might emerge from the crowds swirling around her. As if finding him might just be that simple.

Of course, it wasn't. Her luck didn't run that way.

She'd known what she wanted. Known who she was. Or had until Cam had walked back into her life. Until he'd shaken every sense, feeling, emotion, and memory like a child's kaleidoscope. Twisted the pattern of her life into something new.

Since then, she'd been riding a runaway horse toward a cliff edge. Blindfolded.

"Are you sure Corporal Rastus wasn't feeding you a story? I haven't felt anything since yesterday."

"I'm not sure of much anymore," Cam confessed. "Rastus said Doran's been moving up and down the river. But always staying within the city itself. He's frustrated. And working on a very short fuse. Sergeant Lester was one of his own by Rastus's telling."

Morgan closed her eyes. Allowed the power to well from

the most secret places within her. Channeled it. Sent it forth to discover what it might.

She didn't have long to wait. The faint scent of mage energy clouded her head. She freed her mind. Let her unconscious tease the wheat from the chaff. Was this Doran? Some random *Other* who'd crossed his path? No, she recognized Doran's powers. Saw them in her head as a twisting double rope of red and purple, though the breadth and depth of mage energy stunned her.

"Anything?"

She'd put Cam's impatient presence at her elbow out of her mind. So his brusque words startled her. Opening her eyes, she pointed. "That way."

They followed the trail on and off for the best part of the day. Losing it for stretches. Backtracking until they caught it again. Cam let her lead, saying little. As if he'd said everything he meant to last night. Or as if he'd said too much.

Thankful he hadn't brought up their conversation again, she kept her own words to a minimum. It made for an extremely long, awkward afternoon. Too much left unspoken. Too much unresolved.

By the time shadows slid long over the streets, and the sun dropped orange and red behind the church towers and chimneys, her legs ached, her mind felt like mush, and she'd decided Doran's trail had been all flash and no substance. Too random and yet too pat. As if he knew exactly what she'd do and had led her on like waving a red flag in front of a bull.

She sighed. "He's gone, Cam."

He followed her into a nearby chop house, the heat steaming the damp from their clothes. Making her nose run. She turned her mind off to the dyspeptic looks that followed her entrance into this bastion of man. Too tired to care. And perhaps a bit interested to see how Cam would handle her.

He never flinched. Simply followed in her wake. Fell into a chair across from her.

She closed her hands around her coffee. Hated the sick ache of defeat shriveling her insides. "It's long odds, but there may be someone in London who can help."

"An *Amhas-draoi*?"

She laughed. "A librarian."

That caught him off guard. He lifted a brow in question.

"Lord Delvish. He's a friend of the family. What he doesn't know about the old ways isn't worth knowing. His library is immense. Bigger than my aunt's and that's saying something."

"And he lives in London?"

"On Cheyne Walk. He's a bit odd, but the sweetest man. I can pay him a visit. See if he has any idea why Doran would flee to London. Any ideas how to track him."

"You really think he's going to be able to help?" The skepticism coming through in his voice.

"He's a link to *Neuvarvaan*. If we understand the goddess blade, we may be able to predict what Doran will do next. And why."

"We know why Doran's hacking his goddamn way through the British Army. Because he's looking to create his own personal army of Undying."

"Don't snap at me. I'm grasping at straws here. He's using the *Morkoth*'s dark magics to cloak his powers. And I can't track what I can't sense."

"Then if we can't find him, we'll have him find us. I'll have Rastus pass the information to Doran. We'll flush him out into the open."

"And if he doesn't take the bait?"

Cam's eyes glittered, a ruthless smile playing over his face. "He'll take it. He'll not chance leaving us alive. He's running because he's scared, Morgan. Scared of you and me. Fear can make a man do all sorts of things he shouldn't." His gaze stabbed right through her, leaving her unsure if he intended a hidden meaning. Was he trying to tell her he had regretted revealing so much to her last night? That he didn't mean it? She couldn't tell. Wished she had the true *Fey*'s ability of mind-reading.

His eyes flickered over her, flat and cold, every emotion hidden from view.

Mayhap it was just as well she couldn't read minds. Some things were best left unknown.

The charred front door was their first clue. The gray-faced butler who reluctantly opened the door to them their second hint that things were far from right at the home of Lord Delvish.

"His Lordship is not at home to visitors."

Morgan, being Morgan, didn't take that as a no. Instead she oozed her way inside using three parts female flattery. One part brute *Amhas-draoi* force. The poor fellow didn't stand a chance in hell.

Once they were inside, it was more than obvious something very bad had occurred.

As if a bomb had gone off, furniture stood askew or toppled. Books lay on the floor. Glass smashed underfoot. A rug sat curled in a corner, the dark stain seeped through to the backing an indication of why.

Maids with red eyes and suspicious faces worked to clear the mess here and in the adjoining rooms, but it would take an army of servants to restore order to the chaos wreaked on the Delvish household.

"A break-in and robbery at a gentleman's home," Cam muttered to himself.

"Hmm?" Morgan frowned, her frightened, worried eyes scanning her surroundings.

"I read about this in the paper a few days ago. What do you suppose they wanted?"

"Who knows? Jewelry? Valuables easy to pawn?"

"Maybe." Cam eyed the destruction. "It looks like they broke more than they stole."

"So they weren't very bright robbers."

The butler showed them through to the back of the house, the destruction lessening as they went, although evidence of the earlier mess could be seen in hastily patched chair legs, empty spaces on walls where pictures once hung.

He stopped at a closed door. Beckoned them on. "His Lordship is in his library."

If a bomb had gone off in the rest of the house, ten such had exploded in here. A sea of ripped pages and broken-spined books covered the floor. More books lay scattered and fluttering on tabletops. Bookcases. A large oak desk.

Cam took a step, his boot coming down on the crackle of old vellum. He bent, picking up the manuscript, his eye falling upon a jumble of indecipherable squiggles. Beautiful to look upon, but complete gibberish to his mind.

Morgan took it from him, her face whitening as her gaze scanned the page. "A scrap of the ancient teachings by the philosopher Taog. Do you know what this is worth?"

Cam glanced again at the artful curved writing. A headache blooming behind his eyes after only a few seconds of examination. He shook his head. "Not much in that condition."

Morgan's gaze went hard as nails. "Aunt Niamh would weep if she saw this."

A man knelt upon the floor, sorting through a sea of ripped pages. Hearing their voices, he looked up, a tired smile crinkling his lined face. "So you've come at last, Morgana girl, though I'd hoped it would be sooner than this. My prophecies aren't what they were in my youth. Time was when I could have foretold your coming to the second. Now I'm near as blind as if I'd no ability at all." He rose slowly, the creak of his limbs almost audible. "And you've brought the colonel. Good to see you, my boy. You're much better looking in person."

Whatever that meant.

Cam didn't even bother to ask. A definite sign he was growing a little too comfortable with Morgan's magical way of life.

She waded through the mess to reach Lord Delvish, throwing her arms around his thin shoulders, kissing his parchment-dry cheek. "Uncle Owen, you're all right."

He patted her back. "Spent the evening with friends. Came home to this."

Morgan held him at arm's length, checking him over. "What happened? Who did this?"

His smile dimmed, sorrow clear in his watery eyes, the shaking of his hands. "I'd no warning of an attack. Not even the merest snippet of a vision. If I had, Mrs. Fisher might still be alive, poor thing."

Morgan helped Delvish to a chair. Looked around for another and came up empty. Instead she perched on the edge of his desk. "Now one step at a time. Who attacked you?"

His gaze sharpened, and Cam caught a glimpse of the man Delvish might have been in his youth. Shrewd. Far-seeing. Formidable. "The *Amhas-draoi*. Not alone, mind you. There were others. It was one of them murdered my housekeeper. But the *Amhas-draoi* knew what he searched for."

"What did he search for, Uncle Owen? What is Doran Buchanan trying to do?"

But already the man had slipped back into vagueness. He plucked a book from the desk next to Morgan. Began leafing through it in a distracted way. "Magic of that sort is best locked away from those who might be tempted. It's why I kept it hidden. Not out amongst the lesser writings. Look at this. A collection of poems by Flann Manistrech. Destroyed."

"Magic of what sort?" Morgan urged. "What did Doran take?"

Delvish straightened. "Where are my manners, Morgana girl? Would you like some tea? Let me ring for Mrs. Fisher. She'll bring us a tray."

"Uncle Owen, Mrs. Fisher is—"

Cam caught Morgan's eye. Drew a line across his throat. "Icksnay on isher-fay," he muttered. To Lord Delvish he said, "No doubt she's busy elsewhere, sir. And tea isn't necessary. We've only come to find information on *Neuvarvaan*, the sword of Undying."

Delvish shuddered. "An ill weapon. I wonder Andraste doesn't destroy it once and for all rather than allow such *Morkoth* evil to linger on." He stood, adjusting his jacket. Removing his spectacles to wipe them on his handkerchief. Replace them on his whipsaw nose. "I foresaw this happening, you know. Years ago. Tried to warn them, I did. But the true *Fey* are ever arrogant in their dealings with *Other*. Always believe they know everything. Ha, for all their wisdom, they didn't see this one coming, did they?"

Cam came farther into the room, careful to step around the disaster underfoot. Who knew a page under his boot might not be the key to solving this puzzle? "What can you tell us of the goddess blade?"

Delvish moved to a bookcase, half the books gone or lying willy-nilly. "To create an Undying takes mage energy. And lots of it. But not any old magic will do. Oh no." Running his fingers over the titles, he plucked one from the pile. Handed it to Cam. "It must be power derived from a living source. Not the stale energy of standing stone or barrow mound." Moved to a shelved cupboard. Pulled first one, then another of the shelves out, removing a parchment. Tossed it to Morgan, who juggled the unexpected missile.

The pile grew as the old man moved through the wreck of

his library, searching out tidbits of information. Scraps of knowledge from a past Cam hadn't even known existed except in fable. Some were written in the same illegible handwriting of the earlier page. Others in ornate monkish Latin. Still more in an archaic cross of Gaelic and what read to him like a slightly odd version of ancient Greek.

Morgan had no trouble reading through the densely packed writings, but for Cam, only a few moments of study sent the room spinning, sent his stomach into his throat as if he'd had too much to drink. Before he humiliated himself by heaving onto the floor, he got up, stretched the worst of the nausea away. Moved to a window for a breath of air.

Morgan held at it, her head perched in her hand, her eyes scanning the pages, her lower lip caught between her teeth in concentration.

"She's quite a woman."

Lord Delvish had followed Cam to the window, his indulgent gaze fixed on Morgan. "She reminds me of her mother. A fiery beauty with the heart of a lion. She led young Davydh Bligh a mighty chase before she allowed him to catch her."

"Was she *Amhas-draoi*?"

"Morva Bligh? No, though she could have been. She'd the soul of a crusader. More than likely where Morgana girl gets her spunk, though the Blighs are all fighters. They've had to be over the years. Times are never easy for *Other*. 'Tis a challenge walking that line between worlds."

Delvish turned his gaze on him, creating a sensation in Cam of millions of fingers probing his brain. Millions of eyes piercing his thoughts. He gripped the sill as his vision narrowed, pinwheels spinning across his line of sight.

"You tread a similar line, Colonel, between the twin sides of yourself. The man you've been and the man you will be. A nudge in either direction could tip the scale."

Some prophecy. Tell him something he didn't know.

But curious, he motioned toward Morgan. "So if you're so good at reading the future, what do you see for us?"

"You and my Morgana girl?" Delvish's face tightened, his eyes going distant as stars. "I see grief. And struggle."

His body strained to see images invisible to Cam, his pallor growing chalky white. Would he pass out? Pitch over dead? All because Cam wanted to know if he'd end in Morgan's bed or not? He put a hand on the man's shoulder. Tried jarring him out of his trance. "Forget it."

But Delvish remained fixed upon some distant vision.

Cam tried again. A little more force behind his hand. "Stop. I don't want to know. It doesn't matter." His movement caused a book to fall with a loud clap to the floor. Snapped Delvish awake. "I said forget it."

His Lordship shook his head, dazed. Shaky. "I saw *Neuvarvaan*. And you. The great sword descending in an arcing slash of power." His eyes widened into circles of alarm as he fought to swallow. "The creation of an Undying."

Chapter 21

Morgan raised her head, eyes weary after so many hours shuffling through pages, but a new fear pricking her heart. "I don't believe it. No one can use the *Other* like this."

Caught dozing, Uncle Owen opened his eyes. "What's that, Morgana girl?" Cleared his throat. "It's old magic. Difficult magic. But anyone who can steal away one of the *Fey*'s chief treasures from under their noses is certainly up to this task."

"But if he succeeds in puzzling out the Guenguerthlon text and taps into the mage energy lying within the city, he'll have more than enough magic to call forth the spell of Undying."

Resettling his spectacles, Uncle Owen sighed. "You've stated the case quite succinctly. And from what you've told me of this Buchanan fellow, he's neither hindered by the strictures placed upon him by the Order of *Amhas-draoi*, nor does he seem worried about the penalties meted out by the *Fey* on those who betray them."

"He sees *Neuvarvaan* as his route to rivaling the *Fey*. Becoming immortal. All-powerful. And with an army of unkillable warriors who's to say he won't do it."

"Isn't that why you've come? You and Colonel Sinclair? You're the two who will see that Doran Buchanan is stopped."

She stretched the kinks out of back and neck, her gaze sweeping the library. Speaking of Cam, where had he run off to? He'd been quiet for hours, seemingly lost in thought, but she'd never heard him leave.

Uncle Owen paused in the midst of rooting through the ruin of his desk. "Your colonel's gone to rustle us up some supper. Ah, there it is," he said, finding what he searched for.

"Not my colonel. We're only working together. Though I can't fight what I can't track. And the fog of *Other* mage energy makes it impossible to pick up any one strand."

Flipping open an enamel snuff box, he took a pinch. Sneezed once. Twice. "What's that? Not your colonel?" As if he hadn't heard anything she'd said after. "Well, you know best, Morgana girl. You know best." He blew his nose with a great honking snort. "Probably just as well considering."

That caught her attention.

"Considering what? What's that supposed to mean?"

"Hmm? What's what supposed to mean?"

Morgan just shook her head. Pinning Uncle Owen down was akin to nailing jelly to the wall. Best to let him follow his own train of thought to whatever end.

Stuffing his handkerchief back into his waistcoat pocket, he stood. Gave a thoughtful rub of his chin. "Here, I have something that might help. If I can find it."

They'd made some headway in cleaning away the worst of the mess, but it would take an army of servants to restore the Delvish library to its former glory.

Instead of moving to the shelves, Uncle Owen crossed the room to a locked chest. Removed a ring of keys from a peg beside it. Fitted the largest into the rusty lock. Lifted the lid with a groan of hinges.

"I'm surprised Doran and his thieves didn't bother that old trunk."

He rummaged inside the trunk, his voice echoing.

"Didn't need to. They'd found what they were looking for." Straightening, success lighting his features, he waved a leather-bound book over his head. "Aha! Knew it was here."

"What is it?"

"A copy, my girl. A more recent version. Not as extensive in footnotes and sources, but still invaluable." He set the book on the table in front of her. "Found it in an estate sale in Dublin last year."

Morgan ran her hand over the warped cover. Leafed through the furred edges and water-stained pages. Some stuck together. Others hopelessly illegible. "Unless it tells me how to track Doran or how to combat *Neuvarvaan*, it's not going to be much use." Disappointed, she closed the book. Pushed it back across the table toward Uncle Owen.

He pushed it back. "Keep it. A gift to my favorite goddaughter."

"But—"

He laid a fatherly hand upon her shoulder. "A piece of advice, Morgan, from an old, broken-down fortune-teller. Not even the wisest of the prophets know for certain what the future holds. We see possibilities. Probabilities. Of both past and future. From this we can deduce the most logical path, but nothing is writ in stone. Nothing is immutable. You may be wrong about the young man."

Leave it to Uncle Owen to cut to the crux of things with the delicacy of a pickax. He meant well, but it was a conversation she didn't want to have. Not when her emotions were as jumbled as the room around her. She sought to end it. Quick. "Cam and I live in different worlds, Uncle Owen. Our paths—logical or not—aren't meant to cross." She hoped her tone said, Leave it alone. But in a tactful, respect-your-elders way.

Uncle Owen ignored it. He took her chin in hand. Tilted her face to his just as if she were four and not four and twenty. His eyes, a lightning flicker mix of brown and green, trapped hers. Carried her into his vision. A mirror within a mirror within a mirror. And every one an image of Cam. Of her. A million futures. One past. His words sounded like a drum in her skull. "To be a great seer, you must never discount the messiness that is the human heart."

A door opened. "Things are still muddled in the kitchens, but I've found cold ham and bread. Some soup."

Startled, Uncle Owen swung around to Cam.

The connection severed, Morgan dropped her gaze. Focused on the wood grain of the table. A frayed corner of the book. Anything to keep her thoughts from what she'd seen. How she felt.

Cam looked from one to the other, his face questioning. "Did I miss something?"

She tried to play it off. Tossed him a smile. "Not much."

And knew Cam knew she was lying.

Morgan woke to the *shink* of curtain rings being pulled open and silver light falling across her bed, her face. Instinct had her reaching for her knife even before she'd come fully into consciousness. But then the dark form outlined against the window moved, and she relaxed back against the pillows.

"Did I frighten the spell-wielding Amazon Morgan Bligh? I hadn't thought it possible."

His words fell as harsh as his expression, revealed as he stepped out of the shadows and the same moon-glow that had roused her fell upon him. More telling still was the sour whiskey scent clinging to his clothes as if he'd spilled on himself and hadn't bothered to change.

"You're drunk," she answered swiftly. "Again."

"I wish I were." With one hand, Cam clung to her bedpost. With the other, he plowed a hand through his hair. "In fact, I'm feeling extremely clearheaded. For the first time in months. In years, even."

She pushed herself up against the headboard, her stomach knotting at the cruel slice of his words. She didn't like where this was going. Understood it less. What had happened to make Cam drop into the self-destructive behavior of their early days together? "Then you can explain yourself."

"I'll do better than that. I'll explain you," he said, pointing an accusing finger in her direction.

A cold knot of fear settled deep in her stomach, her limbs leaden and unresponsive. She showed Cam none of those things. Instead, she lifted her chin, offered a look that said, Give it your best.

"You, Miss Bligh, are a tease and a voracious man-eater."

His best turned out to be pretty damn good. Morgan winced under the insult.

"But as it turns out, I'm all right with that. After all, the sex is amazing." Hard to make someone as impossibly gorgeous as him ugly, but he managed it with the smarmiest of greasy smiles. "And it's not like we were ever going to marry for real, now, was it? I mean, look at you. Not exactly the kind you take home to meet the family."

She glanced down at her simple white shift, the only thing virginal about her. Not that she'd ever cared for such social niceties before. But now seeing herself as Cam must see her, she withered, a hot, angry flush stealing over her face. "Why are you saying these things?" she whispered through lips gone dry, but he didn't hear. He just kept on with a litany of her failings as if now that he'd started, he couldn't wait to lay it on as thick as possible.

"You're easy on the eyes, for certain, and if I'm ever in need of a she-male to watch my back, I'll call on you, but I need someone who'll be an asset to my position, not simply . . . an . . . ass."

He trailed off, apparently out of nasty things to say for the moment. And Morgan chose that moment to attack.

"Get out." She slammed to her feet. Grabbed him, easy to do in his inebriated state, and quick-marched him to the door. "Get the hell out of my room, you damned bastard. Quick enough to enjoy the tease, weren't you? No questions about my assets then."

She pushed him into the corridor. Stood, rigid with fury as he weaved in front of her, glazed eyes raking her breasts as if he hadn't just insulted her.

Before good sense took over, she balled her fist, her heart racing. Reared back and gave him the hardest, jaw-breaking crack across the face she could . . .

. . . and came awake still feeling the tingle all the way to her elbow.

She lay back, her heart still racing, her palm damp with memory. She rubbed it down her shift, willing her breathing to come slower. Focusing on the rain pattering against the window, plinking through the gutter. Listening to the wind as it shook the casement, causing the curtains to billow with every damp draft.

Burrowing deeper under the quilts, she tried to clear her mind of the disturbing images and twisted dream dredged up by too much claret and a less-than-savory meal. No doubt one too many pieces of cake at dinner tonight.

The wind picked up outside, slamming twigs and leaves against the glass. Bringing with it the tang of metal, a scent of death and evil. At the same instant the familiar red and purple double rope of mage energy burst into her brain like a red-hot dagger thrust straight to the base of her skull.

She screamed, or thought she had. But the voice wasn't hers. Despite the excruciating press of power, she'd managed to bite off her shout. The scream came again. From down the hall.

Oh gods! Cam.

Kicking out of her covers, ignoring the fact she wore next to nothing, Morgan raced for the door. Pounded down the dark corridor toward Cam's closed bedchamber. After the initial explosive screams, all had gone quiet. More frightening than any sounds of struggle would have been. At least that would have told her Cam still fought. Still lived.

Sliding to a stop in front of his door, she breathed deeply. Prepared herself for the fight ahead. The eerie silence on the other side preyed on her already frayed nerves. She clenched her jaw. Donned the focus of the warrior. And turned the knob.

Nothing.

The door wouldn't open. Something or someone heavy lay in front of it. As she shoved hard with one shoulder, the heap moved. Allowed her to thread her way through the narrow gap. The room felt as charged as if lightning had struck, the air alive, the mage energy almost visible, raising the hairs on the back of her neck.

The heap turned out to be only the carpet, askew and blocking the door. She stood, scanning the room. The bed lay unoccupied, the window stood open, rain pouring in to drench the floor.

"Cam." Her voice sounded overloud in the seemingly empty room. But she knew he was there. As was Doran. Her wards had failed. The battle upon her.

"Your persistence is unexpected. Even admirable. But you knew it had to end this way." Doran stepped from the doorway leading to Cam's dressing room, his dead eyes glowing with a darkling *Fey* light, though in no other way did he seem changed from the arrogant *Amhas-draoi* she remembered. Still as conceited as ever.

Any effect of the *Morkoth* blade lay beneath the surface. In the otherworldly strength that staggered her. The buzz in her ears, the sticky dryness of her mouth, the sweat slithering down her back just from being in the same room with him.

"Where's Cam?" She wished for the comforting grip of her sword hilt. Hell, even clothes would make her feel less vulnerable. Instead, she wiped her hands down her sides. Met his gaze, refusing to look away, though the pain of it was enough to bring tears to her eyes.

He stepped back into the darkness of the sitting room. Reappeared, supporting a body that he tossed toward her. Rolling him over with one booted foot. "Here's your colonel."

Cam lay trussed and insensible, the slight rise and fall of his bare chest enough to give her hope.

"Despite your troublesome nature, I'm offering you the ultimate reward. Immortality. Invincibility. Or rather, I'm offering it to the colonel."

Morgan conjured the first spell that came to mind, releasing it at the black *Amhas-draoi*.

Doran doubled over, his shoulders hunching, a grunt of pain coming from his thin lips.

But not for long.

In a moment, he'd straightened, his death stare potent enough to freeze her to the floor, wipe her mind clear.

Throwing his heavy cloak over one shoulder, he stepped up to Cam's body. Drew forth his sword.

Neuvarvaan.

There was no mistaking the *Fey* intensity of the blade. It glowed with a gray-green cemetery light. And Morgan was suddenly reminded of Ensign Traverse's words. A feeling like the first shovelful of earth hitting your coffin. Although in her case, the soil heaped higher and higher, burying her beneath the avalanche of raw, naked *Morkoth* power.

She choked, her lungs burning as she swallowed over and over. Her whole body shook until she knew she was going to be sick.

Doran laughed. And *Morkoth* magics burned their way through her. Bones grated, muscles went lax, and she felt herself falling. She bit hard on her lip to hold the screams back. She'd not give Doran the satisfaction.

Even as she collapsed, she heard the cut of air as *Neuvarvaan* plunged, and the wet suck of steel meeting flesh.

Cam's body jumped, the blade quivering in his chest. His head lolled to the side, his eyes wide with shock, a moan escaping from lips frothy pink with blood. And as she watched, the change overtook him.

Not the strength and skill of the Undying, but a shriveling of limbs and features, years passing within the space of seconds. A ravaged face. Curled and crooked hands. A body wasted by age and magic. Only the eyes remained the same. Their icy blue luster searching hers for help. Begging for the release of death. "*M'eudail,*" he whispered.

And this time, she did scream.

Over and over until a hand covered her mouth, a voice whispered in her ear, a heavy weight as someone knelt beside her on her bed. "Morgan, *mo chride*, my sweet. *Shhh*, it's a dream. It's all right."

And just like that, six months evaporated, leaving her crazy in love and heart-achingly destroyed. Torn in two.

"The dream was so real. Too real." Morgan shivered, curling closer into the crook of Cam's arm, the warmth of her naked body stirring him back to life. He should be exhausted. Drowsy with the afterglow of lovemaking. Instead, every part of his anatomy stood to attention. It was almost embarrassing.

To fight the urge and because he hated to break the spell of cold room, warm bed, and hot body, he brushed a chaste kiss upon the top of her head. "The worst dreams always are."

She lapsed into silence, her breathing slow and even. Probably asleep again. And no wonder.

She'd clung to him after first waking, the thrum of her

heart as fast as a bird's, her breathing ragged with suppressed tears. But terror had quickly melted into something else. Something greedy and possessive that gave him barely space to breathe. Fast. Angry. As if she needed to prove to herself that this time he was real. Not another night terror.

Even when they lay spent and dazed, Morgan seemed twisted taut as a clock wire. The weight of her dreams still holding on. She inhaled a quick, shuddery breath. Curled into his body as if needing the comfort of his heat.

"Cam?"

Pulled from a near doze, he ran a hand down her arm. *"Hmm?"* Felt her tremble.

Another long silence, then, "I want to show you . . . me. All of me. Not just . . . well . . . all of me."

He started to say something smart along the lines of what parts of her hadn't he seen when some quality of her quiet resolve broke through his randy thoughts.

He opened his eyes. Leaned up onto one elbow.

She watched him, alert as a wild animal, frightened and ready to run if he made any startling move.

"What is it?" he asked.

She closed her eyes. Turned back the blankets, uncovering herself so that she lay exposed, the flat plane of her stomach, the high, round peaks of her breasts, the slope of her broad shoulders, and the long bones of her throat where her pulse beat as swiftly as it had when he'd first found her tonight.

"Look at me," she whispered, closing her eyes.

How could he not?

He frowned, clamped down hard on the sinful thoughts flitting through his dirty brain. "What are you trying to—"

"Look. At. Me. All of me," she repeated.

And as she spoke, it happened. A ripple of air like heat from the desert floor, and a prickly sensation that seemed to jump between them skin to skin. His eyes burned, but he wouldn't blink in case he missed something.

A shiver of change passed over her body. Where before had been a creamy expanse of golden skin, unmarred and unbroken, now stood out a swirl of color, blue black, a twining of symbols curling over her left shoulder. Down her arm to her elbow.

His gran-da's voice spoke to him from some long-ago memory. Mage marks. Symbols of magic and power.

"How did . . ."

You get them? You hide them from me?

Even though he left both questions unspoken, she seemed to sense what he asked. A sly smile crept over her features. "I received the first markings after my third year with Scathach. The *fith-fath* disguises them, a bit of household magic easily conjured and easily sustained. I barely even need to think about concealing them anymore."

He should be disgusted. Repulsed at the outrageous scarring. No woman with any hint of breeding would allow such self-mutilation. And yet wasn't this just more evidence—as if he needed it—that Morgan wasn't entirely human? Or at least not like any human he'd ever known. She was *Other*. A species with its own rules, its own traditions—and now that he was forced to confront it—a freedom he envied.

Without thinking, he took a finger. Traced the swooping tattoos from their origin at the base of her neck. Followed their path across her shoulder. Her arm.

Morgan remained absolutely still, though her flesh pebbled under his light touch, her nipples pearling into hard buds, her stomach tightening. Her eyes locked on his, a wary expectancy darkening her wolf-bright irises.

She'd never seemed more foreign to him. A creature of legend and ancient mythology. How had he ever thought he could capture the heart of a being like this? A whirlwind of light and fire who carried the blood of another world within her veins? He'd been fooling himself. Immersing himself in a fantasy where he could give her what she wanted. Where he could be what she needed.

But that was insanity. Might as well try to catch a lightning bolt in his hands or cage a mountain lion in hopes of taming it to the leash.

Her expression went grave. "So say it and be done."

Another test. But this one made the foul mouth and take-no-prisoners attitude she'd used earlier to check his reaction seem like child's play. Like threading a field of caltrops, what he did or said here would affect all that came after.

He cupped one breast, his thumb rubbing the sensitive aureole, her hiss of pleasure making his own temperature rise. "Actions speak louder than words."

He lowered his head, his tongue following the same path his finger had moments earlier. Her flesh tasted salty, smelled with a heady mix of her normal woodbine and meadowsweet overlaid with the musky scent of sex.

His hands skimmed her body. Her breasts. He took it slow, knowing his patient thoroughness frustrated her need to have him inside her now. She arched against him, willing him to end the long, teasing strokes, the graze of his teeth and lips. But he held back, even though he felt his own restraint growing thin. This might be as close as he ever came to bottling the wild ferocity of a Highland storm; he'd string out the pleasure as long as he could.

"Cam," she urged, her voice breathy and rushed with passion. "Please, Cam. Finish it."

"I need to be sure you know exactly what I think. No mistakes."

He laughed as she lifted her head, shot him a withering glare. "I'll tell you what I think," she began. Cut off by a slow, drugged kiss that caused both of them to forget everything but the pleasure they shared for the space of minutes.

Capturing her hands in his, he positioned them around the dowels of the headboard. Showed her how he wanted her to hold on to them before drawing himself up onto his knees between her legs.

With a steamy look that set his blood roaring straight to his center, Morgan gripped the headboard. Lay back letting him look his fill. And where before there had been a hesitancy, now she seemed to revel in the effect. Her head thrown back, her lips parted slightly in a take-me invitation that had his whole body alight and scraping the edge of explosion.

The tattoo's pattern, the gleam of moist skin, the red-gold hair loose about her head like a crown. Hers was the sleek, muscled body of an Amazon, the voluptuous temptation of some prehistoric earth-goddess.

He dipped his head to hers, tasting, then devouring. She opened to him, showing with her tongue and teeth that she was more than ready for anything he wanted to do to her. His fingers found her woman's place, a gentle pressure enough to bring a moan to her lips. He breathed it in along with the whimpers of near ecstasy, loved the way she asked for more, her whole body alive beneath his hands and then his mouth. She cried out, her body quivering beneath him as he lapped at her slick heat.

She released the headboard, squirming free of his assault. Lifting his head, he took her mouth again. Let her taste her own essence on his tongue.

She answered with temptation of her own as she ran her fingers over his member, just that slight touch enough to make his pulse leap into his throat.

He groaned, his body poised and throbbing at the brink of abyss. "Have I said enough? Or do you need more persuading?" His voice came out sounding almost normal, despite the live-wire quiver beginning in his belly. Sizzling like liquid fire through his veins.

"Always better to be sure," she answered, the smoky sultriness of her voice as she guided him inside her, pushing him to the point where rational thought ended and pure animal lust took over.

He thrust deep, her hips rising off the bed to take him. She writhed against the steady increase of rhythm, her eyes black with urgency.

Climax took only moments, both of them already caught in a slippery tangle of arousals before their bodies ever joined.

A shuddering riptide of feelings broke over him as she clung, her head thrown back, eyes closed, the sculpted beauty of her face awash with moonlight. He crushed her to him, unwilling to release her, unwilling to uncork the bottle and free the storm. Because once he did, she'd be gone. And instead of a Highland storm he'd hold a frozen burn. Hard. Protected. The rush of heat and life frozen away beneath a shell of ice.

At that point, he might lay in bed with her, their bodies still damp from a joining that rocked him to his core with its wanton passion. But the real Morgan would be walled away from him. He'd yet to find the key.

And if Lord Delvish's prophecy was right, his time might be fast running out.

Chapter 22

Cam folded the completed note to Rastus. Dripped the blob of wax across the edge, pressing his seal into it. Amos would take it to Arthur's. Pass it along the chain to Rastus. And the trap would be set. The next move would be Doran's.

But it wasn't Amos who answered his summons.

"Look who I found skulking around outside."

Brodie stood in the doorway, dwarfing the figure he held by the upper arm, crushing the wine-red velvet pelisse she wore.

She threw a dagger glance up at her captor. "I was not skulking. And I have as much right to be here as you. More so, he's my brother."

Brodie looked completely unfazed. In fact, he seemed almost amused. "The wee mousey can speak."

Color infused her face, her gaze growing hard as diamonds. "How dare you?"

Cam cut her off before she worked herself into a rage. "Euna, what are you doing here? Aunt Sylvie's probably worried sick."

She straightened. Gave a conspiratorial grin. "That's where you're wrong. It was Aunt Sylvie who sent me."

That knocked him back on his pins. Aunt Sylvie must be desperate if she allowed Euna with naught but a footman for a chaperone. She protected her niece as if she were made of spun glass, no matter that Euna was tough as nails and clever as a fox. Fortune hunters, rakes, dilettantes—they were all held at bay by Uncle Josh's haughty condescension and unpredictable temper as well as Aunt Sylvie's enveloping protectiveness.

No wonder Euna looked positively triumphant at being out from under their thumb, even for a moment.

She shook off Brodie's restraining hand. Rushed forward. "Cam, Aunt Sylvie's worried about you. She says this woman you've brought home with you is trouble. She doesn't understand why you'd marry in such a helter-skelter way. She worries—"

"Sit," Cam commanded, his voice like a gunshot. Euna dropping into a chair like a sack of potatoes. "Brodie? What's your excuse?"

He blinked. "For being here? A desire to see your bride again. She may be trouble, but wrapped up in that body, who cares?"

Euna huffed her disgust. Crossed her arms, chin up.

"Morgan's with Amos," Cam explained. "As I would be if certain people"—he glowered at Euna—"didn't make it their business to poke their noses into my business."

She flushed, but held firm. "You can roar at me all you like, but I'm not frightened by you."

"No?" He stepped toward her. "More fool you, then."

She persisted in the face of his growing wrath. "I know Charlotte—"

"Is dead." He cut her off, his tone accepting no argument. "And Morgan's my wife now, so if Uncle Josh and Aunt Sylvie want to strip me out of the family tree, fine."

A spark of anger lit Euna's eyes. She rose, her hands clutched in her skirts, but her head high. "Don't be dramatic. You know they wouldn't do that. They want you to come to the Abercrombies'. They're having a party the day after tomorrow. Here." She handed him a gold-edged invitation.

"You must be joking. I wouldn't let Morgan within ten leagues of so-called society. They'd fall on her like a pack of rabid dogs."

"You make them sound like monsters."

"I have heard rumors Lady Wesleyan eats her young," Brodie quipped, eliciting freezing stares from twin sets of icy blue eyes. He held up his hands in mock surrender. "It's just rumor, mind ye." He cleared his throat. "I think I hear Susan calling. If you'll . . . ah . . . excuse me?"

"Coward," Cam muttered at his retreating back.

Euna sighed. "Really, Cam. All they want is a chance to find out what's going on."

"Why the Abercrombies'? Why not simply come here and do it?"

She didn't say anything.

He nodded. "That's what I thought. They don't want to know the truth. They want to quash the rumors. The *ton* smells another Sinclair scandal, and Uncle Josh is hoping to head it off before it grows legs."

"They love you, Cam. They've just forgotten how to show it. Uncle Josh's business interests. His standing among his political friends. Aunt Sylvie's work with her committees. They're so caught up in appearances. In stepping a foot wrong. They're afraid."

Cam crossed to the sideboard. Plucked the decanter from its place. Poured a whiskey, bringing it halfway to his lips before he paused, his gaze fixed on the amber liquid. Pure gold. And the very shade of Morgan's eyes.

He slammed the glass to the table, where it shattered, spraying glass and whiskey over his breeks. "Tell them to join the queue."

* * *

So he didn't want her within ten leagues of his precious society?

Well, to hell with him.

Morgan stomped her way around her bedchamber where she'd fled upon hearing those gut-wrenching words thrown out like a live shell.

Ashamed of her. That's what he was. Ashamed that Morgan Bligh would make a fool of herself and him in the company of his erudite, sophisticated London acquaintances.

The latch clicked, sending her spinning on her heel.

Cam stood, his eyes gliding over her with a decided lusty look. "I've managed to get rid of everyone. For the moment. And I've sent Amos with the instructions for Rastus."

All he had to do was stand there, and a pathetic thrill zinged up her spine. Wicked ideas springing into her filthy mind. She quelled the swooping drop of her stomach. Reminded herself of Cam's hypocrisy.

The quiet words—made more powerful by the very reluctance to speak them. The weaknesses he'd revealed. And the weaknesses he'd revealed in her. So convincing. Wrung from the heart.

And all lies.

He wanted her in his bed. That had been made perfectly, deliciously clear to her the last few nights. What he didn't want—and that also had been made clear to her—was Morgan in his life.

She conveniently forgot the part where she'd wanted that as well.

He'd caused her to doubt herself. Wonder if she'd made the right decision. And then pulled the rug out from under her, leaving her for the second time in a year feeling like a complete fool.

She plastered a smile on her face. Hoped she didn't look too manic. "A real London soiree? Sounds exciting."

He cocked a frown in her direction. "You heard that, did you? As the Spanish Inquisition is exciting. I'm not going to give the bloodsuckers what they want. The only reason we've been asked is so they can sharpen their claws on us. Cut us to ribbons with their rapier smiles and false goodwill."

"You think I can't handle the pressure?" It took every ounce of acting ability not to crack something heavy over his head.

"I think I'd rather face ten such Dorans with matching swords before I'd set foot within the halls of Lady Abercrombie's gossip abattoir."

She knew as well as anyone the stifling atmosphere of being onstage for a roomful of people all waiting for a misstep to pounce upon. She'd lived with that kind of scrutiny her whole life. Even with hiding their lineage as her family had, there had always been hints of their gifts. The neighborhood's subsequent curiosity mingled with fear had always been one more obstacle to her fitting in. Another excuse to snub that odd Bligh girl.

"I've sent Rastus word. He'll let Doran know we're alive. We need to be ready." The firm, no-nonsense tone to his words told her it was useless to argue any longer. It would avail her nothing but a sore head from banging it against a wall.

"I still don't know if this is the best way—" she began.

"Do you want to prolong this, Morgan?"

She wanted Doran killed, the sword returned, the mission a success. Of course she did. But a small guilty part of her knew that with that accomplishment, her time with Cam would be over. And also knew that once he was gone, he would not seek her out again.

She used him. And he allowed it. But there was a limit to what he would accept—even if it cost him as much to sever their renewed connection as it did her. That as much as everything else made her blood burn with a fierce need to find a way to cling for just these few days longer. Enough time to regain the equilibrium that would let her turn her back once more on Cameron Sinclair and leave him behind.

As if she'd been sucker punched in the gut, every bit of breath and strength left her. She slumped down on her bed, rubbing her temples against the headache that blossomed behind her eyes. "No, of course not."

He made it as far as the door before turning back. "This will end it, Morgan."

Left alone, she flopped back on the bed, staring up into the bed curtains. With no way to tell which *it* he referred to.

Cam balled up his latest attempt at a suitable reply to his uncle's gently couched order and threw it on the fire. Euna's impressions notwithstanding—her message had clearly been meant as a command from on high: Come or, once again, you will have disappointed us.

Tired of being the family's black sheep, Cam wanted nothing more than to confront Sir Joshua and lay it on the line. Mayhap then he'd find a peace with his family he could live with.

Plowing a hand through his hair, he made his decision. Left the library to look for Amos and found Susan, letting her know where he meant to go and when he'd be back.

Susan paused in the midst of supervising a pair of day workers, the girls shrinking away from him as if they expected him to breathe fire.

And no wonder.

A glance in the hall mirror on his way out the door showed him a man girded for battle, a face etched in grim lines, a mouth pressed thin, shoulders bunched somewhere around his ears.

The walk to his uncle's house in Curzon Street took less time than he'd hoped and soon enough, he stood facing Sir Joshua's long-faced butler, Beasley.

"Colonel Sinclair." The man bowed him in, curiosity alive in his pale eyes.

"Is my uncle at home?"

"Just preparing to go out, sir. But I shall let him know you're here," he answered as he led Cam to a sitting room to await his uncle.

As Cam crossed the hall, another door opened, a man bowing his way out. "Good day, milady. Miss Sinclair. I'm sorry the necklace turned out not to be yours, but I'll not complain. For it allowed me to beg an introduction to the most beautiful woman in London."

Cam gave a sneer of contempt. Please, that was laying it on a bit thick.

"I hope to see you both at the Abercrombies'." The man turned and, spying Cam, tipped his hat on his way by. "Your servant, sir."

Cam offered a stiff nod at the ass prowling around his sister. God help her if that was the sort she preferred. As drab as paste.

Left kicking his heels, Cam moved restlessly from hearth to windows to desk and back. He caught his hand reaching for his cross, and cursed himself for a superstitious coward. He didn't need courage to face his uncle. Only resolve.

The door opened behind him.

"Cam, you've come. I knew you would. Will you join us at the Abercrombies'?" Euna hurried to grab up his hands, her face awash with delight, a new womanly ripeness to her features he'd not noticed before. No wonder his aunt and uncle guarded her so closely. And no wonder that poor excuse for a man had been sniffing around her.

"Who was that fellow just here? Not your type, I hope."

Euna wrinkled her nose. "Hardly. His name's Lieutenant North. He came calling to return a necklace he'd found on the street outside Gunter's. Someone thought it was mine, though I've not lost any jewelry, and told him so." She dismissed the annoying lieutenant with a toss of her gold curls. "Enough about North and his necklace. Did you decide to answer Uncle's invitation?"

"I'm not made for dancing and I've always been a poor flirt. The women would be disappointed."

Euna dimpled. "If you think that, you've not looked in a mirror lately."

He lifted an eyebrow at Euna's choice of phrase.

She linked her arm through his and pulled him toward a couch. "Although your hasty marriage has definitely soured the hopes of more than a few. Tell me about her."

"About who?"

She shot him a disgusted sister look. "Don't be coy. About Morgan. She frightens me. And amuses me. And makes me want to know her better all at the same time. How did you two meet?"

"At a military ball in Edinburgh last winter."

"See, so you do dance."

"No. That's what brought us together. Our mutual disinclination to shuffle about the floor, looking ridiculous. We found each other behind a forest of potted palms, hiding from the crowd."

He smiled, remembering back to that long-ago night. The way Morgan's eyes sparkled with mischief, then deepened with a hint of the reckless passion that brought her days later to his rooms. His bed.

Then as now, there'd been no flirtatious conniving. No false pretense. She'd desired him. He'd found her irresistible. And they'd become lovers.

"I'd wanted you to meet someone. He'll be there." Euna's words brought him back with a thump.

"That sounds ominous."

"His name's Henry Lisle. He's a stepson to Lord Bruton."

"I don't like him already." The Earl of Bruton's tastes ran to racing, gambling, and women, not necessarily in that order. Fortunately he had the wealth as well as the character to know just how close to play his game without losing his shirt. Any relation of his was someone to watch—especially if that relation were making eyes at his little sister.

"Beast. Henry's not at all like his stepfather. He's gallant and honorable and as respectable as a church mouse."

"And poor as one too, I imagine. Bruton's got three sons of his own to spend his blunt on."

Euna huffed. "You're as bad as Uncle Josh."

Being compared to his uncle? Talk about frightening.

The door opened again. This time on his uncle's sober countenance. "Don't tell me. You've brought home another wife. A love child, perhaps?" He jerked his head toward Euna, and she rose in a flurry of skirts, leaving Cam behind with a final pleading look for restraint.

Cam sketched a bow, any momentary peace wiped out with one black look from his uncle. "I came to tell you I wouldn't be attending the Abercrombie rout."

"It wasn't a request."

"I'm aware of that. But unless you're wearing a general's uniform under that outfit, I'm not forced to bow to your command. Not anymore."

"How about a major's uniform?"

Instantly on his guard, Cam waited to see where this was going. "Sir?"

His uncle drew himself up. Still a good six inches short of Cam's height, he seemed to fill the room with his presence. "The woman living under your roof is not your wife but your latest mistress. Is that true?"

Like a physical blow to the chest, his uncle's question knocked Cam back, drove the air from his lungs. His first thought was Brodie. The big, cabbage-headed jaw-me-dead had let something slip. But no, Brodie was the soul of discretion. As many beds as he hopped in and out of, he had to be. "What makes you come to that conclusion?" Cam brazened.

"A letter I received. The latest Mrs. Sinclair is really a young Cornish woman of dubious reputation and lax morals. Can you deny it?"

Only a handful of people knew the truth of Morgan's identity. But only one person came to mind with enough motive to throw him to the wolves by revealing the secret. What the hell was Eddis playing at?

His uncle pinched the bridge of his nose. Squeezed his eyes as he fought for control. When he opened them, he'd swallowed whatever anger he'd shown. "I've known you to get into the worst sort of scrapes. And I've tried to make allowances for your behavior. After all, your father was a volatile hellion, and you've always held more than a comfortable share of his nature. The only one of your siblings to do so, thank heaven." He offered Cam a weak smile. "But to establish your mistress in a place of honor within your household. Parade her in front of the world as a wife. That I cannot let stand. If those in high positions found out, they'd—"

"Add it to my long list of supposed crimes?" Anger soured his stomach. "Damn it, Uncle Josh. Can't you see I don't care anymore what they think of me? I just want to be left in peace."

His uncle—as usual—ignored Cam's rough tone. Glossed over it with soothing words. "I want you at the Abercrombies', Cam. I've someone I want you to meet."

"Let me guess. Henry Lisle."

"That popinjay? Euna's been bending your ear with her nonsense, has she? No. I can handle young Lisle. It's Mrs. Kennett-Holmes. After hearing about you, she's anxious to make your acquaintance."

"Kennett-Holmes. Wasn't he an intimate of Sir Robert Peele's? The man must have been seventy when he finally died."

"That's him. His widow's barely twenty-five, though. And left rich as cream."

"I don't need the money."

"No, but she's political connections of her own. Those relationships could make or break Sinclair whiskey. Among the family's other holdings."

"So I'm the bull staked out to lure in the cash cow?" He couldn't keep the edge of bitterness from his voice. Didn't even try.

"You're asked to think of the family and do what's right."

Cam had heard enough. What his uncle asked of him was another empty marriage. More long years of playing the London game. Not this time. The farmstead in Strathconon pulled him northward. He'd not give up the call for the dubious charms and fortune of Mrs. Kennett-Holmes. Not even to repair frayed family relationships. He started for the door. "There's no more to be said. Good day, Uncle."

His hand had barely gripped the knob when his uncle's answer curdled his innards. "I'll ruin her, Cam."

The knob went slippery in his hand, sweat springing out on his palms, chilling his skin. He turned slowly back as if he'd not understood.

His uncle stood solid as a mountain in the middle of the room, his arms crossed in defiance, his face pale but set in rigid lines. "I'd hoped to avoid stooping to this. Hoped you'd see the wisdom of attaching yourself to a woman of Sally Kennett-Holmes's caliber. She could take you far."

"I don't want to be taken anywhere. And not by her."

Uncle Josh sighed. "It's for your own good. If you won't see the wisdom of this match, think of Miss Bligh. That's her name, isn't it? Think of her. She'll be ruined."

"Blackmail? You wouldn't dare."

Uncle Josh spread his hands as if in apology. "I know you think I'm being harsh. But I'm tired of watching you distance yourself from the life rightly due you by your name and position. Memories are short in this town. It wouldn't take much to be welcomed back. You need a wife." He paused before letting the final shoe drop. "Miss Bligh needs my silence."

"One thing I don't need is a wife."

As if he felt he'd crossed too far over the line, his uncle withdrew. Sought conciliation. "How about this? Come. Speak with her. Play the war hero bit. If things work out, consider the possibility of remarriage."

Cam felt the weight of Uncle Josh's expectation like a noose around his neck. His throat went dry, the blood pushing its sluggish way through a body suddenly cold.

His uncle let him stew before nudging. "Well, Cam? What's it to be?"

"I'll be there." He chewed the words like glass.

Uncle Josh turned his attention to the correspondence on his desk, effectively dismissing Cam. His parting words, "And without the martyred attitude, I hope."

Cam's vision went red, fury uncoiling with whiplike speed. "I said I'd be there. Beyond that, don't push your luck." He heard his response as if coming from another's mouth—overloud and rough with emotion. But it was the expression of shock on his uncle's face that set Cam's heart racing. Sent him stumbling heartsick and shaking from the house.

Because until then he hadn't known how close to murder he'd come.

Chapter 23

Morgan escaped the growing claustrophobia of the town house for the freedom of London's streets. Though freedom might not be the most suitable word choice. She'd felt the disapproving eyes of at least half a dozen passersby as she'd walked the short distance to Green Park alone. As if she couldn't risk stepping into the street without fear of being clubbed over the head and sold to white slavers. Or worse—exchanging unchaperoned words with a man unrelated to her by blood or marriage.

She pursed her lips, stared down the worst of the offenders, while folding herself deeper into the collar of her spencer to avoid the rest. This was just the sort of confining restrictions that made the remote wilderness of Skye so appealing. A freedom from expectations. From duty.

But duty to what? To whom? And what kind of freedom was she really looking for? When had the oath of fealty to the *Amhas-draoi* become like a stone about her middle, weighing her down? Taking away choices she didn't know she'd had.

Picking a rock from the leaf-strewn path beneath her feet, she kicked it out ahead of her. Followed it, kicking it again.

What did Cam want? The pebble skipped ahead. Rolled to the verge.

What did she want? This time it ended amid a group of stones. She recognized its shape. Knocked it on farther.

Could she give up one dream to pursue another? Kick. Follow.

Take that leap of faith that a life with Cam wouldn't be the drudgery and grind Scathach warned her it would be? Follow. Kick.

That they could find a way to fit their worlds together. Mold them into something new. Something greater than the individual pieces.

She'd seen that kind of love. A love that allowed for all things. That gave as much as it took. Her cousin Conor had found it with his wife, Ellery. They'd beaten back every obstacle to be with each other—including death. If they could do it, mayhap she and Cam could make it work as well.

This time, the pebble skipped and bounced, rolling into the grass. Lost among the piles of leaves and autumn bracken. And Morgan gave it up as gone. Dropped with a sigh onto a bench to let these whirling thoughts settle, take root.

The easy autumn weather had turned cold, the air carrying an icy crispness that froze her breath, made her nose run. Half-naked trees stabbed limbs of gold and red and green into the gray sky, their tops lost in the low smoke from thousands of coal fires and fog off the river. Ice rimed the edges of puddles and spread a spiderweb of lace across the park's reservoir. But not even this glimpse of beauty could blot out the jostle and rub of so many people. So many *Other*. All crushed within the span of miles. All pounding against her skull like the drone of a million bees.

Could she live here? Would she lose Cam if she couldn't?

She pulled off a glove, twisted the wolf-head ring as if she could channel her family's communal wisdom through it. If only Gram were here to talk to. Or Jamys. He always managed to cut through to the heart of a problem. Morgan was all emotion. Driven by feelings. Never by common sense. So was this a case of passion over practicality? Or had her mind simply caught up with her heart?

It was the sound that alerted her first. The far-off echo of a perfect round note. Then another. And soon, the faint chime of bells surrounded her. Coming from nowhere and everywhere.

A movement caught the corner of her vision. Figures passing through the trees nearby. Indistinct, almost murky, the outline of their bodies blurred and ghostlike.

She knew that sound. The sensation of time and place folding in upon itself. Her body's heightened sensitivity as if she were one big funny bone.

No disapproving Londoners this time.

Oh, to be that simple.

Morgan pressed her hands palm-down onto the frozen stone of the bench. Felt the chill through her gloves. The scratch of her stockings. The rock that had worked its way into her left boot. All real. As real as the true *Fey* passing like shades through the park. As real as the bells clanging in her head like a toll of doom.

Scathach had lost control.

The *Fey* had breached the walls.

She followed the disappearing figures, breaking into a run to catch them before they left the security of the heavy trees for the edge of the park. The nearest roads. Her chance to question them lost once they crossed away into the city.

"You," she shouted, grabbing the shoulder of the last *Fey* in the group of three, the zing of his touch cracking the air like thunder.

He turned, his raven hair tossing in anger, his silver eyes flashing a warning. He bore the same crystalline elegance of all true *Fey*, a brittle surface beauty that hid the cruel arrogance marking all their race. "You risk much to approach me as equal, *Other*."

The insult tore through Morgan's lingering hesitations. She faced him, calling on her own high blood to match him spark for spark. "I approach you as one of Scathach's own. You owe me respect if nothing else."

His gaze registered shock, but his manner remained as superior as ever. "*Amhas-draoi*? 'Twas your order's failures that have reduced us to hunting the *Duinedon* lands in search of the sword."

"A sword Andraste lost. Not us."

His mouth twisted into a sneer of contempt. "Lost? Stolen, you mean. And by one of yours. Your task is over, *Amhas-draoi*. Leave this to us. We will find the sword. And the *Other* responsible for its theft."

"I'll get you your sword. And, Doran. I only need a few days more."

"There are no more days to give. Andraste senses *Neuvarvaan*'s power building. The *Other* wielding it does not understand the *Morkoth* forces at work. They will consume him in the end, but by then it will be too late. He will have unleashed an evil not easily checked or turned back."

She wanted to argue. To fight their arrival tooth and nail. But already she sensed the stares of nearby strollers. The cocked brows and mumbled whispers. To them, she spoke to naught but wind and sky. They couldn't see the *Fey* hovering like spirits. Moving with impunity through their world. Not yet. But if Doran weren't stopped soon, they would. And by then, the collision between *Fey* and *Duinedon* would be irreversible. The harm almost as great as an army of Undying under the command of a madman.

No. Right now, they saw nothing. Only a madwoman. And mayhap, she was.

She'd actually been contemplating walking away from the

Amhas-draoi. Straight into Cam's open arms. But there'd be no arms. No world where she or any *Other* might live with any sense of freedom if she didn't hold firm now.

The *Fey* sought to pull away from her and join the others already heading into the street, but she jerked him back. Caught and held his swirling iridescent gaze, though it cost her a headache to do so. "The *Duinedon* colonel and I will find the sword. I swear on my life. Tell your mistress that."

He bowed, but didn't look convinced.

Despite her firm words, neither was she.

"You're still studying Lord Delvish's book?"

Morgan wheeled around, her heart in her throat, shocked she'd allowed anyone to sneak up on her. Even Cam, though she'd come to acknowledge that in ways unmagical his talents rivaled her own.

He put up his hands in mock surrender. "I'm unarmed, I swear."

He leaned against the door, but it was obvious he worked at this pose of nonchalance. A boiling storm gathered at the darkest edges of his gaze, and his jaw jumped with suppressed anger.

Rubbing her temples, Morgan put aside Uncle Owen's book. She'd been reading for hours. Puzzling out the arcane language, the faded diagrams, the riddles within stories within puzzles that marked so many of the old texts. The basic idea seemed simple enough. It was the execution that brought on the headache.

"It doesn't look as if your uncle accepted your regrets."

"I'll be spending a few hours at the Abercrombies'." When she opened her mouth to argue, his gaze warned her she spoke at her own risk. "I don't want to. I have to. There's a difference. We'll adjust, Morgan."

"Adjust? The board's set. The pieces are moving, and

you're going to step away for a night of hobnobbing with the best and brightest? It's not a matter of adjusting. It's insanity."

Cam's face went hard as stone, his hands tightening to instant fists. But whatever he thought to say, he bit back. Instead, he crossed to the hearth, slowly uncurling his palms to warm them over the fire.

"I've seen them, Cam. The true *Fey* are crossing over. And their numbers will only grow as Andraste's patience wanes until there won't be any stopping them. No barriers the *Amhas-draoi* erect will hold them back."

He spun to face her. "You've seen them? Where? Why didn't you warn me?" His questions came like bullets.

"In Green Park. Others moving east on the streets toward the river. More fanning north toward Regent's Park. For now groups of twos and threes. But it's only beginning."

He rubbed his chin, his gaze trained inward as if he was considering. "It complicates things, but there's no help for it. I have to go tomorrow night."

She waited for his reasoning. Even a halfhearted excuse. His uncle's tyranny. His aunt's pleading. His sister playing the guilt card. What had caused him to reverse course? To decide that a night out in the company of his old London friends was more important than ending the looming threat of Doran and his mastery of *Neuvarvaan*'s black magics? Or worse in her mind, a dropping of the walls as the true *Fey* sought to succeed where she and Cam failed?

The silence grew, the air charged with suppressed emotion and anger.

She broke first. "Very well. If you go, I go."

"No."

"Excuse me?" She cocked her head, unsure if she'd misunderstood. Hoping she'd misunderstood.

"No, I said. I go alone." Misery stamped his features.

But a rough-edged misery that didn't allow for comfort or even question.

"Well, if we're supposed to be newly married, won't it seem a bit strange if you show up without me?" She tried to sound reasonable. Conciliatory. It wouldn't help to lose her temper. Cam was doing that enough for the both of them.

"I need to do this alone, Morgan. It's not about you and me. It's about my uncle, and he's warned me that bringing you is not part of the bargain."

Now they were getting somewhere. "What sort of bargain?"

He shrugged. "Forget it."

"I think I'm entitled to know what your family thinks of me."

He braced his hands on the mantel, his gaze focused on the fire as if he couldn't—or wouldn't—face her. "Uncle Josh has asked that I come without you."

"I see."

And she did.

Like an icy dousing, his words froze straight through to the pathetic part of her that wanted to be part of that glittering world. Yearned for his love. And wasn't that just more proof of her own pathetic wishy-washiness? She was supposed to be hard as nails. A fighter. An *Amhas-draoi*. Not some debutante in search of a suitable husband.

She squared her shoulders, laced her fingers together in her lap. Fought to regain the warrior mantle slipping from her shoulders.

His scalding gaze met her new cool remoteness. "You think I want to go? Or that I think those things?"

She kept silent. Afraid she might reveal the truth.

It only angered him further.

He grabbed her by the arms, hauling her roughly to her feet, his grip almost painful. What she saw in his face set her back. A glimpse of that part of him he kept chained within.

Released only at peril to his sanity. It swam close to the surface. Howled for escape. "Answer me, damn you."

She let his rage wash over her. Remained as untouchable as her heart. "You want an answer? I'll give you one. I thought I could do this, Cam. I thought I could separate myself like an egg. A part of me for Scathach. A part of me for you. But I can't. I need to commit with all my soul. Be it the *Amhasdraoi*. Or you. And I chose my path long ago."

He stood erect as if he faced an executioner, grim-faced but resigned. As if he'd known this was coming. And wasn't surprised.

She hardened herself to the inevitable. "I think it's as well you seek out your own kind. We're too different, Cam. And I'm not in the market for a man. Not even one as tempting as you."

Her arms remained captured in his grip, his face so close that she need only lean forward to brush her lips against his. His body hummed with slow-fading anger and a tension that held him rigid, his steel-blue gaze impenetrable. "I don't believe you. I'm this close to you, and I don't believe you."

She frowned, wishing away the heat pooling deep within her. "My body may desire you, but my heart is my own."

He released her, almost flinging her away from him as if he couldn't bear to be near her now. "You can say the words, Morgan. But I know you feel it. It's more than lust. More than the bump and grind of two people pleasuring each other. I've had that. Know what it feels like." He plowed a hand through his hair. "This is more." He let out a disgusted breath. Flung himself toward the door. "Forget it. You'll come to your senses or you won't. I just hope I'm still around when it happens."

"And where would you be? Off with your high-in-the-instep London friends?" God, she sounded petty. Childish, even. What the hell was happening to her? She felt as if the old Morgan were cracking to pieces. Every new Cam-inspired emotion another body blow to the woman she thought she was. The woman she had to be if she was going to succeed before the *Fey* did.

He smashed a fist against the jamb. Closed his eyes and inhaled a deep breath in an effort to calm himself. Letting it out slowly, he fixed her with a grim stare. "According to your uncle, I don't live to see the end of this battle, Morgan. I become a creature of the sword. An Undying."

Like a slap to the face, she came up short. Uncle Owen? "What did he tell you?"

"He foretold my death—or should I say my rebirth?—as an Undying."

Her throat closed, her mouth suddenly parchment dry. "No. It's a mistake. It can't be . . ."

He shrugged. "I may live forever, Morgan. But I won't wait forever. Not even for you."

Amos bustled in, carrying a second decanter and glasses, his displeasure clear. Seeing him looking round for a place to set down his burden, Cam lifted his head. "You can put it here," he said, clearing a place on the table by his chair, pushing the books, papers, and a hideous dish of Sevres china to the floor with a crash.

The dish survived. Too bad.

It had been one of a set Charlotte had purchased shortly after their wedding during her buy-her-way-to-happiness phase. Expensive, but ultimately harmless. A shame she'd given it up for less benign means of making him pay.

And now Uncle Josh asked him to set his foot in the trap again. With a woman he'd never met whose only appeal lay in her political affiliations and the funds she had invested on the Change.

"Thank you, Amos. That'll be all for tonight." Amos

seemed hesitant to leave him alone, so Cam lowered his best officer's glower on his hovering servant. "I said, good night."

Amos knew when arguing was fruitless, part of the reason he made such a good valet. So giving a curt, wordless nod, he left. Only the firm closing of the door evidence of his disapproval.

Left alone, Cam poured out a glass of whiskey. Downed it without pause. Refilled the glass, the second one following just as quickly. After the first blast of throat-burning fire, the whiskey's heat sang through him, relaxing muscles, loosening the taut knot in the pit of his stomach.

His uncle had him by the balls. Wouldn't hesitate to twist if he thought it in Cam's best interest. He hadn't told Morgan about his uncle's threat. Or about the woman who awaited his best all-women-love-a-uniform chivalry.

Why bother?

She remained determined to keep a distance between them—a distance that seemed laughable when they'd already shared so much. But a distance uncloseable despite his best efforts. He needed to stop tilting at windmills and accept the inevitable. He and Morgan weren't meant for each other.

And did it matter now? Lord Delvish had foreseen Cam's death at Doran's hands. A living death as a creature that could never die. Could never be killed.

What Delvish had not foreseen was whether Cam lived on in defeat as one of Doran's puppets or if the *Amhas-draoi* was defeated, the price being that Cam remained trapped evermore. An immortal doomed to see those around him perish as he lingered on to the ends of the world.

Could he watch Morgan age while he remained young? Could he hold her in his arms as she died? As his children died? And his children's children?

A thought to drive anyone to drink.

Cam pressed the heels of his hands to his eyes, wishing himself in the flagstoned parlor of his grandfather's little house in Strathconon. Imagining the tang of a peat fire, his gran-da's cheerful whistle as he sat blanketed in the Windsor chair by the hearth, his hands working in a flurry of carving.

As his dream took shape, the reality shifted until past and future melded into a single vision. Gran-da's eyes warm with affection as he talked to the woman in the chair across from him, her red-gold hair brilliantly lit by the fire's glow, her head resting on her elbows as she laughed at something the old man had said.

Their voices rose and fell as they shared stories and exchanged information, Gran-da nodding from time to time as she confirmed what he'd always assumed, but never been able to prove.

He looked up, his piercing blue eyes excited. "Ye see, lad? It's just as I told ye. The divide between *Fey* and *Duinedon* isn't a wall of stone and mortar. 'Tis a veil of silk, a swirl of mist, a ripple upon a mountain pool. All it takes is the desire to see past the end of our noses, to believe in a world we can't ken for certain except in dreams or through sheer good fortune."

Cam sighed, his own voice tired, his whole body weary from battling Uncle Josh's sticky manipulations. Lord Delvish's Sight. "You're a result of too much whiskey and not enough sleep."

Gran-da chuckled, his knife a blur and flash of silver as he worked, the ghostly apparition of Strathconon's cozy parlor superimposed over the elegance of the London salon. Almost blotting it out. Even Gran-da seemed more solid. And younger. No longer the feeble old man held by aching joints to the warmth of his hearth. Instead, he bore the booming voice and thick, dark hair Cam remembered from his childhood. "'Tis for certain I'd nae be visiting if ye weren't in the proper frame of mind, but I'm as real as your love for the lass. And ye do love her, ye know."

"Does it matter now? I'll let her go. It's that or stand by while Uncle Josh destroys her in his bid to save me."

"She doesn't look like a lass to be frightened by the likes of your uncle."

"No, but in this, no amount of *Fey* blood will help. She'll be dragged through the mud, her family with her. I won't let that happen to Morgan or to the Blighs. I've only met them briefly, but they deserve better than that."

"And ye think your uncle would go through with such a villainous plan? Ruin a young woman simply to aid his nephew?"

Cam plowed both hands through his hair, hung his head. "I don't know. But I can't risk it. You didn't see him, Gran-da. He looked pretty determined. He just might think he's doing the right thing. After all, he doesn't know Morgan. Doesn't understand."

Gran-da sat back, the results of his carving complete. The rough figure of a woman lay in the palm of his hand, a faint smile touching her lips, her hair a graceful curve disappearing into the flow of her gown. Like all his grandfather's work, the unfinished edges and rough-hewn surfaces contained a simple beauty that never failed to bring a tingle of delight. He placed the tiny statuette on the table beside him. Leaned back into his chair as if the effort had exhausted him. Closing his eyes, he curled his hands around the armrests. Age again lining his craggy face. "There's only one way to thwart your uncle in his plans. And 'tis simple as working that wood there."

Cam raised a doubtful brow. "And what would that be?"

The warmth of the fire disappeared in a cold draft that whistled down the chimney. The air went dim and smoky, Strathconon's parlor fading, Gran-da growing faint and wavery.

Cam squeezed his eyes shut tight, willing the comfort of his grandfather's presence back. It was his dream. He could make it continue if he chose. But like an outrushing tide, the images thinned until only the scent of his grandfather's pipe remained. "Wait. You haven't told me how to stop Uncle Josh."

The fire leapt back to life, coal shifting and crackling in the grate. Snatching Cam from his doze even as his grandfather's booming voice leapt into his mind like the crash of surf. "Give truth to your tale, lad. Marry her."

Cam's eyes flew open. The room dark, save for the flickering hearth and a much-melted candle at his elbow—the decanter half empty, his glass wholly empty. His head pounded with drink and echoed with his grandfather's words. A crush of longing for the old man hit him with the force of a blow, made him glance with useless hope at the chair beside him.

It was then his mouth went dry, his whole body trembling with fear, disbelief, and renewed loss. He reached for the wooden carving half expecting it to disappear before his eyes, but it remained as solid as the rest of the room, as real as the churning in his stomach and the cold sweat damping his skin. Rubbing his thumb over the woman's face, he couldn't help but smile. The long cheekbones, the arched brows, the smile that could be sly or inviting depending upon her mood. His grandfather had caught them all.

Pocketing the figure, he looked deep into the fire. Sighed. "If only it were that easy, Gran-da. Why not advise me to shift the heavens? Change fate? Morgan's right. Our relationship was star-crossed from the beginning. A fool's hope."

Whether the voice in his head was his own or his gran-da's, he never knew. "Aye, a fool may hope, lad. But his hope is never foolish."

Chapter 24

She watched from the top of the stairs as Amos fussed over the shine of Cam's gold braid, the placement of his dress sword on his hip, the gloss of his boots. He'd been buffed and polished for the drawing room, yet the smoke and thunder of the battlefield still clung to him, evident in the glacial blue light in his eyes, the precision of his warrior's movements.

It had been this way in Edinburgh too. One of the reasons she'd allowed herself to be seduced. She'd recognized the aura of danger surrounding him. And understood it as none of his pretty pastel admirers had. To them, he'd been a hero—dashing, handsome, fascinating. To her, he'd been a man—gorgeous, courageous, and potentially deadly. Though she'd not known exactly how deadly until recently. Or how he struggled with that lethal skill.

As she thought back on it, her heart gave an unexpected jump. She felt the jolt like a burn beneath her breast. Wished she were the woman to help him come to grips with his war between instinct and honor. But still she couldn't make herself go down to him. Couldn't speak for the emotions choking her throat.

Like a schoolgirl too young to be included, she watched

through the railing. Hoped he'd look up so she could turn away with an angry toss of her head.

Childish, but satisfying.

As if he sensed her, he did look up, his gaze unreadable. But for that one moment, she read fatigue and sorrow in the heavy stoop of his broad shoulders, the lines drawing his face into a stern mask. And she remembered the admission he'd thrown at her so carelessly. An Undying. A child of the sword *Neuvarvaan*. She'd not see that happen. Not while she had breath in her body. He might not be hers, but he'd live to be someone's. She'd make sure of that.

"I'll be back as soon as I can get away." When she didn't answer, he sighed. "You gave me your word. You'd do as I say. No arguments."

How like him to bring that up. Did he have to hit her over the head with that ridiculous agreement? This didn't count as part of that deal. She'd agreed to abide by his rules when it came to fighting Doran. Not so that she could watch him gild himself for the London *ton* while she sat at home.

"Morgan? Before I go, can I ask you one thing?"

Her heart snapped shut, and she did it. Turned away. Never heard his question.

Spent the rest of the evening wishing she had.

The lanterns flanking the Abercrombie town house shone on the glittering crowds of guests as they disembarked from the steady stream of sedan chairs and carriages. In a London thin of company, Lord and Lady Abercrombie's party stood out as the place to see and be seen.

Inside, liveried footmen bowed the perfumed, powdered, and diamond-encrusted men and women into the grand hall, while pages in silk knee breeches and stockings dashed through the crush with drinks and trays of savories.

Brodie looked up from between two adoring matrons and their starstruck daughters. Considered too poor to be a prize of the marriage mart, he still generated sighs and heavy fanning as well as the occasional illicit liaison.

Excusing himself, he pushed his way through the crush toward Cam. From the opposite end of the room, his uncle spied him as well. He also made his way over, though his way was eased by his importance while Brodie used simple bulk.

They arrived at the same moment, his uncle sizing him up as if inspecting a steer for slaughter. "Glad to see you understood the wisdom of my request."

"Let's not confuse requests and threats, Uncle."

The words rolled off Uncle Josh's back as they always did. It was like boxing a shadow. "Mrs. Kennett-Holmes is in the next room."

Brodie raised a curious brow. "Kennett-Holmes? Isn't she one of those evangelical do-gooders with a taste for the sermonizing of 'Holy Hannah'?"

Uncle Josh settled a cool gaze on his fosterling. "She's an upstanding Christian, yes, Captain MacKay. Some men prefer their women with a few morals."

Brodie gave a shudder of revulsion. "Sounds dreadful." But he kept needling, bless him. "Does Mrs. Kennett-Holmes know there's a rival to Cam's affections? Can't see that going over too well."

"Cam knows his purpose here. And it's not to be swayed by your dubious influences."

Brodie hid a smile behind his glass of wine. "Just asking, sir."

"Well, stop asking. And go about your business. Surely there's some gullible female waiting to be swayed by your charms into a dalliance. So go find her, and leave us alone."

Brodie bowed and withdrew, almost colliding with a gentleman as they both sought to navigate the narrow doorway into the next room. A gentleman Cam recognized as the pasty-faced bore from Uncle Josh's house. But he'd seen him somewhere else as well. Only where?

"I'm leaving you on your own to sweeten the woman up. I've got to return to your aunt or she's liable to think something's happened to me."

Cam eyed his uncle coolly. "Worried over your health?"

"Hardly. I was set upon by a footpad last night on the way home from my club. The villain got in a blow before a crowd scared him off. But now she's got it in her bonnet someone's out to get me."

Now that he mentioned it, Cam noted the slight swelling around his uncle's right eye, masked by copious amounts of powder. A frisson of warning shot through him. But warning of what? Footpads were common, and his uncle's habit of walking rather than hiring a cab made him an easy target of such an attack. So why did Cam feel as if the first shot in his private war had been fired? "Did you get a look at your attacker?"

"I'd rather have gotten a stab at him. He'd have thought twice before attacking a Sinclair again." His uncle motioned him forward. "Enough stalling. Mrs. Kennett-Holmes awaits. I've told her all about you, and she's anxious to make your acquaintance."

Cam would lay odds the man his uncle had described bore little resemblance to the man he was. No woman in her right mind would take him knowing the truth.

He bore the heart of a killer. Ached to win the heart of an Amazon.

Morgan's wards gave her half a minute's warning before the attack came. And that was being generous.

One moment she'd been whiling away the too-quiet hours with a year-old racing magazine, counting the monotonous ticks of the mantel clock, and wishing she hadn't sent Amos and Susan away for the evening. At least they'd have been company.

The next moment, the air shifted. Grew thick as if the oppressive weight of a thunderstorm approached. A tingle rose the hairs on her neck as if lightning danced across her skin. And with the might of a thunderclap, the broached wards imploded followed by the splintering of a smashed door.

To come for her like this took force. And magic. Lots of it.

Doran hadn't sent someone to fail.

Morgan tore out of the study, skidding to a stop in the foyer just as a pistol blast erupted, the bullet ripping straight across her upper arm, scoring a deep, bloody weal that hurt all the way to her fingers. Biting back a scream, she clutched the wound. Ducked into the study, risking a quick glance to judge her attacker.

He approached from the kitchens, power rippling off him in sour waves. He stank of darkness. And *Morkoth* magic. And she saw her own death mirrored in his evil gaze.

Tossing aside the gun, he drew a sword. Dipped it in a mockery of a salute just before he charged her position, the slash of his weapon barely hampered by the confines of the narrow corridor.

With a desperate flick of her fingers, she released her spell. Felt the tightening of his airways, the crush of his lungs as she squeezed the life from him with the strength of her own sorcery.

He stumbled against the stairs, his face blanched white, shock and a new fear flickering in the dark hollows of his empty eyes.

She didn't give him time to adjust. But hammered him again and again. Each successive draw of her magic enough to keep him off-kilter with no way to defend himself against the onslaught.

His sword fell from a numb hand. Clattered and bounced across the floor.

Blood ribboned its way down her arm. Dripped from sticky fingers. Her whole body throbbed with every beat of her heart, but she willed the pain away. Ignored the black spots narrowing her vision. The dizziness sapping her strength. She needed to end this fight. Before he had time to regroup. React.

And that's when he struck.

Cam used the explosion of a dropped tray of glasses to make good his escape. Mrs. Kennett-Holmes followed the laughter and jibes, craning her neck to find the source of the accident. And before she turned back, he'd vanished.

To his right, Aunt Sylvie sat in company with a group of dowagers, their tongues and fans going a mile a minute. From the room behind him, his uncle's booming voice sounded. No help in that direction.

The gardens were his last best hope.

He threaded his way onto the terrace. Down the stone steps onto the lawn.

Couples strolled the paths. Knots of men and women enjoying a respite from overheated rooms inside. One such couple looked unnervingly familiar, the behemoth dressed to kill in full military regalia arm in arm with a slip of a girl, her glossy curls gleaming silver-blond in the guttering torches. What the hell was Euna doing alone with Brodie? And more importantly, what the hell was Brodie thinking separating Euna from the respectability of her chaperones?

The idea that sprang to mind, he dismissed immediately. Brodie liked it easy. Entanglements with married women who knew the rules of the game were one thing. Playing with the emotions of the uninitiated was something else. And foster brother or no, Cam would tear Brodie's head from his shoulders if he dared try his tricks with Euna.

"The party is that way," he growled, coming up behind them.

"Cameron." Euna started with a guilty flush, while Brodie

remained unfazed by Cam's surly arrival. "The captain came with me to get some air."

Brodie offered the smile of the innocent. "Euna was being pestered by the usual bunch of Bond Street beaux the Abercrombies rely on to fill out these drab affairs."

"And you just happened to be there to play knight-errant."

Amusement lit his eyes. "I admit I had my own angle."

Cam nodded, a slow burn forming in his chest. Clawing its way up his throat. He couldn't believe it. Brodie wouldn't be low enough to seduce Euna—someone as close as a sister to him? Would he? But then he and Brodie had had few chances to connect in the last years. War had split them apart. Tossed them into different regiments. Different circumstances. The time apart had changed Cam. Mayhap Brodie had altered as well. And not for the good.

Cam faced off against him. A convenient outlet for a rage he'd been unable to vent. Menace formed his stance. Fury fired his gaze. "You bloody great bastard."

Euna paled and stepped back, her mouth a perfect O of astonishment.

Brodie's eyes widened. "Ye dinna think . . . ye can't imagine . . ." He laughed. Clouted him on the shoulder. "Hell, Cam. Euna's like my own sister. Save your fireworks for someone else. I'm not the enemy."

Brodie stating it like that made Cam feel foolish, though uncertainty hovered in the corners of Brodie's gaze as he defended himself. A startled surprise that had nothing to do with Cam's sneaking up on them. His white-hot boil lowered to a simmer, though he wasn't willing to let go of all his anger. It felt good. Better than the desperate need dogging him for weeks. "So then, why are you out here?"

"I've been telling ye. Euna's been plagued by sycophants. The sharks smell fresh Sinclair blood in the water."

"And you just happened to be the one to swoop in and rescue her?"

A guilty flush stole up Brodie's neck, his gaze hard with an unspoken message.

"Well, MacKay?" Cam pushed, ignoring Brodie's attempt to dodge the question.

Brodie shrugged. "Fine. If ye must know, I was avoiding a certain lady of my acquaintance. She's been a bit"—he searched for the word—"persistent in her attentions."

Cam's anger rushed out of him with a whoosh of spent breath. Of course. Leave it to Brodie to avoid an embarrassing scene with an old lover. Though London must be littered with such by this time. If he weren't careful, he'd be spending all his days hiding from such "persistent" acquaintances.

"Why didn't Morgan come with you tonight, Cam?" Euna asked, the clumsy attempt at changing the subject welcome to everybody.

He snatched at the first excuse he thought of. "She's unwell."

"I don't like her."

Cam's hard gaze fixed unwavering on his sister. "Excuse me?"

She held her ground, but Cam noted how her hand tightened on Brodie's arm. "Mrs. Kennett-Holmes. I don't like her."

"She's not for you—or me—to like or not like. What's important is that Uncle Josh likes her."

She lifted her chin. A hint of the Sinclair stubbornness in the jut of her jaw, the flash in her blue eyes. "He thinks he knows what's best for you, Cam. He thinks he knows what's best for everyone." Her gaze flicked to Brodie, then embarrassed as if she'd revealed too much, she dropped her gaze to her slippers. "He doesn't know anything."

* * *

Mage energy ripped through Morgan, frying every nerve, crushing her skull as if he cracked an egg. She dropped to her knees. Clutched her head as if she could keep her brains from oozing out. Glanced up in time to see him diving for the weapon.

Throwing herself forward, she fought to reach it first. Her fingers barely touched the cold knob of the hilt before he kicked it from her grasp. The metal clang as it spun end over end into the drawing room, echoing through her pounding head.

Dragging a dagger from its sheath, her attacker aimed it at her exposed back.

She spun. And spun again. Avoiding the downward plunge. The fire in her wounded arm. Coming to her feet with the quickness of a cat.

Closing her eyes, she whispered forth a new attack. Felt the invisible bonds reach for him. Hold him fast.

Then with deliberate slowness—in part to concentrate on the binding spell, in part to keep her wobbly head on her shoulders—she bent to retrieve the sword. Her hand curling around the hilt bringing instant reassurance. It wasn't her weapon. But it was a weapon. And with it, the tables turned. Instant control.

She approached—close enough his mage energy enveloped her like a poison cloud. Close enough to let him see the depth of her power as an *Amhas-draoi* and know he'd been bested.

"Where's Doran?" she demanded, capturing his gaze. Refusing to let him break the contact.

"Fuck you." His breathing came fast as he struggled. His fists clenched, and Morgan knew if he managed to get them around her neck, she'd be dead in seconds.

"Is that any way to talk to a lady?"

"You're nothing more than that *Duinedon* colonel's whore."

She didn't take the bait, though his words slid beneath her

well-armored exterior. Pinched the place in her that wondered if that wasn't just what she'd become. A well-armed mistress. "I'll ask you again—where's Doran?"

A cruel smile lit his eyes; his face went hard. And he made the move she'd anticipated yet underestimated.

Had Doran been giving bloody lessons?

The man not only held power, he knew just how to wield it effectively. The binding spell unraveled and with it her hold on the situation. He sprang, his hands going for her throat.

With only one arm, she could do little to hold him off. Instinct brought her own hand up in defense, the sword extended. With momentum behind him there was no time to stop or even slow. The blade's point drove into him. Through him.

The wet sucking plunge of the weapon roared in Morgan's ears, the actions spinning out into slow motion so that the changing expressions on his face—shock, pain, terror, and the slow gray of death—imprinted themselves on her brain. An instant forever memory to haunt her nights for years to come.

He fell sideways. Gravity wrenching the embedded sword from her grip.

He clawed the curtains, the chair. Reached for her as if she could hold off death. Pull him back from the oblivion awaiting him.

And in the moment when life left him, the rage, the hate, the venom poisoning his soul fell away and left a man. Scared. Pitiful. Wanting only the comfort of not dying alone.

Had he deserved such a death? Had Doran lied to him? Tricked him into believing his cause was just? If she'd been better skilled, could she have avoided taking his life? The questions whirled through her tender brain. Unanswerable. But imperative.

Morgan stood, chest heaving, shaking, incapable of looking away from the sprawled figure, bleeding his life into the carpet.

Her mind cleared as if a giant hand had wiped it clean. She swallowed over and over. Tried taking a deep breath, her nose and mouth filling with the acrid metal tang of blood and sweat and excrement. Her stomach clenched, making her heave.

Wiping a hand across her mouth, she somehow managed to make it to a chair by the fire. Sat down before she fell down.

The battle over, her energy drained in a whirlpool rush that left her light-headed. Or was that loss of blood? Hard to say.

She pressed her opposite hand to the wound in a feeble attempt to stanch the sluggish flow, gritting her teeth against a stinging pain she could see.

She'd sit here for a minute. Just long enough to catch her breath. Then she'd go in search of a tourniquet. Something she could use to bandage her arm.

She leaned back against the cushions. Just a moment more. It couldn't hurt to lie back. Cam would be here soon. Or Susan and Amos. Gods, she hoped not them. That would surely lead to some unanswerable questions.

Warmth eluded her. Thought grew useless. Except for a voice—Cam's voice that came at her from the not-so-distant past. *Have you ever dealt death with your own hand? Looked a man in the face while his life drains in front of you?*

She'd mocked Cam's concern. Shrugged off his warnings. She could take it. She was the big, bad *Amhas-draoi*. The best of the best. How bad could it be?

She drew her knees up. Leaned her head upon them, squeezing her eyes shut tight. She knew now. And it was worse than she could ever have imagined.

Chapter 25

Cam found her there hours later. Curled in a chair by the dying coals of a fire, shoulders hunched, face pale and tight with pain.

He'd shaken off the determined flirtations of Mrs. Kennett-Homes, evaded his uncle's evil eye, and pointedly ignored the disturbing friendship of Brodie and Euna. These were all problems to be dealt with another day. He'd done what was asked of him, albeit with little enthusiasm. If Uncle Josh chose to reveal his hand and Morgan's identity, Cam would deal with it then. More terrifying and more immediate? A dead body lying impaled in his drawing room, his servants missing, and Morgan fevered and bloody.

He decided to forget the body for now. From the looks of him, he wasn't going anywhere. And after casting a quick hope that Amos and Susan had been well out of whatever had happened here tonight, he gathered Morgan into his arms. She needed him now. The rest could wait.

Ignoring the cloying stench of death that clung to her, he carried her to bed. Undressed her. Tended to her wounded arm, ugly but clean.

All the while, he spoke to her. Nonsense phrases in the soft

Gaelic of his childhood. Endearments any mother would use to soothe a grieving infant.

A red-hot fury held him at her side long after she'd drifted into a fractious doze. Fury that she'd been alone and vulnerable. Fury that he'd not been here for her. She'd trusted him. And he'd betrayed her trust. Again. It didn't matter it hadn't been by choice. The damage had been done. Had it ended with her death, he'd only have had himself to blame. Another death laid at his door.

Shadows crossed the floor as the moon dropped into the west, and he remained. Her fever rose, peaked, and fell away, and still he remained. By the time he made it back downstairs to deal with the losing half of the battle, it was well past four, his eyes gritty with exhaustion.

The corpse lay faceup and spread-eagle, blood pooling greasy and brown beneath it. Dark eyes stared unseeing from a long narrow face shadowed by new beard. A face Cam knew he'd seen before. But where? This sense of déjà vu was becoming increasingly annoying.

Yanking free the sword, Cam wiped it clean. A cavalry saber. Well used, but well cared for. He tossed it back on the floor to be dealt with later.

Kneeling, he searched the body for any hint of identity. Pockets revealed string, a pocketwatch, loose coins, a much-folded playbill from Drury Lane for a play held three nights previous. His coat held no tags or marks identifying the owner. He wore no rings. Carried no letters. No calling cards. The dead man's past had been wiped as clean as his sword.

"Who are you?" Cam whispered to the empty room.

He didn't expect an answer. He didn't receive one.

Dreams and dreams of dreams.

These were the foggy images passing like ghosts through

Morgan's mind. *"Fada siar air agh-aidh cuain."* A voice singing plaintive and low. *"Se mo dhuan-sa cruit-mo-chrith."* Soft words sung in a language that conjured a shimmering winter aurora over Skye. A crash of icy surf. Stolen hours spent tumbled in an Edinburgh bedchamber.

A steady heartbeat sounded beneath her ear and strong arms wrapped her in a tender embrace as she was carried. The chill of air pebbled her bare skin, and skillful hands tended to the throbbing agony of her arm. *"Guth mo luaidh anns gach stuaidh. Ga mo nuall-an gu tir."*

She swam in and out of these sensations, these pictures, cringing from the staring, accusing eyes of the dead man. A man whose waxen face morphed into Cam's. Whose muddy eyes lightened to an eagle's blue. She reached for Cam, needing to feel the safety of his touch. Knowing that if she could only hold on to him, she'd not fall back into the fevered tide pulling her away from shore—away from him.

But even as she touched him, his face changed again to the flat, challenging arrogance of Doran Buchanan, whose cruel laughter taunted her with failure. Changed again to Scathach's disappointed black gaze. And on to the cool contempt of the *Fey* in the park. The shifting sands finally settling into the friendly, grizzled patience of an old man, his piercing blue eyes twinkling with amusement. Of them all, he was the only one who spoke. His words threading their way deep into her heart.

"Love isn't a chain, lass. Sometimes 'tis within the arms of a lover we find our greatest freedoms. Our greatest strengths." He laughed, shaking his head. "Remember, the *Fey* may hold the wisdom of ages, but in matters of the heart, they ken less than nothing."

Like taffy, she felt pulled in all directions. Stretched and thinned until nothing of Morgan Bligh remained. Only an empty shell holding the assumptions and expectations of all of them. Knowing that however she chose, she'd be letting some part of her down.

She opened her eyes to darkness. Heavy blankets. An ache in her stiff and bandaged arm. The solid weight of Cam lying beside her in bed, still half clothed as if he'd fallen asleep in the midst of undressing.

She shifted positions, expecting a dagger slash of pain. Discomfort definitely, but beneath the taut constraints of bandage, the worst came and went.

She'd live.

Cam lay inches away, so close she felt the warmth of his breath, saw the stubbled angle of his jaw. Asleep, he lost the predator watchfulness. Became for a few moments the boy on the loch, racing the geese. Enjoying the swift freedom of the wild birds. Wishing for that same independence to follow the pull of the spirit.

Reaching out a tentative hand, she traced the dark brows over the deep-set eyes, the long bones of his cheeks, and the sensual curve of his mouth. Felt the familiar tug at her heart that every moment in his presence created within her. A tug that frightened her with all it promised. With all that might be lost.

She leaned forward, daring to brush her lips against his.

His mouth opened beneath hers, his tongue dipping within to taste, then devour. His eyes flicked open, the frozen blue of his stare at once both wary and excited.

"You're awake," she accused, feeling suddenly self-conscious. Embarrassed as if he'd caught her at something forbidden.

He answered with a sly smile. "I am now, but I have to say that's not how I expected to be roused."

The night's events rushed into her like air to a vacuum. What the hell was she doing simply lying here? Letting the stirring of her body drag her away from her purpose. She fought to sit up. "Susan and Amos . . . the man . . ."

Cam's smile vanished, the warrior once again. The only remnants of his earlier brilliance, the gleam of his boots, the muscle-sculpting cavalry breeches. Fatigue and worry shrouded his gaze. Rage overlying all. It radiated off him like heat from a stone. "Taken care of."

Swinging his legs over the bed, he ploughed a hand through his hair. Scrubbed his face to wake himself up. When next he met her eyes, his gaze held the power to scorch. "Do you know how frightened I was to come home to that . . . to you . . ." His jaw hardened to the point she thought she heard his teeth grinding. "Damn it, Morgan. I should never have left you alone."

And she understood. His rage wasn't directed at her. "I'm all right."

Her words never sank past his own self-guilt. "You don't understand. I could have lost you. It could just as easily have been you lying down there."

"But it wasn't, Cam."

She pushed out of the blankets. Rolled up on her knees, letting the light-headedness pass. She dropped her eyes. Fumbled with the bedclothes. "I don't fear death. Or battle."

He took her by the shoulders, careful to avoid her arm, but still with an iron grip. "What do you fear, Morgan?"

She met his hard gaze unflinching, knowing that what Cam asked moved beyond tonight's attack. "I fear imprisonment. The gilded cage that traps all women if they let it. I yearn for a greater life than bearing children and waiting on my husband's attentions as a hound waits upon the word of his master."

He laughed, though the warmth of it never reached his eyes. "You have a jaded view of marriage if that's all you see when you look upon it."

"And can you tell me it's otherwise? You who hid from your marriage first in war and then in a mistress's bed." She refused to look away, though her eyes burned, and the throbbing in her arm seemed to move to her heart. "You're right.

I have seen another kind of marriage. One where love outweighs all else. My cousin found it. And did I see even half a hope of that kind of love, I might risk the trap."

"And you don't?"

Her lips curved in a sad smile. "You yearn for freedom. A life without fetters of any kind. I've seen it." Her gaze dropped to the cross around his neck. "And know it's true."

He saw where her eyes rested. Fisted his hand over the cross as if warding her off. "What have you seen?" His grip on the cross tightened until the knuckles turned white. "What have you seen? Did you scry my stone? Is that it? When? When did you do it?"

She remained silent, too weary to fight. Too confused to argue.

He leaned in, his body rigid as if he held his temper by the merest thread. "Bloody hell, Morgan. You haven't answered my questions."

His rage was now directed squarely at her. He seethed with it. And like a match to dry tinder, intimacy burned away, leaving naught but ash. "No, but you've answered mine."

Cam lay in his bed, one hand behind his head, one fingering his necklace. His first thought had been for whiskey. His second to seek out Rastus and end the traitor's life. Both impossible. And so he'd been left to stare into the black corners of his room. Feel the oppressive crush of memories. Imagine Morgan's sickened reaction to seeing his deeds played out before her. Conjured from his cross just as she'd conjured the memories of Traverse at the standing stones.

He'd played a part in so many killings. So much death. The creature inside him thrilling in the hunt. Glorying in the power that came from being feared.

And the Serpent Brigade had been feared.

Almost as much by the English army as the French. Their reputation for cold-blooded brutality mixed with the secrecy and special nature of their missions made them outcasts among the ranks and pariahs among the officers.

He hadn't cared at first. In fact, he'd enjoyed the independence of his position. Part of the lure of the brigade. A group of select men with their own rules. Their own standards. It had only been later he'd realized the cost of such freedom.

And now Morgan knew it too.

She'd been right to keep her distance. Hadn't the general come right out and said what Cam had only suspected? That the brigade had been a collection of criminals and madmen? So where did that leave him?

He closed his eyes, knowing sleep wouldn't come easily. Disgust soured his stomach. Rose in his throat like bile. Lifting his hands, he studied the calloused palms. The strength in the long fingers. Morgan had witnessed all these hands had done in the name of war. Had used her magic to steal his memories for herself. Betrayed his trust by taking from him a time he wished only to forget. She'd watched the murders he'd committed. Some deserved. Some not. He could imagine her horror—her loathing. Was it any wonder she cringed at giving herself up to him? He was as much a beast as the man tonight. A hired gun. A natural-born killer.

The dead man's face swam into view alongside so many others. But this time Cam recognized him. His features clicked into place like so many puzzle pieces.

Devonshire. Outside Ensign Traverse's house.

The scarlet-jacketed officer.

That connection made, another leapt forward. Stunning him with its implications. Bringing a sheen of cold sweat to his body.

The man at his uncle's house with Euna. The man at the

Abercrombies' tonight. He'd been the bawdy drunkard at Mrs. Cabot's brothel.

A coincidence? No. Cam didn't believe in coincidence.

Doran had upped the ante. He didn't just seek to destroy Cam and Morgan. He looked to destroy any and all around them.

That Cam would not let stand.

He'd bring this fight to Doran. Take his chances against the goddess blade. And immortal or not, if success should be his that day, he'd stick to his plans.

Finish this last mission and retire to Strathconon.

Alone.

Unable to sleep, Morgan found her way to the kitchens. Thankfully, unscarred by the attack and still neat as a pin. Just as Susan had left them.

Daggerfell's kitchens had always held the power to soothe, and many an hour she'd spent with Cook, her arms to her elbows covered in flour. Or pounding dough as if she practiced in the tiltyard.

A cup of tea and a buttered roll later and she'd managed to eat away the worst of her guilt. Cam had been right to be angry. She should never have ventured to scry his cross. To delve into thoughts and memories not freely offered. It had been a break of faith. A lapse in honor.

So what had prompted her to go against her better judgment? Risk his wrath? Had she done it to convince herself of the Cam she knew? The conniving, lying aristocrat who'd tempted her with everything and brought her nothing but pain and humiliation.

Perhaps in part.

But what she'd found had only confused her. Instead of a scion of an ancient house who wielded his wealth and position with the cutting strength of a blade, she'd seen a boy as wild as the Highland mountains. Wanting only to fly from his responsibilities. To feel the wicked pleasure of freedom. A boy who'd become a man. Crushed within a loveless marriage. Trapped by duty and family. And later by war and the guilt that followed.

She swirled the cold tea around and around in her mug.

Was it wrong of Morgan to need surety in a mate? To have no what-ifs before she took a step that could end the life she'd carved for herself? Was that kind of confidence in her decision an impossibility? Did anyone truly know the future before they pledged themselves? The questions hurricaned through her head. If nothing else, taking her mind from the biting sting in her arm.

Her cousin Conor had wed with the belief that he'd not see another dawn. His bride, Ellery, had agreed with the understanding she'd be a widow within hours—days at most. And yet they'd ignored the future they'd seen and taken that final step. Found a treasure beyond price if the lovesick way they looked on each other was any indication.

Cam too might be facing such a fate, though Morgan refused to believe it. To imagine Cam struck down would only undermine energy best used for fighting Doran. She'd ignore the niggling fear. Concentrate on what she could change. Not what lay outside her power.

Love isn't a chain. It's our greatest strength.

The thought once within her head couldn't be shaken. Where had she heard such before? Gram? Uncle Owen? It sounded like both of them and yet she was almost sure neither one had ever said such a thing to her.

But the words remained. The force of the truth undeniable.

And with a flash of insight that burned away all else, she knew what she needed to do.

Chapter 26

Cam came awake to the snick of a turning lock. A rush of cool air from the hallway.

And then she was there.

Red-gold hair spilled loose over her shoulders. Down her back.

Her candle's light silhouetting the dusky flesh of her breasts, the muscled curve of her hips, the determined tilt to her chin, she was his every fantasy. An impossible desire. Inches away and forever out of reach.

He fought to stay angry. To hold tight to the knot of betrayal that kept the worst of the pain at bay. He struggled to harden his heart against the apology clear in the bronze of her gaze.

The rest of his body hardened on its own.

"What the hell do you want?" He slammed to his feet. Winced at the ache of need centered in his groin. He could act as furious as he wanted; Morgan could tell all too clearly how he really felt. "Stooping to your *Other* tricks again to get in?"

"Didn't need to." She smiled, coming farther into his room. Tossed a knife on the bed beside him. "Compliments of Brodie. He's a man of many talents, you know."

What she did next, he'd never anticipated. Not in his wildest imaginings.

And he'd had a few over the last weeks.

She kissed him. Brushed his lips with a touch as weightless as down yet holding the promise of so much more if he let her continue. And why the hell not? It was what he'd wanted, wasn't it?

Instead, he grabbed her wrists. Forced her to step away. Saw his coldhearted fury reflected in her eyes.

This didn't make sense. She didn't make sense. And he grew tired of being strung out and reeled back like a child's toy. "What's your game?"

Her face grew shuttered. "No game. Not this time."

"And you expect me to believe you? After all that's gone between us?"

"I don't expect. But I hope."

What had he said to his grandfather? A fool's hope?

She stood so close he saw the rise and fall of her chest. The flicker of caution in the lightning depths of her gaze. Smelled her cool floral fragrance mixed with the earthier scent of desire in her hair, on her skin. His hand came up, touched the bandage wrapped taut around the muscle of her arm. A reminder of how close he'd come to losing her forever.

She refused to surrender. "Send me away, and I'll go. Tell me it's over between us, and I'll believe you. But if you can't, I'll stay. And I'll make you forgive me."

There stood a challenge if he'd ever heard one. He swallowed.

Uncle Josh's disapproval. Gran-da's advice. The dangling uncertainty of Lord Delvish's warning. There were a million reasons he should push her away. Throw her from his room. Relock the door. And forget her.

And only one reason to hold her fast.

He lowered his mouth to hers, her body swaying as she

opened to him. His tongue dipping to taste the heat of her as the air left his lungs in a punching rush of emotion.

That one reason prevailed.

But damned if he'd make it easy for her.

Morgan's hands splayed across the cool marble of Cam's chest, deliberately avoiding the cross, the reason for his anger. His heart raced beneath her palm, his breathing coming quick and fast. His kiss sent a lightning strike of emotion straight to her center, making her knees buckle, eliciting an involuntary moan.

He caught her before she fell, rolling her under him as they both crashed onto the bed. Trapping her. Pinning her with his weight and the furious hunger in his gaze. A gaze that singed wherever it lingered. And it lingered just about everywhere. Her breasts, the flat of her stomach, the junction of her legs.

Unable to move, she lay still as his eyes devoured. Enjoying the slow knotting of her insides into a tighter and tighter coil. The way her blood roared through her veins. The way he rubbed against her, letting her feel the hard shaft of his erection.

She answered his hunger with her own, wanting him to push himself into her. Fill the yawning uncertainty she fought to crush under her overpowering desire for Cam.

"Take me," she murmured. "Fuck me. Now."

But he held back. Instead his head lowered to her breasts. Laved the sensitive flesh until her nipples hardened to dark pearls. Until she arched, wanting him to take more into his mouth. Wanting him to feast where until now all he'd done was sample.

He withdrew, but only to rake her again with another hellion's gaze. To adjust his grip upon her wrists. To let the sweet friction ratchet up another full notch. Every muscle taut and waiting. Every breath quick and sharp with arousal.

His mouth found hers again, his tongue plunging into hers. Forcing her head back. Forcing her to answer with an assault of her own. A war of tongues and lips and teeth that left them both breathless.

One wrist came free, but only for a moment, and then he'd captured both in one hand. His other skimming her side. Brushing the hair between her legs. Finding, then teasing the nub hidden within.

She bucked against his touch, whimpers of near climax coming from deep in her throat. Was this his way of punishing her? Hold her captive in a web of spiraling need with no release in sight?

To hell with that.

The twist of her torso, the throw of a well-placed leg, and Cam found himself blinking up at her from his back, his expression inscrutable even if his body told its own tale. But before she could answer his desperate hunger with her own, he tore away. His gaze hard as flint, his chest heaving. "You've seen my crimes. You know the evil I'm capable of. The madness that lies just beneath the surface."

She shook her head, trying to focus on his words and not on the bodywide throb that threatened to consume her. "I stole only one memory from you, Cam. There was a sailboat. And a storm. Hugh and Euna were there."

He went still as if considering her words. Sifting through memory. "I remember. It was the last week before the new school term. The last week of freedom before I was sent south. Away from Strathconon."

"And the storm?"

Pride lit his face for a moment and the faded edges of an ancient grief. "We beached on the rocks. Smashed by the waves and the wind. But I got us safe there before she broke apart. Wet, bedraggled as drowned rats, and more terrified of Uncle Josh than the storm."

"Then what? I saw no more."

"I could tell you. But mayhap, you'd rather see what happened with your own eyes?"

Before she could refuse, he forced her palm open. Forced it closed again over the sharp points of the jet cross.

The power within the stone dragged her under in mere seconds, tumbled her into the midst of lashing rain, shrieking winds, the jink and lurch of the little yacht as Cam fought it to shore. Cliffs rose sheer before her. All but for a shale-strewn beach, a thin slice of safety between the jagged rocks. Cam made for that narrow gap. He could do it. He knew he could. Hadn't Father always told him he had the devil's own skill? He'd prove it now.

Slapping his hair out of his eyes, he screamed at Hugh and Euna to hold to the railing. Twine the ropes around their hands for a surer grip.

The crunch of staved-in wood, the crack of a splintered mast, and the boat came to rest, heaved on its side, pieces strewn across the beach. Cam bent double over the broken tiller dangling useless in his hand.

The three of them shaking and laughing and faking a disregard for Uncle Josh's upcoming discipline as they climbed the path to the house. Met Gran-da coming down. Braving the storm and the plummeting path to find them and bring them to Uncle Josh.

Cam caught Gran-da's gaze. A gray-faced mix of sympathy and anguish. That's when the awful realization dawned. Father and Mother weren't coming back. Not today. Not ever. Dead of fever. No time to even say good-bye.

As if a stray piece of wood had impaled itself within his breast, he felt something hard and numbing sever him in half. The part of him before he knew. The part of him after.

Even as his heart grew leaden, he caught the telltale wailing of the *caoineag* from the rocks below. Or was that Euna's sobbing? Hugh's stifled blubbering? He couldn't tell and then the sound was gone. Blown away by the wind.

Morgan's fingers fell away. The memory spun out to its end. The strength of the moment finally understood.

"There's more if you care to watch." His voice came harsh. His expression serious. "Much more."

Morgan shook her head, still off-kilter from what she'd already witnessed. "I told you once that all you've done is just a part of who you are now." She brushed the hair from his face. "The man I love."

Love. Had she really said that out loud? The word felt strange on her tongue, but not as distasteful as she once thought it might. She tried again. "I want you, Cam. Even as I shrink from stepping into that cage eyes-open."

"Must it be a cage?"

"There's no way the warring sides of myself can coexist. To have you is to turn my back on the *Amhas-draoi*." She tried not to let her grief show through. She'd grow accustomed in time to the hollow sense of loss as if a part of her had been cut away. "But since I must choose, I choose you."

Cam caught her chin. Made her face him. "I don't ask for that kind of sacrifice. I don't want that kind of sacrifice."

"But I—"

"Damn it, Morgan, don't force that responsibility on me. If there's any future for us here, it's not over the grave of your buried dreams."

"Do you want me?"

"Are you jesting? Can you really lie there and ask me if I want you? My whole body is ready to come apart at the stitching if I don't fuck you right now."

It was her turn to move against him. Feel the tip of his cock poised to enter. Her earlier need resurfaced, sharper for the wait, the tingly heat between her legs unbearable.

He took a deep, moaning shaky breath. Cursed. And pushed

himself away. "I may live or die in the next few days. I don't want my last thought to be that you regret what you feel. That I'm placing you into some kind of prison."

She lurched for him. Refused to let him escape. "Can't you let me mourn the loss of one dream even while I revel in the realization of another?"

He didn't look convinced. In fact, he looked bloody pissed and ready to murder.

She lowered her head. Slanted her lips across his, smelling the heady clean scent of him. The odor of man and sex and sweat. "If you want me as much as you say you do, you'll finish what you started. You'll end this. Now." Her words came as hard and angry as his own. And she didn't bloody care.

She wanted this throbbing pleasure-pain to end in the crashing rush of orgasm. Wanted to feel him slam into her with a power that would send her out of herself. Prove to her the choice she'd made was right.

Caught beneath her, his gaze hardened to a frozen blue chill. "You're damned right. I will end it."

Gone was even the pretence of tenderness. Forgetting the bandage on her arm, or mayhap remembering it and not caring, he shifted. Flipped them over so that once again he lay on top. Dominant. In control. Mad as hell.

He spread her legs. Buried himself inside her, every thrust staking a claim. Proving a point. He watched her as he pleasured her, his eyes as sharp and focused as a mountain eagle.

She arched against him as their rhythm increased. As the supple coil of her body vibrated beneath him.

Cam's body hardened. His arms flexed, every muscle stretched tight even as a shudder exploded through him. Into her.

She clung to him, fighting the riptide of emotion and sensation as each crashing wave tore her apart as easily as they had the little yacht. But looking up, she saw through the shroud of rain and wind, the glowing lights of home.

"Colonel?"

Cam pushed the hand away. Burrowed deeper under the blankets. Encountered naked flesh, which jolted him out of sleep.

Morgan.

So it hadn't been a dream.

He spooned up against her, nuzzling the flesh of her neck.

"Colonel Sinclair, sir. Wake up. Please."

Shit. Amos. What the hell was he doing here? Cam opened one eye to see the old batman's face inches from his own. "Go away."

"I'm that sorry, sir." Amos's idea of a whisper was anything but. Cam shrank under the volume. Hoped Morgan didn't wake. "Sir Joshua's belowstairs. Says he's needin' to speak with ye."

Cam groaned, rolling away from Morgan's delicious heat. Rising to take the banyan Amos held out for him. "Did he say anything else?"

"No, sir. But he's brought Lady Sinclair and Miss Euna with him. I'd be on my guard if I were you, sir. He's preparin' for battle, by the looks of him."

Uncle Josh. The perfect beginning to a perfect day. More than likely here for his expected recount of last night's progress with the completely forgettable Mrs. Kennett-Holmes.

"So be it," he grumbled, plowing a hand through his hair. Yawning. Stretching the kinks out. "Bring me my clothes."

"But . . . Sir Joshua . . ." Amos motioned toward the door.

"If Uncle Josh comes round at dawn, Uncle Josh can damned well wait until I make myself presentable."

But though he said it, Cam dressed in haste. Breeks. Boots.

It was time to end the charade once and for all with his uncle. Be sure he knew Cam appreciated his advice and support. But he didn't need it. Not anymore.

There'd be fireworks—Cam glanced back at Morgan, still somehow asleep—perhaps more threats. Still, if a chance existed that he'd pierced Morgan's armored heart, he'd risk any amount of his uncle's bullying.

"Cam?"

Morgan stretched one arm over her head, a come-back-to-bed invitation lighting her eyes. Cam wanted nothing more than to crawl back between the sheets. Wrestle her to delicious surrender again. Sheathe himself inside her velvety heat. Find release.

He imagined ice water. And lots of it. "My family's downstairs."

"What do they want?"

"No doubt they've come to be sure their rabid dog remains muzzled and leashed."

"Interesting turn of phrase." Her gaze ran over his bare chest, centered on his groin with a sleepy-sexy smile that almost unmanned him.

He sighed, his voice grave. "It's going to be ugly."

"Do you know a family fight that isn't? I've told you, Cam. I'm not afraid of talk. Your uncle can do his best, but it won't change me. Only you've been able to do that."

She gave nothing away, but he understood her now. Knew the reaction was her way of hardening herself against expected pain.

His gaze fell on her bandaged arm, a knot of near loss still uncomfortably squeezing his innards. He'd prove to her she'd been right to trust in him. This time he'd make it come right.

"My uncle may command my respect—even my loyalty—but he doesn't own me. He'll find that out soon enough," he growled through clenched teeth as he stormed out of the bedchamber, drawing on a shirt as he went.

He surprised Uncle Josh in the drawing room in the process of running his hand over the stain in the carpet, Aunt Sylvie sitting primly on the sofa by the fire, twisting a handkerchief between her fingers. Euna beside her.

Arrayed for battle. The space between them as charged with emotion as any front line.

Brodie's presence was a bonus Cam hadn't expected. He stood at the hearth, a boot on the fender, his shoulders hunched as he stared into the flames. What he did here was a mystery, but Cam wouldn't turn away an ally.

He looked up when Cam entered, the tight-clenched jaw relaxing a fraction. His eyes searching Cam for injury.

Aunt Sylvie started as if she might rise and go to him. She didn't. She held back, but her hand slid into Euna's sitting beside her, a watery smile of relief lighting her eyes. "Thank heavens, you're all right," she murmured.

Her concern sent a wash of regret through him. Forever a square peg in a round hole, Cam had spent his life asking for forgiveness for simply being himself.

No more.

They'd take him as he was. Or they'd lose him.

Uncle Josh took his time straightening. "Can you explain this?"

Cam noted the track of his gaze. His bloodstained fingertips. "Hangnail?"

His uncle's face went white, then red. "Don't sport with me, lad. You'll lose. I've not gotten as far as I have by putting up with jokesters."

Cam's whole body tightened. Why had he ever thought he could find a way to make his family understand? He shrugged. "We had a break-in last night."

Brodie stiffened, his gaze searching out Cam for the truth.

Aunt Sylvie's hand flew to her mouth. "Was anyone hurt?"

Uncle Josh turned a hard gaze on his wife. "That's not wine, Sylvie. It's blood. And lots of it."

Cam smiled, an imperceptible nod to Brodie that he'd be told more later. "No one we need worry over, Aunt."

Apparently satisfied with Cam's abbreviated answer, his uncle dismissed the wreck of the carpet. His aunt and sister less easily. They both focused on the stain with wide eyes.

His uncle jerked his chin at the ceiling. "Has Miss Bligh gone?"

"No. She hasn't." He couldn't help it. Despite the shock he knew he'd inflict, he offered his uncle a look that told a story of its own.

Brodie swallowed a laugh, but his uncle remained unfazed. "Mrs. Kennett-Holmes—"

"Will need to look elsewhere for a new husband. I'm sorry, Uncle Josh. I can't woo a woman whose sole enticement is her money, her connections, and her calming influence."

His uncle changed tack. His face softening into less belligerent lines. "Cam, are you prepared to jeopardize your future? Your sister and brothers' futures for this woman? We're your family, Cam. We need to hold together."

"Family?" Cam spat, his earlier weakness burned away. "A family's supposed to accept you as you are. Not as they wish you would be. I tried for years to be the man you wanted me to be. And spent more years apologizing when I didn't measure up. I can't do it anymore."

Finally, his words seemed to get through.

Uncle Josh dropped into a chair, his hands curling over the arms, his expression full of self-contrition. "I blame myself." He sighed. "You've inherited too much of your father. Even my upbringing was not enough to hold back the worst of his excesses coming to fruition in you." He straightened. Pointed an accusing finger in Cam's direction. "But I'll say one thing—

your father may have been a reckless gadabout, but he knew the importance of family. To him, being a Sinclair meant honor. Pride. He'd be as disappointed as I am to hear you've spurned it all for a woman of Miss Bligh's character."

Cam's hand unconsciously reached for his cross. "We won't ever know what my father would think. But I do know what Gran-da thinks. And he's given me his blessing."

"You've seen . . ." Uncle Josh jerked back against the chair, a flicker of something Cam might take for belief at the corners of his gaze. And why not? Joshua Sinclair had been raised in Caithness. Had walked the same lonely mountain tracks. Stood on the same fog-shrouded shores. Heard the same stories of the old days when a winter's storm held families close to the fires.

A warmth filled the emptiness in Cam where the last shreds of family duty had been pounded to dust. A healing that let him see his uncle as the tired, besieged old man he was. A final gift from his grandfather? A product of Morgan's love?

"So you're calling my bluff. You don't think I'll ruin her?" His uncle's question froze the room to silence. A final desperate attempt to hold Cam within his orbit.

Brodie's hand went to his waist as if he might draw steel.

Euna jumped, her gaze sweeping from her uncle to Brodie to Cam.

"Joshua!" Aunt Sylvie stood, her nervousness whipped to steely resolve. "Do you hear yourself? Do you see what you're doing?"

His face seemed to melt into defeat, shoulders slumped. "I see Cam throwing away a chance to put his unsavory past behind him and start fresh."

"And can he only do this in the arms of Sally Kennett-Holmes? Can you not put aside your stubborn Sinclair pride long enough to hear your nephew out? Morgan Bligh may not be our choice, but if she can bring a smile back to Cameron's face, I'm willing to withhold judgment."

His uncle snorted, but remained silent. Again, Cam had the feeling that mention of his grandfather had tipped a scale somewhere in his favor.

This time, his aunt did cross the room. Cupped his cheek. "It's been too long since a true smile lit your eyes, Cameron." She mouthed silently, "Leave him to me."

He'd never noticed the stubborn jut of her chin before, or the dogged gleam in her eyes. But they were there.

And for the first time in a long while, Cam saw hope for the square peg.

Chapter 27

Doran trusted few. It was how he'd survived as long as he had. First as a soldier in the *Duinedon*'s army, fighting his way beside his brothers across India until one by one they'd fallen. Later as student and soldier in Scathach's order of *Amhas-draoi* where he'd finally understood firsthand the discrimination of *Other* by true *Fey*. The way the most potent magics were held in tight-fisted secrecy by the *faery* world. Any excuse to keep the *Other* away from real power.

Well, the all-seeing Scathach hadn't seen everything, had she?

So arrogant in her superiority, she'd never gleaned his reasons for such diligent study, such single-minded determination in becoming the best of the *Amhas-draoi*. Only one within the order holding greater innate ability. And he'd gone soft over some woman.

So who really was stronger?

But now this miserly bestowal of his favor proved a difficulty. Three of his closest followers dead. Just one remaining he believed in enough to follow through on his instructions. And the dubious talents of the sewer rat, Rastus.

"You have your orders, North. Bring the woman back to me here." He caught a look cross the man's face. "Untouched."

"And you, sir? While I'm snagging the bait, what are you doing?"

"Laying the trail. Traceable, but not obvious. I want Bligh and Sinclair to find me. I have plans for those two."

Neuvarvaan spoke through him in the black speech of the *Morkoth*. It was the sword that instructed him in what to do. How to proceed. How to rid himself of these two problems and increase his numbers in one dramatic move.

An army of Undying must begin with a single soldier. Or two. And who better to lay the foundation for all who would follow? A man with the ruthless savagery of a wild creature honed to lethal precision. An *Other* only one generation away from the true *Fey* whose battle skills, though roughly cast, were no less deadly.

He tasted success. All had come together as planned. The abduction of the sword. The deciphering of the *Morkoth*'s magics. The drawing of enough power together and in one person to start the chain reaction of mage energy that would spark the transformation. Create deathless perfection from the clay of mortality.

"And after you get what you want? I want the woman for my own," North whined. "Want to wipe that cool disdain from her face."

"The Sinclair woman?" In a generous mood, Doran shrugged. "As you wish." Then thought better. "If there's enough of her left, that is."

"Cam?" Brodie's voice—but different—sounded in the hall. The deep baritone threaded with pain. Or anguish. "Cam!" Definitely anguish.

He ducked his head out the door to the library.

And went dead-cold.

Gone was the starched and polished officer of a few hours ago. Brodie leaned heavily against the door, his eyes wild. Dangerous. Trained inward on some horror only he could see.

Cam's heart galloped, a hard ball of fear lodged in his throat. "Brodie?"

Nothing.

Cam placed his hand on Brodie's shoulder.

The reaction was instant and explosive. And if Brodie had been armed, Cam's head would have been on the floor.

Even so, the force of Brodie's blow threw a surprised Cam to his knees. A stinger in his neck that left his arm numb to the fingers. "What the hell—"

Brodie stood, shoulders squared. Legs spread. Chest heaving. Poised for battle.

"Euna's been taken."

A leather jerkin over his shirt to turn aside a knife blade. Slow a pistol shot.

Boots, supple as a second skin, allowing for silence as he selected his position. Waited for his best opportunity at a clean kill.

At his belt, a cartridge pouch, a pistol holster, and a scabbard for his dagger. Another dirk in his boot.

After wrapping the untested rifle in fabric to avoid a telltale glint of sun off the weapon, he sighted along the barrel. Noted its weight. The cool wood of the stock against his cheek. Squeezed the trigger, feeling the hammer-spring slam forward. The surge of vicious exhilaration that followed.

He'd understood long ago that someday he'd be called to account for his crimes. That a reckoning would be owed. But the depth and cruelty of that divine justice he'd not foreseen.

The swift retribution of a lightning bolt. That he could have handled. But this . . .

Let him taste happiness. Glimpse heaven.

Then slam the doors. Douse the lights.

Bring on hell.

His glance fell on the all-too-familiar whiskey decanter. And the need for the relaxing heat of his family's malt sank its claws into him. A few drinks might dull the howling storm of blood-hate singeing every vein. The overarching power of revenge.

He deliberately turned his back on the alcohol, wanting the fire of vengeance in his belly. It was the only way he'd save his sister.

If he was heading to hell, he'd bring Doran right along with him.

What he'd told Morgan had been the truth. The churning gut, the weak knees, the choking fear. He'd experienced them all. And buried them deep. It was the only way to survive the war. To survive the savagery.

The emotions had broken the surface for a time, bringing the chilling memories with them, the faces of the dead threatening to destroy his peace. His mind.

For Euna, he would bury them again. Rastus had been right. He needed every trait of the Serpent to bring Doran down. Cameron Sinclair could fight the darkness within him. Or Sin could embrace it.

He chose Sin.

And once he had chosen, there would be no coming back.

Morgan leaned against the doorjamb, the mage energy filling her senses overpowering the wobbly-legged light-headedness. She'd doctored her arm as best she could, using the limited medicines she'd found in the house. The bullet-scored tissue burned, hampering her mobility, but she'd no choice. Doran had captured a pawn. Check. But the queen and two knights moved onto the field of play. It was up to them to match his moves with a check and mate of their own.

"It's begun," she announced.

"Doran?" Cam broke off his conversation with Brodie, the guilty flush stealing over the captain's face and the way he avoided looking directly at her an indication she'd been the object of their discussion.

But it was Cam's expression that sent her heart straight to her toes. The empty blue of his gaze, the square jut of his jaw, the careful way he held himself as if any slight movement would cause him to crack chilled her to the marrow of her bones. This was not the same Cam who'd left her bed this morning, a man she could have pledged herself to. This man radiated pure feral rage. Assumed the mantle of a creature bound to kill. Knowing only how to destroy. Never how to love.

Cam might return from this mission alive. But she understood now, never whole.

Brodie's knowing gaze sought out hers, the sorrow she saw there for both of them. For he stood to lose a friend just as she lost a lover.

But regrets would have to wait.

Now was for Euna. Doran. And the reclaiming of *Neuvarvaan*.

Firmly locking away the grief and the heartache that would come in time, she turned her mind to what she could control. Once they succeeded in freeing Cam's sister and sending Doran to the deepest pit in the darkest hell, she'd retreat to the sanctuary of Daggerfell and her family's arms. To nurse her broken heart for a second time.

But this time, there'd be no third chances. She would have Cam. Or she would remain alone. There was no middle ground.

Her hand fell to the basket hilt of her sword, using the

comforting presence of the weapon as a way to draw her mind off distractions. "Doran's letting himself be found. All but forcing us to follow the trail he's laid."

"So we indulge him. And we end it. Today." Cam's voice as emotionless as his gaze.

"Cam and I've discussed it. I'm coming with ye." Brodie pushed up from the table, the giant Highlander needing only a plaid and a claymore to assume the guise of one of the brutal clansmen of his ancestry. She could almost hear the bagpipes. Smell the heather.

Morgan offered him a curt nod. "If I'm right in my thinking, it's going to take you and an army of such to best Doran."

Brodie smiled, though it never reached his eyes, which were grim, lit with shadows of their own. He spread his empty hands. "I'm only one, lass. But I'm a great strapping brute for all that. Together, the three of us may contrive." He glanced at Cam, his smile fading. "She mayn't be blood, Cam. But she's a sister to me, nonetheless. We'll see her safe."

Cam seemed to flinch, but in no other way did Euna's abduction register in the ravages of his face.

Morgan closed her eyes. Whispered the words of the *fith-fath*. At once her leather breeches and jacket became a simple gown, the raiment of a woman hiding the weapons of the *Amhas-draoi*.

"Come," she said, wishing she could hide her grief as easily behind such a mask. Surely Cam knew how she must feel. But if he did, he gave no sign he cared. "Doran's calling."

Despite the swell of humanity crowding the wharves, warehouses, and shipping basins, few trespassed into the morass of dirt and debris around the entrance to the half-constructed Regent's Canal. Complications in management had temporarily halted the anthill of construction between the docks and the canal's terminus in the heart of the city, leaving a cemetery of abandoned machinery, tools flung aside as if the workers were expected back at any moment, coils of heavy rope, mountains of dirt and clay and silt embedded with shards of pottery, broken bricks, rocks blasted from unfinished locks.

Morgan picked her way around one such pile, the size of it dwarfing her. A slide and she'd find herself buried beneath a ton of crushed rock and earth.

"Doran," she called, the double coil of his mage energy a living thing moving within her skull like a snake. If she closed her eyes, it was all she could see. The earlier red-purple signature now almost completely black, shot with gray and blue and yellow. The *Morkoth*'s magic binding with his own into one huge supply of power. "I know you hear my voice. Bring out the girl."

Silence, but she knew the bastard heard her.

"Show me she's safe," she shouted. "She's no part of this."

She kept her eyes firmly on the battle-scape around her, never once glancing up to where Cam and Brodie held position. Cam with his sniper's rifle trained on her. Brodie playing backup in the case of unforeseen trouble.

To all who saw her, she was alone. Vulnerable. Easy pickings.

Just how she wanted it.

"Where's Sinclair?"

The voice was Doran's. She'd know that smug, condescending rasp anywhere. It bounced off the man-made ravines and blasted cliff walls of the half-finished lock. Swirled like a noxious evil wind around her.

"Near death," she answered, thanking the gods an empathic ability was not among the rogue *Amhas-draoi*'s talents. He'd never pick the lie from the truth. Not if she did her job right. "A belly wound. Your assassin was lucky. For a time. Before I killed him." She let the reality of her words sink in. "If Euna Sinclair's kidnapping was intended to punish him, it's too late.

He'll be dead by tomorrow." She swallowed. "If he's fortunate." She scanned the ground for signs of movement. "Let Euna go."

"Is that her name? My men and I have simply been calling her bitch as we rode her."

Morgan's stomach clenched in spasms, making her want to heave. By the sweet mercies of the White Lady, she prayed the girl dead or mad if gang rape had really been her fate. Somewhere above, she knew the men heard the taunt as well. She willed them to hold it together. Focus not on Doran's words, but on the end goal. Killing the little shit.

Doran stepped into view like a being spat from the *Unseelie*'s Dark Court. A sour, fetid stench wrapped round him, the odor of death and darkness and the wicked strength of the *Morkoth*. Even his physical shape seemed affected by the ancient evil. Grown gaunt and gray, his once mighty body bent with invisible burdens, only his gaze remained razor sharp, yet bore a millennia of hate. *Neuvarvaan*—Andraste's stolen sword—rested against his leg, but she knew it listened to her words as avidly as Doran.

"A shame the colonel's not here. I'd a deal to set before the two of you." He gave an offhand shrug. "But one's better than none."

She slid her sword from its scabbard. "Enough games, Doran. Spill it."

He straightened. "Very well. You in exchange for Miss Sinclair." Confusion must have flashed across her face because he smiled. "Come with me willingly. Let *Neuvarvaan* create you as an Undying."

Just the thought made her shudder. "And in exchange?"

"I allow Miss Sinclair to walk out of here unharmed."

She flexed her fingers on the worn grip of her sword, adrenaline jumping along every nerve. "And if I tell you to bugger off, you miserable piece of shit?"

Doran laughed, though the humor never reached his

soulless gaze. "Do you eat with that mouth, Bligh?" He settled a long, hard stare on her. "It's your choice, of course. But know this. If you fight, you'll lose. And Miss Sinclair will return to her home in very small pieces. I've already begun."

He signaled to someone out of her range of vision.

A man appeared from behind a pile of stone to her right, bearing a struggling, weeping woman in front of him, her once fashionable walking dress now a sodden, filthy mess of almost rags.

"Show us, North."

Doran's henchman shoved Euna roughly ahead of him. She stumbled to her knees, her hands tied behind her, unable to break her fall. She looked up, meeting Morgan's stare, her eyes hot with fear and shame and red with tears. As Morgan watched, North reached around, ripping Euna's gown from shoulder to waist for Morgan's inspection.

And Morgan wanted to be sick all over again. A brand burned into the white of Euna's flesh just above her left breast. A mark of ownership. Possession.

One word.

Slave.

Chapter 28

Cam had never been so close to madness.

Not during the bloody chaos of Talavera when he'd had to pick pieces of offal from his hair and his clothes after the cannon shot that had destroyed the squad of soldiers beside him. Or afterward when the grass fires raged, sweeping over dead and wounded alike, the stench of burning carcasses filling his nostrils.

Not even during the storming of Badajoz when he'd climbed the bodies at the breech like a human ladder. Ignored the pleas for mercy from the dying. The screams of those fleeing the battle-crazed British out for blood. Then he'd calmly picked his way past the carnage in his search of his target. The man he'd been sent in to kill.

In every case, he'd held to his duty. Put aside the sickening twist of his own disgust and ploughed on. Unthinking. Uncaring.

But this time . . . this place . . . this was Euna. A wild battle-frenzy reddened his vision. Tightened his finger against the trigger. And a quick death was no longer good enough for the half mortal, half *Fey* walking corpse below him.

He adjusted his sight. His aim now centered neatly on the

man's left thigh. He'd splinter bone. Sever an artery. And when the bastard lay writhing on the ground, the fun would really get started. Cam's palms itched to make it happen. A few feet more and he could take his shot. And then they'd see who took who apart piece by bloody piece.

Morgan spoke again, her words lost to him amid the deafening roar of his own pumping heart. But whatever she said, it lured Doran farther into the open of the worksite.

Instinct took over as he walked himself mentally through his checklist. Took clear aim. Let the clarity of the sharpshooter take him over.

He'd end this threat once and for all. Destroy Doran Buchanan with one perfectly placed bullet.

"Come on, ye prick. I'm going to fucking kill ye right now."

Had he really screamed that aloud?

No. He might have thought it, but it was Brodie's shout of anger. Brodie who'd lost control and revealed himself.

To Cam's right, the damned fool was scrambling for a foothold on the piles of shale, a hand out to control his wild plummet to the floor of the dry canal bed.

And what had been a calculated extermination blew up into calamity bordering on farce.

Brodie's pistol came up even as he ran, the report a crack like the lash of a whip.

North went down, a bullet to the chest, shock at the unexpected attack by the hulking, screeching madman his last expression.

Euna sank to the ground, head bowed as if fighting to make herself invisible to the horror around her.

Only Morgan and Doran remained unmoved by the chaos.

Doran lifted a hand, palm out, fingers spread, and the very air seemed to shudder in a silent clap of thunder.

The rocks around Cam clattered and bounced. He fought

to remain upright as the earth under his feet jinked and settled back.

Morgan fell to her knees, even as her own arms rose over her head. Palms out. Face pale with what seemed great pain or great concentration as if she alone held back the earth around them. Kept the walls from caving, the rocks from spilling into the base of the canal.

Brodie turned his second pistol on Doran, but the *Amhas-draoi* merely flicked a finger at him and, like batting a fly, Brodie was swept off his feet, his pistol skittering out of reach, his face going white as flour.

Cam knew that anguish. The mind-exploding pain of the body being scythed apart with invisible knives. As if your very soul were being chopped to bits.

Morgan cried out and a wave of gold light pulsed from her hands, wrapped Brodie and Euna in a cocoon of star-shot air. But even that much seemed to drain her. How long could she hold, weakened by that bullet wound? When would she finally collapse under the force of Doran's power?

He couldn't wait for the perfect shot. It was now or maybe never.

He raised the barrel a second time. Took aim at the center of the *Amhas-draoi*'s chest. Squeezed off a shot.

From behind came a bone-snicking crunch. Just before the world exploded around him.

Went black.

Morgan felt her wards collapsing just as the crack of a rifle sounded above and behind her, the bullet passing so close she imagined she felt the slice of air as it stung by her ear. Buried itself with a puff of dirt in the ground beside Doran.

He glanced up, his eyes homed in on her with a diamond hardness.

And Morgan chose her moment.

Flinging the binding spell with the force of a sword thrust, she drove in under his guard, sliding her dagger from its sheath. Burying it into his stomach with a howl of fury.

He stumbled back, screaming, a look of stunned surprise in his pale eyes. But with a roar of pain and triumph, he whipped up a tornado of choking, blinding dust.

Morgan threw her arms over her head, dropping to the ground, hoping to avoid the hailstorm of dirt, glass, rocks, and splintered wood.

And when the worst passed, she rose on shaky knees to see Euna beside her whimpering, a layer of dust blanketing her cowering body.

Brodie and Doran?

Vanished.

Euna lifted her head, peering around her cautiously as if judging a trap. The heavy fall of her silver-blond hair disguised her wretchedness, but Morgan noted the sagging defeat of her shoulders, the uncontrollable shaking.

She crawled to her, freeing Euna's hands. Pulling the other woman into a reassuring embrace.

She gathered the ruin of her gown over her chest. Tremors shook her body, her teeth chattering as if she were freezing. But it lasted only minutes. Then she looked up, her eyes hard with a bravery Morgan had glimpsed in memory, but thought lost forever under the stern protectiveness of Sir Joshua. Euna seemed to gather herself together, swallow her shocked terror.

Something in Morgan's expression must have given away her unspoken question. Because Euna shook her head, her eyes drilling the corpse of the dead man as if she'd love to put her own bullet in him.

"It's not true. They didn't hurt me." Her gaze fell as she lifted a hand to her breast, before letting it fall. Unable to touch her scar. The slur she'd bear forever. "At least not the way they said."

Before Morgan could comment, Euna scanned the wreckage of the canal bed. "Will he be back?"

"Not likely. He's crawled into a hole to lick his wounds."

Morgan hated to admit it, but after that display of power, her dagger probably hadn't killed Doran. Simply slowed him down. Made him mad.

Euna's gaze narrowed. "Where's Brodie?"

Morgan didn't know for certain, but she'd a good idea and it didn't bode well for the captain. "He's been taken."

"In my place?" Euna asked, a tremble returning to her voice.

Morgan could think of only one reason Doran would bother with Brodie. But to explain why to Euna was impossible.

"I don't know," she said, hating the lie on her tongue. If anyone deserved the truth after living through what she had, it was Euna Sinclair. But Morgan would leave it to Cam to fill in the blanks. She needed to track Doran while the trail remained fresh and burned into her skull. But where was Cam? He should have been down here as soon as the spell had dissolved. As soon as his sister had been freed. A plunging stab of fear hit her with enough force to throw her back on her heels.

"Stay here. I'll be back."

Euna looked like she wanted to argue, but again she gathered her strength. Nodded.

Morgan rose, her eyes searching out Cam's position. "Cam?" she shouted, but no voice returned her call.

Picking her way through the wreckage, she climbed up from the half-completed lock. The path treacherous with shifting dirt, loosened scree that broke and tumbled beneath her feet. She adjusted her steps. The shot had come from this direction. Up. Left. Dodge a hole. Push through a tangle of rope and crates and busted barrels.

And there it was. The rifle, lying abandoned. A smoothed

place in the dirt where someone had rested. Waited. And been dragged away.

She knelt, gleaning what she could from the marks. The second man coming from behind. The unexpected attack.

Fighting panic, she followed the broken route away from the lip of the canal, her eyes burning, her throat closing around a dry choking fear. And just as she half expected, the trail ended. Cam and his captor disappeared.

Fisting her hand around her sword, she looked up, the wall of the city looming above her like a tidal wave, the sounds and smells and pounding energy of its millions flooding her senses. Drowning her power.

And now Doran had two.

Morgan knew it was wrong. Knew she should accompany Euna to the door. Hand her off to her aunt and uncle with explanations and assurances. But she'd no time for either. Not if she was going to track Doran. Find Cam and Brodie. Save them from *Neuvarvaan*.

Uncle Owen's premonition rose up, hitting her with the force of a blow. Her only solace his other admission that no future was writ in stone. She could alter fate if she hurried.

Oh, and why not just hold back the tides, rope the moon, and single-handedly align the stars while she was at it?

Euna seemed to understand her impatience. She stopped Morgan at the corner. Squared her shoulders. Lifted her chin. The *fith-fath* Morgan had flung over the other woman had gotten them this far, but Euna would have to cross the last few yards alone. Exposed.

Euna mustered the tattered edges of a smile. "I'm not the china doll you think me."

Morgan raised a surprised brow. Cocked her head, seeing Euna in a different light. "What will you tell your family?

There will be questions. Not to mention . . ." Her unthinking gaze fell on Doran's mark.

Unspilled tears shimmered in Euna's eyes. Tears she fought to hold back. She gave a quick up-and-down of her shoulders. "Truly? I don't know."

Then with a slap of torn skirts and a duck of her head, she flung herself away from Morgan. Out of her shadow. Up the street. And into the supposed safety of her home.

Free at last to concentrate on the greatest problem, Morgan retraced her steps, her long, ground-eating strides swallowing the miles. Up Piccadilly. Through Covent Garden and Holborn. Into the City. Past St. Paul's and the Tower. Back to the river. Back to the unfinished canal. Back to Doran.

Cam swam up out of unconsciousness, a drumbeat pound in his head, cramped muscles in his shoulders and back. He tried shifting his weight, coming up against the heavy rasp of rope, binding his wrists. His ankles. A slow drip of water echoed every thud in his skull, making thought nigh impossible. But he didn't have to think too hard to realize who'd struck him from behind. Who'd brought him here. In confirmation, the spine-crawling snap of Rastus's cracking knuckles sounded off to his right.

Dim, murky light illuminated a rounded misshapen ceiling, pools of brackish oily water, the flotsam of shovels and spades, crates of what he hoped weren't explosives.

No more than ten yards away, in the center of the room, stood Doran Buchanan, a hand pressed to his side, over the prone figure of another. A man bound just as Cam was. A man he recognized with a sick churning in his gut.

Brodie.

But if Brodie was here, where was Morgan?

He tried craning his neck to search the room for any signs

of a third body, but his range was limited, and he didn't want to call attention to himself. If they thought he remained out cold, all the better.

Think, Sinclair. What now?

As he struggled to form even a ludicrous plan of action—better than giving in to the defeatist idea that he alone still lived—Doran stirred. Words ripped from Cam's memory slit the air.

"Airmid gwithyas a'n fenten. Ev sawya." A language that in Morgan's sultry voice heated his blood spilled now like the speaking of a curse. *"Dian Cecht medhyk a'n spryon. Ev sawya."*

A wounded Doran sought to heal himself.

Uncurling from his place by Brodie's side, seeming more creature than human, he unsheathed *Neuvarvaan*.

And Cam got his first sight of what he'd risked his life and soul to find.

Double spirals decorated the pommel, more of that ancient, headache-inducing script etched into the hilt's quillion. Seeing the mottled reflection off the wide-leafed blade, he knew he stared death and life in the face.

Apparently whatever magic Doran had used worked. With the toe of his boot, he shoved Brodie onto his back. Raised the sword high overhead, point poised over what Cam knew would be Brodie's heart.

A high-pitched whine like that of a mosquito began, an incessant uncomfortable buzz that dropped in octaves even as it lengthened, the buzz stretching to individual pulses of sound as the seconds passed. It was hardly perceptible at first, Cam chalking the steady throb up to the lump in his head, the rush of blood in his ears. Yet this low pulsing thrum came from around him. Vibrating through the air. Carried through the soil.

Finally it became like the growl of the ocean or the whoosh

of the wings of a thousand geese as they rose from the fields. But not at all like any of them. It was a tribal chant. A barbaric call for blood. A sound he knew signaled the beginning of the end.

Part of Cam wanted to curl into a ball, hunker farther behind the cluttered stack of barrels and boxes, and pray Doran forgot about him. Another part couldn't tear his gaze from the dreadful action playing out before him.

Even as it grew louder, it grew more focused. Buried itself in Doran, expanding him. He seemed taller. Burned brighter. Crackled with a sinister light.

Then just as the sound became a deafening crescendo, silence fell over the room, but for Rastus's useless prayers.

With a primal scream, Doran plunged the sword downward, Brodie's body heaving with the force behind the blade's descent into his flesh.

Writhing against his bonds, Cam swallowed his own scream. Bit his lip until blood flowed.

Waited for Brodie to age. To die.

Wished it had been him.

The trail couldn't have been clearer if Doran had marked it with a big arrow. Drawn down into the empty warehouse cellars by the combined scents of blood and mage energy. Compelled by the sudden gripping in her chest as if a giant hand squeezed her heart. Pulled the part of her that was *Other* from between her ribs. Stole it. Used it for Doran's black arts. His *Morkoth* sorcery.

The narrow corridor opened into a larger room. Doran stood fifty feet away, the air quivering around him, Andraste's sword still embedded in the chest of the man lying spread-eagle on the ground.

Cam. She'd been too late. Uncle Owen had spoken truth.

Shrieking her fury, she hurled the darkest, deadliest spell she knew at Doran's exposed back. Let the voraciousness of the *nownek glas* burrow into his blood, where it would eat him from the inside out, leaving the shell of a carcass behind.

Focusing on his victim's expected transformation, Doran wheeled to face the unexpected attack, catching the spell in the face. Eyes bulging, the bones of his skull collapsing in on themselves as the spell worked its destruction.

Morgan advanced, sword drawn, the solid weight of her blade like an extension of her arm, the justice of her fight pushing away any doubts. Any hesitation.

And coming closer saw with mingled relief and sorrow the dead man's face. Still young. Still lifeless. But not Cam.

One more twist of his wrist and Cam would have secured enough give in his bonds. Hard to do without altering Rastus. But not impossible. Besides, from the few fearful moans and prayers for deliverance he heard behind him, the traitorous bastard remained completely focused on the doings at the far side of the room. Not on him.

He chafed at the thick rope, the flesh of his wrists tearing, the sticky blood from the cuts slicking his hands.

And then he was free. Unarmed, but free.

But even as he slid his wrists out of their restraints, a movement caught the corner of his eye. A rise and fall of Brodie's chest? A twitch of his fingers?

Had Doran actually succeeded?

Cam took opportunity as it came. He'd not get another such.

Rolling to his right, he came up swinging. Rastus going down with a whoosh of stunned surprise.

But the fight hadn't completely left him. He struggled for the pistol caught in his holster. Came up instead with a knife. His actions quick and clever, but not near enough to stop Cam.

Behind him, the sounds of battle rose and fell. But all Cam's focus was on the bastard who'd turned on him. Smashed him over the head. Thought he could best him.

None had fought and survived the assassin, Sin. They'd all died with his name a curse upon their lips. His pitiless stare their last glimpse of life.

It would be the same with Corporal Rastus.

He lunged, the knife ripping through Cam's coat. Again. And again, the blade catching flesh, a searing slash of heat grazing Cam's ribs.

Did Rastus really think he could win? That he even had a chance against him?

Cam dodged the next attack. Drove in, catching Rastus's wrist. Bending it until the knife clattered to the ground.

The ground beneath his feet shook, dust gritting his eyes, tipping barrels, scattering boxes. The air seemed to grow thick, the room's walls pressing in on them. It was all he could do to keep his feet.

But if he was having difficulty, so was Rastus.

His hand fumbling for the pistol, he scurried for the exit even as Cam lunged for the loose knife.

The pistol's report slammed through the room with a gut-loosening roar at the same moment Cam released the dagger, threw himself down and to the left.

Rastus's aim was good. The bullet slammed into Cam's shoulder.

Cam's aim was better. The knife ended hilt-deep in Rastus's chest.

Doran lowered his head, stared out at her from beneath heavy brows. And Morgan felt that same compression in her chest as he strove to use her own power against her. The spell's feeding slowed. Stopped. The parasitic magic of the *nownek glas* crushed under the combined weight of Doran, Morgan, and all the *Other* of London.

"It's begun," Doran said, from the lipless orifice that had been a mouth. He gestured to Brodie, whose sightless eyes stared up at her as black as death. "My first recruit in my army of Undying. The *Fey* will take notice now. Realize they're not the dominant race any longer. A new order has arisen."

Morgan's sword came up, her tattooed arms flexed in anticipation, her stance one prepared for battle.

Doran merely laughed, yanking *Neuvarvaan* from Brodie's body with a wet suck that made her want to throw up. "You desire to be next?"

Doran raised *Neuvarvaan*. The sword no longer held the deathly green glow as if lit from within. Instead, light seemed to be drawn into the blade, swallowed by the dark power of Andraste's sword. Causing it to grow. Stretch. Feel its new strength. Its new creation.

The world tilted on its axis. The ceiling above, the floor beneath, the slime-dripping walls, all a whirl of color and sound, and then she felt nothing. Heard nothing. Saw nothing as if she'd been blasted into the emptiness of a *Fey* passage between worlds. Stranded outside of place and time.

She opened her mouth on a silent scream. Knew the madness of such an entrapment would claim her in a matter of minutes.

But they were minutes she could use to fight back. With the only weapon she could think of. If Doran had shown her it was possible, Uncle Owen had given her the means.

Taking a deep mental breath, she let her mind expand. Cracking the door of her consciousness wide. Seeing the universe of mage energy as a crackling horizon of writhing light. Pulsating in all colors and patterns. The endless power a well that could be drawn on for infinity. Giving her the strength of millions.

In Doran, the *Morkoth* magic had tempered that energy.

Allowed its use without ill effect. She'd not that luxury. Unwarded and defenseless, such a violent surge in power could kill. But she'd run out of options.

The gathering of mage energy into her body filled her until she felt as if too many shared her skin. They warred within her, crushing the breath from her lungs, warping her muscles, clamoring in her brain until the din deafened her. And still she called for more to come to her aid.

Light infused her. Filled her vision until it scorched her eyes from their sockets. Until all was flame. Until she became a living firestorm of energy and power.

"Kuntell galloes. Ladra galloes. Gul devnydh a galloes." The words came thick as ropes. Binding Doran. Tightening around him. Wrapping him in the same fire that consumed her.

"Merwel re'm galloes." Flinging out her arms, she released the fusion of *Other* energy. Let it pour from her eyes, her mouth, her fingers. Let it tear into the *Morkoth*-tainted *Amhas-draoi*. Set him ablaze.

Blinded, still she felt him falter. Felt his power ebb. The tremble in the air as *Neuvarvaan* and Doran fought against her control.

A gun blast from the other side of the room broke through her control. Set the energy rippling and curling through her body.

It was time.

A maelstrom of light and sound, earth and air threatened to shatter her bones to dust. Pull her body apart nerve by nerve. So many thoughts not her own. So many dreams and hopes, skills and spells. She wove them into a weapon not even a *Morkoth*-aided Doran could withstand.

Screaming her defiance and with the last of her strength, she torched his very soul, shriveling him to ash and choking smoke and a few floating embers.

Remembered nothing after.

Chapter 29

She had no recollection of Cam, dazed and wounded, carrying her out of the warehouse. No memory of Brodie Mackay's explosive awakening, the death glow of *Neuvarvaan* marking him as Undying even as he made an anguished escape into the confusion and anonymity of the city. No recall when they spoke to her of the dark hours she spent between life and death when all had despaired but the one man who'd never left her bedside.

Until the day she'd awoken.

Cam had walked away even as she struggled up out of the swamp of unconsciousness, whispering his name through cracked lips. Sending a silent plea for the comfort of his strong hand in her own. The steady weight of his presence reassuring her when all her dreams left him for dead.

There were others there to welcome her back to the world of the living—Gram, whose silver-gray eyes burned clear with relief and love, her father enveloping her in a bear hug that threatened to crush the breath back out of her lungs. Scathach, who stood as one among three other *Fey*, two men and a single woman whose brilliance outstripped her companions' as the sun's bright light eclipses the stars.

Dressed in shimmering white, her silver hair coiled against her head, her upturned eyes a fathomless whirl of blue and gray and green, she stepped to Morgan's bedside, dropping her hand to the scabbard at her hip. *Neuvarvaan* safely back in the hands of the warrior-goddess Andraste. She bowed her head. "We owe you a debt, little sister."

Heat crawled up Morgan's neck at the tribute. Stung her cheeks. "I only did what I was asked to do. Nothing more."

A ghost of a smile tipped the corner of Andraste's lip. For her, probably the closest thing to laughter she'd ever get. "Even so, the *Fey* do not forget an owing. You have only to call upon us."

Gram stood, shooing the group of *Fey* before her like ill-behaved children. "That's enough. All of you. You'll tire her out with your grand bowing and scraping. She needs her rest."

The two males tossed their dark hair, flinging the tiny woman black looks before blinking out of sight. But Scathach and Andraste both allowed the rough use, no more than indulgence in their cool gazes. Gram might have given up a life among them for a mortal's love, but she still held a strong whip-hand among the children of High *Danu*.

"Wait," Morgan called.

Andraste turned back, her perfectly arched brows raised in question.

"I do have a favor to ask. Ensign Traverse, the soldier who survived *Neuvarvaan*'s attack. Can you help him? Restore him to the way he was?"

The warrior-goddess tilted her head. "This is what you truly wish?"

Morgan swallowed. Eternal youth. Riches unimaginable. Great power. She knew she had but to ask and Andraste would see it done. The *Fey* didn't favor mortals with wishes very often. But their honor required a fair reckoning when they felt a debt owed.

Morgan lifted her chin. Faced Andraste with all the strength of the *Amhas-draoi* behind her, her tone final. "It is."

"Not even the true *Fey* can undo all the *Morkoth*'s black magics."

Morgan's shoulders slumped.

"But"—Andraste lifted a finger—"we will do all we can to aid this young man. You have my word."

"Thank you." Morgan bowed her head. Sent a silent *I did my best* to Cam. Hoped wherever he was, he heard it.

"You have a visitor." Gram's voice stirred Morgan from a doze. Sent a tingle of anticipation through her weighted limbs. He'd come.

But it wasn't Cam that peeked a shy head around the door.

White-knuckled hands squeezing her purse, a shawl draped across her thin shoulders, Euna Sinclair took a seat beside Morgan's bed. Offered a shy smile. "They told me you weren't at home to visitors, but I insisted." She bit her lip. Dropped her gaze to her lap. "I never said thank you for saving me. I only wish Captain . . ." Her words died away.

Morgan still felt the sting of failure at Brodie's disappearance. What must he be feeling—thinking? "Have you heard from him?"

Euna lifted her head and the sorrow and sleepless nights were visible in the flat blue of her eyes. "Uncle Josh inquired. A man resembling Brodie took ship for the continent. But nothing more's been heard."

"He's alive, Euna. At least we know that much."

"Does he see it that way? Or does he see what they did to him as simply a living death?" Bitterness stung Euna's words. Then her chin firmed, her shoulders squared. "Forget I spoke. He *is* alive. Somewhere. I can live with that."

Was there more than concern for a foster brother in Euna's

tone? Had there been feelings between Brodie and Cam's sister severed by *Neuvarvaan*'s killer stroke?

Morgan reached for Euna's hand. Squeezed it, worried at the fragile press of bones beneath the skin. "But how are you? Truly?"

Euna's courageous smile reassured Morgan. The young woman was tougher than she looked. "Uncle Josh and Aunt Sylvie have been dears. They worry over . . . I mean, what husband wants . . ." She pressed a hand to her breast. "If I dress in the dark, I don't see . . ."

Morgan fought to sit up, ignoring the spinning room, the woozy light-headedness. As an Undying, Brodie was lost to them all. And Traverse had no guarantee he'd ever regain his youth. But Euna . . . here was someone she could help. Or at least her grandmother could.

"Do you trust me?"

Euna tilted her head, her brows furrowed in question. "Of course."

"Gram?" Morgan called out, knowing her grandmother remained close by. "There's someone here I'd like you to meet."

Alone once again, Morgan waited for Cam to come to her. And waited.

Then followed a day and a night and a day of unanswered questions, awkward silences, and sidelong worried glances when they thought she wasn't looking.

To be honest after the first few days, she hadn't tried overhard to discover the truth of Cam's defection. It was enough to know that he'd abandoned her, his promises as worthless now as they'd been last year.

She worked at furious. Not hard to do through frustrating days of lying flat on her back. Longer maddening weeks when the shortest walk could bring tears to her eyes and a spinning dizziness that sent her reeling like a drunk for the nearest chair.

She'd been a fool. A fool twice over, which made it worse. She'd fallen for the lost little boy and been blindsided by the rotten bastard of a man. In the end, all he'd really wanted was a good lay and she'd given it to him. Repeatedly.

Well, to hell with him.

She didn't need him. Didn't want him. Couldn't care less where he was or what he was doing.

The anger burned bright and hard in her heart, squashing out the teeny voice that said he needed her still. That his words had been truth. His final actions that of a man who'd been pushed to the edge and over. Who ran from her in a vain effort to outrun a past he could no longer deny.

It was only in her sleep she dared to remember. When her dreams brought her visions of a windswept barren landscape, an isolated farmstead, and a quiet firelit room. His face swam before her, grief and loneliness clouding his gaze, and she ached for the calloused touch of his hand on her skin, the teasing heat of his kisses. Those nights she woke shaking with dry, wracking sobs, her throat tight, her eyes hot with unshed tears.

Autumn passed beyond her bedchamber window, Daggerfell's woods a vibrant collage of scarlet and orange, yellow and gold. Friends and family came and went. Books read. Letters written. The little moments of life pieced together into a Cam-less existence.

The first snow fell. Heavy, wet flakes whispering in the lanes, blanketing the gardens. Morgan spent the day tramping the fields. Watching the icy hiss of white slant out across the Channel. Her lungs burned with use and the frozen air, her hands went numb in her gloves, her hair frosted white before she turned her steps toward home. Creeping to the quiet of her room, she collided head-on with her grandmother.

She motioned for Morgan to sit. "*Myrgh-wynn*—my granddaughter, we need to speak, you and I."

One look at the determined glint in Gram's eyes and Morgan squared her shoulders for the argument to come. "I wondered when you'd apply the thumbscrews."

Gram let a smile curl her lips, but her chin remained stubborn with purpose. "You have hidden yourself away for too long. You are full recovered, yet you remain here rather than return to Skye. Can you tell me why that is?"

Vying for time, Morgan shed her sopping wet cloak on a chair. Pulled off her gloves, tossing them on her bed. Shook the snow from her hair.

"It is long past time for you to go to him."

Morgan felt Gram's words like a body blow. She whipped around, hating the revealing sting of tears. Cam wasn't worth it. "Go? To him? Are you insane? That's just what I'm not going to do."

Gram remained as unmoved as stone. With a patience that Morgan had always envied and hated, she settled into a chair by the fire. Folded her hands in her lap. Obviously, this wasn't going to be a lightning assault. More like a drawn-out siege. "You would rather hide behind the safety of Daggerfell's walls than join with the enemy? Take the battle to him?"

"You've hit the nail on the head. Enemy. As in opposite of love. As in he's not worth my time." She stomped to the hearth. Made a great show of warming her hands. Ignoring Gram's unasked-for advice.

"Your actions reveal the lie of your words. I have seen your heartache in the somber light of your gaze. In the sorrow of your heart. In the tragedy of your dreams."

Morgan remained silent. If she let Gram have her say, mayhap she'd give up and leave. But every accusation battered Morgan's already bruised heart. Tore open a wound barely healed over.

"His sorrow is no less than yours, *myrgh-wynn*. And perhaps affects him more. He does not have the comfort of family. Nor the peace of his own conscience to offer reassurance."

Gram had the persistence of an army sapper. Tunneling under Morgan's defenses. Weakening walls. Pulling apart her arguments one brick at a time.

Morgan clamped her mouth over the harsh words that threatened to spill from her lips. Remained with eyes focused on the fire. Did everything but plug her ears with her fingers.

Still, Gram wouldn't let it rest. "He is a proud man with the soul of a warrior. It will take a powerful woman to match such strength."

The breech forced open, Morgan had no choice but to swing around to challenge Gram. "He left me. Remember? I offered him my love"—she beat her chest with her fist—"I sacrificed my future for him. And what did he do? Walked away from all of it. It wasn't good enough." She swallowed around the final truth. "I wasn't good enough."

And there it was. The real reason she sheltered within the safety of her rooms. Her greatest fear.

Gram nodded as if she'd already known what Morgan hadn't admitted even to herself. Mayhap she did.

"Don't you see, Gram? All I did, and I wasn't enough." She hated the crack in her voice, the weakness behind it.

"Perhaps the colonel thought leaving you *was* giving you what you wanted. Perhaps he thought he wasn't enough for you."

Morgan sank onto her bed, clutching the bedpost as she rested her head against the gnarled wood. Could that have been Cam's reasoning? Could he have assumed that by bowing out he offered her back her freedom? Released her from what she'd stupidly referred to as the prison of his love?

Why had she even said that? Why hadn't she seen then what stared her in the face now? That no amount of *Amhas-draoi* power mattered if she'd no one to share her days with. Or her nights beside.

Taking a deep steadying breath, she closed her eyes, hating the spiraling doubts, the complete blindness of men. He should have known. He should have asked.

She should have told him.

When she opened her eyes, Gram stood, a smile of success lighting her face as if making Morgan cry had been her sole purpose. Her job here accomplished.

Morgan swiped a sleeve across her face. Sniffed. "If you're so wise, where is he now?"

Gram laughed. "You two are more alike than you wish to believe. Like you, he fled to the one place he felt most at peace. Home."

She stood on the shore of a loch, its icy blue brilliance mirroring the mountains surrounding it. The dirty storm clouds overhead.

Old snow curled in the corners of the rocks, blew through the cliffs. The sad cry of a loon sounded lonely across the waters. Returned in echo.

She rubbed her arms briskly, trying to warm her courage before climbing the path that led to the solitary farmstead.

It was just as she'd dreamed it. Built of local stone, the house seemed to grow from the hillside behind it. Bleak and storm-scarred with thick walls mortar-chinked to keep out the Viking winds howling down from the Orkneys and a slate roof sprouting chimneys, though smoke rose from only one. Scraggly trees leaned like old men in a garden left fallow and waiting patiently for spring.

Morgan knocked, though she knew Cam wasn't home.

She'd reconnoitered before plunging headlong into what could be an amazingly awkward situation.

Strathconon's tenants spoke of the colonel as a solitary man, taken to spending long days on the moors and mountains. Never rude, yet holding himself apart from the life of the valley. No trips to the village. No evenings spent in the company of his neighbors. No visitors to his isolated holding on the edge of the estate.

Still others told—though always in a frightened whisper—of a mysterious woman who came to him only at night. And disappeared with the first gray smear of dawn in the east. On those days, the colonel seemed darker and more forbidding than ever. And though none understood why, they all took great pains to avoid him on those occasions.

If the exterior of the house exuded strength and age, the interior welcomed with snug rooms and a beeswax shine. Comfort and wealth combined to create a homey, cheerful atmosphere. Thick colorful rugs on the floors. Expensive paintings on the walls. A chimneypiece scattered with souvenirs of a life in the Highlands. Part of a stag's antler. A clamshell. Weathered pebbles of an unearthly blue. A small bird's skull. And in the center of it all, an urn of delicate antiquity. Worth a king's ransom by the looks of it.

Like Cam, an odd mixture of high class and native ruggedness.

A pricking at her back spun her on her heel straight into the unblinking portrait stare of a hawk-nosed, strong-jawed gentleman whose frozen blue gaze was all too familiar. She lifted a hand, as if she could speak with him. Tell him he'd been right. Love wasn't a chain. And in matters of the heart, at least one former *Fey* knew more than enough.

Morgan and Cam might circle each other endlessly unless one of them chose to end it. She would brave the first step.

And please, God. Let Gram's hunch be right. Or it would be one hell of a long trip south.

Cam tumbled the stones in his pocket as he pushed open the door, shut it against a wind shrieking with a promise of the storm to come. There'd be snow before morning. Lots of it. And he'd be trapped inside. No endless wanderings to tire his body and his mind enough for sleep to come. Morgan's shade would visit him in his tossings and turnings. Punish him with second-guesses. What-ifs.

Had he been right to leave? In the chaos after Doran's destruction when he'd been half mad with pain and grief and fear, the slithering coil of the serpent had convinced him to walk away. That he'd fallen too far for even Morgan to drag him back.

It had only been in the last weeks the voice had died away and he'd almost convinced himself—almost—that she might have stayed. He might have made her happy.

He crossed the hall to the back parlor—one of the few rooms he'd reopened upon his arrival. The upper floors remained shut.

Who needed a bed when sleep was the enemy?

At the threshold he slammed to a stop, the breath punched from his lungs, his heart banging against his ribs.

It couldn't be.

He squeezed his eyes shut. Opened them again expecting her to be a dream. He'd had them often enough to be wary. Morgan seated at the table, her red-gold hair gleaming in the light of a fire, her whiskey gaze hot with a love he thought forever lost to him.

But she remained. And the smile she turned on him smashed through the brittle barriers he'd thrown up to keep the worst of the hurt from taking him completely over.

He crossed the room in two strides, sliding to a halt an arm's reach away. So close he smelled her enticing perfume, sensed her tension.

She clutched the arms of her chair, bit her bottom lip, but her eyes held his. Refused to let him look away. Retreat. "This is the second time I've had to track you down."

His hand closed around the pebbles, reassuring him he wasn't imagining. "I thought it best to disappear. Make it easy for you."

Her jaw jumped. "You think what I've been through the last months has been easy?" She settled back, taking a deep breath. "One question, Cam. That's all I've come here for."

She squared her shoulders. Chin up. Eyes bright. Must be one hell of a question. She paused. Just long enough for dread to knot his insides. For sweat to break out on his chilled skin.

Apparently deciding she'd spun out the suspense long enough, she inhaled and asked, "I need to know, Cam. Do you love me, or were the last weeks just a way to get me naked into your bed?"

"I—"

But she didn't give him a chance to finish. "I once told you I didn't look for marriage. Had no need for love. I was wrong. Like it or not, I love you."

Love. The word plunged a burning brand into the icy fist of his heart. Cam dropped into the chair beside her, leaned forward, elbows on his knees, head bowed. Without looking up, he asked, "Can you know what I am—what I'm capable of—and love me anyway?"

Amusement colored her words. "I could ask you the same question."

He couldn't move. Couldn't think. Here was the dream. Morgan in his house. In his life. Not for a day or a month, but a lifetime. All he had to do was answer. But words wouldn't come. His throat closed, his mouth dry. He lifted his eyes to hers. "Why?" was all he managed to choke out.

She lifted her eyes to his, her expression as fired with purpose as if she stood on the battlefield. "Because I'm tired of waiting on my knight in shining armor to sweep me off my feet. He's damned overdue. This damsel decided to do her own sweeping. Write her own happy ending."

She smiled, sending a violent wave of heat straight to his center. Months of snow and ice and cold baths had dulled the desire, but never extinguished it.

"So what's your answer?"

Whether it was her words or some slight movement toward him, he couldn't say. All he knew was one moment, he sat reeling in stunned excitement. The next he'd grabbed her up, knocking her chair on its side, swinging her around before settling her against his heart. Sliding his hands into the spill of her hair, he slanted his mouth over hers. Dipped his tongue between her lips. Felt her answering invitation in the plunge of her tongue, the slow sucking of his bottom lip, the suggestive grind of her crotch against him.

She broke away, her eyes glassy with lust and a consuming need as pressing as his own. "Well?"

He'd forgotten the question in the agonizing torture of having Morgan in his arms and still fully clothed. Something he meant to remedy in the next few minutes. But her question hung like the treasure it was. "Oh gods, yes, Morgan. I love you." His hands curved around the swell of her rear, lifted her onto the hard bulge in his breeks. "But we do it right this time. Proper."

He looked up into the eyes of his grandfather's portrait. Offered a nod of acknowledgment.

"Marry me, Morgan." His tone brooked no dissent.

"You? Proper?" She moved against him, the friction making him hiss. "Aye, Cam Sinclair. I'll marry you." She leaned close to whisper in his ear, "And they lived happily ever after."

GREAT BOOKS, GREAT SAVINGS!

When You Visit Our Website:
www.kensingtonbooks.com
You Can Save Money Off The Retail Price
Of Any Book You Purchase!

- **All Your Favorite Kensington Authors**
- **New Releases & Timeless Classics**
- **Overnight Shipping Available**
- **eBooks Available For Many Titles**
- **All Major Credit Cards Accepted**

Visit Us Today To Start Saving!
www.kensingtonbooks.com

All Orders Are Subject To Availability.
Shipping and Handling Charges Apply.
Offers and Prices Subject To Change Without Notice.

More by Bestselling Author
Fern Michaels

__About Face	0-8217-7020-9	$7.99US/$10.99CAN
__Wish List	0-8217-7363-1	$7.50US/$10.50CAN
__Picture Perfect	0-8217-7588-X	$7.99US/$10.99CAN
__Vegas Heat	0-8217-7668-1	$7.99US/$10.99CAN
__Finders Keepers	0-8217-7669-X	$7.99US/$10.99CAN
__Dear Emily	0-8217-7670-3	$7.99US/$10.99CAN
__Sara's Song	0-8217-7671-1	$7.99US/$10.99CAN
__Vegas Sunrise	0-8217-7672-X	$7.99US/$10.99CAN
__Yesterday	0-8217-7678-9	$7.99US/$10.99CAN
__Celebration	0-8217-7679-7	$7.99US/$10.99CAN
__Payback	0-8217-7876-5	$6.99US/$9.99CAN
__Vendetta	0-8217-7877-3	$6.99US/$9.99CAN
__The Jury	0-8217-7878-1	$6.99US/$9.99CAN
__Sweet Revenge	0-8217-7879-X	$6.99US/$9.99CAN
__Lethal Justice	0-8217-7880-3	$6.99US/$9.99CAN
__Free Fall	0-8217-7881-1	$6.99US/$9.99CAN
__Fool Me Once	0-8217-8071-9	$7.99US/$10.99CAN
__Vegas Rich	0-8217-8112-X	$7.99US/$10.99CAN
__Hide and Seek	1-4201-0184-6	$6.99US/$9.99CAN
__Hokus Pokus	1-4201-0185-4	$6.99US/$9.99CAN
__Fast Track	1-4201-0186-2	$6.99US/$9.99CAN
__Collateral Damage	1-4201-0187-0	$6.99US/$9.99CAN
__Final Justice	1-4201-0188-9	$6.99US/$9.99CAN

Available Wherever Books Are Sold!
Check out our website at **www.kensingtonbooks.com**

Thrilling Suspense from
Beverly Barton

__Every Move She Makes   0-8217-6838-7 $6.50US/$8.99CAN

__What She Doesn't Know   0-8217-7214-7 $6.50US/$8.99CAN

__After Dark   0-8217-7666-5 $6.50US/$8.99CAN

__The Fifth Victim   0-8217-7215-5 $6.50US/$8.99CAN

__The Last to Die   0-8217-7216-3 $6.50US/$8.99CAN

__As Good As Dead   0-8217-7219-8 $6.99US/$9.99CAN

__Killing Her Softly   0-8217-7687-8 $6.99US/$9.99CAN

__Close Enough to Kill   0-8217-7688-6 $6.99US/$9.99CAN

__The Dying Game   0-8217-7689-4 $6.99US/$9.99CAN

Available Wherever Books Are Sold!

Visit our website at **www.kensingtonbooks.com**

Romantic Suspense from
Lisa Jackson

See How She Dies	0-8217-7605-3	$6.99US/$9.99CAN
Final Scream	0-8217-7712-2	$7.99US/$10.99CAN
Wishes	0-8217-6309-1	$5.99US/$7.99CAN
Whispers	0-8217-7603-7	$6.99US/$9.99CAN
Twice Kissed	0-8217-6038-6	$5.99US/$7.99CAN
Unspoken	0-8217-6402-0	$6.50US/$8.50CAN
If She Only Knew	0-8217-6708-9	$6.50US/$8.50CAN
Hot Blooded	0-8217-6841-7	$6.99US/$9.99CAN
Cold Blooded	0-8217-6934-0	$6.99US/$9.99CAN
The Night Before	0-8217-6936-7	$6.99US/$9.99CAN
The Morning After	0-8217-7295-3	$6.99US/$9.99CAN
Deep Freeze	0-8217-7296-1	$7.99US/$10.99CAN
Fatal Burn	0-8217-7577-4	$7.99US/$10.99CAN
Shiver	0-8217-7578-2	$7.99US/$10.99CAN
Most Likely to Die	0-8217-7576-6	$7.99US/$10.99CAN
Absolute Fear	0-8217-7936-2	$7.99US/$9.49CAN
Almost Dead	0-8217-7579-0	$7.99US/$10.99CAN
Lost Souls	0-8217-7938-9	$7.99US/$10.99CAN
Left to Die	1-4201-0276-1	$7.99US/$10.99CAN
Wicked Game	1-4201-0338-5	$7.99US/$9.99CAN
Malice	0-8217-7940-0	$7.99US/$9.49CAN

Available Wherever Books Are Sold!
Visit our website at **www.kensingtonbooks.com**